BIG, BOSSY PROBLEM

AN ACCIDENTAL BABY ROMANCE

MANHATTAN BILLIONAIRES
BOOK 3

LILIAN MONROE

1

PENNY

THE CLICK of a dog's claws on polished concrete greets me when I enter my boss's house. As soon as my rain jacket is on the hook by the front door, I drop to my knees and spread my arms. "Bear!"

The dog launches himself at me, tackling me to the ground. His wet snout touches my neck, followed by the rough scrape of his tongue. "Ahh!" I squirm, laughing, scrubbing his fur. I try to catch my breath while sixty pounds of dog plants itself on my chest. "Ack! Get off!"

There's nothing like a pup greeting you like you've been off at war for months, no matter how long it's been since he last saw you. In my case, it's been about eighteen hours. Walking in my employer's front door is my favorite part of my day, because I get tackled by a furry bullet every single time.

Bear's a good boy. Always has been. He's some kind of German shepherd mix, judging by his dark coloring and size, but his hair is quite a bit longer than a full-breed German shepherd, and those pointed ears flop down in the most adorable way. I've loved him since his very first greeting, which was a lot more wary than today's enthusiastic hello.

"Do you know what today is, Bear?" I get to my knees and give him scratches behind those big, floppy ears, just the way he likes.

The dog snuffles.

In the stillness of my employer's empty house, I don't mind talking to the dog like he's a person. Sometimes, I feel like animals are the only creatures worth talking to. Dogs never let you down the way people do.

I stroke Bear's snout and give him a kiss right between the eyes. "Today is our one-year anniversary. I've been walking you twice a day, five days a week for an entire year!"

Bear sits down on his haunches and tilts his head.

"Yep. I've been your dog walker for a whole year." Kneeling in front of him, I bring my crossbody bag to rest on my thighs before sliding the zipper open. Bear follows the movement with great interest.

"Your human said it was fine for me to bring you a T-R-E-A-T to celebrate," I explain, reaching into my bag for Bear's favorite type of dog bone. I pause, arching a brow. "Well, your human's assistant said so. Your actual human doesn't speak to me."

As soon as the treat emerges from the confines of my purse, Bear turns into a vibrating mass of excited doggy energy. "I also made you a special bow tie, fresh off the sewing machine an hour ago. But it looks like you much prefer this part of your present."

I lift the bone, a movement which Bear's gaze traces with laser-like precision. He stays still as long as I ask him to, until I finally take pity on him and let him take the treat. He carries it off to his dog bed by the back door, chewing contentedly.

I love my job. For the past year, five days a week, twice a day, I've done the same thing. This SoHo bachelor pad has become somewhat familiar, even though I haven't seen much more than the foyer and the open-plan living space. Marcus Walsh is in the news every so often, being the handsome, single tech genius he is, so I know he's mega-wealthy. But apart from a few expensive-looking pieces of art on two of the living room walls—and the fact that his home isn't the size of an airplane bathroom like mine—there isn't much evidence that Mr. Walsh is a billionaire.

The front door opens onto a big, open-plan room with the kitchen in the far right corner, complete with double ovens and a big island/breakfast bar area. Cushioned barstools line the island, with a funky, curvy light fixture hanging above. On the other side of the space, the living room wall is exposed brick, with an absolutely enormous television mounted in the center. Speakers and subwoofers halo the television, and a comfy-looking couch faces it all. I say comfy-*looking*, because in the hundreds of times I've been here, I've never actually sat down on the sofa.

I know I'm on camera, after all. I'm sure Mr. Tech Billionaire wouldn't take too kindly to me making myself at home.

Between the kitchen and living spaces, a hallway leads to the bedrooms and living spaces beyond. I've never stepped foot past that threshold. There's an invisible wall keeping me out.

My entry into this billionaire's world has clear boundaries. I get a tiny sliver of a peek into how the other half lives. I have access to the big pantry where Bear's food is kept. I can use the kitchen to replenish his water, and I have permission to use the small powder room beside the kitchen. Once, I snooped through the door beside the powder room because I was looking for Bear's spare leash and saw that it leads into a garage. Yes, a private garage in New York City. The other half never has to circle the block for street parking or take the subway, apparently.

All other areas of this place are off-limits, and that's perfectly fine by me. Boundaries are good. I've spent most of my adult life building my own boundaries back up to healthy levels just to feel safe. I'm more than happy to respect someone else's.

While Bear celebrates with his treat, I do the various small tasks I've gotten used to completing for Bear and his owner. I check the dog's bowl and replenish it with fresh water, tidy a few stray toys, and make sure I have doggy bags and a leash ready for our first walk of the day.

As soon as I jingle it, Bear comes running.

"Last thing," I tell him, kneeling in front of him with his spiffy new bow tie. It clips to his collar with a special clasp I designed myself. The pattern is red with white polka dots, and it looks extremely dashing, if I do say so myself.

I'm probably biased. My dog clothing business has exploded recently, to the point that Bear is the only dog-walking client I've kept. A year ago, I had about a dozen dogs I'd walk every day, but I had to drop all of them to make time for the new business. But Bear's owner pays a *lot* better than most people, so it seemed like a good safety net to keep this particular job.

Also, Bear is my favorite. Don't tell the others.

When I'm not walking Bear, my time is spent hunched

over my sewing machine, coming up with new patterns and styles for bow ties, sweaters, rain jackets, and all kinds of pet clothing and costumes. Thank goodness for Brian, my best friend. He's the one who handles the technology side of things. Without him, I wouldn't have gotten very far with the business at all.

"Did you know," I tell Bear, "that I used to sell my wares at farmers' markets, until Brian convinced me to try doing things online? That was about a year ago, around the time we met." Bear sits while I adjust his bow tie. "I have to say, Brian was right. The internet is like a mystical fairyland I don't understand. I just give Brian the dog clothes, and he gets his little furball to model them, uploads the pictures, and runs the online store. We split the profits fifty-fifty."

Bear listens patiently, and I pretend he understands every word.

My arrangement with Brian works perfectly, because technology has a way of malfunctioning when I'm nearby. My body must be made of magnets. Or maybe I emit low-level electromagnetic pulses every time my heart beats. Screens go blue and freeze, computers start smoking, car alarms go off in my wake.

I'm kidding. Mostly.

The twenty-first century has been tough. Without Brian, I'd still be walking a dozen dogs and barely scraping by. I'm happy to split the business's profits with him equally.

"Another fun fact," I say to Bear, "is that *your* human owns the website where I sell my products! That's right. Marcus Walsh created the online marketplace that made it possible for me and Brian to start this business together. Your human started Sellzy, and that website is the whole reason I was able to start sewing dog clothes full-time. Isn't that cool?" I straighten the red-and-white polka-dot bow tie and give Bear an extra little scratch behind the ears. "This is going to be a bestseller. I can already tell."

Bear sneezes. He agrees.

"Let's show your human," I tell the dog, leading him over to the nanny cam on the shelf by the door. Mr. Walsh's assistant made sure to show it to me and let me know that his security was top-notch when he hired me. I could have guessed that by the military-grade background check he required and the fact that his front door has a fingerprint scanner in place of a regular lock.

Little did my employer know that my fingers don't enjoy being scanned.

When the scanner malfunctioned for the tenth time in my second week of working for him, Marcus Walsh finally gave me a physical key. Unsurprising to me, considering my storied history with electronics, but apparently it was very unusual to my boss. He made a point to come check me out himself instead of sending the assistant I'd been dealing with up until that point.

I still remember the way his green eyes narrowed on me. I felt like a bug on a microscope slide, inspected down to a cellular level. He stared at me like he was trying to figure out if I was lying, if there was some subterfuge with the key. Not a man who trusts easily—but then again, I'm the same way. I can't blame him for being suspicious. Mr. Walsh takes good care of Bear, and that's good enough for me.

Still, the interaction was...unsettling. I don't like it when people—men especially, and *attractive* men like Marcus Walsh doubly so—pay that kind of close attention to me. I learned my lesson in college, *thankyouverymuch*. Male attention is not something I go out and seek on purpose. Not anymore.

But Mr. Walsh finally gave me the key, and that was that. It was the last time I saw my boss in person.

Even so, Bear and I still have a little daily ritual involving the nanny cam, and part of me likes to think Mr. Walsh appreciates it. In reality, he probably doesn't even notice—or he thinks I'm a total dork.

But a dork is better than a victim. A dork is way, *way* better than a target.

I bring Bear to the camera and kneel beside him, slinging my arm around the dog's body. "Smile!" We both look at the camera. I smile brightly, and Bear just gives a great big yawn, complete with lolling tongue.

"Okie dokie," I say, attaching Bear's leash to his collar and leading him to the door. "Let's go! It's a bit wet outside, so I left a towel by the door for when we come back. We'll have to wipe you down before we ruin all this nice furniture, okay?"

I point to the towel. Bear doesn't care; he's completely still, staring at the front door. His ears point forward, fur bristling. Tension turns his body to stone. While I'm busy frowning at his strange reaction, the door flies open.

A young teenage girl careens through the open doorway, sobbing, while an older woman stands on the porch looking like thunder and lightning personified.

"Stay here if you like it so much, you little slut," the woman sneers. I jump at the word. I've been called it, too, and it's a highly unpleasant feeling.

Bear growls while I wrap my hand around the leash to keep him by my side.

The woman finally notices me. She turns the storm clouds in my direction. "What the hell are you looking at?" Without waiting for me to answer, the woman slams the door closed. It rattles for a moment.

Silence crashes down around me, and I stand rooted to the spot, eyes wide. Slowly, I spin around, only to see the girl disappear down the hallway. The sounds of her cries and sniffles echo off the walls, and another door slams.

Bear tugs at the leash, but not in direction of the door. He wants to follow the girl.

I bite my lip, glancing at the dog, then at the hallway, and finally at the camera. "Mr. Walsh, I know I'm not allowed anywhere else in the house, but this seems like an emergency. I need to check on that girl."

For some reason, speaking to a camera in a silent apartment seems infinitely weirder than speaking to a dog, so I pull out my phone and find the phone number I haven't used once in the entire year I've been employed by him. It was given to me for emergencies only, of which I've had none. But this seems like a bad situation. The girl obviously knows my boss, but the way the woman spoke to her...

I have to tell him. He probably doesn't even check the nanny camera. He'd want to know a young girl just ran into his home. I would want to know if that happened in my house. Surely billionaires aren't *that* different from the rest of us?

I have an old flip phone because smartphones are the devil. If they don't malfunction, I usually end up accidentally dropping them in the toilet or down a sewer drain, like they're doing their best to get away from me even if it means diving into a dirty, watery grave. But with an old flip phone, texting isn't exactly easy. I try to keep texts short and sweet, if I send them at all.

Penny: Bear OK. Girl came crying. Please txt/call. Ty.

I wait a few seconds, staring at the scratched screen of my flip phone, waiting for it to vibrate with a response. I'd know a message was incoming anyway, because one of those expensive-looking speakers on the wall would start beeping and buzzing if a text message was on its way to my phone. They remain silent, though, and for the first time in my life, I wish I had a smartphone to tell me if my message made it to its recipient.

Nothing happens, so I snap the phone closed and slide it into my purse. Then I unclip Bear's leash and follow him down the hallway toward the sounds of a very upset teenager.

2

MARCUS

I'M through my office door and on the way to the elevator bank by the time my phone vibrates with a text message from Penny. I stare at the screen and frown at the short, grammatically incorrect message. My dog walker texts like it's 2004. I did not expect that.

Lots of emojis and acronyms and overuse of exclamation marks, sure. That would fit her bubbly, cutesy personality. The sheer number of hours of video footage I have of her talking to my dog in a singsong voice and clipping ridiculous bow ties and rain jackets on his body—which Bear dutifully endures and might even enjoy—points to the fact that her texting style would include at least one emoji.

She didn't even write in full sentences.

Marcus: I'm on my way.

I stare at my phone's screen as the elevator descends, my own message stuck in the ether, remaining unsent. Damn elevator. Clicking through my phone to the camera footage, I watch it again from the beginning, when Bear tackled Penny by the front door.

Then I realize what I'm doing, mentally punch myself, and fast-forward to the point when the door opens and my niece comes flying through. The angle doesn't allow me to see my sister, but I hear her voice clearly enough.

I can tell by the slurring that she's been drinking. My sister's always been a mean drunk. Has been ever since... Well, ever since I let her down. Her struggles with alcohol are a constant reminder that I messed up.

And she called her own daughter a vile word. I'm going to kill her.

Anger winds its way through my chest, making me hot and uncomfortable. I unzip my jacket and glance up at the numbers above the elevator door, cursing myself for getting an office on the fifty-second floor. I waste too much of my time on a damn elevator.

As soon as I hit the underground garage, I have my phone to my ear, but neither Penny, nor my sister, nor my niece answers their phone. By the time I make it to my Ducati, I'm fuming.

My sister Stephanie relapsed—again. I don't even know why I'm surprised. But the way she spoke to Mackenzie...

Unacceptable.

It's raining outside, so I'm forced to drive slowly. If the city's meteorologists could get *one* forecast right, I'd damn well appreciate it. It would save me getting soaked on the back of a bike when it's not even supposed to be wet outside.

Traffic is terrible, but I'm able to maneuver between screaming cab drivers and dopey tourists to make my way from my office's high-rise to my home in SoHo. It's a refurbished factory that has been my home since my business first exploded. Emil and Leif, my two best friends, keep trying to convince me to buy something nicer, something gleaming and pristine with the word "penthouse" attached.

As if I'd want to spend even more time in an elevator. My place is just fine. It's more than fine.

An eternity later, I slide into the garage at the back of my place, cut the engine, and toss my helmet aside.

My anger is a burning flame. Stalking through the garage door, I enter the back of the house near the kitchen. Bear doesn't immediately appear to greet me, which means he's with my niece. I shed my jacket and kick off my shoes, then head toward the hallway leading to the bedrooms.

Halfway down the hall, I hear the sound of voices. Slowing, I pad on sock-clad feet to just outside the guest-room door.

"...and he's so *mean* to me." Mackenzie sniffles. "I didn't even do anything. I was just lying on my bed and he burst through the door and started yelling at me. I don't want to go back there."

The anger inside me flares brighter, but I pause when I hear another voice.

"I'm sure your uncle will let you stay here as long as you want. Do you have your textbooks?"

"Yeah," Mackenzie responds, sounding as downtrodden as I've ever heard her. "But I didn't have time to grab any clothes. Everyone at school will make fun of me if I have to wear day-old clothes tomorrow and the day after."

"We'll figure that out," Penny answers. "Don't worry."

"I hate my mom's boyfriend." I can almost see the mulish expression on Mackenzie's face. It's a Walsh specialty. My father passed his stubbornness on to all of us. I take a step toward the door, then—

"My dad remarried when I was eleven," Penny says.

I freeze. I know nothing about my dog walker. I saw her in person one time when she couldn't get the front door open, and that interaction was enough. She's not the kind of woman I need in my life. Just look at the ridiculous outfits she makes for Bear.

"Did you get along with your stepmom?"

Penny hums. "Kinda," she answers. "We didn't hate each other or anything, but I sort of became a second-class citizen, especially when she and my dad had my little brother. It sucks to be pushed aside by your own parent."

Mackenzie groans. "I hope my mom doesn't get pregnant with Kyle's baby."

A tinkling laugh. It sounds different than when I hear it through the recording on my nanny cam. Fuller. Warmer. "Well, we can't do anything about that. You're here now, and we should make the most of it."

"Are you the one who makes Bear's bow ties?" Mackenzie asks in an abrupt topic change.

"Sure am." A pause. "Does your uncle hate them?"

I frown, leaning closer to catch every word.

"He pretends to," Mackenzie says. "But I think he secretly likes it when you dress Bear up."

Another little laugh, and the two ladies quiet down.

There's a short silence, then I hear a sharp sound, like someone clapping their hands together, followed by Penny's voice. "You know what we need to do? Yoga."

My niece lets out a surprised giggle. "What?"

"We need to stick our butts in the air and do some deep breathing. I promise it'll help."

"I don't know how to do yoga," Kenzie says, but I hear the rustling of fabric, like she's moving off the guest-room bed.

"It's easy." Penny's voice is bright. It makes me lean closer to the door. "Now, we'll have to stand this way so we have enough room. Yeah, stand here. Okay, ready? Sweep your hands up, up, up while you breathe in...and out."

A short silence follows, then Penny's voice floats through the doorway again, more muffled this time.

"Good. Now put your butt in the air." A little giggle. "Yeah, like that. Wow, you can already get your heels on the ground. I wish I was fourteen years old again."

"No you don't," Mackenzie responds.

"You're right. I don't."

More giggles.

"Okay, let's drop down like—*oof*."

My niece laughs again, and the corner of my lips tips up. I inch closer to the door.

"Let me try that again," Penny says. "Downward dog. Just like that. Arch your back..."

I poke my head around the doorjamb to see two sets of legs facing me—and yes, two butts in the air. I lean a shoulder against the doorjamb and wait for them to finish.

And if my eyes roam over the expanse of leg revealed below the hem of Penny's dress, well, I'm only human.

"Now rock back and drop your head—"

My dog walker and I make eye contact through the vee of her legs. I arch a brow.

Penny sucks in a breath, lets out a gurgled scream, and promptly loses her balance. She tips over into Mackenzie,

LILIAN MONROE

who falls over into the side of the bed. Bear's tail is in the way, and my dog leaps up and off the bed in surprise, landing on top of the two women.

Groans escape the mass of limbs and fur and fabric. Bear hops off them, then nudges his nose next to Penny's head. He starts licking her face, and she screeches.

"Not now, Bear. I love you too, buddy but—*gah*! Stop—" More laughter. "Bear, stop it!"

Mackenzie disentangles herself from Penny and Bear, sitting up with her back to the bed. She starts laughing, leaning her head against the mattress. "Hey, Marcus."

"Sorry to interrupt."

"Penny was just teaching me how to do yoga."

"I can see that." I watch Penny sit up, her copper hair a wild, staticky halo around her head as it falls out of the ponytail still valiantly clinging to a few strands, her navy dress hiked up high on her legs. Both women sit against the bed frame, legs sticking straight out.

Bear collapses on top of the two ladies with his head on Mackenzie's lap, hind legs on Penny's outstretched thighs. Without a second of delay, Mackenzie starts scratching his ears, and Penny gives long, slow strokes along his fur.

Lucky dog.

Penny pushes her hair off her face and clears her throat. "Mr. Walsh. Hello." She gives me a nod, calm and professional, as if I didn't just watch her collapse into a heap on the floor. There's a strange buzzing in my chest and an unfamiliar feeling around my mouth, like I actually want to *smile* at her.

It's the relief of seeing Mackenzie giggling when she could've been crying. That's why I feel this way.

She clears her throat. "I'm sorry, I hope you don't mind me coming to check on Mackenzie, it's just—"

"It's fine," I interrupt. "Has Bear been walked yet?"

Penny looks at the dog, her face flushing red. I'd forgotten how many freckles she has. It's not a fine dusting across the bridge of her nose, or a few choice beauty marks dotted over her cheeks. The woman is covered in freckles. Every inch of her skin is dotted, even her ears. When she turns her head, I see that she's wearing a polka-dot bow in her hair that matches Bear's.

She made matching outfits for her and my dog. I don't even know what to think about that. I hate those polka dots. I want to kiss every single one of them, followed by the millions of freckles covering her body.

What a stupid urge. Ridiculous. I curl my hands into fists and crush that thought in my palms.

Penny shakes her head. "No. We'll go right away. Ready, Bear?" She pats his flank and gives it a scratch.

Bear rolls over to give her better access to his belly.

Penny laughs, the sound bright and carefree. Her face lights up, pink lips parting in a bright smile. A lurch occurs in my chest. There's something wrong with my heart. I need to schedule my yearly physical—I've been too stressed lately.

I clear my throat, and Penny glances up.

"Right. Let's go. Come on, bud. Time for us to go for a walk."

Bear jumps off the ladies' legs and doesn't even look at me on his way out. He knows I interrupted his scratches, and he's not happy about it.

I lean against the wall as Penny exits the room with the dog. Both Mackenzie and I listen as she makes her way out of the apartment. She talks to Bear like he's a person the entire time, which is absurd.

"Here we go, buddy. Just wait while I put my jacket on. You're such a good boy, you know that? Oh, no, not right now. Put the toy down. Yes, I'm serious. Listen, how about I give you some peanut butter when we get back? Yeah, I'm resorting to bribery. Uh-huh. Right now we need to go do your business outside. Yep. That's right, boy. Okay, here we go!" A second later, the door opens and the two of them are gone.

The house feels empty as soon as the door closes behind her. I scowl.

I turn my attention to my niece. She's straightened herself up and is climbing back on the bed. When she's settled side-on, with her back against the wall and her legs straight out on the bed, she starts picking at a loose thread on the coverlet, not meeting my gaze. Her dark, near-black hair hangs in messy hanks across her face, and she doesn't bother pushing it back.

But there's a flush on her cheeks, and a minute ago she was laughing with Penny. That's more than I could have managed on my own.

Sighing, I take a seat beside her. God, I suck at this. What am I supposed to say? Finally, when the silence stretches on and on, I manage a gruff, "Your mom's been drinking?"

Mackenzie nods.

"How long?"

One shoulder lifts, and Mackenzie finally gets the thread loose from the comforter. She rolls it between her fingers. "A while."

"And she has a new boyfriend living at her place?" It's a fight to keep my voice level.

My niece nods. "Yeah. Since September."

It's the middle of October now. I grit my teeth. "And that's when she started drinking again? When she started going out with him?"

Mackenzie jerks her chin. "Yeah. It's gotten worse since he moved in."

A familiar ball of emotion writhes in my stomach. Anger and frustration and guilt, twisting like a mass of angry vipers in my gut. I want to punch something. I want to cry.

We sit in silence for a while. This isn't the first time Mackenzie's had to stay at my place, but the last time was nearly three years ago. I actually thought Steph had put her drinking days behind her for good, but obviously I was wrong.

I know I should treat her with grace and understanding. I know that addiction is a demon that's not easily vanquished. I know I'm partially to blame. But she hurts her own daughter with her drinking. She causes Mackenzie *actual* pain and subjects her to the presence of all her deadbeat boyfriends. That's unconscionable. Unacceptable. *That's* what makes me angry.

It takes a superhuman effort to wrestle my temper down to manageable levels. I don't speak until I know my voice will come out almost calm. "I heard you say her boyfriend was mean to you. Can you tell me about that?"

If this guy has fucking so much as *looked* at Mackenzie wrong...

"He just yells a lot," Mackenzie says in a small voice. "He told me he'd get my mom to kick me out of the house. He said I was a nuisance." Her bottom lip wobbles. "I don't want to get kicked out, Marcus. I just want to go to school and get good grades. I have a science project to do, and I want to try out for the volleyball team, and...and..."

My ribs constrict. I sling an arm around my niece's shoulders and pull her in close. As soon as she hits my chest, she dissolves into tears. I lean my cheek against the top of her head and let out a sigh.

I've got six nieces and six nephews, and Mackenzie is the one I'm closest to. She's the eldest, and she's been my little girl since she was born. Steph needed a lot of help when Mackenzie arrived. It was around the time my company was taking off, so I was able to help out financially, even if Steph resented every cent I gave her. I moved the two of them to a new apartment, paid Steph's medical bills and living expenses, made sure she was stocked with all the necessary baby things. My sister did her best to pretend she didn't hate it. Still, I fell in love with her little girl as soon as she held on to my finger in her surprisingly strong infant grip, staring up at me with huge, green eyes. Mackenzie feels more like a daughter than a niece.

"I'm glad you came here," I tell her. "You know you can always stay with me, right?"

Mackenzie nods. "Yeah." She sniffles. "I don't have any clothes for school tomorrow. I don't even have my shampoo or my toothbrush or anything. I just had time to grab my backpack before Mom dragged me out of the apartment."

The fire that had banked inside me blazes to life again. I'm going to kill my sister. My teeth grind, and it takes a few long moments for me to get myself under control again.

"We'll get you some new clothes, Kenzie. Don't worry."

"I don't have any money."

That makes me laugh. "Well, you're in luck, kiddo, because I've got shitloads of it."

She huffs a sad little laugh, sitting up to wipe her eyes. Big black smudges appear across her cheeks, and I frown. She's wearing makeup. When did she start wearing makeup?

"There's black shit on your face," I tell her. "I'll give you a few minutes to get cleaned up, then we'll figure out where to get you some new clothes."

Mackenzie hurls herself off the bed and rushes to the bathroom to look in the mirror. A teenage shriek splits the air. I shake my head and walk out to the main living space. I text my driver to get him to come pick us up, then lean against the kitchen counter and scrub my face.

Where the hell do teenage girls get clothes these days? What kind of clothes am I supposed to buy? And *makeup*? Really? She's only fourteen. Am I supposed to get her makeup now too?

Overwhelmed doesn't even begin to cover how I feel. I should be at work, going through the endless tasks on my to-do list, instead of agonizing over my teenage niece wearing eyeliner. I'm supposed to be acquiring a small company within the next few months, and this is the time that Steph decided to start drinking again?

The front door opens, and Penny appears. "Sit. Good boy. We need to get you dried off, buddy." She reaches for a towel she must have left by the front door. I watch from across the space as she dries down my dog, taking extra care around his paws. Bear just sits patiently, panting, looking like the happiest dog in the world.

I can't blame him. I'd probably look that happy if a beautiful woman was rubbing a towel all over *my* body.

Ugh. I turn away from the two of them. I need to get laid.

Penny Littleton is not the type of woman I go for. She's so damn cute it gives me a headache to look at her. When I first saw her a year ago, all I wanted to do was wrap my arms around her and bury my face in the crook of her neck to see if she smelled like bubblegum and strawberries. I bet she smells sweet. Bet she tastes even sweeter.

Instead, I handed her the key to my house and told her what I expected from her as a dog walker. She'd stared at me with those big blue doll's eyes, her lush mouth calling to me, freckles painted over every inch of her face, and nodded. "No problem," she'd said. Her mouth had stretched into a big, happy smile, and it'd made my cock so hard I had to make a hasty exit as soon as she got the key in the door.

It makes no sense. The women I go for are sensual and sexy and happy to leave once the deed is done. They understand that I'm far too busy to do anything more than scratch an itch. I don't do bubbly. I don't do *cute*.

But that day, I very much wanted to do cute. Over and over again. On every surface in my home. I wanted to do cute so bad I thought of Penny Littleton every time I wrapped my hand around my cock for the next two weeks.

Fine—three weeks.

So I've avoided her ever since. I don't have time for women, and I certainly don't have time for my dog walker. Bear loves her too much to mess with.

Penny finishes drying him off and unclips his leash, hanging it up by the front door on its designated hook. She straightens his new bow tie and stands, giving a little yelp when she sees me. I hadn't realized I'd turned around to watch her again.

Her tinkling laugh sounds again, and that strange lurch in my chest occurs once more. Another lurch happens further down. I ignore them both.

"Sorry," she says with a stupid, cute little flush on her cheeks. "I'm usually alone in here. I wasn't expecting you."

Wasn't expecting me in my own damn home. Like she owns the place.

I wait for a flash of annoyance...and it doesn't come.

Bear finally deigns to come say hello to me. I pet his head as I meet Penny's gaze across the open-plan space.

"You don't need to come this afternoon," I tell her. "I'll walk Bear. I'm taking the rest of the day off. I'll still pay your regular fee."

Usually when I give people paid time off, they perk up. Penny actually looks disappointed. She glances at my dog. "Okay. I guess I'll see you tomorrow, Bear." My dog trots to her and demands scratches. Penny obliges. "Bye-bye. Be a good boy while I'm gone."

Bear huffs, gives me a disappointed look, and walks to his water bowl.

"You're leaving?" Mackenzie appears in the mouth of the hallway.

Penny turns around again and meets my niece's gaze. "Yep. You feeling better?"

My niece shrugs. "I guess. Marcus is taking me to get new clothes."

"Oh, lovely!" Penny exclaims. "Where is he taking you?"

The two women look at me expectantly. Even Bear stops lapping at his water bowl to look my way.

I gulp. "I, um..." My eyes dart between Penny and Kenzie. My niece's face is blotchy and red, her eyes still a bit watery from her tears. I don't want to let her down. Turning to Penny, I jerk my chin in her direction. "Come with us. I'm sure you know more about what a teenage girl likes than I do. I'll pay your normal hourly rate."

Penny tilts her head. She turns to Mackenzie. "Do you want me to come?"

That one little question makes the ground tilt beneath my feet. Right then, when Penny doesn't just accept my offer to pay her an admittedly great hourly rate to tag along and actually checks with Kenzie to make sure my niece wants her there...that makes me feel unsteady.

I rub a spot in the middle of my chest and make a mental note to get that doctor's appointment scheduled.

I'm used to having employees, and it's a clear relationship. I pay them for their time. They do the work. Hell, most of my relationships have followed that same script. I pay for dinners, for drinks, for weekend trips to the Caribbean, and I get something clear and defined in return. It starts when I say it starts, and it ends when I say it ends.

It never goes any further than a few months of fun. Never goes any deeper than the surface of my skin.

I know that if my niece told Penny not to come shopping, Penny would turn down the few hundred bucks out of respect for a fourteen-year-old girl's wishes. Not everyone would do that. Not everyone would go against my requests just to heed the preferences of a teenage girl.

"Yeah," Kenzie says, smiling brightly. "I like your style. Maybe you can help me find a dress like yours."

"Oh." Penny flushes again, sliding her hands down her

front. She's wearing a navy-blue dress with a high neckline and a flouncy skirt. Her rain jacket is rubber-duck yellow, and there's a scarf tied on her purse that matches her hair bow. I never would have imagined my ripped-jeans-and-T-shirt-wearing niece would want to look like that. I can't imagine *anyone* would want to look like that. It's ridiculous. Completely, utterly ridiculous.

Penny smiles at my niece. "Well, we'll see what we can find, okay?"

Mackenzie nods and runs to the guest bedroom to get her purse. After putting my shoes back on and grabbing my jacket, I find myself beside Penny by the front door. My fingers decide to brush across the back of her hand.

Her skin is very, very soft.

"Thanks," I say quietly.

Penny glances up at me, and my eyes drop to her lips. I bet those are soft, too. "No problem," she answers. "Mackenzie's lucky to have you."

3

PENNY

I'D FORGOTTEN how gorgeous Marcus Walsh is, but boy, have I gotten one hell of a reminder. He makes me feel like I have a trapped bird in my chest. It flaps its wings against my ribs whenever he looks at me.

His eyes are almond-shaped, slightly uptilted—and bright, emerald green. His hair is coal-black, a bit longer than strictly professional. He's big—tall and broad—to the point where I barely reach his shoulder. He could probably pick me up and throw me over his shoulder without any effort whatsoever, just by using a single one of those big hands of his.

Why do I enjoy that thought?

I adjust and readjust my crossbody bag, just to do something with my hands. I'm sweating under my rain jacket. Under his gaze.

Dangerous—this man is dangerous.

And don't I know better than to get close to a dangerous man?

I zip my rain jacket all the way up my neck and pull the

hood over my head. Marcus's eyes follow the movements like a predator watching his prey.

I try not to squirm, but I'm surprised to find I don't feel the usual slimy discomfort of a man's gaze. Instead all I feel is...heat. A long-forgotten heat tightening in my chest and stomach—and lower.

Frazzled, I clear my throat and bat imaginary hair off my cheeks. I feel itchy all over.

This isn't like me. I haven't been attracted to a man for a long, long time. Hell, I do my best to not attract them right back! My stepmother loves to inform me that if I didn't dress in such silly clothes, I'd have no problem catching a man. She doesn't seem to understand that catching a man is the exact opposite of what I want to do.

I want to stay as far away from men as possible.

For obvious reasons, I don't speak to my dad or stepmother much.

Dogs are a much better choice. Dogs don't show up at your door and follow you to work. Dogs don't stalk you for months and months, to the point where you're afraid to leave your house. Dogs don't hack into your computer and read your personal emails. The police would probably be much more helpful if a dog was bothering you compared to a man.

I know that for a fact. I learned the hard way.

"Ready!" Mackenzie comes rushing from the hallway and stabs her feet into shoes. "Let's go."

There's a car waiting for us outside, and from the way Mr. Walsh nods at the driver, I assume he's an employee. We take off. Mackenzie has brightened right up and is listing all the clothes she'll need, along with toiletries and makeup. Marcus is answering noncommittally, one arm on the edge of the car window, his other arm resting on the center console.

I'm in the back seat with Mackenzie, so I have a good view of his profile. His jaw could cut glass. His nose is strong and straight, and his throat is strangely sexy when he leans his head back against the headrest. I close my eyes and turn to the window before opening them again.

The rain beats down a steady drizzle on our car. It washes New York City in shades of gray, making the city look hazy and foreboding. Inside the car, I'm warmed by heated seats and enclosed in a leather-upholstered cocoon. I feel safe.

The thought jars me. I feel *safe*. I'm three feet away from a powerful man, and I'm not afraid.

That in itself is bad. It means my instincts are dull around him. It means he could hurt me.

"I forgot my hair straightener too," Mackenzie says. "So maybe we can get one of those." Her fingers idly stroke Bear's fur as he rests on the middle seat between us. The dog's eyes are closed, and I put a hand on his back to draw some comfort from the heat of his fur.

"Sure," Mr. Walsh answers. His long fingers drum on the center console, and the back of my hand tingles in response. He *touched* me with those fingers. "We'll grab whatever you need, Kenzie."

We turn onto Fifth Avenue, slow down, and I nearly choke. He's taking his teenage niece to get designer clothing on the most famous shopping street in the country. Why was I expecting us to go to Target?

More importantly, what the heck am I doing here?

Mr. Walsh is out of the car as soon as it stops, and the driver is outside my door a second later. He opens it for me and gives me a nod, opening an umbrella for me as soon as I step out. Mackenzie shuffles across the seat to exit on the same side, thanking the driver and taking the umbrella. Bear stays inside, to be kept safe in the heat and shelter of the car while we shop.

My boss is already at the door to the designer department store, nodding to the doorman as he strides through.

"Thank you," I mumble as I follow. My rain jacket squeaks as I take off the hood. Everything around me is gleaming and expensive and terrifying. I'm afraid to move, in case I touch something and ruin it. So I stand in place, dripping water onto the polished floor, watching Mr. Walsh and Mackenzie stride toward a sales associate dressed in all black.

"My niece needs clothes," Mr. Walsh announces. He doesn't ask for help or waste time with any niceties. Like the way he looked at me and said, *Come with us*. He's used to ordering people around.

Barf. The last thing I want is to be ordered around like a dimwitted slave.

With that thought to bolster my defenses, I shove my attraction to him into a mental box tagged, "Destroy at First Available Opportunity."

The sales lady gives Mr. Walsh a deferential nod and turns to Mackenzie. "Can you tell me what you're looking for, miss?"

"Well..." She glances at Marcus, a question written in her eyes.

"Whatever you need, Kenzie," he replies, putting his hand around her shoulders and tugging her close for a quick hug. "Just tell the lady what you want."

Mackenzie takes a deep breath. "I have nothing," she

finally says. "I need jeans, tops, and probably a dress or two. Underwear. A hair straightener. And I like Penny's dress, so if you have something like that, can I please try it on?"

She points at me, and all eyes turn to land on my soggy, dripping self.

I die. I just expire right there on the shiny stone floors.

"May I see the dress?" The woman smiles at me, gesturing for me to unzip my jacket. She clasps her hands in front of her stomach, waiting patiently. Her voice is calm and respectful, and I wonder if she would've used that tone if I'd walked in here on my own, without the great Marcus Walsh beside me, stinking of money.

I'm guessing the answer to that question is a big, fat *NO*.

I clear my throat. "Of course."

So, surrounded by clothes worth thousands and thousands of dollars, I unzip my rubber rain jacket and open it up to reveal my dress. It's a thrift flip. It started as a floor-length maternity dress, and I deconstructed it and re-sewed it into a 1950s-style circle dress. Now, it has a high neck and cap sleeves, and I was particularly proud of the darts I added. The original dress cost me two dollars. Two. Dollars. I was proud of that fact until I stood in the lobby of this store, surrounded by stupidly expensive clothing, being inspected by the Designer Gestapo.

I'm wearing a *homemade dress* while a fancy saleslady examines it with an expert eye.

"I'm not sure I recognize the designer," she says, groomed eyebrows pulling together.

No shit. My heart starts hammering, the weight of her gaze, and Mackenzie's, and Marcus's burrowing into my skin. Especially Marcus's.

That mental box flies open, and lust hits me like a high-speed train right between the eyes. Unfortunately, the impact severs the connection between my brain and my mouth.

"It's a Littleton," I blurt like an absolute nincompoop. "From the spring/summer collection this year." A deranged smile spreads over my lips. "I couldn't believe it when I found it."

I flounce the skirt, then my mouth clamps shut as my brain catches up to my words.

What the hell did I just say?

Did I really just claim that I am a designer called Littleton and that my dress was part of a *collection*? What the actual heck is wrong with me? I need professional help.

Well, I need *more* professional help.

Oh, God. She's going to look at me like I'm dirt. She's going to know I'm poor, that I run a dog-clothing business, that I chopped and sewed this dress myself.

But the sales lady just gives me a knowing nod. "Of course. Groundbreaking. I particularly loved Littleton's use of color blocking last year."

I am a deer in headlights, and I just about manage to nod. The funny thing is, she's not wrong. I did do a lot of color blocking in my thrift-flip projects and my dog clothes collection alike. But somehow, I don't think the sales lady knows that.

I also don't know if I'd describe myself as "groundbreaking." More like "broke." Groundbroke?

With those nonsensical thoughts coursing through my head, I make the mistake of meeting my boss's gaze. His eyebrow is arched, green eyes steady on mine. Is it just me, or did his lip twitch the tiniest bit?

No. He's not smiling. Look at his face! He looks like he thinks I'm the stupidest woman to ever grace his presence, and at this point, I'm not sure he's wrong.

"Follow me!" The sales lady does a graceful sweep of her arm and takes us deeper into the store. I end up walking a few feet behind Mackenzie, and Mr. Walsh falls into step beside me.

His voice is like honey, warming me down to my toes. "Did Littleton do a lot of color blocking in last year's spring/summer collection, or was that sales associate full of shit?"

I flick my gaze up to his, then immediately look away. I can feel the flush rising up my neck. "You heard her. It was a groundbreaking collection." I speak out the side of my lips, my steps stiff as we move deeper into the store.

"And let me guess. Fall/winter is seeing a polka-dot trend?" I catch his gaze flicking to the bow in my hair. There's definite amusement in his eyes, but it's not the nice kind of amusement. It's cynical and mocking. Damn him! How can he look so pretty when he's making fun of me?

My cheeks are on fire. I'm not the type of woman who can blush prettily. I'm extremely fair, freckled, and ginger. When I blush, every inch of my head, chest, and shoulders grows bright red. I must look like an absolute fright right now. I can't imagine a red face, yellow rain jacket, and polka-dot bow is a good look.

"I can't presume to guess what kind of genius Littleton will come up with next," I answer primly, lifting my chin. I steal a glance at the man beside me, just in time to see the corner of his lips tilt up the tiniest bit once more. My heart does a Cirque-du-Soleil-worthy cartwheel, then sticks the landing and gives the rest of my organs a deep bow.

But the hint of a smile on Mr. Walsh's face fades as quickly as it appears and is replaced by a deep scowl.

Well, then.

Clearly, this man doesn't like me.

Why does that thought bother me?

While I'm busy untangling my whirling thoughts, my brain malfunctions again. This time, it's my feet that lose their connection to my spinal column, and I trip over a perfectly flat section of the floor. Arms flailing, stomach lurching, I pitch forward—toward a very fancy and very expensive-looking display of mannequins wearing glittery evening gowns.

At the last moment, an arm wraps around my stomach, and I'm hauled up onto my feet again. My back is pressed against a strong, male body. An arm made of marble bands across my stomach. The touch feels like wrapping my hand around an electric fence. My whole body jolts, desire searing through me in a hot wave. My skin grows sensitive, my breasts feel heavy, and an awareness of the space between my legs becomes impossible to ignore.

His palm presses into my navel, his chest a firm wall at my back.

Shocked, all I can do is stand still while my body is pressed against a man's for the first time in years.

No. Not "a man's." Against *Marcus Walsh*, my billionaire boss's very nice, very gigantic body.

"You okay?" he asks, his hand sliding across to the dip in my waist. His fingers shift down the slightest bit, and I know he's feeling the waistband of my underwear.

My suddenly drenched underwear.

I give a jerky nod. "Thank you," I pant, pulling away.

He steps away from me, but the back of my body still feels like it's on fire. My stomach has a brand across it, and I almost want to excuse myself to the bathroom to check if his arm left a mark. I put my hands on my cheeks in a futile attempt to cool them down, finding my boss, Mackenzie, and the sales lady staring at me.

I point at the glittery monstrosity in front of me. "It's just so pretty."

The sales lady nods sagely. "A common reaction."

I give her a pinched smile. We keep walking. My steps are wooden as my thoughts whirl around me, the sensations in my body quickly spiraling out of my conscious control. The heat of my boss's body is a blaze at my side. His arm brushes my jacket, and his steps echo on the gleaming marble floors. I'm so painfully, keenly aware of the distance between the two of us that it's hard to focus on anything else.

I'm off-balance. This isn't right. I'm not supposed to feel this way about men.

There's only one man around whom I feel safe, and that's my business partner Brian. He's proven himself time and again to be reliable. He's been my friend for five years, and he's the only man who hasn't tried to sleep with me. I trust him—only him.

But other men? Ones who look at me like I'm only good for sex or cleaning duties? They're best kept on the other side of my thick, spiked defensive walls.

I'm absolutely sure that Marcus Walsh should be on the far side of the wall, with big bazooka rifles aimed at his head. He's rich, powerful, and so painfully beautiful that looking at him hurts my eyes. If normal men are dangerous, Mr. Walsh is deadly.

The echo of his touch still burns along my stomach, my back. My shoulders feel singed where they crashed into his chest. My throat is tight and my heart beats unsteadily.

As we stop in front of a display of ridiculously expensive clothing, I know that the best thing for me to do is stay far, far away from him.

Problem is, I'm not sure I'll be able to.

4

MARCUS

MY PHONE RINGS. I leave Penny and Mackenzie as they head to the fitting room for the hundredth time and step aside, answering the phone.

"Marcus," my mother says, exhaling sharply. "I got your message. Mackenzie is with you?"

"Mm," I answer. "Have you heard from Steph?"

"Not a word. She's not answering my calls."

The knot of snakes returns to my gut, twisting, spitting, biting. I hate this. Hate that Mackenzie is in the middle of it, hate that I'm to blame for it all.

I'm supposed to be the one to take care of my family. I'm the one they rely on.

My mother lets out a breath. "I'll keep trying her. Is Kenzie okay?"

"She's fine. I'm grabbing some clothes with her now."

"You're a good man, honey," my mother says.

I grimace. I don't feel like a good man. I feel like I'm being crushed by the weight of it all. My familial responsibilities, my business—all those lives relying on *me* to make things work.

Penny's voice floats across the space. "You look *amazing*, Mackenzie. No, I'm serious." She...squeals. I don't know how else to describe the noise, and I do my best to block it out.

"Marcus," my mother continues, drawing my attention back to the phone call. "I just heard from Ollie. Little Anna just broke her arm, and their insurance didn't cover the entire bill. She'd never ask you herself, of course, but could you..."

"I'll take care of it," I answer automatically. "How much do they need?"

Ollie is my youngest brother. He has three kids—Oliver Jr., Anna, and baby Eric—and works for the in-house legal team at my friend Leif's company. I introduced the two of them and got him the job three years ago. My brother's wife had to stop working due to medical issues after having Eric. They must have been struggling more than I knew. I should have taken care of this sooner.

"Do you want to pay the hospital directly? I'll get Ollie to send you the information."

"It's okay, Mom," I say. "I'll take it from here."

"Love you, honey," my mother says. "Mr. Rosebury says hello, and he says thank you for getting his oven fixed."

My mother's neighbor was ancient twenty years ago. Now, he's prehistoric. When I was a kid, he'd pay me to help bring his groceries up the three flights of stairs and other odd jobs. I saved up for my first computer with the money he gave me. The least I could do was send someone over to fix the old man's oven, especially when he wouldn't let me buy him a new one.

"It's no problem, Mom. Tell him hello from me."

"Will do. I have to go now; Tara's kids will be here soon, and I haven't prepped anything for lunch. Bye now. Give Kenzie a big kiss from me and tell her I can't wait to see her new outfits. Oh and honey, don't forget this weekend!"

I frown. "This weekend?"

"Oliver Jr.'s birthday," my mother chides. "You said you could make it."

I close my eyes. "Of course. Yeah. I'll be there."

"See you then."

I hang up the phone and let out a breath. My mother is a force of nature. She's the glue that holds us all together—family, friends, community.

I touch the fabric of the dress hanging in front of me. The fabric is fine, the beadwork exquisite. I didn't grow up with any of this. My mother still lives in the same three-bedroom apartment in Washington Heights where I grew up with my two sisters and two brothers. I'm pretty sure my childhood bedroom, complete with bunk beds and dressers dominating the tiny room, is just as I left it. The only difference is now my mother owns the apartment and I pay the ongoing expenses. She never wanted anything nicer. Said the place was full of memories that couldn't be replaced by a fancy, million-dollar home.

I can't blame her. I've stayed in my SoHo factory for years. There's something to be said about stability, about knowing where you came from.

I lifted my family out of near poverty. I did it. I made it.

So why do I feel so hollow? Why do I feel like it'll never be enough? There's always another emergency. Another mouth to feed. Another oven to fix.

I don't mind being the person they all turn to. In a way, I

like it. I'm the one that my family and friends rely on, the one that makes sure we never end up in the place we started.

But sometimes, it's just…never-ending. It feels like there's no point to any of it, except to make sure that everyone else is happy. I'm constantly chasing something, and I don't even know what it is.

Mackenzie's laughter makes me turn, and I see her emerging from the fitting room with Penny. Wisps of anger still curl around my chest at the thought of what my sister said. How she treated her daughter this morning.

Is it any wonder I feel like I haven't done enough? Stephanie could have been anything she wanted by now if I'd been there for her. If I hadn't been so selfish that day, when it all turned bad.

"Marcus, look!" Kenzie lifts up a blue dress. "It's not exactly like Penny's, but it fits really well. Can I get it?"

I shrug a shoulder. "Whatever you want, baby girl."

Her eyes shine, and she throws her arms around my neck. "Thank you."

Over her shoulder, I meet Penny's gaze. She's holding her yellow rain jacket in both hands, and there's a bright-red flush on her cheeks and neck. Her skin is smooth, silky, touchable. I wonder if her copper-colored hair would feel soft between my fingers. If she'd enjoy it if I wrapped it around my fist.

I tear my eyes away from her and nod to my niece. "Got everything you need?"

"Yeah. Except makeup and undies. And hair stuff. So you need to go do something else because I do *not* want my uncle to see me buying underwear." Her nose wrinkles. "Gross."

Penny's lips twitch. "I'll help you, Mackenzie. Come on."

They turn to follow the sales associate to another section, and I find myself wandering through the aisles, seeing nothing. My mind is whirling. My phone keeps buzzing, and I know I should answer it. My assistant Todd probably needs a hundred and one things from me. Maybe my mother forgot about another person that will struggle unless I lend a hand.

But I ignore it all, because all I can think about is how soft Penny's skin was and how good she felt when I caught her and pressed her against my body.

Taking care of my family and employees feels hollow, but having her body cradled in mine felt very, very real. I'm edgy, unsettled. I hate feeling like this.

I end up next to a jewelry case containing colorful, funky pieces. A pair of earrings catch my eye. They're flower-shaped, with one gold flower nested inside a blue one. The center of the flower is a bright blue stone.

They'd look great on Penny. She'd probably pair them with an outrageous bow in her hair or another piece of the Littleton "spring/summer collection" and look as good or better than any of the designer duds in this place.

A sales associate materializes on the other side of the counter. "See something you like, sir?"

I shouldn't. She's my dog walker. You don't buy your dog walker jewelry.

Then again, Penny spent her day making Mackenzie feel better about what happened this morning. Not only that, but she's been working for me for a year, and she hasn't missed a single day. Bear loves her. I could call it a yearly bonus.

"Those earrings," I say, pointing to the case. "The blue ones with the gold."

"Beautiful choice, sir," the man says. He has slicked-back

blond hair and is dressed in black from neck to feet. "Bea Bongiasca makes very unique pieces. The Flower Power Double Hoop earrings have been particularly popular."

I have a feeling he would have said that about literally any piece of jewelry I point out, but I let it slide. Before I can over-think it, I buy the earrings and slip them in a pocket.

Then I realize what I've done, and I want to shoot myself in the head.

My niece and dog walker reappear, arms laden with about a dozen bags, looking flushed and exhausted.

"Ready to go?" I ask.

"Yes," Mackenzie says. "I'll show you everything I got when I'm at home." She hands me back the credit card I'd given her earlier, and I slip it into my wallet.

When we get outside, Penny clears her throat. "I'll just grab the subway from here," she tells us, then meets my gaze. Under the awning, we're safe from the steady drizzle coming from the overcast skies. Penny looks like a bright spot against all the gray drab surrounding us, in yellow and blue and red, a riot of copper hair and freckled skin.

Lust blazes through me.

It's not *her*. Penny herself is just too...cute. Too much.

I just need to get laid, and she's the closest woman, that's all. But I can't deny it—I want to have her pressed up against me like she was earlier, feel the heat of her body through our clothing, have her panting breaths coasting over my cheek. As we watch each other over the small distance that separates us, desire wraps a tight fist around me.

Would she taste good under that dress of hers? Would she sigh and moan for me with the same abandon with which she laughs? Would she beg and plead me for more? I need to know the answer to all those questions and more. Would she be shy and demure if I undressed her, blushing like crazy, or would she get a little wild?

Wild. She'd let go, I decide.

Heat whips through me, scorching everything in its path. I need this woman beneath me. Tonight. Right now.

She clears her throat. "Well. See you later."

Ice water dashes across my face, dousing my misplaced lust.

I scowl. What the hell is wrong with me? The last thing I need right now is another distraction. I'm dealing with an important acquisition at work, worrying about my sister's relapse, and now have to take care of my teenage niece. I don't need a woman to complicate things.

I certainly don't need *this* woman to complicate things.

I wave a hand. "Fine. Goodbye." Ignoring the way Penny flinches, I duck my head and dive into the waiting car, holding Bear back when he tries to launch himself out toward Penny.

Mackenzie appears a second later, frowning at me. When we start driving, she meets my gaze. "Why were you so rude to Penny? You could have at least given her a ride home. She was really nice today, and she helped me a lot more than you did."

"My credit card helped a bit, as I recall," I grumble, not meeting my niece's eyes.

There's a silence, then a sullen answer from my niece. "Well, *I* like her, even if you don't."

I stare out the window and don't answer Mackenzie's

comments. When we get home, I take the stupid earrings out of my jacket pocket and stuff them in the bottom drawer of the desk in my home office, slamming it shut with a bang.

5

PENNY

WHEN I DON'T SEE Mr. Walsh for the rest of the week, I'm glad. Without a clear explanation for what exactly occurred the day Mackenzie arrived, I can only push all my strange, lustful thoughts and feelings aside and pretend they never happened.

I still visit his home twice a day to walk Bear, and I see evidence of Mackenzie's presence with sweaters thrown over the big leather sofa, a few extra pairs of (designer) shoes by the front door, and various bits of schoolwork piled on the edge of the kitchen island.

Oddly, it makes me more comfortable. Like an actual human being lives here now, and I'm not walking a dog that lives in a museum.

One time, six months ago, I found a sock under Bear's dog bed. It was the first evidence I saw that my boss actually lived here. I ended up folding the sock and placing it on the corner of the kitchen island with a note explaining where it was. It was gone the next day.

I've run into cleaners and cooks and Todd the assistant, but mostly the house is empty apart from me and Bear.

The sock was the most contact I'd had with Marcus Walsh, tech billionaire and entrepreneur—and it very well could have been dealt with by the cleaning crew. Still, one sock was enough for me. Yes, my online shop was hosted on Mr. Walsh's website, but that didn't mean I had anything to do with the CEO. My working for him was more of a strange connection, a footnote in my life. It didn't mean anything.

Now, walking into his house makes my heart twist and stumble. It's Monday morning, and it should be like any other Monday, when Bear greets me like a long-lost sibling finally returned.

But today, I'm *nervous*. It's ridiculous.

I tiptoe into the house and let out a breath of relief when Bear comes clicking along the concrete floor toward me. He tackles me to the ground and gives me doggy kisses as I laugh, and finally extricate myself and stand. I check his bowl, tidy his toy area, and then grab his leash.

"Ready for your walk?" I ask.

Bear woofs. I glance at the nanny cam, but after what happened last week, it feels weird to pose and smile. I did it every day for a year, and it became part of my routine—but that was before I had spent a day with Marcus Walsh. In a way, waving and smiling for the camera with Bear was a way to assert myself. Yes, I was in a man's house, walking his dog, but I wasn't powerless.

So many of the things I do are to prove to myself that I *can*. I'm sick of living a small, terrified life. I'm sick of flinching anytime a strange man comes near.

Smiling for the camera every day made me feel in control. A silly thought, really, especially now that I've spent more than thirty seconds with the man who owns it. I was in his car. I saw him treat his niece like a daughter.

Now, there's someone on the other side of the lens, and I don't feel in control at all.

"Let's go," I say brightly, and Bear seems happy to comply. We head out onto the streets. There's a little park and playground just two blocks away that's part of our regular route. Bear does his business, then sits patiently while a small child comes up to pet him, soon joined by her mother and two other children. Bear accepts rubs and scratches until the kids move on, and then we head home.

I love walking this dog. He stays directly beside me and always puts himself between me and people who might approach. He's growled a warning at a few men that have tried to strike up conversations, and I always gave him an extra treat afterward. He's protective and perceptive and makes me feel safe when I walk beside him.

He reminds me of my old dog, Margie (short for Margarine). I got Margie when I was thirteen and took her with me after I moved out from my dad and stepmom's place. She was my best friend and a great judge of character.

If only I'd listened to her advice. A lot of the pain I went through in college could have been avoided if I'd paid attention to my dog's opinion of my ex-boyfriend. Unfortunately, she died of cancer a year before things between me and my ex got really bad. Sometimes I wonder if saying goodbye to Margie made me more vulnerable to the torture that Billy put me through.

"Penny!" a voice calls out from behind me. "Penny Littleton?"

I turn to see a tall, lithe woman with blue-black hair. She's wearing a deep red corset and tight, dark-wash jeans. A long wool coat falls off her shoulders and opens to reveal glimpses of the outfit. Her hair is sleekly curled and piled on top of her head in a vaguely retro, pin-up style. Her lipstick matches her corset. She looks sexy and chic and totally put together.

Unlike me, who's wearing a rubber-duck-yellow rain jacket, matching boots, and pigtails.

I freeze, shocked. "Nikita."

She laughs, spreading her arms. Before I know what's happening, my college best friend wraps her arms around me and hauls me into a tight hug. "I haven't seen you in years!" Her perfume is floral and sweet, and her hugs are just as great as they were nearly ten years ago.

Pulling away, Nikita drops down to one knee and gives Bear a big scratch behind the ears. He sniffs at her hands, approves, then shoves his head under her palm to ask for more pets.

Nikita obliges him. "What have you been up to? Love your dog. Bit bigger than Margie was, though!"

"He's not mine," I answer. "I just walk him. I, um... I never got a dog of my own after Margie died."

"Oh." Nikki gives me a look that's part sad, part questioning. "Well, you're lucky." She gives Bear another scratch, then stands up. "Is that what you do these days? I haven't seen you in so long. You dropped off the face of the earth."

I grimace. She's not wrong. I open my mouth, wanting to explain what happened and why our friendship ended, but nothing comes out. Instead, I just say, "I actually started a business a couple of years ago. I make dog clothes and sell them online. It's going pretty well these days. Been doing it full-time for about a year."

Nikita's face splits into a broad smile. "That is *amazing*. I love it! You were always so creative. I knew political science wasn't your true calling."

My heart warms, and I know my face is flushed. I shrug. "It's all right."

"All right? Penny, you started a business!"

I laugh, shaking my head. I've never been very good at accepting compliments. "What have you been up to?" I have to crane my neck to meet her eyes. She's wearing patent leather platform heels on top of being a tall woman to begin with. At five foot nothing on a good day, I'm not exactly on her level.

Still, some deep part of me relaxes. I don't have many friends, and Nikita was always good to me. After everything that happened in college, I completely isolated myself. Nikita was the only one who kept trying to call me, even years later.

Ignoring her was one of the only things that truly made me feel shame. But I was in defensive mode, barricading myself against the outside world. Even now, years later, I don't allow myself to get close to many people.

But Nikki's looking at me with those same chocolate-brown eyes, full of kindness and warmth. She's confident and hot and has always carried herself like she'll fight anyone who challenges her. Standing in front of her, I wonder if I could have dealt with my past troubles differently. If I could have been more like her.

"I manage a vintage clothing store. It's not bad." She shrugs. "Tell me more about you, though. What happened to you? One minute we were going to class together every day, and the next you deleted all your social media and disappeared. I was worried! I ended up calling your dad just to make sure you were still alive. And now, here, in the city? You said you'd never come here."

A long breath escapes my lips. "That's a long story, Nikki."

She grins. "Lucky for you, I'm a good listener. What are you doing tonight?"

There's a brief pause; it's no more than a second or two. But in that moment, my world expands and shrinks and tosses me around like a rag doll.

I open my mouth to tell her I'm busy, like I normally would. That's what I should do, right? Because it's safer to stay alone, at home, where I can't be found.

But I stop myself at the last moment. Maybe it's the week I've had, dreaming of a man with green eyes, feeling things in my body that I thought I'd never experience. Maybe it's the confidence of having Bear's bulk and warmth leaning against my legs, or the fact that I *do* run a successful business, and Nikki's right, damn it. It *is* amazing!

Whatever the reason, some old wound inside starts to knit itself shut. Or maybe it's been shut for a long time, and I only now realized I was healed enough to move on. I find myself straightening my shoulders and meeting my old friend's gaze.

"I have no plans tonight. Are you free?"

Nikki gives me a blazing, bright smile. The same smile she gave me when we first met in a big auditorium on the first day of freshman year, when she moved her bag so I could sit next to her.

Just like that, a broken connection is mended. We decide to meet up for drinks in the evening, and she gives me another tight hug before saying goodbye. "I'm not going to let you disappear this time, Littleton," she answers, sticking a long, perfectly manicured black nail in my face. "So you better not bail on me."

I grin. "I won't."

"Good."

We part ways. When I make it back to my boss's house, I still have a smile on my face.

Until I open the door and see Marcus Walsh standing in the kitchen wearing nothing but loose workout shorts, socks, and sneakers.

I freeze in the doorway. I grow roots. An earthquake couldn't make me move.

He's...

My mouth grows dry as a desert sandstorm. Something sizzles in a pan that he shakes around, the muscles in his back and shoulders writhing with the movement. Bear tugs at the leash I'm still holding tight, and I remember where I am. I unclip Bear's leash, and he goes trotting toward his owner. Mr. Walsh makes a noise that sounds like a grunt and a growl all wrapped up in a coating of surprise, then bends over to say hello to his dog.

From the side, I can see the thick bulk of his abdominal muscles rippling with the movement. He's not built like a bodybuilder. He's built like an athlete. Like a boxer or a swimmer.

Heat gushes through my thighs, my stomach. I squeeze

my knees together, still unable to move from my spot by the door. Wiggling my toes to make sure I can still feel them, I tear my gaze away from the image of male perfection in the kitchen and turn toward the row of hooks by the door.

I use a few moments to gather myself while I hang up the dog's leash. My body buzzes with electricity, every hair standing on end. My clothing feels rough against my skin. My nipples have gone rock-hard, and I check the front of my rain jacket to make sure they're not poking through.

When I finally gather the courage, I turn to face my shirt-less, sweat-slicked boss. I want to lick him. Is that gross? It's gross. Even in my lust-addled brain, I know it's gross. But I still want to do it. Run my tongue right over his nipple and see what he'd do, how he'd taste.

I find him staring at me, his eyes narrowed, brows tugged low.

Gosh, he's beautiful. Even though he looks grumpy as hell.

"Mr. Walsh," I say with a nod.

"Call me Marcus," he grunts, one hand absentmindedly scratching Bear's head. Bear leans against his owner's leg and enjoys the attention.

"Okay," I croak. "M-Marcus."

This is bad. I'm feeling things that are dangerous to my self-control, to my sense of self. For the first time in eight years—more—I have an urge to strip down and ask him to touch me. To throw myself at him and hope he catches me. I want to feel his stubble on the inside of my thigh until my skin is rough and red and sore. I want his skin against mine. I want those big hands shaping my body. I want his cock to split me in half.

I jab a thumb at the door behind me. "I'm gonna get going."

I turn to make my escape and have my hand on the door-knob when I hear, "Wait."

Freezing, I listen to the rushing blood in my ears and try to keep my breath steady. I don't want to wait. I want to run. I want to go somewhere cold so my body won't feel so over-heated. I want to jump in the shower and wash this feeling off my skin.

I'm attracted to my boss. Desperately. Dangerously.

Rotating slowly, I swallow past the constriction in my throat and lift my gaze to meet Mr. Wal—to meet Marcus's.

He still looks angry, or at the very least unimpressed. And damn my stupid hormones, but it still turns me on. That dark look in his eyes, that gleaming, sweat-slicked skin, it's...

It's demented, is what it is. I need to get my head checked.

"You've been very reliable this past year," he says, his voice a low rumble. It sounds like he's forcing himself to say the words even though he'd rather be doing literally anything else. "And I wanted to thank you for helping my niece last week."

"Oh," I answer stupidly, shifting my weight from foot to foot. I paste on a smile. "Right. Well, it was no problem. She's a good kid. I remember being her age and living with a stepparent. It was hard. I could relate. Plus, I probably would have died of mortification if my uncle had to help me buy underwear, you know? So I was happy to help." I clamp my lips shut to stop myself from babbling and adjust my rain jacket so it won't cling to my bare, clammy arms underneath.

My boss stares at me for a moment, then jerks his chin at

the shelf near my shoulder. "You didn't smile for the camera this morning."

My whole entire head gets hot so fast I'm worried it'll pop right off my neck like some sort of gruesome, bloodied rocket. I didn't *actually* think Marcus watched the nanny cam himself. I assumed he had staff for that. I never thought I'd speak to him ever again after our first meeting outside the front door. The posing was just a funny tradition I started with Bear. It was me, asserting myself in the silliest, stupidest way I could.

I stammer, gulp, glance at the nanny cam, then let out a nervous laugh. "No, I guess I didn't."

Marcus turns back to the stove. I hear the gas turn off, and he slides an omelet onto a waiting plate. I stare at his back for a bit while I try to pull myself together. It's like an anatomy lesson. I didn't know half of those muscles even existed.

But then Marcus turns back around, catches me staring, and arches a brow. "You can go now."

I jerk. "Right. Okay. Bye-bye Bear!" Then I practically tear the door off its hinges, run down the street, and don't stop until I'm around the corner and can catch my breath.

I stare up at the overcast sky and feel the first raindrop hit my cheek. I let out a long breath. My heart still hammers uncomfortably, and that hot, sticky feeling clings to my skin. I close my eyes as the rain starts in earnest.

I liked this job better when I didn't have to interact with my boss.

THANKFULLY, Marcus isn't home when I go back for Bear's afternoon walk. And just because I resent the way he made me feel this morning, I make a point to bring a particularly bright, dog-sized rain jacket with me (neon green with orange polka dots), put it on Bear, and pose for the camera.

"Smile for Daddy, Bear!" I say brightly, painting a big, fat smile on my own face. In my head, I'm sticking out my tongue at the man on the other side of the lens, and maybe even sticking up a rude finger.

Bear pants, happy, and shoves his cold, wet nose in the crook of my neck. I shriek and laugh, pulling away and promptly falling on my butt in the process. "You did that on purpose," I accuse the dog, trying my best to scowl. A laugh falls out instead.

In response, Bear yawns, then trots to the front door and sits down, waiting patiently for me to put his leash on so we can go out for a walk. He glances over his shoulder, looking smug.

I pull myself up and shake my head, planting my hands on my hips. "You're lucky you're such a good dog, Bear."

Otherwise, I'm not sure it would be worth dealing with his owner.

FOR THE FIRST time in many, many years, I have plans after work. Nikita texted me with the details after we parted ways, saying she knew one of the bartenders at a brand-new, trendy cocktail bar in the Meatpacking District. She could get us free drinks, she said, so I had no excuse to bail.

I check the message for the millionth time as I stand in front of my closet, wondering what people wear to bars these days. Unlike Nikki, I don't have a red corset and glamorous wool jacket to wear when I'm out at lunchtime. Once upon a time, I did. When we were friends. When I was in college and I felt safe going out with no more armor than eyeliner and a few pre-drinks to keep me warm.

I touch the skirt of my favorite dress, a citrus-colored number with a Peter Pan collar. I doubt it's appropriate for a trendy cocktail bar. My phone appears in my hand and before I know what I'm doing, I've typed out a message to cancel.

But my thumb hovers over the "send" button, and something holds me back.

It's been *years* since I've been out with a girlfriend. I haven't let myself go out since college. I count on my fingers and feel my eyes widen. The last time I was in a bar was nine years ago. Nine. *Years.*

Now, I don't think it's necessary to go to bars to enjoy your life. Plenty of people have fulfilling lives without bars or alcohol.

But I don't.

All I have is my sewing machine, Brian, and Bear. Even though it terrifies me, I want to go out with Nikki. I want to sit next to her and feel something new. What I experienced when I walked into Bear's house and saw Mr. Wal—*Marcus* standing shirtless was so electric, so visceral, it made me realize that I've been living a flat, gray existence. I haven't *felt* anything in years.

Nothing except fear.

I've had a good excuse, of course. But I think I'm finally ready to move on.

So, with a deep breath, I grab my orange dress with the Peter Pan collar and put it on. It's a cute dress, damn it, and I came up with the pattern myself and cut it to fit my body perfectly. It looks awesome on me.

Instead of pairing it with my usual white sneakers, I kneel next to my bed and reach past the dust bunnies to an old shoebox I hid there years ago. Lifting the top off, a pair of white Mary Janes with a chunky heel stare back at me.

My heart starts to thump, but a smile drifts over my lips.

For eight years, I've covered myself up. I've dressed either in dowdy clothes or clothes that made me look sickeningly cute. No cleavage, no figure-forming items, and definitely no heels. I thought it would stop men from approaching me, but it didn't.

Men still catcalled me in sweatpants, messy hair, and stained shirts. They catcalled me when I wore bright colors and when I wore black. What I wore didn't change a thing except make me feel like I was in control. So I started hiding. Existing—not living.

I've lived a smaller life than necessary, and for what? To still feel unsafe when I walk on the street unless I have a sixty-pound overprotective dog next to me?

I'm wearing heels tonight, damnit—if I can still walk in them.

With shaking hands, I slip them over my feet, tie the ankle strap, and stand. I totter, the old, knotted pine floorboards creaking under my soles. Then I turn to the full-length mirror.

My heart pounds as I smooth my hands down the skirt of my dress, spinning around to check out the back. The white zipper dives down my spine, leading the eye to my bare legs. I won't pretend that my legs look a mile long. I'm five foot nothing. I'll never be a gazelle.

But they look long*er*.

And dare I say...they look *good*.

"My feet are going to be so sore tomorrow," I tell my reflection. "This better be worth it."

Then, because I'm feeling indulgent, I take a cab instead of the subway to go and meet my college bestie for after-work drinks.

Who even *am* I anymore?

6

PENNY

A BARTENDER LIGHTS a drink on fire when I walk in. He's tall and handsome, wearing a little black vest and a white shirt. The sides of his head are shaved, and the top is slicked back from his angular face and light-brown skin.

Nikita watches on with faint amusement, a dark eyebrow arched. I stumble over a perfectly flat piece of floor, catching myself against a high-top table.

I have *got* to stop doing that. Seriously.

The man sitting there reaches over to stabilize me. "Whoa," he says, smiling. "You good, babe?" His hand grips my upper arm as he helps me stand up straight.

Fear arcs up inside me with a vengeance at the touch, and I flinch back.

"Okay, whoa. I get it." The man laughs, pulling his hands back.

I stare at him, mumble some gibberish, and scurry to Nikita's side. As soon as her gaze makes contact with mine, the fear subsides. She's here. I'm safe beside her.

My friend slips off her barstool and gives me a tight hug. "You made it!"

"I almost didn't come," I say, my voice muffled in her cleavage.

My old friend laughs, pulling away to hold my arms. Her eyes crinkle at the corners. "I thought we had a fifty-fifty chance of actually meeting up. I'm glad you're here."

I let out a harsh breath that's supposed to be a laugh and slide onto the barstool next to hers. My already-aching feet let out a cry of relief. These heels might be cute, but they are far from comfortable.

The bartender places Nikita's finished cocktail on a coaster in front of her, then gives me an assessing stare. "Let me guess. You'll enjoy something fruity, but not too sweet."

I blink. "Um."

"Let Carlos work his magic, Penny," Nikki tells me.

Shrugging, I glance at the bartender. "Sure. Magic sounds good."

Carlos winks at me, but it doesn't make that sick, bitter fear rise up. When he starts working, my shoulders relax some more. That's when I realize that I was nervous about *ordering a drink*. Pathetic! Ridiculous! I'm so, so out of practice.

In an effort to calm down, I let my eyes drift over the space.

The room oozes cool. The lighting is dim, the music is low and pulsing, and the whole place has a speakeasy vibe. A little bit vintage, which appeals to me. All of the bartenders are wearing white shirts, black vests, and black bow ties. They all have slicked-back hairstyles like Carlos. The women have high ponytails and short skirts.

Nikki smacks my thigh with the back of her hand.

"Lookin' good, Penny. Are those the same heels you used to wear for special occasions in college?"

A flush rises up my neck and I let out a nervous laugh. "Will you be disappointed if I tell you I haven't worn them since we went to that birthday dinner for Jackie?"

She gapes at me.

I bite my lip. "I actually haven't worn any heels since then."

"That was, what, seven years ago?"

"Nine."

She clutches her imaginary pearls. I laugh. It feels good, I realize, to be somewhere new, laughing with an old friend. I've isolated myself for so long that even sitting at a bar feels like an adventure.

My drink is placed in front of me. "Enjoy, beautiful," Carlos says with another wink.

I pause for a moment, waiting for the familiar discomfort of being called a pet name by a strange man. Surprisingly, it doesn't appear. Maybe it's the fact that there's a chunky wooden bar separating us, or maybe it's Nikita beside me.

Or maybe I'm changing. Growing. Moving on.

Carlos leans his hands on the bar, nodding to the drink. "Try it," he says. "It's my own creation. I'm trying to convince my manager to put it on the menu, but he's stubborn. So when I give you the signal, make a big production about how this is the best drink you've ever tasted."

"Oh, shut up, Carlos." Nikita rolls her eyes.

Carlos grins at me, wipes the bar in front of us, and moves on to the next customer.

I take a sip, and my eyes bug. I stare at the orange-and-pink-layered drink in my delicate martini glass. "You know, this might be the best drink I've ever tasted." I meet Nikita's stare. "And I'm not even joking."

She laughs, touches the edge of her glass to mine, and we fall into easy conversation. We talk about our work, what we've been up to, she catches me up on all our old friends. Unsurprisingly, she's kept in touch with a lot of the people we were friends with in college. She's always been the sun around which people revolve in any social situation.

I remember meeting her and being incredibly intimidated. Here was this tall, gorgeous woman who was completely comfortable in her skin at only eighteen years old. After that first lecture, she practically dragged me out of my dorm room and glued her hip to mine, and we became best friends.

It feels like the same thing is happening now, more than a decade later. She's dragged me out to this bar and made me feel like I belong.

But when our second round of drinks are placed in front of us and we've caught up on all the highlights of the past eight years since I disappeared from college, Nikki gives me an assessing stare.

"So," she starts. "This is when you tell me what the hell happened after the end of junior year."

Every muscle in my body seizes.

Nikki must see it, because she puts her hand on my arm. "It's okay. You don't have to say anything."

Her touch is warm, soft, and comforting. I've had so little physical human contact in so long, even her fingers on my arm feel like a jolt.

Maybe it's the alcohol I just ingested, or the fact that I'm in a bar for the first time in years. Maybe I need to talk just to get the image of a shirtless Marcus Walsh out of my brain.

Whatever it is, I hear myself speak words I haven't said out loud to anyone in a long, long time. "You remember my ex-boyfriend, Billy?"

Nikita grimaces. "The creep who tried to get you to stop talking to me?" Her eyes widen. "You didn't marry him, did you?"

I snort. "No. I tried to break up with him. He..." I gulp. "He didn't take it well."

My old friend tilts her head. She was always a good listener. Beneath the sexpot, intimidating exterior, Nikita is the most loyal, loving friend you could ask for.

And I pushed her away.

Gosh, I've made mistakes. So many of them.

"Tell me," she says.

Music wraps me in its pulsing rhythm, and I take a sip of my delicious, fruity-but-not-too-sweet drink to steel my nerves. Then, I talk. "After I broke up with him, Billy started showing up at my apartment. Remember when I broke my lease and moved? It was because he'd stand outside my window at all hours of the night. I'd catch glimpses of him on the other side of the street multiple times a week. He'd call me incessantly. He threatened to kill himself if I didn't take him back. Then it got weird. Well, weird*er*." My throat grows tight. I close my eyes and take a deep breath. Nikki's hand appears on my forearm as it rests on the bar, and I draw comfort from her touch. "I started getting all kinds of messages from random social media accounts. I'd show up for appointments and they'd been canceled without my knowledge. My professors were getting emails from my email account. Rude emails. Emails that made me look like I was insane. He sent in a blank assignment from my account, and I nearly failed the class because the professor didn't believe me that I wasn't responsible."

"It was Billy?" Nikki asks in a low voice.

I nod. "I went to the police. They didn't do anything. They said if he approached me or hurt me physically, I could try to get a restraining order. But it wasn't against the law to stand outside my apartment. I think..." I take a deep breath. "I think they didn't really believe me. I mean look at me. I'm tiny, and female, and I have this squeaky voice—"

"You have a great voice, Penny."

"And the cops just thought I was some dumb girl going through a breakup. Nothing serious. Or at least that's the sense I got."

"That's fucked up," she says.

I nod. "Billy would call in sick to work on my behalf. I lost my job because of it—remember, the one at the campus café?"

"You loved that job," Nikki says quietly.

I nod. "Yeah. One time, I swear a knife in my kitchen disappeared. I thought maybe I'd misplaced it, but I was so paranoid..." I shake my head.

"You ran," Nikita says.

It feels so good to talk about my past. The words keep coming and coming, and I can't stop them. "I was so paranoid, I didn't know who to trust. I tried to talk to my dad, but he kept telling me to get back together with Billy. Billy had talked to him and convinced him I was having some sort of mental breakdown."

When I meet Nikki's gaze, her eyes are glassy. "I wish

you'd talked to me," she says, her voice tight. "I would have killed him."

I give her a sad smile. "Right now, I wish I'd talked to you too. But we'd had that big fight after Jackie's birthday—"

"Which Billy instigated."

"Which Billy instigated," I agree. "I was isolated. I had no friends, no family. I didn't know who to trust."

"Holy crap, Penny." Tears pool in her eyes, and I shake my head. I don't want her to cry on my behalf. I'm the one who made mistakes. I'm the one who pushed her away.

Throat tight, I keep talking. "I ended up dropping out, leaving Long Island, finishing my degree at a community college here in the city. My reputation was completely destroyed with all the professors and professional contacts I'd made." I swallow thickly and let out a huff. "Nikki, it went on for *years*. Even as recently as three years ago, I got a weird email that sounded like Billy's old messages."

"He stalked you," she says.

My stomach gives a lurch. I nod. "I was terrified for a long, long time." *Still am.* "So I just became a hermit. I moved into the city, because I knew Billy hated it. I figured it was so big I could be anonymous. I started walking dogs. Bought a sewing machine and spent all my free time making clothes for myself, and finally for dogs. And now I have a business selling dog clothes," I say with a watery laugh. "So I guess it turned out okay in the end."

Nikita turns back to the bar, her back straight, her head bowed. Then she slips off her barstool and wraps me in another hug. "I'm sorry, Penny."

To my horror, tears spill from my eyes. I try to wipe them, and I'm sure I make a mess of my makeup in the process.

Nikki helps me mop up my snot. It feels better than I can say, to tell someone about what I went through and have them tell me it isn't my fault. She smiles, swiping her thumbs over my cheeks.

"I'm glad we ran into each other," she says. "I missed you. I tried to find you online, but it's like you just fell off the face of the earth."

"I basically did," I answer.

"I'm not going to let you run away from me again," she says sternly. "It was a one-in-a-million chance for us to run into each other today."

Before I can answer, another woman walks up to us and puts her arms around both our shoulders. "Girl! You didn't tell me you were coming here!" The woman leans in, pulling us close.

Still half-crying and trying to wipe my face, I lurch forward and nearly fall off my chair. I give Nikita a confused look, which she returns.

Then the woman says in a low voice, "Help. I was talking to a client and now his creepy business partner won't leave me alone."

I...freeze.

After spilling my guts about being stalked by my creepy ex-boyfriend, I can't even react to what this woman is saying. Twisted, dark fear explodes in my abdomen, and all I can do is cling to my barstool and try not to fall over while the world rocks around me.

Nikita reacts first. She makes a big show of squealing and hugging the woman, then calls over the bartender for a drink. She gets off her stool and lets the woman sit down in her place, moving to shield us both from the rest of the bar with her body.

I let out a breath.

So does the woman. "I'm Bonnie," she says. We introduce ourselves, and I take a moment to study her. She has a pretty round face with deep dimples in both cheeks. Her hair is blond, shiny, and falls down to her shoulder blades. The ends are curled in a way that makes me think she is far more skilled with a hair dryer than I am. Her makeup is tasteful, and she's wearing a black pencil skirt and a royal-blue silk top. A businesswoman of some kind.

We pull up a stool, and Nikita sits between us. I use the moment to pull myself together, while Bonnie surreptitiously looks over her shoulder to scan the bar.

A drunk man stumbles over to us. I stiffen.

Bonnie takes her freshly made martini and pretends to turn, drenching the man's shirt with her drink. "Oh!" she exclaims. "Mike! I'm so sorry. I didn't see you there."

"This is a thousand-dollar shirt," he sneers, mopping his front with cocktail napkins.

"Send the dry-cleaning bill to the office. We'll cover it, of course. My apologies." Then she turns her back to the gaping man, effectively cutting him out of the conversation.

My first thought is that this must be the creepy business partner. My second thought is that I want to be Bonnie when I grow up. I doubt I'd have had the gall to spill a drink over a man's thousand-dollar shirt right before I turned my back on him.

But maybe if I did, I would have seen Billy for what he was a lot sooner.

When the man lets out a few choice curse words and

stumbles away, Bonnie relaxes. "Thank you," she tells the two of us, putting a hand to her forehead. Her nails are almond-shaped and covered in pale pink polish. She blows out a breath and laughs a little, then turns to the bartender to get us all a fresh round of drinks.

"Who was that guy?" I ask after she's made the order.

Bonnie lets out an inelegant snort. "A pain in my ass."

Nikita laughs. "You didn't seem to have any trouble dispatching him."

"If you two hadn't been here, he probably would have expected me to pat down his shirt with those napkins myself." She rolls her eyes. "But he and his partner are hiring my firm, and their portfolio is worth a lot of money. I'm in the schmoozing stage." She makes a barfing motion.

I laugh. "Spilling a drink on him won't put him off hiring you?"

She shakes her head. "His partner didn't even want him to come here. We're not supposed to deal with Mike at all."

We find out Bonnie works in finance. I could have guessed she had some kind of high-flying job, but she seems incredibly down-to-earth. When Nikita lets it slip that I have a business designing dog clothing, all attention turns to me. I end up directing Bonnie to my online store on her phone, and Bonnie squeals at half a dozen designs I've come up with. I look over her shoulder and feel warmth spreading through my chest.

Here's a glamorous, wealthy, professional woman impressed with things *I've* made. My cheeks warm along with my heart. Often, I tend to be dismissive of what I've done. Dog clothes are kind of silly, after all. But seeing Bonnie and Nikita tap through all the products I made with my own hands on the online store that pays my rent and bills, I can take a moment to appreciate all that I've accomplished.

"And you do all this without a smartphone?" Bonnie says, shaking her head. "Girl. How."

I laugh. "I have a business partner. He handles all the techie stuff. Otherwise I'd still be doing farmers' markets and barely making ends meet."

Bonnie ends up staying with us for another couple of hours. Before I know it, it's midnight and I'm stumbling out of the bar on my sky-high heels with two new girlfriends. Then, to my surprise, Bonnie tells us she's having a Halloween party at her place, and she invites us to come along.

To my even bigger surprise, I accept.

Nikki piles into a cab beside me, and I'm reminded of how perceptive a friend she is when she goes out of her way to drop me off at my place first. She used to do this when we were in college too. Without making a big production of it, she'd make sure everyone got home safe. Oftentimes I'd wake up with a hangover only to see a glass of water and two Advil on my bedside table, knowing Nikki had put them there.

"I'm sorry I pushed you away," I tell her when we pull up outside my building.

Nikki gives me a sad smile. "We're together now," she says. "You won't be able to get rid of me so easily. Plus," she adds when I open the taxi door. She nods to the building. "Now I know where you live."

I laugh, say goodbye, and make my way up to my apartment. Once I'm safe inside and my heels have been kicked off and flung across the room, I let out a happy sigh.

I'm glad I didn't cancel. I'm glad I wore heels. I'm glad I told Nikki about Billy's stalking and harassment. I'm glad I met Bonnie and accepted her gushing compliments about my business.

For the first time in as long as I can remember, I think I might be able to move on from what happened to me in college.

And maybe that means I'll be able to get over my fear of men. Maybe I'll be able to start dating again.

Green eyes rimmed by thick, sooty lashes float into my mind. I gulp down a glass of water and push the image aside, then stumble into bed, praying for dreamless sleep.

7

MARCUS

I WAKE up to the sound of loud, thumping music. Pounding bass shakes my walls while some screechy, high-pitched melody dances over it. Groaning, I turn on my side and stuff a pillow over my head. It does nothing to muffle the sound. I toss the pillow across the room, throw my blankets back, and stalk into the hallway.

Fists clenched, I make my way across the hall, barely keeping my temper in check. I count to ten—then I realize I'm counting to the beat of Kenzie's awful music. *Ugh!*

My knuckles make contact with her door, and I can barely hear my knocks over the noise. "Kenzie!"

Pause. No answer.

I pound the door a little bit harder. "Mackenzie! Turn that racket down!" I hear myself from a distance, like an out-of-body experience. When did I become a crotchety old man? Have I always been this way? Did it happen after I hit thirty? Thirty-five?

I pound my fist against the door. "Mackenzie!"

The door flies open and my niece stares back at me,

wrapped up in a fluffy pink bathrobe. "What?" Teenage sass drips off of every letter. She arches a brow, cocking her hip to the side.

"It's six o'clock in the morning," I grit out through clenched teeth. "Turn. The music. Down."

An eye roll is the only answer I get. Then I watch Mackenzie stalk to the stereo on her dresser. She turns the volume knob to the left, maintaining eye contact with me the entire time in some sort of deranged show of teenage dominance.

It shouldn't bother me. I know it shouldn't. But damnit, it *does*.

"Are headphones not hip with the kids these days?" I ask, hating that I'm matching her snippy energy. I'm a grown man. I shouldn't be riled up by a teenage girl.

"I have a morning routine," she answers, turning her back to me. "Can you close the door so I can get ready for school?"

I grind my molars, then do as she says.

Every day—this has happened every single day since she moved in. I'm about to lose my damn mind.

Logically, I know she's a kid. And she's a *good* kid. She's just been thrown out of her home, and she feels rejected by her mother. It's normal that she'd act out.

But all I'm saying is I wish she'd find another way to do it —one that didn't involve a rude wake-up call from across the hall every morning.

Padding on bare feet, wearing my plaid pajama bottoms and a soft white tee, I head to the kitchen. My bleary eyes just about manage to guide me through the coffee-making process, and while I wait for my brew to percolate, I click my tongue at Bear and take him out to do his business. When we're back and he's descending on his breakfast like I haven't fed him in a year, I lean against the counter, only to see a cereal-encrusted bowl beside the sink.

Not in the dishwasher. Not *in* the sink. *Beside* the sink.

Deep breaths. I take three of them.

My brain provides helpful explanations in a feeble attempt to defuse my anger: she's a teen. Her brain isn't fully developed. She'll have poor impulse control for another decade. She's going through a lot.

I know these things. I understand.

But is it *really* that hard to wash up after a midnight snack?

Bear nudges my legs. I scrub his thick fur and stew in my own anger.

I take my rage out on the dirty bowl, scrubbing violently until the concrete-like Cheerios dissolve into paste and wash down the sink. Once the bowl is dried and put away, my coffee is ready. I take a sip, closing my eyes to savor the strong, bitter flavor.

Good. Better. In five minutes, I'll be human again. I'll be able to deal with my niece, her music, and her inability to wash her dishes.

Life has changed in the week Mackenzie's lived with me. I usually get lots of work done from my home office, because I'm able to shut myself away, turn off my phone, and focus. Lately, that hasn't been the case. Since my niece moved in, I haven't been able to work from home at all. With the acquisition I'm working on at Sellzy, I can't afford all the wasted time.

But damn it, I love that kid. I don't want her to be alone in my house, feeling like I've abandoned her too.

Yesterday, I came home mid-morning for a quick work-out. I didn't need anything from the house—I just came here to have the place to myself, for once. I felt almost guilty about it, like I was doing something wrong for enjoying the silence and solitude of my own home.

Then Penny Littleton walked through my front door. The way she looked at me...

I take another sip of coffee and try to turn my thoughts to something more appropriate. Work. My schedule. My to-do list.

But all I can think about are those big, blue eyes, wide and innocent as they stared at me. The flush in her cheeks. The copper hair gathered in a high ponytail. The millions of freckles I want to worship.

Her lips dropped open when she saw me, and I felt a stirring below the waistband of my shorts. She was flustered, embarrassed, and so damn cute. She has no right to be that cute. I don't do cute. I hate cute.

Clomping footsteps echo down the hall, and my niece appears in the opening.

I frown. "What did you do to your face?"

Black-rimmed eyes scowl at me. "It's called makeup, Marcus. Look it up."

I lift my palms in surrender and move out of the way as she grabs the box of Cheerios from above the fridge.

I clear my throat. "Don't forget to rinse your bowl and put it in the dishwasher."

A grunt is the only response I get.

Now that I'm caffeinated, I know to pick my battles. I top up my mug and head back to my bedroom to get ready for work. When I'm showered and dressed, my phone dings.

It's my brother Ollie, thanking me for covering his medical bills. I made sure to send a little extra, to try to ease some of the stress. Hopefully my brother will be able to get Oliver Jr. a good birthday present with the money.

Sometimes I still can't believe what I've built, how far I've come. I grew up close to the poverty line. When Sellzy started making money, the first thing I did was buy my mom's apartment. I've paid for all my brothers' and sisters' college educations and started funds for their kids. I've been their bank for medical expenses, cars, and housing costs. I invested in my brother Terry's company and hired my cousin to work at Sellzy—giving both of them the first stable job they had in their lives. I connected Ollie to Leif's company and gave him a leg up. I've changed my family's trajectory. Me.

I'm proud of myself—but I'm *tired*.

In a way, taking care of Mackenzie is a similar feeling. I've always had multiple lives resting on my shoulders. It's a huge amount of responsibility—one that I often feel like I can't bear. I screwed up once, didn't I? And look what happened to Stephanie. Mackenzie *should* be here, and I *should* put up with her teenage antics, because her broken home is partially my fault. If I'd been there for Steph when she needed me most, her life wouldn't have fallen apart like it did. She wouldn't be looking for the answers at the bottom of a bottle.

"Marcus?" Mackenzie's voice comes from the doorway.

I turn and jerk my chin at her. "Yeah?"

"Can I invite my friend Amy over after school? We have a science project due next week, and she's busy on the week-end. Tonight is the only time we can meet up."

I bunch my lips to the side and pull a cashmere sweater

on over my button-down. "I have meetings until late tonight, Kenzie."

"We're just going to be studying and doing the experiment. You don't need to be here."

I can still hear the bass pumping from her bedroom. Through the doorway, I can just see the tornado-level mess on her bedroom floor.

Now I need to multiply that by two to get an idea of what kind of damage those girls can cause while I'm not home.

"Are Amy's parents okay with her coming here?"

She nods vigorously. "Yep."

Mackenzie is fourteen. That's old enough to be left alone for a couple of hours...right? They're just working on a science project, not throwing a wild party.

"Sure," I answer, slipping my phone into my pocket. "Call me if you need anything."

She smiles brightly, then wraps her arms around my waist to give me a tight hug. "Thanks, Uncle Marcus. You're the best."

I squeeze her back and guide her to the front door. "The car's here to take you to school. Be safe. I'll see you tonight."

A few minutes later, Mackenzie is in the back of my car, being driven to school. I lock up my home office and cast an eye around the open-plan living space for particularly breakable valuables, then shake my head and walk to the garage to get on my Ducati.

I shouldn't worry so much. I'm being ridiculous. How much damage can two teenage girls cause?

. . .

A LOT. A hell of a lot of damage. That's how much two teenage girls can cause.

A fire truck is just pulling away when I rush through the door to my house twelve hours later. The entire kitchen and living room area look like a science experiment gone wrong.

Because that's exactly what happened.

Horror ices my veins as I look at the ruined canvases of two very, *very* expensive paintings. The TV on my wall is covered in some sort of hard, black, calcified substance. Mackenzie and Amy are sitting on barstools at the kitchen island, staring at their feet.

There are char marks on the ceiling. The *ceiling*. The microwave looks like it's been painted black. Every single dish and pan I've ever bought is on the countertops, ruined, covered in the same hard black crust.

I take it all in. I'm not even mad as I look at the destruction. I'm just...wow. I can't believe it.

"Marcus, I'm sorry. It was an accident." Mackenzie slips off her stool and wrings her hands in front of her stomach. "We were just trying to do this science experiment that Mr. Errol talked about, and, well, we might have added a bit too much baking soda, and..." She keeps talking while I notice new details.

Bear comes clicking down the hallway, sniffs at the room at large, and turns around to disappear into my bedroom. I let out a breath. At least my dog is okay. He evidently decided to make himself scarce when the Teenage Girl Science Brigade got going.

Mackenzie's still talking, but I haven't heard a word.

The doorbell rings.

Amy looks up with wide, terrified eyes. "That's my mom."

I turn around, take a deep breath, and open the door.

The woman on the doorstep is made of denim-clad righteous indignation. Bleached blond with dark-wash jeans and a light jean jacket, she has one young boy in her arms and a gigantic purse slung over her other shoulder. She sniffs, then narrows her eyes at me. "What. Happened."

I clear my throat. "The girls were working on a science experiment," I answer.

She scowls at me, then pushes her way past. She snaps her fingers at Amy and points to the ground beside her. "Here. Now. What did I tell you about going to friends' houses? Phone numbers, Amy. I need parents' phone numbers, addresses, and emergency contacts. I had to call the school to find out where you were."

My gaze turns to Mackenzie as my anger mounts. "You told me you had permission," I tell my niece, taking a step forward. My shoe lands in a mysterious gooey substance.

The woman huffs at her daughter. "Look at what you did." She thrusts her free arm to the room. "Look, Amy. What were you thinking?"

The girl's bottom lip wobbles. "It was an accident. We got the measurements wrong, and—" She hiccups, burying her face in her hands.

"You'd better start cleaning right now, young lady. We are not leaving until this place is spotless."

I scrub my forehead. "Look. Um, Mrs…"

"Tilley." She's red-faced and practically shaking with anger. In some twisted way, I'm glad I'm not Amy right now.

I put my hands out, placating. "Mrs. Tilley. I'll call a cleaning company. You just take Amy home. They had a scare, and, um, I think it's best if we leave the cleaning to the professionals."

Mrs. Tilley meets my gaze and gives me a sharp nod. The anger in her eyes fades for a moment, and I see something like fear flash there. "Well, you tell me how much it..." She sucks in a breath. "Tell me how much it costs, and I'll make sure we cover Amy's share. I, um..." She hikes the boy in her arms higher on her hip and clears her throat. The purse slung over her other shoulder slides down to her elbow, and she wobbles. "It might take a little while, but we'll get the money over to you."

I've heard those words before. I've seen the pride and shame warring in my own mother's eyes many, many times. I know if I offer to cover the cleanup cost, Mrs. Tilley will dig her heels in, snap her spine straight, and never, ever agree.

So I just nod. "We'll figure it out," I answer, knowing I'll never ask her for a dime.

"Okay. I'm sorry about this, Mr..." She frowns. "I thought Mackenzie's father had passed away."

I nod. "He did. I'm her uncle." I stick out my hand. "Marcus."

"Ah," she says. "Well, I'm very sorry about all this, Marcus."

"I'm just glad no one was hurt."

I hold the door open for the woman and her two kids, then close it gently behind him. When I see her minivan depart through the window, I take a deep breath and turn around. My eyes land on my niece, who's busy scrubbing a metal baking sheet like her life depends on it.

I'm so completely unprepared for this. I'm not a parent. I have no idea how I'm supposed to deal with Mackenzie. Yes,

LILIAN MONROE

we're close. I've always been a phone call away. But if there's one thing I've learned in the past week, it's that being an uncle and being a parent are two very, *very* different things.

My niece glances over her shoulder, and there are tears streaming down her face. Damn it.

I drop my shoulders. "Stop, Kenzie. Stop scrubbing."

She sniffles, drops the sponge, and wipes her hands and face on a clean dishtowel. It's the only clean thing in here. My feet crunch across the floor as I make my way to the kitchen, and I pick up a plate covered in black residue. I set it back down, and Mackenzie hiccups.

"Hey," I say gently. "Come here."

She buries her head in my chest and cries. She feels so small in my arms. Fragile. Her voice is as thin as ice over a puddle. "I'm really sorry. I'm really, really sorry. Please don't kick me out, Marcus."

Apparently my heart wasn't completely shattered, because another fault line appears. "Stop it, Kenzie. I'm not kicking you out. You hear me?" I pull away, meeting her watery eyes. "I'm not kicking you out."

She sniffles and nods, sobbing so violently snot falls from her nose. "O-okay. We really w-were trying to do our project, Marcus. I promise. I just read the measurements wrong, and...and..."

"It happens," I answer, casting an eye over the destruction, not sure if I'm telling the truth. I sling an arm over her shoulders and guide her toward the hallway. "Here's what we're going to do. We're going to pack our bags and head to Grandma's house with Bear. I'll find some cleaners capable of fixing this mess. I'll grab a hotel for myself, and as soon as everything's ready, we'll move back in. Deal?"

"You're not going to punish me?" She cringes away from me, eyes wide and worried. It makes me wonder what the hell my sister did to this girl to make her fear consequences so much.

I ruffle her hair. "There will be consequences, kiddo. But it was an accident, and I shouldn't have left you alone in the first place. We'll figure something out. I still love you."

She takes a shaky inhale and more tears leak out of her eyes. "You do?"

Fuck. This kid...what the hell has she been through?

My phone dings. It's a message from my good friend, Leif.

Leif: All set for the weekend?

I frown at the message. The weekend? What is he talking about? My thoughts are like eels, sliding out of my grasp. Kenzie shudders with a hard sob, so I just send Leif a thumbs-up and shove my phone back in my pocket.

"Of course I love you, Kenzie. Come on. When we're in the car, we can come up with consequences together. I'm thinking...a permanent babysitter and dishwashing duty for the rest of your life."

Mackenzie grimaces, and I laugh. Relief floods through me at her expression of teenage angst. That's better. I can deal with loud music and attitude and a few dirty dishes as long as Mackenzie isn't worried about being thrown out on the street, unloved and uncared for.

While I pack my bags and put together Bear's things, resolve hardens within me. Mackenzie isn't just staying at my house for a little while. She's family. She's my little girl. She's going to feel loved and supported, but she's going to have more structure while she's living here.

She ruined my kitchen and living room, and I should count myself lucky that nothing worse happened. She was doing schoolwork, after all. What if she'd been doing something worse? What if she'd dug into my alcohol cabinet? What if she got drugs from someone at school?

This past week, I treated Mackenzie as a roommate. It's time for me to step up and be the parent that my sister can't be for her.

As soon as we get to my mom's house, I'll make good on my promise. I'll find some after-school care for Mackenzie, get my place cleaned up, and make sure my niece has a real home with me. I never want her to worry about being thrown out—but I also never want to walk into a failed science experiment. We both need to do better. Especially me.

When I grab Bear's leash by the door, an idea pops into my head. I look down at my dog, who's panting up at me with a big doggy smile on his face, excited to go on an adventure with me. I know one person who gets along with Mackenzie. Someone who already works for me, who knows my house, who passed all the background checks.

It would only be temporary, after all. I need someone to keep an eye on my niece until I finalize the acquisition at work and my schedule becomes more manageable.

Surely my dog walker wouldn't mind a couple of extra hours of work every day...right?

8

PENNY

I WAKE up to a blaring phone, which I promptly knock off my nightstand along with the half-empty glass of water I'd set out last night. Swearing, I stumble out of bed and answer the phone, thankful it didn't land in the fresh puddle of water on my carpet.

It's Todd, Marcus's assistant, telling me I have the day off due to "unforeseen circumstances at Mr. Walsh's home." My services won't be needed to walk the dog for the rest of the week, but his boss requests a meeting with me on Friday. At his office.

Yikes.

I croak out a "no problem" and shut my phone with a snap. Then I stare at the alarm clock on my nightstand and groan. It's nearly nine o'clock, which is the latest I've slept in about ten years. And my mouth feels like something fuzzy and alive grew in it overnight, then died a horrible death.

Alcohol. I'd forgotten about the consequences.

It's sometime in the middle of my shower, after I've cleaned the water on my bedroom floor and washed that awful taste from my mouth, that the cobwebs are cleared from my mind and I'm able to form coherent thoughts again. They bring me back to the phone call. I stand under the boiling-hot water, watch my skin turn its usual shade of lobster red, and stare at the tiles on the wall.

I agreed to a meeting with Marcus Walsh.

I *agreed* to a meeting with *Marcus freaking Walsh.*

Shampoo suds fall down the sides of my head as my heart starts beating a little bit faster. He's not going to fire me...is he? If he were firing me, he'd probably have Todd do it. And he wouldn't do it at his office. He'd do it at his home, where I usually am.

Right?

It's not like I need this job to survive, but I like Bear and it provides some stability. Sure, the dog-clothes business is booming right now, but what happens after Halloween? I have so many orders for custom-made costumes that I've been working day in, day out to get them done. After that, who knows?

The holiday season is usually okay too, I reason. I make winter- and holiday-themed sweaters for dogs. They usually sell out by the first week of December.

But still. What if they didn't? What if my patterns aren't quite good enough? What if I didn't buy the right fabrics? What if something happens on the tech side, Brian can't fix it, and the whole house of cards collapses?

I close my eyes and dip my head under the stream of water. Shampoo gets in my eyes, and I wince, tilting my head back up to clear them. I massage my scalp, then put a huge glob of conditioner in my hair and try to talk some sense into myself.

There's no point panicking. Marcus is probably not going to fire me. He just wants to meet one-on-one for some other reason. At his office. Where he probably hires and fires people all the time.

I grab a loofah and scrub myself raw. It's not an appointment to get sacked. Last night's alcohol must have killed off too many brain cells. I'm just having a perfectly normal meeting with my boss. It's all aboveboard. Friday, I'll find out what he wants, and everything will be absolutely, one-hundred-percent *fine*.

In the meantime, I have Halloween costumes to sew, and I'm meeting with Brian to get today's batch of orders packed and shipped. I don't have time to wonder about the inner workings of a billionaire's mind. I have my own business to run.

Sure, it's not some fancy-schmancy technological wonder, but it pays my bills and I'm proud of it, damnit.

With that thought snapping my spine straight, I finish my shower and ready myself for the day. Today is a liquid eyeliner day, with an extra-snappy flick at the corners of my eyes.

I sit at the vanity in the corner of my bedroom—a tiny desk barely wide enough to fit my legs under—and do my best to put my makeup on like I know what I'm doing. Then I dress in one of my polka-dot house dresses and pad on bare feet to the tiny kitchen/living/dining room.

Also known as my workshop, and the center of my business.

I have a small, two-seater couch that was a hand-me-down from my elderly next-door neighbor. Its original fabric is 1970s brown-and-orange floral chic, so I sewed a navy-blue slipcover to match my decor. It's currently buried beneath mounds of fabric and half-completed projects that need to be finalized before we can put them up for sale. My sewing machine is opposite the couch, about two feet away from it in the small, narrow room. It's surrounded by ceiling-high mountains of fabric in all patterns and colors.

I live by the motto that She Who Dies With The Most Fabric Wins. And I smell victory.

Finished items are folded neatly in a plastic bin next to the couch, right beside my padded shipping bags and label maker.

Calm descends over me like a weighted blanket at the sight of all the implements of my business. I cross over to the little kitchen, which is really just a small counter, a fridge, and a tiny stove with a strip of linoleum in front of it. The coffee maker comes to life with the push of a button, and within minutes, I've got fresh, hot brew in a mug.

I bring it to my sewing machine and set it down on a coaster I keep for that exact purpose. Then I turn my sewing machine on, warm yellow light flickering to life. I check the bobbin, the needle, the thread, and all the mechanical parts that move in tandem, and take a deep, happy breath.

Then I sew.

For the next four hours, I sit hunched over my machine, ticking items off my to-do list. I cut a new pattern for a ladybug costume with an adjustable clasp. I make six bow ties with a pumpkin pattern. I clear my mind of all thoughts of Marcus Walsh, Bear, Mackenzie, Nikki, Bonnie, and insecurities about my business's longevity, and I do what I do best.

Creating something with my own hands is a special kind

of pleasure. I start with flat bolts of fabric, and I end up with cute dog clothing that people pay a premium for. That's something to be proud of, no?

My coffee is ice-cold when I take my next sip, and I'm surprised to see a shaft of sunlight burning across my living room. I blink. It must be early afternoon, judging by the light. Straightening my back with a number of alarming crackles and pops, I stand up and pad to the window.

Steam rises out of manhole covers below, and the sounds of the New York streets rise up toward me. Honking cars, yelling voices. A siren wails in the distance. I tilt my head toward the sun until a cloud drifts by to cover it.

It's a beautiful October day. Soon, the world will be cold and gray and dreary, but today is one of those special autumn days that reminds you that summer will come again. I should go out and enjoy it. If I'm about to get fired by my sexy-as-sin boss, I might as well grab every bit of pleasure I can until then.

My buzzer rings.

I step over a mound of neatly folded fabric and around a tub of clasps and buttons as I make my way to the intercom. "Yes?"

"It's me." Brian's voice comes clearly through the speaker.

I push the button to open the building's entrance, then step over to my apartment's door, open the deadbolt, and crack the door. Two steps take me to the kitchen, where I dump the stale coffee and start a fresh pot. The machine is busy gurgling when the door opens and my friend and business partner Brian steps through.

Brian is a tall man with brownish-blond hair that curls in tight ringlets. He keeps the sides cropped very tight and the top a bit longer. His hair must add at least an inch or two to his height. His old satin Yankees bomber jacket is unzipped to reveal a white tee underneath, and his jeans sit low on his hips. His leather Converse sneakers are a pristine, gleaming white, as usual.

Brian's dog, a stout, slobbery bulldog named Paulie, trundles across the floor and crashes into my shins. I kneel down to give him a nice, long scratch behind the ears. "Hi, Paulie."

"Hey, Penny," Brian says, nudging the door closed with a hip and crossing to give me a hug.

I stand and melt into the embrace. "Hey, Brian."

He sniffs. "You making coffee?"

"Just put on a fresh pot."

He grins. "You're the best." He hands me a wrapped package. "Got you an egg and cheese sandwich from the bodega. Figured you would've missed breakfast."

"My hero," I say, snatching the sandwich from him.

He laughs and pulls a paper from his back pocket. "Here's the list of new orders to be made. I have some time today, so I can help you do the labels and packing for the last batch."

With my mouth full of food, all I can do is widen my eyes as I look over the orders listed on the pages he gave me. I swallow. "This is more than you said."

"Halloween rush."

"Wow."

His smile is bright. I've always loved Brian's smile. His mouth is ever so slightly too big for his face, and he has long, lean dimples that crease his cheeks whenever he smiles. Which is often. "Glad I went into the dog-clothes business, that's for sure."

"What do you think, Paulie?" I ask, reaching for a bag of

dog treats I keep specially for him. Paulie's eyes gleam in canine excitement and he sits down at my feet, waiting to be fed. I grin at Brian. "Paulie agrees."

"Paulie would agree to anything in exchange for food."

I laugh, give Paulie the treat, then turn back to the kitchen. "Your dog and I have that in common." I stuff the rest of my sandwich in my face.

We have coffee and get started on packing. Brian works the label maker. It's just techy enough that I sometimes mess it up, and plus, this gives me the chance to fold and wrap the orders just the way I like. We work well together—always have. I wrap a bow tie and a tiny, pug-sized rain jacket in tissue paper and use a sticker with my logo to keep it closed. Then I slip the whole thing with a little thank-you card into a shipping bag and hand it over to Brian, who affixes the label.

Paulie lies on his side on the only space on the couch not taken up with fabric, his eyes closed, four legs stuck straight out in front of him.

After a few minutes, I feel Brian's eyes on me.

"What?" I ask, my voice teasing.

He smooths a label onto a shipping bag. "You look tired, and you're quiet. Everything okay?"

My cheeks flush, and I'm not sure why. Brian is so thoughtful. So kind. He worries about me. But why am I embarrassed that I had a few drinks last night? I'm a grown woman, after all. "I went out to a bar last night," I admit.

He freezes, his long fingers frozen around a padded bag. "You did?"

I shrug a shoulder. "Ran into an old friend," I tell him.

There's a pause, then Brian clears his throat. "Oh," he

says, placing the bag in the large Tupperware container with orders ready to go out. "What's his name?"

I throw him a half-laughing frown. "*Her* name is Nikita," I answer. "I knew her in college."

It's weird that Brian would assume I went out to a bar with a man. He knows about my past—or at least, he knows the broad strokes. I told him I had a bad experience with an ex-boyfriend and left it at that. He knows how hard it is for me to trust people of his gender. People in general.

A tiny bit of tension melts out his shoulders, and something flashes across his face. An emotion I don't have the time to read. As quickly as it appears, it's replaced with a teasing smile. "Good. I was feeling a little protective there for a second. Was about to ask where I could find this guy to make sure he knew how special you are."

Of course. Protectiveness. That's what he's feeling. I shake my head and laugh. "Come on, Brian. You know how I am with guys. The last thing I want to do is go out drinking with them."

"I know. You won't even go out drinking with *me*." He nudges my shoulder and grabs the next order from my hands, taking the appropriate label to stick on the front of the bag. "I'm a little jealous of Nikita, to be honest. She finally got to take you out."

"She's amazing. You'd like her."

He grunts in response, and we work a while longer in silence. Paulie, busy dreaming dog dreams, lets out a fart that stinks up the entire apartment so much I have to air the place out. I laugh, plugging my nose, and push my stiff window up, propping it open with a piece of wood I keep for that purpose. Paulie opens his eyes and glares at me when he feels the breeze.

"You brought this on yourself, pup." I give him a flat stare, and he drops his big head back down on the couch and goes back to sleep.

Brian grins at me as I make my way back beside him and get back to work. Then, out of nowhere, he says, "Where did you go?"

I glance at him. "Hmm?"

"The bar. Which bar did you go to?"

"Oh. A little cocktail bar in the Meatpacking District. Nikki knew one of the bartenders."

A line appears between his brows. "Right." He clears his throat. "Did you have fun?" The tone he uses isn't exactly friendly or casual. There's color on his cheeks, and he focuses on the label maker with a touch too much intensity.

I pause in the middle of folding an order of three bow ties and look at Brian until he meets my gaze. "Are you mad at me?"

He must see something in my eyes, because he blinks a few times and shakes his head. "Of course not. I'm glad you went out. Wish you'd invited me, though."

I huff a little laugh, then shake my head. "Oh. I think you're overthinking this. I was just catching up with an old friend. It wasn't some crazy night out or anything."

He nods, the corner of his lips tilting up. "I sound like a jealous asshole, don't I?"

"A little, yeah." I answer with a smile. "But hey—Nikki and I are going to a Halloween party in two weeks. Maybe you could come."

His brows jump, and he nods. "Wow, a party."

"I know, crazy, right? I haven't been to a party in years." I fold another outfit and throw my friend a smile. "So you'll come."

Brian nods. "Sure. Sounds fun."

We finish packing up the orders in silence, then decide to head out to the post office together. Paulie walks along with us, sniffing at everything, demanding scratches and pats from anyone who will give them. Brian waits outside the post office with him, and I catch him watching me through the window. He gives me a smile and a wave, then kneels down to give Paulie more scratches.

Once the orders are sent, we decide to grab some lunch. We get tacos, eating them standing up while Paulie waits patiently for scraps. The last embers of my hangover melt away, and I fall into the comfort and security of my friendship with Brian. He makes me laugh, distracts me from all the things I don't want to think about, then walks me home. He gives me a long hug when he drops me off at home again.

"I'll see you later. I can help you pack up the next batch," he says while I kneel down to say goodbye to his bulldog. "I'm free on Friday, if that works for you. Should be enough time to finish sewing them, right?"

I grin, giving Paulie one last kiss on the head. "Sounds good."

Brian starts to walk away when I call him back.

"Oh! Brian! I'm actually busy on Friday. Maybe we could do Saturday?"

My best friend frowns at me in question, tilting his head. "Saturday would work." An unasked question hovers between his words.

For some reason I can't quite explain, I don't want to tell

him I'm meeting with Marcus Walsh. I give him a bright smile. "I have a work thing on Friday," I explain, then change the subject. "Saturday sounds great. Bring the camera. I'm working on Christmas sweaters, and I'd like to have Paulie model for us."

He holds my gaze for a long moment, then nods. "No problem."

I wave the two of them away and head back inside. When I get back to my silent apartment, I lock the door and lean against it, letting out a long breath.

There's an icky feeling swirling in my stomach, and I'm not quite sure why. I shake my head, stalk back to my sewing machine, and start cutting fabric to make a new Christmas sweater.

When all else fails, at least I can distract myself with sewing...

Except today, apparently, because my thoughts keep circling back to my meeting with my boss. Why does Marcus want to see me?

...And why didn't I want to tell Brian about it?

9

PENNY

THE SELLZY OFFICES are on the fifty-second floor of a high-rise made of glass and steel and elegance. The elevator ride takes an eternity, and with every floor that passes, my nerves crank tighter.

I'm ejected into a bright, white space with a funky circular couch around a glass coffee table and an immense contemporary sculpture of swooping acrylic curves. To my left, a reception desk curves to capture people arriving before they can walk into the open space beyond.

Behind the desk is a beautiful blonde wearing a lipstick-pink dress that's cut high on her neck but flatters her figure perfectly. My stress levels double. I don't belong here.

She smiles at me. "Hi. May I help you?" The nameplate on her desk says Amanda.

"Um," I answer, wiping my sweaty palms on my black polyester pants. Why did I wear these stupid pants? Why not something nicer? "I have a meeting with Marcus Walsh?" It comes out as a question.

Amanda's smile remains in place. "Of course. Your name?"

"Penny Littleton."

She taps away on a keyboard I can't see over the desk, checks her monitor, then nods. "Have a seat. He'll be with you shortly. Can I get you something to drink while you wait? Coffee? Tea? Water?"

I want to hate this woman for being beautiful and put-together while I feel anything but, but I can't. She's really nice, and she seems genuine. Hating her would just be an outlet for my stress, and that wouldn't be fair.

I shake my head.

"No problem." Amanda smiles at me again, then stands and struts away from her desk into the office space behind. Doesn't look like *her* heels make her feet ache the minute she puts them on. Damn her.

I sit back on the couch, my rain jacket squeaking against the leather. I unzip it, already sweating.

Staring into nothing, I jump when the receptionist reappears in front of me. She gestures deeper into the office. "Marcus is ready to see you now."

She's on a first-name basis with him. Hmm.

I stand and shake my head. What do I care that my boss is on a first-name basis with this gorgeous woman? He's also on a first-name basis with me. Maybe it's just how he operates?

We walk around the desk onto a vast space. There are bean bags in the corner and a Ping-Pong table beside them. Glass-walled conference rooms are in use along the opposite wall, with a large, open kitchen visible beyond. We walk around the Ping-Pong table and down a corridor to another space full of desks and co-working spaces. No cubicles in sight.

A few offices line the far wall. We walk to the very farthest one, and Amanda gestures to the open door. "Go on ahead. He won't bite." She smiles, her eyes lingering on me like she's assessing something.

That irks me. Both her words and her gaze. But I'm just projecting my stress onto this woman, and that's not fair. I give her a curt nod and walk past her, into the inner sanctum of Marcus Walsh's office.

It smells like him.

As soon as I step inside, I nearly trip over my own feet as the scent of him assails me, flooding my senses. A now-familiar heat circles low in my belly, tightening not-quite-uncomfortably in the area below my navel.

Behind a white desk is Marcus Walsh, in all his black-haired, green-eyed glory. He taps on his computer for a second, then looks up at me. His expression doesn't change, but he does stand up and gesture to the couch and armchairs to my right.

"Penny," he says. "Thanks for coming in. Please."

I follow his gesture and arrange myself on the couch, clearing my throat. Marcus prowls across the office and shuts the door. He does it gently, but the sound echoes in the space. He's wearing dark pants and a forest-green sweater that clings to the muscles of his arms and shoulders. I watch the fabric stretch as he leans to look out the window next to the door, lifting his arm to scratch behind his ear.

A little strip of skin is exposed by the movement, just above his belt. My mouth waters.

I squeeze my eyes shut and take a deep breath. I'm sitting

here, probably about to get fired, and I'm lusting after my boss?

Who *am* I anymore?

"Is everything okay?"

My eyes spring open. I find Marcus standing across from me, one hand on the back of an armchair, his long fingers leaving a slight depression in the dark fabric. His eyes are dark, stormy, and unreadable as they study me.

I nod. "I'm good," I squeak. "Just, um... I'm just nervous."

His expression softens, and he slides into the armchair. "Don't be nervous."

"That's like saying, 'don't think of pink elephants,'" I answer. "Doesn't really work that way."

His lips might have twitched ever so slightly, but I'm not sure. His face is like stone. He props an ankle over his knee and leans his head on his thumb and index finger, watching me. "True. What are you nervous about?"

"Well, gee, I don't know," I answer sarcastically, running my hands down my thighs before tossing my ponytail over my shoulder. "Maybe the fact that I'm pretty sure you're about to fire me?"

He smirks. *He smirks.* That is not something he should be smirking about! I am not a laughingstock!

Still, as outrage mounts inside me, an equally loud voice in my brain tells me to admire the sight of those male lips curling, those eyes crinkling. He's handsome on a regular day. I don't even want to know what he looks like when he's smiling for real, with no hint of cynicism on his face.

"I'm not going to fire you, Penny," he answers.

I'm still busy trying to understand why his mocking smirk sends all kinds of fizzles and pops darting through my body, so it takes me a while to understand his words. I blink. "Oh. You're not?"

He shakes his head, gaze sliding to my lips. "No."

My shoulders drop. "Oh," I repeat. "So why am I here?"

Just then, my stomach decides to join the conversation. It growls so loudly we both look down at my torso. My cheeks heat.

"Are you hungry?"

Embarrassing. "Huh?"

"Have you eaten lunch?" He stands again, moving to the door. It gives me a nice vantage point from which to view his ass.

It's a nice ass. Round buns. Very squeezable. Exceedingly bitable.

Focus, Penny.

"No, I haven't eaten anything today," I answer. "I was too nervous to eat."

That makes him scowl, for some reason. "I'll be right back."

As soon as he's out the door, I sit back on the couch and groan. If he's not going to fire me, then why am I here?

Just as soon as he leaves, Marcus is back bearing donuts. My stomach grumbles loudly enough for Marcus to glance up and frown, like my stomach noises offend him. He sets the tray down on the low table between us and gestures for me to help myself. "It's all I could find on short notice in the kitchen. I could order something in for you if you prefer, or get Amanda to grab you a sandwich downstairs."

"No," I blurt. "No, donuts are fine." I don't want anyone going out of their way to feed me. I just want to know why I'm here.

Marcus nudges the tray toward me. Three donuts stare back at me, gleaming with fat and sugar and deliciousness. My stomach makes itself known again.

We both pause.

Marcus stares at me expectantly. "Eat, Penny."

Welp. Might as well.

I grab a napkin and a Boston cream donut and take a bite. *Ohmigod*. Orgasmic. I can't help the little groan that escapes my lips as I take my first bite.

Marcus watches for a moment, then leans back, satisfied.

"I asked you to come here because I wanted to ask you if you'd like to expand your hours."

I frown, chocolate glaze and cream and donut dough filling my mouth. It takes me a while to chew and swallow. "My hours?"

Marcus's gaze flicks to my top lip as I lick a bit of chocolate glaze off it. I set my donut down on my napkin. Why did I choose the messiest one? Why didn't I just say *no, thank you* like a normal person? No, I had to stuff my face with deep-fried dough and cream and chocolate right in front of my boss. Why? What's wrong with me?

"There was an incident this week," he finally continues after I've dabbed my mouth to remove the worst of the chocolate glaze. The napkin comes away embarrassingly dirty. I must look like a toddler who took her chances with an unattended bottle of Nesquik syrup. "Mackenzie had a science experiment."

"For Mr. Errol's class?" I ask, eyeing the oozing cream from my donut, wanting another bite. I didn't eat breakfast, and now that I've had one bite of sugary deliciousness, my body seems to be remembering that I'm starving. I take a quick lick of the cream, closing my eyes. This is a good donut. A *really* good donut.

Marcus clears his throat. When I open my eyes again, he shifts in his seat and glances at the table between us. "Yeah. Mr. Errol's class." His voice is a touch rougher than it was a moment ago.

I try to bring my brain back to the matter at hand: Mackenzie, science experiment, my working hours. I set the donut down on the napkin on my lap. "Mackenzie told me about her experiment when we were shopping. She was excited about it. She said chemistry is one of her favorite classes."

Marcus nods, gaze sliding back up to mine, then to my lips, and back up to my eyes. "Well, she and her friend ruined my kitchen and living room," he finally says, that roughness gone from his voice.

"Oh. I'm sorry." My brain is chugging along with great difficulty. Why is he telling me this? Why am I sitting in my boss's office eating a donut?

Marcus nods. "And I realized that with my schedule, I'm not able to watch Mackenzie as much as I should."

That poor girl. I don't know what to say, so I take a bite of my pastry instead. Cream oozes out onto the corner of my lip, and I lean forward to stop myself from dribbling it all over the front of my top.

This is the most embarrassing and confusing moment of my life. Why can't I be like Amanda? I could have drifted in here wearing sky-high heels and a tight dress, flashed a nice smile, and acted like a normal person. Instead, I'm a stomach-grumbling, donut-eating gremlin who can't even manage to stuff her donut-hole like a civilized person.

The donut crushes in my hand, the dough too weak to hold the immense amount of cream stuffing. I drop a big glob of it onto the napkin, and I know I look like a mess. Panic is quickly taking hold. I don't understand why I'm here or what he's trying to say. I'm just glad there aren't any mirrors around.

Then Marcus's hand appears next to my face. His fingers touch my jaw, and his thumb sweeps over the corner of my mouth, picking up the cream filling that didn't make it inside my gob. His hand is broad and warm, and it sends fire rushing through my veins.

And his eyes.

God, his eyes.

They're dark and low, focused on my lips and the movement of his thumb. Picking up the cream on his digit, he leans back in his seat and brings his thumb to his mouth, sucking off the sweet, sugary goodness between those beautiful lips.

And I die.

I just die right there. I expire. I implode—explode.

I must sit still for a stupid amount of time, staring at his mouth, at his thumb, feeling the imprint of his fingers on my cheek.

I— *What just happened?*

"I need someone to be at my place when Mackenzie's home from school," Marcus says, as if nothing at all just happened. "And I want you to do it."

My heart is beating a mile a minute. My head is about to explode. My lady-parts are throwing a wild party, soaking through my panties in record time.

Finally, the ability to speak returns to me, even as my

body riots. "You... You want me to be Mackenzie's babysitter?" My voice is nothing more than a croak.

His throat bobs as he swallows, his tongue darting out to lick his lips, as if he didn't quite get every bit of sugar in the first swipe. Another wave of heat washes over me.

The man across from me seems unaffected. "I just want someone to be there on evenings and weekends when I have to work. A couple hours a day. I'd pay you your usual rate." He pauses. "Eat," he says, gesturing to the donut. "Your stomach keeps grumbling."

There is no *freaking* way I'm eating any more of this donut. Absolutely zero chance that's happening, ever. I shake my head and set the donut down on a napkin, grabbing another to wipe my hands. They're trembling.

"So?" Marcus prompts. "Can you start on Monday? Say, three hours on school nights?"

I nod. "Right." I clear my throat, cheeks flaming. It's hard to think through the haze of lust and confusion. I'm not used to this. My body doesn't react to men like this. The sugar is going straight to my head, making it hard to reason. "I appreciate the offer. I really do. But Mr. Walsh—Marcus, I have a business that takes up all my time outside of walking Bear."

The billionaire's brows twitch together.

My cheeks flush. Gosh. I'm sitting across from a man who started a *tech empire*, and I'm really going to explain to him that I make dog bow ties for a living?

I press a hand to my cheek in a futile attempt to cool my skin down. My fingers are sticky from the donut. My mouth still burns from where his thumb stroked it.

Then I just launch into the explanation: "Those bow ties I make for Bear? I sell them. Along with costumes, winter- and holiday-themed sweaters, rain jackets, and all kinds of clothes and accessories."

His face remains utterly expressionless. "Dog clothes."

I'm sure my entire head, all the way to my scalp, is bright red. I shrug one shoulder. "It's kind of silly, but people really eat it up. Actually, my business partner and I use your platform. Our shop is on Sellzy, but I also do a few farmers' markets a year. Brian keeps trying to get me to start our own website, but all that technical stuff... I don't know." I exhale and stare at the coffee table, at the ruins of my donut. "I was featured in *Pets* magazine last year, you know. It doubled my business for the following six months. It's kind of crazy how many people buy my products." *Am I* bragging *to Marcus freaking Walsh? About dog clothes?* I take a deep breath. "So, you see, I can't just give up my livelihood to be a babysitter. I'm sorry."

The door opens. Amanda's head pops in. "Your two o'clock is here, Marcus."

He shakes out his watch and scowls. "Tell them to wait."

She glances at him, at the donuts, at me. I'm sure I look like I have the worst sunburn of my life.

When she disappears again, my boss regards me from his chair, his forearms resting on its arms, fingers tented in front of his chest. Fingers that were *on my face* right before they were *inside his mouth.*

It takes all my self-control not to squirm. I feel like a tiny little ant staring at the bottom of a very big shoe. Who do I think I am? Marcus Walsh could kick me off the Sellzy platform, and I'd lose ninety percent of my sales. He probably thinks I'm ridiculous for selling dog clothes. I mean, *I* think I'm a little ridiculous, and I'm the one who came up with the idea. But people love them! Even Bear struts around when he has a bow tie on, and he always stands beside his rain jacket if it's wet outside, waiting for me to put it on him.

Marcus clears his throat. "That's very impressive, Penny. I had no idea you were a business owner."

I blink, then search his gaze for some kind of sarcasm. I see none.

His eyes drift down to my lips, then slide away from my face altogether. His scowl deepens. "So it's the time away from your business that's the issue?"

I nod. "I'm already drowning in orders. I can't afford to take that many hours off every week."

"What if you worked from my place? I've got a spare room we could set up as a base of operations."

Surprise makes me sit up straighter. "Oh. I mean..." My mind is racing, stomach is gurgling again. I should *not* have eaten that donut. For multiple reasons. I shake my head and try to focus. "Wouldn't it be easier to find a real babysitter? I'm not exactly qualified."

A bitter huff escapes his lips, and he gives me a shrug. "Maybe. Maybe not. Mackenzie likes you. And she hasn't had very many constant adult role models in her life. I'd rather not have to go through a long hiring and vetting process to find someone she clicks with." Emotion clouds his eyes— concern. He's worried for his niece.

And I mean, I met her mother. I can imagine that Mackenzie's had it tough. It was hard enough growing up in a blended family without the chaos and drama that I witnessed when Mackenzie burst through Marcus's front door.

"I get it," I say quietly. "But I'm sorry, I just don't see how it would work. Even if I have a workshop at your place, I'd have to watch Mackenzie. I wouldn't be able to work while she's there. And I'd have to double up on all my supplies."

He gives me a nod. "True."

There's a pause, and I'm able to catch my breath. Everything will be okay. He's not firing me, and he's not going to kick me off the Sellzy platform. Everything will go back to normal once I leave this office. Whatever that moment was with the donut and the thumb and the licking, we'll both forget it.

Well, he'll forget it. I'll replay it in my mind for the rest of my life.

Then Marcus speaks again. "What if we set up a full-time workshop for you in the spare room? You could come in the morning, work from my place, then spend time with Mackenzie in the evenings." He spreads his hands, that sweater stretching over his pecs.

I frown. That *could* work, I guess.

Marcus must sense his advantage, because he leans forward. "You'd be saving time by not commuting twice a day to come and walk Bear. Even if it's slightly less efficient when Mackenzie's around in the evenings, the extra time will make up for it. And I could talk to her—she could even help you. I'm sure there's admin that she'd be able to do. She's good on a computer. Social media!" He points at the ceiling. "She's always on her phone. It would be good for her to meet a female entrepreneur."

Blinking rapidly, I struggle to get my thoughts in order. He thinks I'd be a good role model? He considers me an entrepreneur, even though my business is so silly compared to his?

And logistically, his proposal could work.

My heart thumps. It takes me about an hour and a half every day to make the two trips to his house and back, and they often break up my flow while I'm sewing. If I could work straight through the day, I could probably get a lot more done. I might even be able to catch up on orders and get ahead on winter sweatshirts and Valentine's Day bow ties.

If I got more done during the day, I wouldn't have to stay up quite so late. My weekends wouldn't be dominated by sewing. Maybe I'd have more free time. I could see Nikki more often. Brian and I could hang out without talking about the business. I could have friends.

The shackles clamped around my ankles could finally loosen, and I'd be free to start my life over, for real this time. No more hiding from relationships, from people, from men. Billy's shadow could finally be burned away by a new dawn.

But—"I work weekends too, Marcus. What if I need to do a rush order? What if something comes up and I need to work?"

"So we'll get you another sewing machine. You can set it up at my place, keep your own gear at yours. Work at your place on weekends."

I shake my head. "No. I can't afford that."

"I can."

My spine stiffens. "This is my *business*. I don't need your misplaced charity. Plus, it's not just the machine. It's the patterns, the clasps, the fabric, the labels, the shipping supplies. I can't just snap my fingers and double all my expenses just to babysit your niece. I understand you might be accustomed to throwing money at a problem, but I built this business on my own sweat and time. I won't let you trample all over it."

He exhales, lifting his hands in a placating gesture. "I'm sorry. I didn't mean it that way."

I smooth my hands over my lap, toying with the cheap fabric of my pants. The outrage inside me banks. "How long do you need someone to watch Mackenzie?"

"A few months," he responds. "Nothing more. Just until things at work calm down. Look—you could have access to my place anytime. Weekends too."

I bunch my lips to the side, thinking. What's making me hesitate to refuse him outright is the commute. That's a huge chunk of my day eaten up by going to see Bear and coming back home twice a day, five days a week. If I eliminate that, maybe I won't have to work weekends. Or I could split my time so weekends are spent packing and shipping, and the week is for sewing.

Marcus's eyes study me intently. He leans back, victory written on his face. "You'll do it."

I open my mouth. Close it. Open it again. "I didn't say that."

"But you will."

My glare doesn't seem to faze him. "You're being very pushy, Mr. Walsh."

His lips spread into a wide, triumphant smile, and my heart stops. Just—stops. Dead. Right there in the middle of my chest. His smile transforms him from untouchable-male-model good looks to something more approachable. More human.

I thought his smirk was hot. It was a pile of hot garbage compared to this.

And gosh, that smile works for me. My thighs clench as everything from nipples to knees grows taut.

This isn't just a crush. This is a flattening. I'm so, so attracted to this man. I'd lather myself in cream just for him to lick it off me, which is a problem. How can I stay safe if I'm already feeling overwhelmed in his presence? How can I make sure that what happened with Billy doesn't happen again?

A dark brow arches. "So?"

I bite my lip, drawing his gaze to my mouth. The heat in his eyes must be in my head, but it still makes my breasts feel heavy and sensitive. It was that stupid donut. And the thumb-licking. That's what's got my head in a muddle. That's the only reason I'm even considering this crazy plan.

Clearing my throat, I try to ignore the sensation. "I *might* do it. But I have to see the spare room first, and I'll need help moving all my supplies over. Oh, and my business partner might need to come by. He manages the orders and helps me do the packing. And it's possible I'll need to come by on weekends, so I hope you're serious about access. This is my livelihood. I can't afford to fall behind, especially not this time of year. It's my busy season."

"Done." Marcus stands up and extends his hand toward me.

I'm slower to stand up, but I eventually extend a hand. His hand wraps around mine, warm and strong. I feel dizzy.

"Thank you," my boss says quietly, his fingers still holding mine.

The touch forks through me, electric, sizzling. I...don't hate it. I'm not afraid. I don't want to recoil.

For the first time since my ex-boyfriend made my life hell, I don't want to run from a man's touch. I can hardly breathe. A man is touching my hand in a way that feels incredibly intimate, even though logically I know it isn't. He had his hands on me earlier, in an even more intimate way, and all it did was turn me on.

I need to pull my hand away, or else these feelings will lead me straight into deep trouble.

With great effort, I do just that and give Marcus a jerky nod. "Don't mention it. When do you want me to start?"

"The cleaners said they'd be done this afternoon. How's Monday? We could move your stuff over tomorrow or Sunday, if you like."

So soon. I gulp. "Okay."

"I'll send my driver to your place to help you move your stuff whenever it's convenient for you. Would you like to view the room right now? I'll clear my schedule for the afternoon. I just have to talk to my two o'clock meeting, but it shouldn't take longer than ten minutes. Can you wait?"

"I... Okay. Sure." Things are moving fast. I just agreed to move my business to Marcus's spare room. Logically, the decision makes sense. Not only will I save time on the twice-daily commute to walk Bear, but I'll also make some extra cash from Mackenzie's after-school hours. Not to mention how much she might help me, if she decides she wants to.

But in the not-so-logical areas of my brain, alarm bells are ringing. It all sounds like a great idea, if I ignore the blazing-hot ball of desire consuming the lower half of my body.

As Marcus calls Todd over and asks him to clear his schedule, my mind reels. This attraction is a very big problem. If I can't get myself under control, things are going to go very, very wrong.

10

MARCUS

By the end of my meeting with Penny, a tight knot of tension in the pit of my stomach has loosened. She'll watch Mackenzie.

She'll be there when I get home every day.

The thought rises unbidden, and I push it back down, even as my hand tingles from where I touched her. I wanted to kiss that cream off her face and taste it on her tongue. When she said she'd help me, I wanted to pull her across to my armchair so she'd straddle my hips and press herself against me.

I close my eyes. I need to get this under control. I need a warm body that isn't Penny's to take care of these urges.

A little voice in my head tells me this arrangement is a bad idea. This nonsensical attraction to Penny means I should be keeping my distance, not ensuring that she'll be at my house nearly every day. I *can't* get involved with a woman. I learned my lesson years ago. I already have enough responsibilities as it is—I can't deal with a relationship too.

As I walk out after my meeting to take Penny to my place,

I find her in the reception area, staring at the artwork on the office wall. Her fingers slide her pendant necklace back and forth along its chain. Her chest is covered in freckles, which I can see above the neckline of her white top. Thousands of them. It would take days to count them all. She shifts in her chair and the shoulder of her jacket falls away, revealing more freckled skin beneath.

My mouth waters with the need to taste her skin, to peel her clothes off and see what else is revealed.

I mentally backhand myself across the face. Those are not thoughts I should be having. I blink and shift my gaze to Amanda. "Transfer my calls to Todd."

Amanda nods, face perfectly blank. She's worked for me for years, from nearly the start of Sellzy. She used to be part of the software engineering team and is well-versed in all the back-end systems of the website, but she chose to take a step back so she'd have more time with her husband and young child. Now she's the office manager, and she's damn good at it.

What I'm saying is, Amanda knows me. And she must have seen me panting after Penny just now.

What the hell is wrong with me? Penny is my employee, and she's going to be my niece's after-school babysitter. She's not dating material. Not even a little bit.

But she's intriguing. Take her business—she makes dog clothing for a living. What kind of person does that? What kind of person has that kind of idea in the first place, and the drive to follow through?

Then there's her looks. The big, blue eyes. The shimmering hair that begs to be wrapped around my fist. The lush, pink mouth. The lean curves on her short figure. The way she laughs like she knows she shouldn't. The glimmer in her eyes when she says something cheeky.

It's like she was made to be attractive to me from some template I didn't even know existed. She's *cute*. I don't get why she drives me so crazy. It's infuriating.

When we walk into the elevator, I can't quite resist the urge to place my hand on her lower back to guide her into the little mirrored box. Her cheeks grow pink, and a deep, satisfied feeling spreads in my chest.

Then I catch myself, and I pull my hand away.

Maybe hiring Penny wasn't such a shit-hot idea after all. But I still lead her to the lobby, my eyes tracing the graceful curve of her neck as she does her best to avoid my gaze. We head out to my waiting car, and I take her to my place to inspect her future workshop.

There's a big cat inside my chest, stretching in satisfaction at having her near. At knowing she'll be near for the foreseeable future.

Penny stares out the window the whole drive, her legs clamped together, hands clasped between her thighs like she's trying to make herself as small as possible, whole body squeezed into the opposite corner of the back seat.

I comb my fingers through my hair. "So what are your requirements for the work room?" I ask, just to fill the silence, to distract myself from my thoughts.

She turns to look at me, the gray light from the passing scenery making her eyes look stormy. "Well," she answers, "it just has to be big enough for my sewing machine, fabric, and finished projects. A table for cutting patterns and ironing would be useful."

I nod. "We can make that work."

She shifts in her seat, facing me. "You're really serious about this," she says quietly.

I lift my gaze from her legs to her face. "About what?"

"About me being there with Mackenzie."

I huff, then pull out my phone. Flicking through the photos until I get to the ones of my destroyed living room and kitchen, I pass it over. "This was the carnage from the failed science experiment."

She takes the phone from my hands like it's a priceless vase and her eyes widen. "Oh my goodness."

I snort. "Yeah. It was worse in person."

"Your *paintings*. Your TV." Her mouth forms a cute little O that I want to kiss away.

I clear my throat. "The paintings are with a specialist. They think they can restore them with little to no permanent damage. The TV didn't make it."

Her pale auburn brows arch. "Wow."

"You get it now? Why I can't leave Mackenzie alone?"

Lush, pink lips start to curl. It's a teasing hint of that cheeky smile, the one that never fails to make my cock grow hard. She dips her chin. "I get it now."

I shift in my seat, keep my eyes off her mouth, and think pure thoughts. "She's a good kid, but she's still a kid," I say. "You can flick through the photos. There're closeups of the kitchen. It was a disaster."

Penny's gaze drops to the phone and a line appears between her brows. She brings her finger to the screen like it's some kind of foreign object and flicks awkwardly. When the picture changes, she does a little jump. Has this woman never used a smartphone?

Everything she does intrigues me. Every twitch, every movement, every noise.

"Oh. Your Le Creuset Dutch oven," she mourns before sucking her lips between her teeth.

I lean toward her as we turn onto my street. "It was bad. Mackenzie thought I would kick her out."

"You'd never do that," Penny answers absentmindedly, still flicking through the photos.

I turn to look at her, frowning. "How do you know that?"

"Because Bear loves you," she answers, flicking to the next photo. "People with dogs—" She lets out a yell, fumbles the phone, and drops it to her feet. "Oh, no. Oh, gosh." Her face is bright red when she retrieves my phone and hands it over. She doesn't meet my eyes. "Sorry. Is the screen okay?"

"It's fine," I answer, unlocking the phone. A photo of an ex-fling in red lingerie fills the screen.

Oh...shit.

I swipe away from the photo app and lock the phone, shoving it in my breast pocket.

There's an awkward silence. Then Penny says, "I'm sorry. I didn't see anything except, you know. Skin." She flaps her hands in the area of her torso and clears her throat. Her chest, neck, and face are bright red. "Is that your girlfriend?"

"No," I answer through clenched teeth. "We used to see each other a few months ago. She sent me that photo last weekend. It must have saved automatically to my camera roll."

And I never answered. Heather and I were purely physical for about six months. It was never anything more. When she texted me on Saturday night, she wouldn't have been hurt when I didn't respond. Things between us are—were—

simple. If I'd wanted to sleep with her, I would have gone over to her place after she sent the photo. I didn't want to sleep with her, so I didn't respond, and she didn't text me again. I'm sure she had no trouble finding a man willing to keep her company on Saturday night.

I don't explain that to Penny. I know it would make me sound like a womanizing asshole. That wouldn't bother me normally, but I'd like Penny to think better of me. I don't want to examine why. I want to howl at the pressure inside me, the heat and emotions I can't explain.

The silence stretches between Penny and me as my driver parks the car in front of my place. That stupid photo. Penny's uncomfortable, and it's my fault. My fucking fault. She'll probably tell me she doesn't want to move her workshop. She'll come up with some bogus excuse, all because I didn't check my camera-roll settings.

My fists clench. I want to punch something.

When my driver gets out to open my door, Penny finally meets my gaze. I don't know what to say. We slide out of the car and stand on the sidewalk, the space between us impossibly wide.

Then Penny lifts her gaze to mine, an expression of sympathetic pity pulling her features down. "You know, I also get women sending me sexy photos at all hours of the night." She turns toward my house and flicks her ponytail over her shoulder. "It's a curse, really."

A surprised chuckle falls from my lips, and Penny flashes me an impish grin over her shoulder. She marches to my front door, head held high.

But despite her joke, she stands a bit farther away from me and is careful not to brush my arm with hers when we enter. She immediately steps over to the hooks on the wall and fiddles with the leashes before hanging up her jacket. I suspect it's to put more space between us.

It's probably a good thing. There *should* be space between us. She works for me, and I don't want her. I'm just horny because I'm going through a dry spell and I'm stressed at work. Whatever this is, it'll pass.

I'm better off with women like Heather. When the relationship is clear, uncomplicated. When the woman in question doesn't make me think of anything beyond getting her undressed and leaving when it's done.

"The room is this way," I say, gesturing down the hall. "Keep your shoes on. The cleaners aren't done, and there's still crap all over the floor."

Penny nods and follows me down the hall. My place is a five-bedroom converted factory. Three of the bedrooms are fully furnished: the master, Mackenzie's room, and a spare guest bedroom often taken over by hordes of nieces and nephews. One room is my home office, and the fifth and smallest room is vacant. I've been meaning to renovate it into a third bathroom, but like everything in my life, the project has been pushed back until work calms down.

"Here it is," I say. "It's small, but it gets good light."

Penny lets out a choked laugh. "Small, he says," she mutters. "It's bigger than my living room." She spins in a slow circle, then crosses to the wall of built-in wardrobes and pulls one open. It's empty. She glances at me over her shoulder, and I lift my gaze from where it was glued to her ass. She jabs a thumb at the shelves. "Can I use these?"

I nod. "Sure. I have a spare desk in the garage I could move in here if you like."

I watch her circle the room, inspect the windows, measure the cabinets with spread hands. She paces the room and mutters to herself, looking at every corner and every outlet.

Finally, Penny faces me, her hands clasped at her breast. "Oh, Marcus." Her eyes are shining.

A strange tightness occurs in the center of my chest. I shift my weight to the other foot. "It's adequate?"

Before I know what's happening, Penny throws her arms around me and squeezes me in a bone-crushing hug. Her body is soft as it presses against mine. A bolt of pure arousal pierces through me. Having her this close to me...

I stand there, arms hovering just above her body, trying to angle my hips so my stupid, sudden boner doesn't come in contact with her. The top of her fiery red head comes up to the middle of my chest, and I just stand there and grit my teeth till it's over.

Then, just as abruptly, she pulls away. "Sorry. Whoops. I got overwhelmed." A nervous giggle punctuates her words. She turns her back to me and wipes at her eyes. I take the opportunity to readjust myself. She lets out a breath and faces me, beaming. "I forgot that I'm the one doing you a favor here."

This woman is so fucking adorable and sweet and beautiful it makes me ache all over. I hate it. I need to call Heather later, deal with this problem. The thought makes my jaw clench.

Penny has both hands on her cheeks, her eyes scanning the space again, a dreamy smile tugging at her lips.

I want to put that look on her face over and over. I want her to smile and laugh and blush because of *me*.

But isn't that what I do? I provide. I take care of everyone who relies on me—and then I fuck up and let them down. I have enough on my plate taking care of my family and employees and all the people who depend on me. The last thing I need is another person to add to the list.

"I'll have the desk moved in," I say, my voice full of gravel. Then I turn my back to her and stalk out of the room. "You can start moving your things in tomorrow. I'll send a truck."

Later, when the house is quiet and night has fallen, I let my fingers hover over Heather's name on my phone's screen. But it's late, and I'm tired, and Mackenzie's in the next room.

I lock my phone and go to sleep.

FABRIC. So much fabric. Swags and rolls and stacks of it. Every cupboard door in my spare room is open and quickly being filled with all manner of sewing supplies. My assistant, Todd, joins me in the doorway as Penny directs a mover to shift her sewing machine desk closer to the window. I hired two men to help Penny move, but I didn't expect quite so much *stuff*.

Mackenzie is hard at work sliding plastic containers full of buttons and snaps and bows into the bottom shelf of the cupboard. There's no scowling and rolling eyes and attitude. My niece looks...happy.

Todd's dark-brown eyes survey the scene in one quick, all-encompassing glance.

"Don't say it, Todd," I grumble.

"I haven't said a word."

I throw him a sideways glance. "You're thinking it."

Todd's expression is perfectly neutral. "I'm not thinking anything, sir."

I snort. "Anytime the 'sir' comes out, I know I'm in trouble."

"I'm not sure the trouble will come from me, though." He arches a brow. Todd is a tall man with rich brown skin and close-cropped hair. He's a wizard with scheduling and not afraid to defend my time like a knight with a day planner. I'd be lost without him.

He's also opinionated as hell, and just about the only employee who's ever had the guts to stand up to me, apart from Amanda.

"You think this is a bad idea," I say, walking down the hall as Todd falls into step beside me.

"You invited your dog walker to set up her business in your home because you needed a babysitter," he notes. "I wonder about the logic behind the decision, is all."

Todd Garrison: diplomat. He should go into politics.

"We might have something in common there." I pause at the mouth of the hallway, glancing back toward the room where Penny is still chirping out polite orders. "I'm not sure logic was involved at all." Unless you count the logic of my dick-brain. That made perfect sense twenty-four hours ago.

Scrubbing my jaw, I make my way to the coffee machine in my freshly cleaned kitchen. I arch a brow at Todd, who nods. We both customize our coffee with the appropriate additions (cream and half a spoon of sugar for me, almond milk for my lactose-intolerant assistant), and take our first sips.

"We have another meeting with Feldman on Monday morning. I saw that you made progress with the IP section of the acquisition contract," he says, one hand holding his phone, the other holding the coffee mug.

I sip my slightly sweetened coffee and nod. "The contract is still not where we want it, but if I can get Feldman to move a little bit more, and if he meets us on price, I think we'll be able to push the purchase through."

Todd starts answering when the door flies open as a hurricane of blond hair flies through.

"Uncle Marcus!" Isla Sorensen screeches, sprinting toward me.

Bear jumps up from his bed at the intrusion, head swinging toward the door.

The girl crashes into my legs, causing my coffee to slosh dangerously close to the edge of my mug. I set the mug down and pick the girl-sized tornado up, throwing her over my shoulder. She screeches, laughing, as her frazzled-looking father rushes through the door along with a nanny carrying an empty car seat and a massive diaper bag.

"I just found a nine-year-old girl," I say. "Did you lose her?"

Bear comes padding over to me, lifting his snout toward Isla's face as she hangs off my back. Then he moves toward the door to inspect the other visitors.

"Isla, I told you not to go inside until we had Madeline out of the car," the girl's father chides. He gives Bear an absentminded pat.

His daughter shifts on my shoulder, lifting herself up so fast I have to clap her legs down against my chest to keep from dropping her. "Oops," she says innocently.

Isla Sorensen isn't my niece by blood, but she's part of my chosen family. Her father, Leif, is a good friend.

Leif snorts. He turns to help his wife, Layla, come through the door. She's holding their eleven-month-old daughter, who's busy tugging at her hair and ears. The baby lets out a squeal at the sight of Bear, wiggling until she's let down. Then she scoots toward Bear and shoves her face in my dog's fur.

Bear endures the less-than-gentle pets with fond canine patience.

"Gentle, Madeline, gentle," Layla says, demonstrating how to pet the dog for her daughter. Madeline copies the motion with clumsy baby movements, and Bear rewards her by licking her hand. Madeline is so startled she flops onto her back with a giggle, both legs sticking straight in the air.

Leif grins, crossing the distance to shake my hand. "As you can see, my life has devolved into pure chaos."

"So has mine, apparently," I answer, then take a few steps toward the couch. Isla screams as I tip her over the back of it so she bounces on the cushions. She laughs, falling to the floor. Bear bounds over to investigate, playfully jumping on Isla as she giggles.

I turn back to Leif. "To what do I owe the honor?"

Leif's blond brows tug together. "You forgot."

I blink. "Forgot what?"

He exchanges a glance with Layla, then turns back to me. "You were supposed to take the kids to your mom's. It's Oliver Jr.'s sixth birthday party this afternoon. Layla and I are having a date night."

"The first night out we planned since the wedding," Layla adds.

My stomach bottoms out. Shit. *Shit*. Leif texted me about this the day Mackenzie ruined my kitchen. I completely forgot. My mother even mentioned the birthday party to me.

I glance at Todd, who points to the garage. "Your nephew's gift is wrapped and waiting on the shelf. There's a reminder in your calendar, but..." He clears his throat. *But your mind has been elsewhere*, he leaves unsaid.

There's too much going on. I deflate, rubbing the bridge of my nose, then take a deep breath and face my friend. "I'm so sorry. I forgot. There's a lot going on at work, and—"

"There are just two more boxes of fabric," Penny calls out, coming down the hallway with Mackenzie and the men I hired to help her move. "And the desk in the garage to be moved over to the corner of the room." She comes to an abrupt stop at the mouth of the hallway, blinking at all the new people. "Oh. Hello."

Leif arches an eyebrow. "Moving in?" His gaze turns to me, a question written in his eyes. "A lot going on with *work*, huh."

I don't dignify that comment with a response. His snark is worse than Mackenzie's, and Leif doesn't have the excuse of being a fourteen-year-old girl.

All eyes turn to my dog walker.

Penny clears her throat. "Um. Sort of moving in. Not permanently."

"Hi, Leif," Mackenzie says, dispelling the tension as she appears behind Penny. "Layla. Isla. Madeline. Harriet." She gives a polite nod to the Sorensen's long-time nanny, who smiles back. Harriet's husband was ill when Layla and Leif met and got together, but she seems happy to be back with the family and the new baby.

I introduce everyone by briefly barking their names and pointing. I turn to the blond-haired girl on the floor, currently wrestling with my dog. "The devil-child is Isla, and the toddler currently trying to eat dog food is Madeline."

Layla yelps and dives toward her daughter, hauling the laughing baby up in the air as kibbles go flying out of her chubby little fist. Harriet sets down her bag and offers to take Madeline from Layla, who agrees, then tries to brush off baby drool and kibble powder from her silky top.

Bear bounds over and makes quick work of the spilled food at their feet, glancing up at Madeline, looking for more.

Isla's head pokes over the top of the couch. Her blond hair is nearly white, and her eyes sparkle with mischief. She tilts her head as she looks Penny over from head to toe. "I like your skirt."

Penny smooths her hand over the orangey-brown corduroy fabric that hits her just above the knee. I also like Penny's skirt. I especially like how the skirt looks from behind, and I'm sure I'd like the skirt even more if it were rumpled on the floor of my bedroom.

Penny smiles. "Thank you."

"Is that a Littleton fall/winter design?" I ask, my voice wry.

My redheaded dog walker glares at me, and my cock throbs in response. She's extremely adorable when I make her angry. I want to do it again. And again. And again. And then kiss the frown off her face and replace it with an expression of bliss.

Ugh. I grimace. Todd was right. Moving Penny in was a terrible idea.

"It was indeed a Littleton fall/winter design." She lifts her chin. "Groundbreaking. Excuse me," Penny says primly. "It was lovely to meet you." She nods to my guests, then prances out the door. I watch the way her hips sway back and forth and reconfirm that her skirt is fantastic.

I come back down to earth and find Leif and Layla staring at me with curious expressions on their faces, so I cross the room, pick up my coffee, and take a big gulp. Then I turn to my assistant. "Todd, call the car. We'll have to leave soon to make it to my mom's house in time. Leif, Layla, have a good date night. I'll see you this evening. I'll drop the kids off around eight o'clock."

Layla draws her brows low over her eyes. "Look, Marcus, it seems like you have a lot on your plate. It's no big deal. We can go with Harriet"—she nods to the nanny—"to the birthday party and take the kids home after." She glances at her husband. "We can give the tickets to the show away, right? Maybe we can go another night."

"Broadway tickets aren't exactly easy to come by, babe," Leif says quietly. "And if Marcus says he can take the kids, he can take them. He won't miss his nephew's birthday."

"Leif's right," I say. "It's just a minor scheduling hiccup. I'll manage. You two have fun."

"You're sure?" Layla asks. "I could call my sister, see if she's free..."

"Your sister's busy with college. Please. It was my mistake. But I'll head over to my mom's for the afternoon. Everything is fine."

An uncomfortable feeling squirms inside me. This is what happens. I let people down. I can't live up to the responsibilities that are thrust upon me.

But, as the chaos in my home buzzes around me, I do what I always do: I take a deep breath, push down my doubts, and take care of everyone that needs to be taken care of.

11

PENNY

I CAN'T BELIEVE I agreed to this. I can't even explain what came over me when I was in the Sellzy offices, or why I decided it was a good idea to move my workshop from my living room to Marcus Walsh's spare bedroom.

It was greed, I think. The thought of all the extra money for twenty-odd hours a week of watching Mackenzie. Or maybe I was blinded by the glass and chrome and fancy-looking tech people.

It was the donut. It was the thumb, and the lick.

Marcus put a spell on me. That explains it. That's why I agreed to move my entire business operation to his house.

Or maybe I simply lost my damn mind.

When I walk back into the main living space, my boss's hair is sticking up in all directions. Isla is launching herself off the couch to try to tackle him, and he lets out the biggest, most surprised laugh I've ever heard. It booms through the room as he collapses on the floor, girl and dog tackling him to the ground with vicious tickles.

I freeze, watching.

This is a side of Marcus I've never seen. He's always so serious, so reserved with me. Just a shade of a smile on his lips to betray any amusement, nothing close to a full-blown laugh.

Isla's parents watch on and try to calm their daughter down, but the baby starts crying and distracts them.

Mackenzie bumps into my shoulder, holding the last box of fabric scraps I carted over from my apartment. "He's like this with all my cousins," she says. "Uncle Marcus was always the best one to play with when I was a kid." She grins at me, then walks toward the hallway.

Throat tight, I follow. I'm in over my head.

When I walk into my new workspace, my worries melt away and a spark of excitement ignites in my gut.

This is why I agreed. There's more space in this room than in my entire apartment. I have storage and *light*. I have a large, solid table to cut and pin and iron. No matter how many doubts still circle in my mind like sharks, I can't deny that this workspace is far, far superior to my cramped apartment.

If I can get lots of work done in the next few months, I might actually be able to expand the business and get ahead of my orders, instead of always playing catch-up.

The sound of screeching floats down the hall, and Mackenzie lets out a giggle. "Sounds like Marcus is winning."

I give her a small smile and turn back to the cabinets to unload the last box of fabric. Mackenzie disappears from the room to investigate the noises coming from the living room, and I take a deep breath.

This is a weird situation, but I need to set aside my own lust and confusion. I have a feeling deep in my gut that it'll be good for me. Good for my business. To have space to work...that's a lot more valuable than the extra paycheck from watching Mackenzie. Plus, Mackenzie already snapped a few pictures of Bear in some of my new experimental designs, and she said they got hundreds of likes on her social media account within an hour—which is good, apparently. She sounds excited to help out and even asked me if I could show her how to sew her own dress for her prom.

For the first time in a long, long time, I'm not a hermit shuffling back and forth to my apartment. I'm trying something new. I'm...putting myself out there. Taking a risk.

I haven't done that since college.

There's a knock on the door, and I turn to see Marcus watching me. His eyes are dark, face once again serious. "You looked like you were deep in thought." His voice travels through me like whisky, a smooth burn all the way down to my core.

"I was, I guess," I say.

His broad shoulders dominate the doorframe, but I'm surprised to find I don't feel boxed in. I'm not afraid of him— not even a little bit.

"I'm taking the kids to my mom's house. Do you mind watching Bear for a bit? He's too worked up to ride in the car right now. I want to give him a minute to calm down. I'll come back and get him in an hour or so."

"Of course," I answer. "You...want me to stay here? That's okay?"

"I figured you'd want to test out the new space."

A small smile curls my lips. "I do."

He nods, then clicks his tongue and Bear comes trotting in. The dog falls into a heap next to my sewing machine, glancing up at me like he expects his fair share of ear scratches. I smile and oblige.

"All right," Marcus says, lingering in the doorway.

I meet his gaze. "All right," I repeat. "I'll see you later."

He opens his mouth like he wants to say something, then closes it again, nods, and walks away.

As soon as the group is out of the house, silence presses in. I leave Bear where he's lying and pull out my chair, flicking on my sewing machine and taking a deep breath.

This is temporary. I might as well make the most of it.

I grab the latest list of orders Brian gave me and get to work. My machine hums, fabric glides under the needle, the iron puffs, and I work like a madwoman. I enter the flow state that made me fall in love with sewing to begin with. The feeling of creating something new with my bare hands, of pouring all my focus into the task before me. The rest of the world melts away, and all that exists is my creativity and my skill.

That's why, when my phone rings, I nearly fall out of my chair.

I flip it open and see who's calling. My stomach drops. Oh...*crap*. "Brian," I say into the phone.

"I'm outside your apartment, but you're not answering the buzzer."

I pinch the bridge of my nose. "I forgot we were going to meet today."

Looks like I have something in common with my local tech billionaire. We both forget previous engagements.

There's a pause on the other end of the line. "You're out?"

"Yeah." I clear my throat. "I, um, I'm at my boss's house."

"Oh."

"That's why I met with him yesterday. He needed me to watch his niece after school for a few months, and he offered me a space for a workshop in exchange."

Through the phone, I hear the sound of honking cars and traffic. Something rustles, and Brian says, "I see."

"I've made progress on the orders you gave me," I say, putting false cheer in my voice. "This new workshop is great. I have way more space to work, and I no longer have to keep shifting piles of fabric over and back when I need to iron. It works really well."

"That's good, Pen." A long pause. "I wish you'd told me, though. This is my business too."

"Yeah, but I'm in charge of the sewing," I answer, my voice too defensive, even to my ears.

"We're *partners*. You should have talked to me. Or at least called me to say you couldn't hang today."

I sigh. Bear stands up and puts his head on my thighs, as if he can sense my discomfort. I bury my fingers in his fur. "You're right."

"So I guess we aren't hanging out this afternoon." His voice is distant, and a pain slices through my chest.

"I'm sorry, Brian. Let's meet up tomorrow."

"Forget it, Penny. Just let me know when the orders are shipped. I'll drop the next list of orders in your mailbox."

The phone clicks, and I pull it away from my ear in shock. He hung up on me. Brian hung up on me!

My stomach churns. Guilt and embarrassment and a hot spear of outrage war within me. Brian has helped me so much over the course of our friendship. He's probably the only reason that I was able to talk to Marcus in the first place, because he proved to me that all men aren't awful, harassing stalkers. He's the reason I survived the past few years. He helped me grow my business. He's been my best friend.

And I just made a unilateral decision about that business, moved the base of operations to this house, and didn't even *tell* him.

I sigh, dropping my forehead to rest on top of Bear's.

"Everything okay?"

I jump, spinning around to see Marcus in the doorway. "Yeah. Um. Yes. Everything's fine."

Just once, I'd like to be able to speak to this man without fumbling over my words. *Once*. Just to prove to myself I can.

"Business partner?" He nods to the phone still clutched in my hand, then frowns. "Is that a flip phone?"

I open the phone up and snap it closed again. "Yeah."

"That explains why you text like it's Y2K."

A tiny shard of my guilt melts away, and my lips tilt upward. "Smartphones don't agree with me."

He snorts, then nods to his dog. "Thanks for watching Bear," Marcus says, taking a step inside the room. His presence fills the space from wall to wall, pressing against me like a physical weight.

There's something about this man that's powerful, irresistible. I find myself standing, smoothing my clothes, drifting to the table on the other side of the room to straighten the items I just made. I need to move, do something with my hands, just to deal with the excess energy this man injects into my body.

Marcus joins me at the table, the warmth of his arm bleeding into mine. I keep my breaths level, touching the stitching on a snowman-themed bow tie.

"You're very talented," he says, picking up a custom Bob

the Builder costume I made for a woman's golden retriever. I can't wait to see the photos.

"It's just practice, mostly," I answer. "I've been sewing since I was a bit younger than Mackenzie."

His arm reaches across my body to pick up the snowman bow tie. His bicep brushes the side of my breast, and a zing of heat swan dives down my spine and lands somewhere between my thighs.

I watch his fingers straighten the bow tie, tracing the outline of the stitches I just made. My heart speeds up.

I'm alone with a man. In his house.

"Sounded like trouble with your partner," he says, placing the bow tie gently down where he picked it up. This time, his arm doesn't touch me. I resist the urge to shift my weight so my breast comes in contact with his bicep again.

"I sort of didn't tell him I was moving my sewing stuff here," I answer, flushing. "He was just surprised, is all. I should have cleared it with him."

Marcus hums. He turns to lean a hip against the table and crosses his arms. "He just handles the tech though, right? The online shop?"

I nod.

"So why does he care where you sew?"

I face Marcus, craning my neck to meet his gaze. Slanted, serious eyes watch me.

"I...don't know."

"Does he do that a lot? Ask you to report to him like you're his employee?"

I frown. "No. No, Brian's great. I..." I trail off. There is the way Brian insists on managing everything with the computers. I'm not exactly Genius Bar material, but I'd be able to keep track of lists of orders. I have my ledger, where I keep track of everything by hand. But Brian won't give me the login details. He just gives me lists of orders printed on a sheet of paper, and I have to transfer everything to my ledger one item at a time.

My thoughts derail when Marcus reaches up to tuck a strand of hair away from my face. The tip of his finger is warm and rough against the shell of my ear, and it sends little zips of sensation traveling down my neck. I meet his gaze.

Then, between one breath and the next, something shifts in the energy between us. Tension heightens, and the space that separates our bodies crackles with electricity. My skin grows sensitive, and all the places in my body that remind me that I'm a woman come alive.

My breasts feel heavy, tipped with hard points. I want him to touch them, to use those big hands to cup and knead and pinch me. My stomach clenches along with my thighs. My lips drop open so I can suck in a long breath.

His finger travels slowly from my ear down my throat and across my collarbone. My pulse jumps at the touch, and my hands itch to reach up and touch the stubble lining Marcus's jaw.

His free hand brushes over my hip, and with a smooth, sinuous movement, Marcus shifts his weight and moves closer to me. The pads of his fingers on my hip exert gentle, unyielding pressure until I lean into him. His fingers on my chest move up to my chin, just barely brushing my skin.

My palms are damp. My breaths come staggered and short. My brain has left the building.

I tilt my head up at his touch, unable to move as Marcus's

face descends toward mine. After a brief, breathless hesitation, his lips touch mine.

The kiss starts slowly, tentatively. His lips are warm—just like the hands that hold me in place with the barest touch. He swipes his tongue across the seam of my lips, and I part for him, my body melting where I stand. When the hand on my chin shifts to cup my jaw, I find myself clinging to his shoulders.

The kiss turns deeper, and my head spins. All I can feel is Marcus. His hands, the heat of his body, the warmth of his mouth. My body is made of need, of lust, and I feel ready to explode where I stand.

I haven't felt a man's touch in nearly a decade. I press myself against the length of him, a little moan falling from my lips when his hand slides from my hip to the hollow of my waist and up to my ribs. In a slow, inexorable blaze, my body burns up from my toes to my scalp. I lose myself in his kiss, in the touch of his big, gentle hands on my body. I tumble headlong into the feeling of this gorgeous, grumpy, complicated man kissing me like he's been dying to do it for weeks.

His hand moves from my rib to my breast, and a rough noise escapes his throat. I gasp, utterly lost to sensation.

I'm kissing Marcus Walsh, my billionaire boss. I'm *kissing*—

I flinch back, stumbling, barely keeping myself upright by clinging to the table. Cheeks burning, I turn to face the wall as I try to catch my breath. A stolen glance tells me Marcus is breathing as heavily as I am, his eyes squeezed shut, his lips glistening.

Heart thundering, I try not to dissolve into sheer panic. I

can't get intimate with a man! What if I get hurt? What if he goes all stalker-crazy on me? I'm vulnerable. It's dangerous. I can't. I... I... I...

"My apologies," he grates, like it hurt to speak the words. "I shouldn't have done that."

"It's fine," I squeak, not meeting his gaze. "Takes two to tango."

"I should..." His voice drifts off, then he clears his throat. "Come on, Bear. Let's go see Grandma."

Bear, who had his back to us as he curled on the floor next to my sewing-machine desk, lifts his head and shifts his gaze from Marcus to me and back. I don't know if it's possible for a dog to look unimpressed or if it's just my imagination, but Bear seems to be full of doglike contempt. But he heaves himself up and follows Marcus to the door, and they both pause there.

"You can let yourself out when you're done here," my boss says, not meeting my gaze.

My lips burn. My breast feels branded by the heat of his touch. My panties are ruined. "Yeah," I answer, not moving until I hear the front door close behind them.

Then I let out a shuddering breath, gather my things, and run away.

12

MARCUS

I DON'T KNOW what came over me. I had an out-of-body experience. From the vantage point of the ceiling, I watched myself kiss Penny when I should've stayed away from her.

She does taste sweet. Achingly so. Now that I know it for certain, I can't get it out of my head, can't wash the taste of her kiss from my mouth.

"You haven't touched your cake." My mother's eyes study me while she tidies plates and cutlery from the table.

I glance down at the piece of yellow cake with rich chocolate icing. My mom's special recipe. I take a bite and it turns to glue in my mouth in an instant.

My mother, perceptive as ever, sets down the dirty dishes and takes a seat beside me. "What's wrong, Marcus?"

I chew, chew, chew, and swallow. Then I poke the cake and shrug. "Nothing, Mom."

"Don't lie to me. I carried you for forty weeks and one day, and I pushed you out of my own body. Remember that."

I huff and throw her a glance. "How could I forget when you remind me every week?"

I may be a CEO at work, an entrepreneur, the man in charge—but in my mother's house, I'm her son. It's comforting and frustrating all at once.

She clicks her tongue and leans back in the seat. In the distance, children scream. My brother and his wife used the apartment's outdoor area for the party, complete with balloons and barbecue. There's a definite autumn chill in the air, but with a few rented heat lamps and the energy of active young children, no one seems to mind.

A few of the neighbors have stopped by to celebrate with us, and I know it's down to my mother's presence in the community that they feel so comfortable doing so. She's always been a pillar. A rock. When my father died, Mom rallied the family together and did her best to keep us safe. Things between Stephanie and me still frayed, though, and it was my fault.

"What's got you in a mood?" she asks quietly. "Is something going on at work?"

I shake my head, then pause. "Maybe a little. We're trying to acquire a smaller company, and I'm putting in long hours."

She hums. "That's not it. It's a woman?"

I jerk, then shake my head. "It's not a woman."

There's a short silence, and I lift my gaze to see my mother's arched eyebrow.

"It's not," I insist. "There's no woman. I don't date women. Women have nothing to do with my state of mind, especially not today."

"The man doth protest too much, methinks."

"Now she's quoting Shakespeare at me," I say, lifting my eyes to the ceiling.

My mother's warm laugh wraps me up in a blanket of

comfort and familiarity. Her hand appears on my cheek, stroking softly. "You carry too much on your shoulders, Marcus. You can't bear the weight of the world all by yourself."

I lean into her touch, then pull away. "People rely on me, Mom." And if I'm not careful, I mess up. I let them down.

"Theoretically speaking," my mother says, pulling my slice of cake closer. She plucks a fork from the pile of clean ones and takes a bite. "*If* there were a woman who interested you, would you be opposed to pursuing her?"

"There's no woman."

"Of course not," she says, scraping some frosting from the edge of the cake. I find myself picking up my fork to take a bite from the other side of the slice. My mother chews thoughtfully, then says, "But let's just imagine it for a moment: some woman catches your eye. It surprises you, because she's not what you'd expect. Not at all. She's different, somehow."

I freeze for the briefest moment, and I know my mother notices.

There's a touch of humor and victory in her voice when she speaks again. "This hypothetical woman would draw you out of your self-imposed box. She'd make you think differently. In a lot of ways, she'd tie you in knots. It's natural that it would make you feel uncomfortable, off-balance. You're so used to being in charge."

I stab the cake and stuff a bite in my mouth, glaring at my mother. When I've swallowed, I toss my fork on the plate. "There's no woman." I slash the air with my hand. "This is a pointless conversation, because I don't deal in hypotheticals. I'll date when I have time. When I meet someone who can stand up to me." *The way Penny did at the office. She pushed back on my offer and made me work at convincing her to move her workshop.* "A woman who's my equal." *She started a business with nothing but her own ingenuity and creativity, just like I did.* "A woman that actually gets along with the family. One that you like." *Penny immediately took to Mackenzie. She'd fit right in downstairs among the laughing children and gossiping adults.*

My mother brushes a few crumbs from the table to the empty plate and stacks it on top of the other dirty dishes. "Of course, honey. But these things don't always happen when they're meant to."

"I'm going outside," I announce, standing.

A soft chuckle coming from my mother's throat as she tidies up her beloved kitchen is the only response I get. I make my way outside and am immediately mobbed by a pack of children. My third-youngest niece, Clarissa, attacks my legs with the strength of an NFL linebacker. I pick the four-year-old up and toss her in the air.

Big mistake.

Within seconds, children are clamoring to have their turn. By the third toss of heavier-than-they-look little humans, my shoulders and arms are screaming from the effort.

"Give Uncle Marcus a break!" My eldest sister, Tara, comes to disperse the crowd. "Who wants a marshmallow?"

High-pitched screams answer her, and I'm surprised the glass in my mother's building remains intact. The birthday boy comes barreling across the yard at the promise of more sugar, followed by a pack of young boys close behind.

"A little birdie told me Sellzy is looking to expand operations," a deep voice says beside me. I turn to see Tara's husband, Sean. He hands me a beer and clinks the edge of his own to it. Sean works on Wall Street and has lots of little birdies who talk to him.

I take a sip and give him a flat look. "You're worse than a journalist. Worse than my mother, even."

He laughs, his eyes sliding to Tara, who's handing out marshmallows to each child, as if they aren't high on sugar and cake and candy already. His gaze softens, full of love for my sister.

A knot forms in my throat. I take a sip of beer and try to wash it down, then turn to my brother-in-law. "Your anniversary is coming up, isn't it?" I ask.

Sean's brows jump. "Yeah. Ten years on December first."

"I want to send you and Tara somewhere for a week. Pick a country. I'll organize the rest."

There's a beat of silence, and Sean clears his throat. "You don't have to do that, Marcus."

"I know I don't. But I want to."

There's a pause, then Sean gives me a firm handshake and a thumping pat on the back. When he pulls away, his eyes are glassy, but he clears his throat and looks away to cover it up. "Tara hasn't had a vacation in two years. She's going to love this. Thank you."

I wave the thanks away and give him a nod. Then, before I get mobbed by the next wave of children wanting to be tossed in the air, I slip away to a clump of chairs near the door. My two brothers are there, talking sports, and I join them with a nod.

Oliver works for my friend Leif, and I invested in Terry's commercial cleaning business when he first started it. Both men are successful and settled—something we struggled to imagine when we were crammed in that tiny apartment growing up, three angsty teens butting heads at every turn.

I've been able to help them both.

This is why I do what I do. This is why I work so hard to make Sellzy grow and succeed, why I make sure to put my family first. Nearly every single person in this courtyard relies on me in one way or another. I'm proud of what I've accomplished, of the success I've achieved. I've pulled my family from the brink of poverty, and I've given them joy and stability. My siblings, my mother, my cousins and aunts and uncles and friends...they've all benefited from the work I've done, and I'm more than happy to bring them all along with me.

Well, everyone has benefited except one person. That horrible night—the look on Stephanie's face when I finally saw her—is a dark stain on my memory. I'll never forgive myself for putting my family second the day my father died.

Clarissa is Tara's daughter, but she looks just like my sister Stephanie did when she was that age. Dark hair and big, innocent hazel eyes. Our ancestry is mixed, with a Spanish grandmother and a Chinese grandfather on my mom's side and a very pale Irish-American father. We've all come out looking various shades of white and golden-brown, with a mixed bag of family features. I take after my grandfather in bone structure and the subtle tilt of my eyes, but I got the color directly from my father. My brother Oliver looks like my father through and through. Pale skin that burns bright red when it's touched by the sun and a stocky, solid build. When we were kids, no one believed we were brothers.

As I watch Clarissa laugh with her cousins, it makes me wish Stephanie were here. It's my fault she isn't. I was supposed to be her safety net. I was supposed to take care of her.

I failed.

The reason I failed Stephanie was a woman. A girlfriend. Some chick who didn't like how close I was to my family and convinced me I needed more independence. And like a fool, I believed her.

Now, I'm terrified that I'll fail again. All these people, all these lives. They look to *me*. They rely on *me*. Mackenzie's in my care for the next little while, and my deepest fear is that I'll let her down as badly as I did my sister.

Penny may be cute and sexy and made to make me pant —but she's dangerous. She could easily be the wedge that splits another relationship in my family.

I sip my beer and accept another, then watch the sun go down as the party comes to a close. The Sorensens' nanny stays with a sleeping Madeline as Isla and her gang of new best friends cackle like witches-in-training around a cauldron.

In a way, the hours I spend at my mother's house put everything in perspective. I may work long hours, but I do it because these people matter. And Penny... Kissing her was a mistake. I should never have crossed that line. It's not worth the consequences.

My thoughts buckle under the pressure of it all. The weight of all these lives on my shoulders.

At the end of the evening, I take Harriet and the Sorensen girls home and hand them off to their parents, who look happy and in love and glad to have gone out for an adult evening together. Then I head back to my own place with Mackenzie. She nods goodnight to me and disappears into her room. Pulsing music starts thumping almost immediately.

I pause in my bedroom doorway, then glance down the hall. On soft feet, I make my way to the spare room and glance inside.

Penny's workspace is organized chaos. It smells like her. The bright splashes of color from various fabrics remind me of the clothes she wears, the energy that she brings to every room she enters.

As I stand in her room and stare at the spot where we kissed, I can't bring myself to completely regret it. A part of me feels better for having her things here, knowing she'll be back.

She worked for me for a year, and I only saw her once. Now, within a couple of weeks, I've moved her in under the pretense of looking after Mackenzie.

Our kiss says something different. I wonder how much of my motivation was driven by lust and curiosity, by the need to be closer to her.

Scowling, I leave the room. I don't have time for this. For her. There are enough people for me to take care of. I can't manage another. I *don't want* to manage another. Romantic relationships get in the way of what's truly important.

I learned that lesson a long time ago—I don't need to be reminded of it again.

13

PENNY

MY FOREHEAD DROPS to the edge of the bar, and I knock my head on it a few times.

Nikki throws her head back and laughs. "Tell me again."

"I don't want to," I whine. "I can never go back there. I'll abandon everything I brought to Marcus's house, buy a new sewing machine, and start over."

"What, because you kissed your boss? Come on, Penny. Live a little."

I scowl at my friend. "*He* kissed *me*, okay? Get it right."

She purses her lips, holding back a smile. "Sure."

I glare. "I don't know how it happened."

"I believe you used the words 'electric tension' when you first described it," she answers.

"I should never have called you," I grumble.

Nikita laughs and nudges my shoulder, then calls for another round. We're back in the same cocktail bar, debriefing what a mess I've made of my life in a few short days. Nikki doesn't see it that way, though. She thinks it's great. She thinks I'm finally moving forward in my life.

She says the fact that I broke that physical barrier with a man is proof I have courage and resilience, that Billy didn't win.

Ha. Right.

Kissing my boss doesn't exactly seem like moving forward. Accepting some harebrained scheme to move my entire base of operations to my boss's spare room seems even worse.

"He's too beautiful," I say, straightening. "That's the problem. It blinds me. I can't think straight when he looks at me."

"You're smitten."

"I'm an idiot," I correct.

Nikki grins. She puts a fresh drink in front of me and convinces me to start from the beginning again, to tell her the whole story once more, which I do. When I get to the kiss, she squints.

"So it just...happened. Then he said he shouldn't have done it?"

I nod. "Yeah."

"Who pulled away first? You or him?"

I hate it when Nikita asks good questions. I glare at her.

She grins. "You did."

"I panicked!"

"He would have kept going," she answers. "Interesting."

"It's not interesting. It's a disaster."

"You're funny," she tells me, sipping her drink.

"Yeah, yeah." I sound depressed even to my ears. "You think I should quit? I feel like I've ruined everything."

"You said the new workshop was way better for sewing than your apartment, right?"

I nod.

She sucks her lips between her teeth, then shakes her head. "Don't quit. I think you should act like nothing happened on Monday. You'll probably only see him for a few minutes at the end of the day, right? So just pretend you never kissed him."

"Pretend *he* never kissed *me*."

Nikki's lips twitch, her eyes dancing. "Right. What was it you told him afterward? Something about tango? How many people does it take, again?"

"Shut up, Nikki."

She giggles until I join in. Finally, we both quiet down and Nikki smiles at me. "I've missed you, Penny. It's been too long."

My heart softens. "I know." With a deep breath, I give my friend a hesitant smile. "I feel... I feel like something has changed inside me since we ran into each other. Like I'm finally able to move on from what happened to me."

Nikita wraps me in a hug and crushes me close, and we only pull apart when the charcuterie board we ordered earlier is deposited on the bar in front of us. Then, for the rest of the evening, I listen to Nikita tell me all her best horror stories about online dating over the past eight years, we plan our costumes for Bonnie's Halloween party, and then we say goodnight and part ways.

SUNDAY IS SPENT FIGHTING with my stupid label maker. I briefly consider hurling it through the window, but I finally get it working and manage to pack up all the finished orders I left at my apartment before moving my workshop to Marcus's place.

Then, as the afternoon quickly collapses into a dark, cold dusk, I glance around my living room and smile. It's not big, but without my mountains of fabric and supplies, there's so much *space*. I end up shifting my couch to the opposite wall, unearthing a lamp from the back of my closet to create a reading nook, and planning a DIY wall hanging with fabric scraps I find in a container under my bed.

I finish the project around midnight and hang it up above the couch. It looks freaking awesome. My home is no longer a workshop and business center. For the first time in a long time, my home is a home.

It may be autumn, but my life is going through its version of spring. I'm slowly blooming into the new me, discovering things about myself, my apartment, and my business that I didn't know.

I mean, I *kissed* a man yesterday. Me! The woman who has avoided all male contact for eight years, apart from Brian. And...it didn't terrify me. It probably won't happen again with Marcus, which is fine by me (I swear!), but it marks a big moment in my life.

I thought my ex-boyfriend-slash-stalker broke me. His harassment scarred me so deeply that I felt like the very core of me was violated. I dropped out of college, moved away, and ran from the bright, happy person I was in my early twenties.

But as I stand in my new living room, staring at the woven scraps of fabric I turned into a wall hanging, I wonder if I might finally be ready to move forward. Piece myself together just like that wall hanging, from scraps of the old me.

Eight years ago, I lost everything—even myself. But I finally feel ready to poke my head out of my burrow and see what life has to offer.

.   .   .

ON MONDAY, I wake up feeling much less enthusiastic than I was last night. The feeling gets worse as I approach my new workshop in SoHo and wonder whether my boss is on the other side of the door. If he's topless and sweaty, cooking an omelet in his kitchen, I'm just going to turn around and go home. I can't deal with that kind of assault on my newly awakened sexuality.

A minute later, I'm relieved to find out Marcus isn't home. Bear comes rushing toward me, showering me with the loving attention of a big, scruffy dog, and I take him out for his morning walk. Once all the dog-related chores are done, I put on a pot of coffee and make my way to my new workshop.

And I smile.

The sky is overcast today, but light still floods this room as if it were the height of summer. I notice a new floor lamp by my sewing machine, which arcs gracefully and hangs above my workspace. Everything else is where I left it, so I pull out my list of outstanding orders and get to work.

It's heaven. I no longer have to struggle to unfold my creaky, rusted ironing board, shoving aside piles of fabric to get it to fit across my living room. There's space for every task. There's light, warmth, energy. In four short hours, I finish all the orders on my list. Every single one.

That amount of work would have taken me two days to complete at home. I would've been on the subway right now, heading to Bear for his afternoon walk. My workday would have been interrupted, and it would've taken me ages to get back into the zone once I got back home.

Whatever happened here on Saturday, I can move past it.

I can do like Nikki said and pretend it never happened, because this workspace is worth it. Hell, the extra money I'll get from spending time with Mackenzie will be worth it! I'll be able to buy some of the more expensive fabrics I couldn't afford before, and maybe even upgrade my sewing machine.

With thoughts of my budding dog-clothing empire, I call Bear, jiggle his leash, and take him out for a walk. There's a steady drizzle over the city, the promise of a cold winter. But there's enough sunlight and happiness coming from inside me to ignore the dreary weather.

I took a risk in agreeing to work from Marcus's spare room, but I have a feeling it's going to pay off.

A few hours later, Mackenzie gets home from school. She eats her way through half the fridge while telling me about her day.

"How did your science project end up?" I ask as Mackenzie chows down on a sandwich.

She grunts. "Mr. Errol gave us an extension. Amy showed him the pictures of the room, and I think he was trying not to laugh. He asked her to send the pictures to his email."

My lips twitch, and Mackenzie gives me a flat stare.

"Don't laugh. Now I need a babysitter." She arches her brows meaningfully. "That's so cringe. Imagine if people at school heard about my uncle hiring you just to watch me."

"I'm not so bad, am I?"

Mackenzie shrugs and finishes her sandwich. She puts her plate on the counter, glances at me, then sighs dramatically and moves the plate to the dishwasher.

Lips twitching, I lead her to the back room to show her what I've been working on. Bear follows and sits patiently while we try different bow ties on him.

"You're such a handsome boy," I tell him, tying a heart-print bow tie around his collar. "You can be my Valentine."

Mackenzie giggles and snaps a few pictures. She shows them to me, then instead of putting them on her personal page like she did before, posts them on a brand-new social media account with my company's name on it. I watch over her shoulder, eyebrows rising.

"I checked this weekend, and I couldn't find any of your social media pages," she says, eyeing me. "That's crazy."

"I'm not really good with technology stuff," I admit. "And Brian says social media is a scourge on our society, so we decided not to participate."

Mackenzie's head turns toward me, her expression flat and unimpressed.

I laugh. "It's worked so far, hasn't it?"

"I'm going to do your social media," she announces. "You'll see how much you've been missing out on."

I huff a laugh. "Fine. But first, homework."

A distinctly teenage sigh, but Mackenzie gets her backpack and brings it to the sewing room. We sit back-to-back while she does algebra and I sew half a dozen new bow ties. I find myself smiling. Even though we aren't constantly speaking to each other, it's nice to have someone else nearby. To be comfortable in a room with another human being.

Maybe I've been lonelier than I thought.

"I'm done," Mackenzie announces. "I'm going to my room." She stuffs her homework in her bag and tromps out of the room without another word. A moment later, her bedroom door opens and closes.

I finish what I'm working on, tidy the room a bit, and stretch out my back. Then I pad along the polished concrete floor toward the great room at the front of the house, Bear's claws clicking after me.

And I scream.

Marcus looms just around the corner, putting bags of takeout on the kitchen counter. He's wearing a leather jacket and his hair is disheveled, and he looks absolutely delicious.

A dark eyebrow arches over glittering green eyes. "Hello to you too." His lips shape the words, and all I can think of is how good they felt when they were against mine.

Clearing my throat, I gather my wits and try to keep my voice steady. "I didn't hear you come in."

He doesn't respond, only kneels down and greets his dog. I watch man and dog shower each other with affection, and a sharp tumble occurs in my stomach.

"Okay, well, Mackenzie's in her room," I say. "I'll get going."

"Stay for dinner," he replies, eyes on his dog. He touches the pink-and-red bow tie still tied around Bear's collar, and a flush rises over my cheeks. I forgot to take it off him, and now Marcus probably thinks the heart patterns on that Valentine's Day bow tie are some sort of message for him. As Mackenzie would say, that's really freaking cringe.

"Oh, that's okay," I say, edging toward the front door.

Those magnetic eyes lift up to meet mine. He nods to the bags of food on the counter. "I got enough for everyone." Unfolding his body to stand, I'm once again struck by how very tall this man is. Instead of making me nervous, though, it makes me want to go to him. To feel his arms wrapped around me once again.

Just pretend it never happened, Nikki said. Ha! Right. As if it were that easy.

I clear my throat and am about to refuse when Mackenzie appears and heads straight for the food. "Awesome," she says. "I love Thai food." She glances at me. "You're not allergic to peanuts, are you?"

I shake my head. "Um. No."

"Good. Let's eat. I'm starving." She grabs three plates, sets them down on the counter with a loud rattle, then starts digging in.

Knowing it would be awkward and uncomfortable to make my escape now, I let out a deep breath and decide to stay for dinner. Marcus serves himself last, doing the task with the same focused seriousness he does everything. Heat winds through my core when I realized it's exactly how he kissed me—like every iota of his attention was on me, on devouring my lips and touching my body.

My pad thai turns to glue in my mouth, but I chew and swallow until I can get ahold of myself again.

Then Marcus sits on the barstool next to mine, his knee nudging my own, his warmth flooding my side. The way he smells—a hint of expensive cologne layered with the scent of his skin—makes my head spin.

"What did you learn today, Kenzie?" Marcus asks. He turns his head toward his niece, who's on the other side of me, and his knee rubs the edge of my thigh.

That shouldn't affect me so much. It shouldn't make shivers course through my legs, shouldn't make my heart skip a beat. As Mackenzie recounts the petty dramas of ninth grade, I regain control over my own body...

And I actually start enjoying myself.

It's just like working back-to-back with Mackenzie in the room, or the comfort of actually having a workspace separate from my living space. I feel, in some strange way, like I belong here. It feels *good* to spend time with other people, to share a meal and talk about our days.

When Mackenzie tells Marcus about the new social media accounts, I catch the corner of his lips turning up. He asks me what I worked on and how the space is functioning for me. The three of us chat and laugh like we've known each other for years.

Then dinner's over and the dishes are cleaned up, and it's time for me to go home to my cold, lonely apartment.

"You getting a cab home?" Marcus asks as I zip up my jacket, Mackenzie disappearing into her room again.

I laugh, then realize he's not joking. "Um, no. I'm taking the subway. You know, like a normal person."

"No," he says, reaching beside me for his own jacket.

I frown. "No? What do you mean, no?"

"I'll drive you home."

"No," I blurt.

"No?" A pause. "What do you mean, no?" His face is utterly serious, but I swear I see a glint of amusement in his gaze as he repeats my words right back to me.

I huff and cross my arms. "Marcus, I'm a grown woman who has ridden the subway a million times. You don't have to drive me home."

He glances over my shoulder. "It's dark out."

"That happens when the Earth rotates and the sun ends up on the other side of the planet," I say, sounding, alarmingly, as petulant as Mackenzie does when she's sassing him.

But Marcus just shrugs on his jacket and nods his head to the garage door. "My driver's off the clock. Come on."

"Marcus," I protest, planting my feet.

He just clicks his tongue to call Bear, then disappears into the garage. I stare after him, blinking. The nerve! The arrogance! He must think I'm just going to follow him like his pet dog.

Well. He may be my boss, but he's not my owner. I shove my chin in the air, turn around, and walk out the front door. That'll show him. I'm not trotting after him and letting him order me around. No sir-ee. Not wanting me to ride the subway because it's dark! Does he not realize this is New York City? How else would I get around?

I mean, sure, I don't usually go out after dark because I hate feeling unsafe, but still! I'm turning thirty years old in eight months. I hardly need someone to chauffeur me around.

I hardly need *him* to chauffeur me around.

I'm supposed to be staying away from him! Pretending nothing happened! I can't go accepting rides from him, which would involve being stuck in the warm cocoon of a car, surrounded by his scent and his presence, close enough to touch.

Can anyone say *disaster*? Because that's what it would be.

I'm halfway down the block, keeping myself warm with my hurricane of righteously indignant thoughts, when a car pulls up beside me. The window rolls down and Marcus's face appears.

I scowl, still stomping down the street.

"Penny," he says, his voice flat. "What are you doing?"

"I'm taking the subway." I frown. "How did you get here so quickly?"

"I heard the front door open," he says, turning to face the

street. He inches along while I hurry, my hood up against the rain.

"Penny," he repeats, his voice low and mesmerizing.

Damn him! Why does he get to have a nice body *and* a nice face *and* a nice voice? Not to mention the money and the cars and the doting family and great dog? I need to find *something* to hate about him for times like these.

"What will make you get in the car and let me drive you home?" His car glides along beside me as the chill of the night air seeps through my jacket.

I shiver. "Nothing. I'm fine, Marcus. You don't need to do this." I keep my eyes on the sidewalk in front of my feet, lest it jump up and trip me. I've already fallen over in his presence twice. I don't want to do it again.

There's a pause, then, softly, "Please? I don't like the idea of sending you off into the night. Let me make sure you get home safe."

There's something in his voice that makes me pause. He stops the car beside me, his arm resting on the window opening. Bear's face appears between the two front seats.

Marcus and I hold each other's gaze for a moment, and then I sigh. "Fine."

I stomp in front of the car, through the beams of the headlights, and rip open the passenger door. Ridiculous, I know. I should be grateful, instead of grumpy and off-balance.

"You're rubbing off on me," I say.

He puts the car in gear and starts driving. "Oh?"

"Yeah. I'm all grouchy now. Look at me! I'm a mess."

The sound of his laughter sends tingles shivering over every inch of my body. He stops the car again, faces me, and for a few tension-filled seconds, I think he's going to lean over and kiss me again.

That turns out to be wishful thinking.

Instead, he holds my gaze for a long, *long* moment, shakes his head, and asks me for directions. While I stew in my confusion and lust, Marcus drives me home and drops me off with barely a word of goodbye. I don't take a full breath until I'm up the stairs and locked behind my apartment door.

I strip off my jacket and leave it on a heap on the floor, then knock my head against the wall a few times to jump-start my brain.

What the hell have I gotten myself into?

14

MARCUS

I WAIT until Penny's safely inside before driving away, cursing myself the whole time. My body is a vibrating mass of lust and anger and need.

I loved the way she stomped away from me, how she didn't follow me to the garage the way I wanted her to. It pissed me the hell off, obviously, but I loved it all the same. I loved seeing her relent in the end. I loved watching her click her seatbelt with that little stubborn clench of her jaw.

And I loved it most of all when she lifted her gaze to mine, and I thought I saw my desire reflected back in her eyes.

I loved it too much, I think, because it nearly made me lose control. I would've hauled her over onto my lap and started right where we left off, with my mouth on hers and my hands exploring her body.

It can't happen again.

I won't let it happen again.

As I drop off the woman who owns my thoughts, the city is dark and thriving with wild energy. I drive aimlessly until the fires inside me bank, and then I head home and try to put my dog walker out of my head.

I have work to do. A business deal to complete. A family to take care of.

I don't have time for Penny Littleton.

No matter how badly I want to kiss her again.

15

PENNY

THE REST OF THE WEEK, Marcus gets his driver Will to bring me home. I can't decide if I'm happy or disappointed about it. After all, I'm getting free rides home, which is great...but I'm not getting them from *him*.

In the end, I land on happy. It's a perk of the job—nothing more.

And on Saturday, when I wake up and realize I won't be going over to the Walsh residence for the first time all week, I pretend I don't feel any disappointment.

I'm lying on the (now blissfully empty) rug-covered floor of my living room reading a book when my phone rings.

"Hey, girl," Nikki says when I pick up. "What time should I come over to get ready?"

It takes me a minute to remember what she's talking about. "Oh, right," I say. "Bonnie's party."

"She said any time after seven o'clock is fine. I figure we should arrive just before eight, so we're not the first ones there. I'll come over to yours for a late lunch, get ready, and grab a cab together?"

I nod. "Sure."

"And you have to tell me about your week, post-kiss. I've been dying to talk to you."

My lips curl. "There's not much to tell."

"We'll see about that."

We say our goodbyes and hang up. Then I spend the day doing yoga, reading, and grabbing the last few things I need for my costume for tonight's party.

Me. Going to a party. I can hardly believe it.

A few hours later, when my buzzer sounds, I let Nikki in and feel a growing knot of excitement in my stomach. It's been a long, cold period of hibernation for me. I'm finally ready to come out and enjoy life again.

Nikki bursts through the door carrying bags and bags. She drops them, spreads her arms, and gives me a hug. I laugh and hug her back, still somewhat reeling at the thought that I have a new friend, and we're going out to a party at the house of *another* new friend.

"I settled on sexy vampire nun," Nikita tells me, hunting through her bags until she pulls out a black corset, miniskirt, and wrinkled polyester imitation of a nun's habit. Then she grabs black patent leather spike heels and a face-painting kit. "For fake blood," she explains. "I even got the expensive prosthetic teeth so I'll have the long canines."

I laugh. "You always went all-out for Halloween. Nice to see that hasn't changed."

Nikki winks, then plonks a couple of bottles of alcohol on the counter, followed by a silver shaker and a few other accessories like the long, twirly metal spoon used to make drinks. "I figured you probably don't have a cocktail shaker, so I brought mine."

"You figured right," I tell her. The alarm on my oven dings, so I pull out the bubbling artichoke dip I made and set it on the stove to cool while I grab some chips.

"Is that the same recipe you used to make in college?" Nikki asks, sniffing the cheesy casserole dish.

I nod. "Yep. Haven't had it in years."

"Yummy." Nikki hooks an arm around my shoulder and plants a big kiss on my forehead. "It's good to have you back, Penny," she says quietly, then claps her hands. "Okay. Show me your costume. Let's get ready."

GOSH, I missed having a girlfriend. I haven't laughed so much in years. My cheeks hurt by the time we have our makeup and hair done. My hair in particular took way longer than I'd anticipated, but Nikki helped and we got there in the end.

She went through every detail of my costume, down to the embarrassing granny panties I called underwear. That led us to my underwear drawer, where Nikita discovered the embarrassment of my eight-year-old undies collection. Yet another thing that remained dormant during my period of hibernation.

We had to make an emergency run to the nearest store that sold underwear, which happened to be an—ahem —*adult* shop. And that's how I ended up with scandalously revealing undies, a garter belt, and stockings.

I don't know why I went along with it. The alcohol, proba- bly. And the giggles. And, if I'm honest, the fact that it felt *good* to put something sexy on under my clothes.

By the time my buzzer rings, I've put on the rest of my costume and I'm on my third daiquiri of the evening.

"It's me," Brian says, and I let him in.

Nikki tilts her head. "Who's that?"

"My friend Brian."

"Your business partner?"

I nod. "I cleared it with Bonnie. He's coming to the party with us."

Nikki nods. "Cool."

"What," a male voice says behind me, "are you wearing?"

I spin around and spread my arms. "Whaddya think?"

Brian lets out a laugh. He's got an eye patch, a ruffly white shirt, and a brown vest. My pirate friend wraps me in a hug. "I think you're going to poke someone's eyes out with those things." He touches my hair. "How the hell did you do this?"

With the tips of my fingers, I trace the braids that stick straight out of my head at ear level, ending in little tufts of copper hair. "There's a coat hanger inside the braids," I say. "But it's hard to get through doorways. And at least I'm usually the shortest person in the room, so I'll poke people's shoulders instead of their eyes."

"Or their carotid artery." Nikki grins. Her vampire fangs gleam in the lamplight. Creepy...and very sexy. Even with the nun's habit on her head. Damn her!

"Never thought I'd say this, but Pippi Longstocking is *hot*." Brian's eyes drop down below the denim pinafore dress I'm wearing to the two mismatched thigh-high stockings. One is solid white, and the other is striped red-and-white. I had to buy two sets at the sex store, which seemed like a good idea at the time. At least Brian can't see that the stockings stop at mid-thigh.

Maybe it was the excitement of being with an old girlfriend, or the idea of connecting with the younger, carefree me, but I decided I wanted to feel a little more attractive than usual tonight, so buying the garters and stockings seemed like a good idea. I've spent so long hiding behind high collars and ankle-length cutesy dresses, and for what? Men still catcall. I still feel unsafe when I walk down the street on my own.

Maybe the change has to come from within. I have to live my life *despite* the catcalls. And that includes sexy undergarments that I wear for no reason other than wanting to. My little secret.

"I figure the hair balances out any hotness," I say, "along with the long-sleeved shirt."

"Um," Brian says, arching a brow, his eyes coasting down my body. "Sure. It balances it out, all right."

I flush. Brian's never looked at me like *that* before.

"Aren't you going to introduce me?" Nikita says.

"Of course." I smile. "Brian, this is Nikita, the college friend I was telling you about."

A strange moment follows, but maybe I'm reading too much into it. The two of them shake hands and study each other, and something like suspicion draws Nikki's brows together. Combined with the vampy lipstick, the protruding canines, and the dramatic smoky eye, not to mention her mass of black waves falling out of the bottom of the nun's habit and tight dominatrix outfit, the results make *me* nervous, and I'm not even the recipient of the look.

"You want a drink?" I ask brightly, to dispel any awkwardness.

"We should get going," Nikki says. "It's already past seven o'clock."

LILIAN MONROE

"Party ahoy!" Brian says, pointing a plastic sword at the door, and the weirdness of the moment evaporates.

I laugh, finish my drink, grab my purse, and hook my arm through Nikki's to head to my first Halloween party in close to a decade.

We arrive at Bonnie's apartment forty minutes later. I don't know what I expected, but I'm shocked to see she lives in a luxurious apartment the size of a regular three-bedroom house. It's huge. And beautiful.

As soon as I step over the threshold and hear my Mary Janes clack on her solid hardwood floors, a tempest of emotions rises up inside me.

Anxiety knots my stomach at the sight of strangers drinking and laughing like old friends. Awe lifts my heart at the high ceilings, the city skyline glittering through the massive windows. Excitement at being here gives me the jitters, at being invited in the first place. A touch of embarrassment burns my cheeks at the elaborateness of my costume, when most people seem to be wearing regular clothes plus cat ears.

Nikki squeezes my arm and tugs me deeper into the apartment, and Bonnie appears in front of us holding drinks. "Welcome!" she cries, doing double air-kisses with everyone and foisting alcohol upon us. Her blond hair is curled and pinned around her face, her mouth is painted deep red, and she has a beauty mark above her lip. Oh, and she's wearing a dramatic cone-bra bustier that hits me right at eye level.

"Madonna," I say with a smile. I take the champagne flute she hands me and stumble through the double kiss, accidentally going in the wrong direction so she almost kisses my lips.

Bonnie just laughs, then takes a step back and looks at me from head to toe. "I love it. Pippi Longstocking. Genius." She turns around and grabs another guest by the elbow, tugging the woman closer. "Dani, look at Penny's costume. Finally, someone understood the assignment! If one more person walks through with stupid cat ears, I'm canceling the party."

Dani looks at my hair and arches a brow at Bonnie. "Congrats. Your boobs are no longer the most lethal thing in the room."

We're shuffled inside, and Nikita—obviously—is immediately adored by everyone. Brian stays close to me, which I appreciate. I sip my drink, nod, shake hands with a few partygoers, and generally try to soak up the atmosphere.

"You okay?" Brian asks. He's moved from champagne to beer, and he tips his bottle against his lips.

I nod. "Yeah," I say, surprised to realize it's true. "I think I am."

A squeal escapes the pack of bodies where Nikki's currently standing. She looks over her shoulder at me, eyes glimmering, then shuffles off with Bonnie to the corner of the room.

The music dies down, and Bonnie's head pops up over everyone else's. She must be standing on something. "We've reached an important point in the night," she says into a microphone. "Karaoke!"

Groans and cheers sound in equal number. Then Nikki joins Bonnie on the stage or the riser or whatever they're standing on—I can't see from here—and gives someone to the side a nod.

Then she looks straight at me. A screen drops down from the ceiling to rest against the wall beside Bonnie and Nikki.

When the screen lights up, my stomach drops to my feet and splatters all over my bestockinged legs. "Good Old-Fashioned Lover Boy" by Queen is stamped on the screen in big, bold letters.

"Penny," Nikita says, leaning over to speak into Bonnie's microphone, "don't you think you should start us off with an old favorite?"

I shake my head so hard my braids go whipping around like a coat hanger-stiffened weed whacker. It doesn't deter Nikki. The crowd between the two of us parts like the Red Sea, and Moses appears to me in the shape of a woman in a sexy vampire costume and a nun's headpiece. It feels like I'm having a fever dream.

"No."

She takes my hand. "Come on."

"I haven't sung anything in years!"

She pauses. "Not even in the shower?"

I know I'm glaring, and I don't care. "The shower doesn't count."

"False," Bonnie says into the microphone, which means it's so quiet in the room that everyone can hear us. "The shower definitely counts."

"I hate you," I tell Nikki.

"Also false," Bonnie says, and laughs sound around the room. I can feel the weight of all those stares on my body. There have to be at least thirty to forty people in here.

Nikki arches her brows at me. "Please?"

"You don't have to do it," Brian says quietly, leaning his head as close to my ear as he can get with my braids in the way.

I glance at Brian, then at Nikki, and something shifts inside me. For nearly a decade, I've lived a smaller life than I should. I've avoided all things that make me uncomfortable—and for what? So I can stay holed up in my apartment with all my fabrics?

Is that really how I want to live? Is that *it*?

"You're the worst," I tell Nikki, but I take a step forward. She cackles in victory, and a few whistles and cheers sound from the corner of the room. I don't remember anyone's name, and their faces are a complete blur.

When we make it to the other side of the room, I see that Bonnie is standing on a small stage, maybe five feet by three feet in size. She helps me up and hands me her microphone, and Nikki grabs the second one.

"Just like the old days," Nikki says with a smile, then she nods, and the first few notes of the karaoke version start playing over the speakers.

I can't believe this. I'm in a fancy high-rise apartment, surrounded by glittering people and expensive furnishings, about to sing freaking karaoke like I'm in a college dive bar. Oh, and I'm dressed like an absolute idiot. Damn this stupid hair! The coat hanger's digging into the sides of my head, and my stupid garter is itching against my thighs.

This is awful.

Then I put the microphone to my lips, and to my surprise, sounds actually come out of my mouth. I'm rusty, and it takes me a few seconds to get into it, but I quickly fall into the old routine that Nikki and I performed dozens of times when we were young and uninhibited.

By the time I'm saying, "Let me feel your heartbeat," and Nikki's answering with, "Grow faster, faster," a small smile tugs at my lips, and I let myself get lost in one of my favorite songs of all time, singing beside a long-lost bestie.

I'll be the first to admit that I'm not an amazing singer. I'm not bad; I can hold a tune, but Nikki is the true talent out of the two of us. She has a gorgeous voice and enough control and power to go professional. I'm not sure how we started performing this song together—probably some variation of the conversation we just had before I came up on stage, plus way more alcohol on my part—but it became a bit of an ongoing joke between the two of us.

We have a whole routine, involving simple, synchronized dance steps, all the important harmonies and backing vocals, and a whole lot of fun.

It's silly. It makes me laugh. It makes me realize that I haven't actually *lived* in years and years.

So why not do it now?

We get to the guitar solo, which is when we're supposed to put the microphones down and do our most complicated dance steps of the number. At this point, Nikki used to swing me around like we're ballroom dancing, spin me, then we'd do a little groovy two-step. In our heyday, it was fast and acrobatic.

My body remembers the steps, even though it's been years since we performed together—then we get to the lift. Nikki wraps an arm around my back and tries to swing me into her arms, but my braids get in the way and whack her across the face. She screams and drops me flat on my ass.

I land, laughing so hard I have tears in my eyes, and dive for the microphone in time to sing, "Dining at the Ritz," exactly when I'm supposed to—except I'm lying on my stomach on the tiny stage with my butt in the air and my hair preventing me from turning my head. So I just sit up on my elbows, kick my legs back and forth, and play it off.

That's when I realize the small crowd is *loving* it. They join Nikki in singing the backing vocals so loud we're definitely going to get a noise complaint from the police. By the time we get to the final note, I have tears of laughter rolling down my face, and I lap up the applause and whistles while handing the microphone off to Bonnie.

Nikki hauls me up to my feet and hugs me, and we both laugh uncontrollably. "I freaking love you, Penny," she says between cackles.

"I love you too." I wipe my eyes and descend off the stage, only to bump into the chest of a man that I never in a million years expected to see here.

Marcus Walsh is standing there, in all his green-eyed glory, wearing a red-and-white striped shirt and a woolly red hat à la Waldo of *Where's Waldo?* fame. His black-framed glasses have no lenses, and they look completely adorable and incongruous on his face.

"Penny," he says, and his voice is so low and smoky that I think I have a mini-orgasm.

The sight is so shocking, so unexpected, that I just gape at him and shriek.

16

MARCUS

I DIDN'T WANT to come to this stupid party, but my friend Emil and his wife Dani basically bullied me into it. They sent Leif and Layla over to my place to make sure I actually showed up. They even brought me this stupid costume and insisted I put it on.

Mackenzie thought it was hilarious and promised not to trash my house while I was out. My mother came over to supervise the non-trashing of the house and any science experiments that might occur while I was at the party.

So, I put the costume on and I got in the back of Leif's Rolls Royce, resolving to show up, be seen, then leave.

But I walked in to the most ridiculous karaoke session I've ever witnessed, starring the one person I least expected to see.

Now she's standing in front of me, her copper hair sticking straight out of her head, wearing an outfit that makes my jeans feel tight. I elbowed my way to the front of the crowd when her friend dropped her, wanting to make sure she hadn't hurt herself, only to see the backs of her thighs exposed with hot, white garters holding up her stockings below the hem of her denim dress.

I can't think straight. It was the sexiest thing I'd ever seen. I want to lift her dress up right now and see it again.

"Penny," I grate as I struggle to ignore the erection trying to bust a hole through my pants.

She blinks those big blue eyes at me and screams.

A frown tugs at my brows.

"Inside voice, Penny," the dominatrix/vampire/nun who provided the backing vocals says, slinging an arm around Penny's shoulders and studiously avoiding the braids.

"Oh. Right." Penny smiles. "Hi."

I clear my throat. "I didn't know you could sing like that."

Penny bites her lip—which makes my zipper groan under the strain I'm subjecting it to—and looks at her friend. "This is my boss Marcus. He doesn't know how to compliment people properly."

My frown deepens, which makes them both giggle.

"Pleasure to meet you," the dominatrix/vampire/nun says. "I'm Nikki."

We shake. "Can I get you guys a drink?"

"Please," Nikki says. "I'm parched."

"After that performance, I believe it!" Bonnie exclaims, walking up to us and handing out beers. "Penny, you've been holding out on us. Here I thought you were shy."

"I am shy," she says.

"You're not shy, you're just out of practice." Nikki sips her drink. "There's a difference."

"Out of practice interacting with other humans?" Penny spins her head around and nearly takes Bonnie's eyes out. "Or out of practice performing to Queen?"

"Humans," Nikki answers.

"That's a little harsh," Penny says, but she's smiling.

Nikki shrugs. "Your words, babe."

I lose track of the conversation for a few moments, because my eyes coast down Penny's legs and back up again. Inches away from me are thigh-high stockings covering the nicest legs I've ever seen. I could reach a hand over and feel how smooth her skin is under the hem of her dress.

"Marcus?"

I blink, seeing Dani and Layla staring at me beside Bonnie. "Hmm?"

Layla speaks slowly. "Bonnie asked how you were doing."

"Fine. I'm fine. Excuse me." I nod, then back away from the group and find a wall to lean against. Then I put my beer to my lips and realize it's empty. I can't breathe. It's too warm, and I'm wearing a sweatshirt and a hat and stupid glasses with no lenses that mess with my depth perception for some reason. Or maybe that's the dizziness. I need some air. I stumble down the hallway and open doors at random. One is locked, which I assume is a bathroom in use. One is a linen closet, and two are bedrooms with itty-bitty windows that won't be of any use.

Finally, I find the master bedroom at the end of the hall, complete with sliding glass doors and a balcony. Perfect.

I don't know Bonnie super well—she's closest with Dani and Emil—but I'm hoping she won't mind me using her balcony for a few minutes. Just to get a grip on myself. As soon as I slide the door open and the cool air fills my lungs, my shoulders relax.

I step outside and lean against the railing, staring out at the city.

These feelings I'm having are out of control. It's bigger than lust. Deeper than a physical need. It's like everything Penny does fascinates me, frustrates me, turns me on. I can't get her out of my head.

It's idiotic. I should have more control than that. I'm annoyed at myself, at her, at my costume, at everything.

I don't know how long I stand there, but it's long enough that my heart rate returns to normal and my thoughts are almost rational. Then I hear a noise behind me. Through the open doorway, I make eye contact with Penny, and I immediately feel off-balance again. Her lips shape a surprised *O* as she freezes with her back to the bedroom door.

Turning to face her fully, I walk to the balcony doorway and point a thumb over my shoulder. "Needed some air."

"Oh," she says. "I needed the bathroom." She points at the ensuite door. "Bonnie said I could use hers if the other one was occupied."

I nod, sweeping an arm toward the door. "Go for it."

She hesitates, teeth biting into her lush lower lip. "Okay, but…"

I arch my brows. "Yeah?"

"Go back outside. I don't want you to hear me pee." She straightens her shoulders, planting her hands on her hips like she really means it. "I have a shy bladder."

"Shy around humans, or shy after you perform to Queen?"

Her eyes narrow. "When did you get a sense of humor?"

My mouth really, really wants to curl into a smile. How does she do it? How does she make me want to laugh every time she's close? Instead, I just nod, close the sliding glass door most of the way, and head back outside.

It's cold out, but I'm comfortable as I stand there. Then I hear the sliding glass door open behind me, and I look over my shoulder to see her standing there.

"All good?" I ask.

A quick, impish grin. "Operation: Tinkle was a success."

I can't help the chuckle that falls through my lips. Then Penny joins me on the balcony, and my tongue suddenly feels three sizes too big for my mouth.

I'm like a damn teenage kid around this woman. She turns me on when she's dressed like Pippi Longstocking, for fuck's sake.

"I like your costume," I say, but it comes out as a growl.

Her freckled cheeks grow pink in the dim light. "Thanks."

"Did you make it?"

She nods. "Yeah. It was easy. I used a couple of old pairs of jeans that no longer fit for the pinafore, and I bought the tights and top. The hair has a coat hanger inside it." She wiggles her head for emphasis.

It would be inappropriate for me to tell her that her hair would make good handles.

A grunt escapes me as my eyes coast down to those stockings.

She sticks the red-and-white one out toward me, level with my hip and the bottom of my sweater. "And we match! It's like we planned it."

It must be instinct that makes my fingers curl around her calf. Her leg is right there at hand level, and it feels natural to grab hold of it. But it must surprise her, because she squeals and hops closer, clinging onto my bicep to hold her balance.

Another little stumble, and I catch her against my chest, my hand sliding up to her knee. I have to close my eyes for a minute, because the feel of her leg hooked over my hip like this makes me want to explode. My other hand moves to the small of her back, and suddenly she's pressed along the length of me, that denim dress riding up to reveal white garters and a bare, beautiful thigh.

Her little breathless pants drive me wild, along with the way her nails dig into my bicep through the bulk of my sweatshirt. My eyes stay glued to the space between us, the sight of her thigh pressed against my hip. Letting my hand slide higher, I run my thumb along the edge of her stocking, where sheer lace meets bare flesh.

"Marcus," she breathes.

An ogreish grunt is the only response I can manage. Her skin is soft as satin and my hand slips higher, fingers sliding under the back garter to feel the soft skin of her thigh and its juncture with her ass.

Thoughts flee from my mind when I feel the edge of the gusset of her panties, the heat of her body between her legs. I drop my forehead against hers, keeping my eyes on that little slice of exposed thigh between red-and-white stocking and denim.

"We shouldn't be doing this," she whispers, but her voice trembles, and she makes no move to back away. Her hands tighten on my arms.

My fingertips trace the seam of her panties, my arm wrapped all the way around her thigh. I love having her pressed up against me like this, where I want us joined. I love feeling her whimper and tremble with need. I love smelling the scent of her skin, her hair, her sex.

I shouldn't. I know it's just an animal attraction—the

natural consequence of a particularly long dry spell. I'd feel this way with any woman pressed up against me like this.

"You want me to stop?" I ask, letting my lips brush against her ear as she buries her face in the crook of my neck. My fingers move slowly, so slowly, coasting along the backs of her thighs, brushing the edge of her panties. She is so soft and warm and perfect. God, I bet she tastes delicious. "Penny?"

I slide my hand over her ass, squeezing gently. In response, Penny pushes her hips against mine, her eyes still closed.

It's enough to make my control shatter. That little movement, the tiniest of invitations. She quivers against me, grinding her core into mine with jerky little movements that make my cock throb behind the placket of my zipper.

"I..." She inhales, finally lifting her eyes to mine. Her arms wrap around my neck, leg still hooked over my hip. In those blue depths, I see deep, unfulfilled need. "I shouldn't want you this much."

Squeezing her lush curves again, I move my other hand to her chin. "I think we've moved beyond that."

"It's a bad idea. You're my boss."

"Not tonight, I'm not." My voice is little more than a rattle of gravel.

A little exhale, and her eyes drop to my lips. It's the only invitation I need to kiss her. Hard. My mouth falls on hers like she's the only thing that will sate me—and hell, she is. I haven't been able to stop thinking about our kiss, or the feel of her in my arms. I've dreamed of her. I've wrapped my hand around my cock every time I've been in the shower, and a few times while I've been in my private bathroom at the office. This woman has invaded my brain, and the plain truth is that

I'm just not strong enough to resist. Not tonight. Not when she's wearing thigh-high stockings and a little denim dress.

She kisses me back just as hard, her hands tunneling into my hair to pull me closer. With one hand still roaming over her ass and thigh, keeping that leg right where I want it, my other hand drops between us. I lift the edge of her dress and find the wet heat of her panties beneath.

She moans when my palm cups her there, arching into the touch. That little movement, the way her lips fall open and go motionless for a brief moment, drives me fucking wild. Holding her leg against my hip with an iron grip, I grind my other palm against her core.

Penny rewards me with the sexiest little gasps I've ever heard.

Glancing at the glass doors and deciding I don't want anyone else to see her like this, I pick her up and walk three steps to the patch of wall at the end of the balcony. She wraps both legs around my waist, and I nearly come at the feel of her against the length of me. I press her up against the wall, pinning her there, then shove the denim skirt up and out of the way so I can see what she's been hiding.

White stockings. A white garter belt. And tiny white panties with lace curving up around her hips. The garter belt hangs on her waist, its material satiny. Beneath everything, silky skin covered in little reddish-brown freckles. Not as many as on her face, but still countless little dots over every inch of her.

"*Ugh*," I grunt. I sound like an animal, but I can't make words. I can't even *think* when I see that. My hips punch forward, drawing a gasp from her lips.

"Um, Marcus," Penny says between breaths.

I rip my gaze away from the mesmerizing sight of her undergarments and meet her eyes. "Yeah, baby?"

"I, uh…" She squeezes her eyes shut. "It's been a while for me. I'm not… I, um…" A nervous little giggle escapes her, and even in the low light of the balcony, I can see her flush. Her hands tighten on my shoulders, her thighs squeeze me close.

I freeze. "Are you a virgin?"

I've only been with one virgin, and at the time, I was one too. My first girlfriend—and that was a couple of decades ago. The thought of being Penny's first…

My question makes her eyes snap open, and she laughs in earnest. "No. No, it's just been a long time since I've been with a man. I'm enjoying this, I am, but…" She bites her lip.

I blink. I am a colossal asshole. "You want to slow down."

She inhales deeply, her legs still wrapped around my waist, her arms still clinging to my shoulders. The breath makes her breasts strain against the top of her dress, and my brain starts trying to figure out the quickest way to get my mouth on them.

Like I said—colossal fucking asshole. I'm not going to deny it. Still want to bite her nipples till I leave my mark on her.

"I don't know what I want," she whispers. "Except that I don't want you to stop."

Meeting her gaze again, I see vulnerability there. It quells my lust just enough that I can think and makes something lurch in my chest. This isn't the type of woman I want to fuck up against the wall at a Halloween party before walking away. Not in a million years.

But—garter. Stockings. Lacy white thong.

I'll die if I let go of her now. I won't make it out the door.

And more than anything, I want to hear what hot little noises Penny makes when she's in ecstasy.

"I'm going to make you come," I tell her, letting my eyes drift down to where her center is pressed against mine. "That okay?"

A breathless giggle that's little more than a sharp exhale. "Um. Yeah. That's fine."

"Good."

Then I get to doing just that.

17

PENNY

AT SOME POINT around the time that Marcus grabbed my leg, I decided to wave goodbye to my brain and let my body take over.

Now I'm pressed up against the wall, with every limb wrapped around my boss and my homemade pinafore dress pushed up and gathered around my waist. My lips feel swollen and kiss-bruised, my panties are soaked, and the last thing I want to do is let go—but my body feels deliciously loose, and as soon as Marcus pulls his hands away from my thighs, my feet drop to the floor.

"Turn around," he grates.

Dazed, I do as he says.

"Hands on the wall."

"Marcus..."

"Do it." His voice is low, rough, sending heat spiraling into my core, so I do what he says and put my hands on the wall.

The heat of his body presses against the back of me, from my shoulders to my ankles. His hands circle my waist below the bunched-up hem of my dress, warm on my bare skin. His jean-clad leg presses the inside of mine, and I step my feet wider, opening myself to him.

With warm breath coasting over my neck and the feel of his long, hard body against my back, I lean against the wall and try to hold on as the world bucks beneath my feet. Then Marcus slides one palm lower along my stomach, dipping beneath the waistband of my panties, and all my breath runs out in a rush.

He groans softly when he feels the small tuft of curls between my legs, then lets his fingers explore lower.

"So wet for me," he says.

I nod, unable to speak.

His fingers delve between my legs, sending shivers coursing through my body with every touch. I can't think. Can't speak. It's been so long since a man touched me like this—touched me at all. My legs tremble and I lean my forehead against the wall, bracketed by my forearms.

I know I shouldn't be doing this. I shouldn't want this. But—

Long, slow strokes bring me up to a fever pitch. I hear little whimpers, and it takes me a minute to realize they're coming from me. Marcus's touch is slow and sure and drugging. His fingertips explore the space between my legs, drawing more liquid heat from me, winding the pressure in the pit of my stomach tighter.

I jerk when he touches my clit, and he responds with a low chuckle and a kiss on the nape of my neck. "You like that?"

I nod and one of my braids scratches against the wall. I can't believe I'm doing *this* while I'm dressed like *this*.

Before I can think too deeply about it, though, his movements grow faster while his other hand slides up my rib cage, slipping under the pinafore—then freezes at what he feels.

"You're not wearing a bra." Marcus's voice is rough as gravel, shivering over the skin of my neck. One hand circles my clit while the other clasps my breast, squeezing.

The sensations are almost too much. I've spent the better part of a decade avoiding human contact—avoiding *male* contact. I'd forgotten what it was like to be touched, to be worshipped. I think it's the heat that surprises me. The heat of his palms, the roughness of them, the blaze of his body at my back.

The heat of my own body as my desire mounts.

He tweaks my nipple through my shirt, sending pleasure forking through my blood. "Why aren't you wearing a bra?"

My whole body jerks in response. "The dress," I gasp. "It hides my chest. Don't need it." I sip enough air to say, "Nikki got rid of all my bras," even though I know that won't make sense to him.

His forehead lands on my shoulder, both hands moving faster. Between my legs, fire erupts as Marcus grinds the heel of his hand against my bud, his fingers curling ever so slightly inside me. The hand on my chest moves across to my other breast, squeezing and pinching with abandon.

And all I can do is lean my head and forearms against the wall and take the onslaught of his ministrations.

When Marcus removes his hands from where they've been torturing me so sweetly, I let out a complaining whimper. He grabs my waist with both hands and tugs me roughly back toward him so my back is arched and my legs are wide.

He grunts low and harsh in his throat. That noise, the way

he touches me like he owns me—turns me on like nothing else.

Then his hand slides between my legs, but instead of wrapping around the front of me, he touches me from behind. Something magical happens then, when he slides two fingers inside me. Electricity makes me jolt, stiffening every muscle. I feel his touch deep inside me, crave more of it. Arching my back and pushing into him, I'm rewarded with another kiss on my shoulder, my neck.

One hand holds me still, clamped around my hip, and the other delivers unimaginable pleasure between my legs. I gasp, writhing, pinned to the wall by his big body.

And I want more.

I don't realize I've said that last part out loud until Marcus lets out a rough, breathy chuckle. "You'll get more, Penny. But first you have to come for me."

"Marcus," I pant.

"Come for me," he repeats, twisting his fingers inside me while his free hand reaches around to touch the little bundle of nerves between my legs.

And all it takes is a touch. The barest brush of his fingers against my bud, and I'm letting out a cry of pleasure so loud I wonder if the whole block can hear me. He wrings every bit of pleasure from me, until I'm worried I'll topple over into a heap, right onto Bonnie's collection of dead potted plants in the corner of the balcony.

Then I'm being spun around, leaned against the wall, while Marcus licks his fingers like they're covered in honey. His eyes are low, hooded, and he lets out a rough grunt. "Better than I imagined."

A dart of pleasure pierces my stomach at his words, and

then he kisses me and I forget everything else. When we pull apart, we're both breathing heavily.

"Um," I say, because I am the epitome of eloquence.

Marcus's lips tilt ever so slightly at the corners, then he busies himself tugging my dress down. He pauses when he's holding it at my hips, eyes staring at the stockings and garters framing my legs. Then, as if it takes an incredible effort of will, he pulls my dress down the whole way, straightening it until I'm completely covered.

Then, slowly, he takes a step back.

I frown. "What about you?"

A slow blink. "Penny, if you come anywhere near my cock right now, I'm just going to want to get inside you. You told me you didn't want that tonight. Is that still true?"

No. Not even a little bit.

Those predator's eyes scan my face, and I'm sure he sees every thought written there. But I just nod. "Yeah. It's still true."

"Let's go back inside," he says after a pause, reaching over to slide the door open. The heat of the interior coasts over my body like a sauna, and I feel too hot, too tight, too...too *much*.

Marcus, on the other hand, doesn't seem bothered at all. He puts a hand on the small of my back and guides me out of Bonnie's room to the hallway, as if he didn't just use that hand to give me the best orgasm I've had in years. *Maybe ever?*

It's hard to think right now. I'm worried that if I start thinking, I'll start *over*thinking. I'll start regretting.

I'm still dazed when we're halfway down the hallway and Brian pops up from some wrinkle in the fabric of reality. One minute the hallway is clear, the next he's right there.

His eyes dart from me to Marcus and back again, his brows drawing together. "Penny. Are you okay?"

"Yeah," I say, but my mouth hasn't quite connected to my brain, because it comes out as little more than a squeak. I clear my throat. "Yeah, of course I'm fine."

We come to a stop, and Marcus stands ever so slightly closer to me. His hand remains on the small of my back. "Did you want something?" he asks, his voice excessively bland, which sends a little trickle of warning down my spine.

Brian frowns at him. "Who the hell are you, buddy?"

Testosterone fills the hallway in puffs of thick black smoke. I watch the two men size each other up, two angry locomotives hurtling toward each other at full speed.

"Oh." I let out a deranged giggle. "Marcus, Brian. Brian, Marcus." I wave my hands between the two of them. "Brian is my business partner. Marcus is my...boss." My voice kind of dies on the last word, but I cover it with a cough.

A tense silence stretches, and the two men study each other for a while. I would try to do something about it, but there are still little darts of pleasure coursing through my thighs and stomach. My panties are wet and clinging to me, and my breasts feel over-sensitized beneath my dress. I don't have enough brainpower to think about some male intimidation ritual. I just let them do whatever they need to do.

Finally Brian's gaze shifts to me. "You ready to go?"

I blink. "Um. I guess? Where's Nikki?"

Brian shrugs a shoulder. "With Bonnie and a bunch of guys. I'm over it, though. I thought we could get some food on the way home."

Marcus goes very, very still beside me. "You two live together?"

I laugh. "No. God, no."

Brian rears back. "What do you mean, 'God no?'"

My face is red again. "No! I didn't mean it like it would be a bad thing. I just meant, you know, we...don't live together."

"It sounded like you meant it to be a bad thing." Brian crosses his arms, his brow full of thunder.

Oh, no. My best friend is mad at me—and why wouldn't he be? I blew him off last weekend, I moved my workshop without telling him, and now I'm acting like he's not a huge part of my life. I blame the post-orgasmic hormones. They're scrambling my brain. I can't think straight.

"If you want to go home, I'll call my driver," Marcus says, finally removing his hand from my back to pull out his cell phone. I suddenly feel cold.

Brian snorts. "Of course you have a driver."

Marcus ignores him, and I shift my weight from foot to foot. I put my hand on his arm. "That's okay, Marcus. We can take the subway. Right, Brian?"

"Right."

"The car will be here in five minutes," Marcus answers, as if neither of us said anything. "He can drop your friend off at his place too. I'll walk you down."

"You are such an overbearing ass," I say, but I can't hide the twitch of my lips.

Marcus sees it, then slides his gaze up to meet mine. A thousand words pass between us in an instant, and I'm left reeling. Words like, *This isn't over.*

Then Marcus gives me a jerky little nod and gestures down the hallway. "Do you have a jacket?"

I can't help it. The twitch in my lips turns into a full-blown smile. I shake my head, then walk down the hallway flanked by Marcus on one side and Brian on the other. I excuse myself for a moment to say goodbye to Nikki and Bonnie, who hug me so hard it feels like we've been friends for ages. Which, in Nikki's case, I guess we have. But as I thank Bonnie for having us and accept praise for my fabulous rendition of Queen's hit, I can't help but laugh.

The stage has another performer on it while partygoers heckle him, and there's a little tug inside me telling me to stay. Tonight has been amazing. Mind-boggling, confusing, exhilarating—and amazing. Why am I going home already?

But Brian wants to leave, and what kind of friend would I be to let him go on his own?

As if Nikki can read my mind, she pouts. "Stay a little longer." Her fake canines stick out onto her full lips. She's lost the nun's habit at some point since I was on the balcony, and her dark hair gleams in the low light of the living room.

I hesitate, then finally shake my head. "I'm exhausted. And Brian wants to leave. It's best if I go."

Nikki huffs. "Ugh. Brian."

"Hey!" I laugh.

She purses her lips and arches a brow. "I don't know, Penny. I'm getting bad vibes."

A chill slithers down my spine. She said the same thing about Billy, way back when she met him after I'd been on a couple of dates with him. I shove the feeling away. Brian is different. Nikita's just being overprotective.

Bonnie lets out an inelegant grunt. "He seems a bit..."

"Possessive of Penny?" Nikki finishes for her.

Bonnie snaps her fingers. "Exactly. Did you see his face when you were singing together?"

Nikki nods sagely.

I frown. "What did his face look like?" I don't give them time to answer. "You're being paranoid. I'm leaving."

Nikki relents, giving me another hug. "Call me tomorrow? You can tell me why you disappeared for a while and came back on your boss's arm looking like you couldn't remember how to speak."

My face goes bright red. The two women cackle.

"Bye," I say, maybe a bit too forcefully, then I turn on my heels, narrowly avoid whacking a nearby partygoer with my hair, and march toward the waiting men.

Marcus's hand slides onto my lower back again, and Brian watches the movement with pursed lips. The three of us ride the elevator all the way down to the ground floor. Maybe it's only awkward in my head, and the two of them are perfectly comfortable.

Sure. That's what's going on.

Marcus makes sure we slide into the back of his vehicle before stepping back to watch as the car pulls away.

I nuzzle into the heated seats, clamping my legs together, and let out a satisfied little sigh. What a night. What a party. What an *orgasm*. I haven't felt that way in so long, I wonder if it's ever been that good. The way Marcus—

"What's going on between the two of you?" Brian's voice is harder than I've ever heard it.

I jump. "What?"

"You know what I mean, Penny."

"I'm sure I don't," I protest.

"He wants you."

"He's my boss."

"My boss doesn't touch my back the way he was touching yours. My boss doesn't pack me into his car and make sure I get home safe. You know he only got us to take this car because he wanted to know whether or not I went to your place, right?"

My brows draw together, and I finally look over at my friend and business partner. "What?"

"You think he won't ask his fucking *driver* whether or not I get out with you? He was all over you, Penny."

"Don't talk about Will that way," I say, glancing at the driver, but it's mostly to give myself time to process what Brian said.

Brian just snorts. It's an ugly, derisive sound. "Oh, you're on a first-name basis with his driver, are you?"

I exchange a glance with Will in the rearview mirror before he shifts his gaze back to the road. I sit up a bit straighter, smoothing my dress down over my legs. It's *very* wrinkly. I wonder what the rest of me looks like as my cheeks grow hot.

"You're embarrassing yourself, Brian. What are you trying to say? Aren't you the one who is always talking about how I should date? How I should put myself out there? Now you're mad at some imaginary connection you think you see between me and my boss."

Shame slicks my throat as the words come out, because I know I'm lying to him. But besides the shame, I feel a hot, burning anger. Brian should be *happy* for me, shouldn't he? I mean, sure, hooking up with your boss isn't exactly a great idea. But I haven't hooked up with *anyone* in eight years! Nikki would probably squeal and demand details, not get her panties in a twist because...because what? What is Brian even upset about?

"'Putting yourself out there' doesn't mean hooking up

with your fucking billionaire boss, Penny. Have you even considered the power dynamic there? It's *wrong*."

"I'm not hooking up with *anyone*, Brian." The lie comes out harsh, loud, and completely unlike me. "And if I was, it would be none of your damn business."

Brian rears back, then his lips curl into a snarl. He leans over the center console. "Let me out here," he tells Will.

"Brian," I admonish. "Come on."

The driver pulls over as soon as he can, and my best friend gets out before I can protest. Then he slams the door harder than he needs to and stalks off.

I let out a huff. "What the hell is up with men? What is his problem?" I turn to look at Will via the rearview mirror. "Huh?"

Will clears his throat, running a hand over his wiry gray beard. "Do you want me to answer that?"

Suddenly I feel exhausted. I slump down and lean my head against the window. "Brian was just a bit drunk, that's all. We'll be back to normal tomorrow."

Will lets out a noncommittal grunt, then puts the car in gear and takes me home.

18

MARCUS

As I slip inside the front door and hear the click of Bear's claws on my concrete floor, I let out a long sigh. "Hey, boy."

I spend a few minutes scratching behind his floppy ears and telling him what a good dog he is, take him out for a pee, then finally come back inside and kick my shoes off. I head to the kitchen for a glass of water, then lean against the counter, rubbing my forehead, wondering what the hell happened tonight.

Penny happened, that's what. In that dress. With that smile. And those legs.

While my brain tries to list out all the reasons kissing her was a bad idea—not to mention everything else we did—I can't quite bring myself to regret it. She was so beautiful, so soft. So *mine*. Having her in my arms felt right in a way that I've rarely experienced.

It felt the same way creating Sellzy did, in those first years, when I was driven by a purpose that came from within. It felt the same as buying my mom's apartment and handing her the deed. Hiring or finding jobs for my family members, giving them a stable salary and benefits and a career.

With Penny in my arms, my soul was singing, telling me I was doing the right thing.

But that can't be right.

She's my employee. I don't have time for a relationship. I was just horny, that's all, and she was incredibly hot.

Walking down the hallway brings me to Mackenzie's bedroom door. I lean a hand against the wall beside it. My niece is important to me in a way I can hardly explain. She's like a daughter to me. I feel responsible for her well-being, for her happiness, her health.

I know, deep down, that although most of those feelings are driven by love for the kid, they're also partially driven by guilt. I wasn't there for Stephanie when my sister needed me most. I let her down. Mackenzie has an unstable home because of *me*.

And now I want to start hooking up with my dog walker? I want to turn this safe haven of Mackenzie's—the only stable home she's had—into a place where she'd potentially feel uncomfortable? I want to subject my niece to an inappropriate relationship between me and an employee?

It's wrong. I should be focused on my business and my family. I have the weight of those responsibilities on my shoulders, and I know if I get distracted, what happened with Stephanie will happen again. I'll drop the ball. I'll hurt someone.

In the guest room, my mother stirs when I poke my head in. "You staying the night, or you want Will to drive you home?"

"Home," she mumbles, and levers herself up. I have a

few blissful minutes of distraction while my mother peppers me with sleepy questions about the party, then pats my cheek and heads to the car. I watch them drive off, sighing.

Then, like it was inevitable, my feet take me to the back room, where Penny's workshop is set up. I step across the threshold and feel the tension between my shoulders dissolve.

As I look around the room, the term *organized chaos* comes to mind. Most of the mountains of fabric are hidden away in the cabinets, but that doesn't mean there aren't piles of projects laid out around the room. Penny's creativity screams from every corner of the room, from the prints to the patterns to the packaging she uses to send her products out to customers. I touch a sticker with her logo—a paw print wearing a bow tie—and my lips tilt up at the corners.

Who thinks of something like this? What kind of person has the drive and determination to carve out such a specific niche—and make it work?

A leather-bound ledger rests on the corner of the work-table, and I find myself flipping it open. In neat, rounded writing, Penny has written a list of every order, itemized neatly down the pages. Printed sheets are stapled to every page detailing various orders, along with receipts for expenses. On a few of the pages, she's circled amounts that I assume are her and her business partner's salary.

As I flip through the pages, those amounts get bigger. Her business has grown.

And the woman doesn't even use a computer.

I shake my head, impressed.

"What are you doing?"

I jump at the sound of Mackenzie's voice, slamming the ledger shut. "Kenzie."

She rubs her eyes. "What are you doing in here?" she repeats.

"Nothing," I answer. "Did I wake you up?"

My niece shakes her head. "No. I got thirsty and wanted some water, then I saw the light. How was the party?"

Incredible. Amazing. Wrong.

"It was fine."

"I don't think Penny would like you snooping around," Kenzie says, turning to shuffle down the hallway.

I grunt in response, because what can I say to that? My niece is right. I follow her out and shut the door behind me, then call out goodnight and head to my room.

When I finally fall asleep, I dream of Penny.

ON SUNDAY, Mackenzie and I head to my mom's house for a family dinner. We're both shocked to walk in and see my sister Steph peeling potatoes in the kitchen, her hands trembling so much she can barely hold the peeler. Her boyfriend is nowhere to be seen.

"Mom," Mackenzie says, stunned.

Steph turns around, drops the potato peeler, and wipes her hand. "Hey, kiddo." She hugs Mackenzie. "How's your Uncle Marcus been treating you?"

"Good," Mackenzie says, squeezing her mom tight.

My sister watches me over Mackenzie's shoulder, smudges dark as ink splotches below her eyes. She shakes slightly when she pulls away from her daughter, inhales deeply, then gives me a curt nod. "Marcus. Can I speak to you in private?"

I gesture down the hall toward the bedrooms. Mackenzie frowns, watching us both walk away. My heart gives a sharp twist. If Steph wants her daughter home again, I won't be able to stop her...and Penny won't have a reason to work from my spare room.

And doesn't that thought just make me the most selfish asshole who's ever lived?

We enter the girls' room, where my sisters shared a space growing up. The bunk beds are still there, although they've been replaced with sturdier versions and new bedding, for when the grandkids come and stay. There's a crib in the corner and a changing table where the desk used to be.

Stephanie nods for me to close the door, then leans against the wall on the far side of the room. I take a seat on the bottom bunk, leaning my elbows on my knees. I wait for Stephanie to start talking. It takes her a few long moments, but she finally takes a deep breath and speaks.

"Thank you for taking care of Mackenzie," she starts, her words coming slowly. "I broke up with Kyle, and I'm getting treatment for my drinking. Mom's taking me to detox as soon as you and I are done talking, then I'm going to a rehab facility for eight weeks. I'd appreciate it if you could keep Mackenzie until I'm back."

My head snaps up, and I search my sister's face. It's drawn, tired, and defeated. A woman who knows she has a long road ahead. "Of course," I say, my voice creaking past the lump in my throat. "What facility are you going to? I'll cover the expenses. Pick the best one you can find."

My sister's face twists. "Stop it, Marcus. Stop trying to pay for everything. Stop trying to carry every single burden on your shoulders. I don't need your money."

I freeze.

She crosses her arms, and her baggy shirt clings to her torso for a moment. My sister is too thin. Her hair hangs in lank clumps that she pushes behind her ears. But her eyes burn when they meet mine. "I don't want you to help me with this. I don't want anything from you." Her words are acidic, cutting. "If I could, I'd ask Mom to take Mackenzie, but God knows she already has enough on her plate with the other grandkids. Plus, Mackenzie's settled at your place, and she likes you. Trust me, if I had another option, I'd take it."

I open my mouth. Close it.

I probably deserve that.

Steph lets out a bitter huff. "That shut you up, didn't it? You don't know what to do with yourself when you don't get to be the hero, paving everyone's way with all your millions."

"It's not like that."

"It's exactly like that." She sneers at me. "But I know how you were before the money, Marcus. You weren't there when it counted."

The hit lands. Pain smarts on my cheek like an open-handed slap. "Steph," I croak.

She holds up a hand. "You and I will never be close, Marcus. But I respect everything you've done for Mackenzie, and even though it kills me, I know her staying with you is the best thing for her. So just do me a favor and stop trying to be a white knight right now. Just let me fix myself up and make things right for my daughter. Otherwise, just leave me alone."

We stare at each other for a moment, until I finally nod. "Fine."

"Good." She pushes herself off the wall, turns her back to me, and walks away.

I sit on the bottom bunk for a while, head in hand, until I hear a soft noise in the doorway. Mackenzie's standing there, watching me.

"Hey, kid," I say, standing. It feels like my body's turned to plaster, hollow and crumbling, like every joint grinds against itself as I finally move from the spot where I've been sitting.

"Mom told me she was going to rehab." My niece glances down the hall, then turns back to me. "You think it'll work this time?"

Christ, it makes me tired to hear Mackenzie speak like that. No child should have eyes that old. I shrug and scrub my hand in my hair. "I don't know, Kenzie. I hope so."

"She said I'm staying with you until she gets better."

I nod. "You and me against the world."

Mackenzie bites her bottom lip, and I suspect it's to stop it from trembling. "And you... You're okay with that?"

My shoulders drop. I stand up and hook an arm around Mackenzie's shoulders to pull her in for a hug. "Of course, kid. I love having you around." I squeeze her tight. "Except maybe early mornings when you crank that racket up to maximum volume."

She lets out a watery laugh against my shirt, then pulls away. "I'll keep it down."

I kiss her hair and turn us both toward the door. "Let's go back. Grandma probably needs help."

"She'll just tell us to get out of the kitchen."

"Yeah, but she'll appreciate us asking."

My mom and Steph are dressed and ready to go. My mother looks tired, but she gives me a nod, then the two of them leave. It seems like it takes forever, but less than an hour later, Mom's back. She gives me a slight nod, and I know Stephanie made it to the detox facility.

The rest is up to her.

There's a knock on the door, and my brother Terry enters with his wife and kids. From there, the chaos of a family dinner explodes in my mom's tiny, old apartment. Grandkids move in packs, my brothers drink beer and talk sports, and everyone carefully avoids saying anything about where Stephanie's gone, glancing periodically at the oddly somber Mackenzie.

And incomprehensibly, I find myself wishing Penny were here. It doesn't make sense, but it's how I feel. She'd be wearing some ridiculously bright outfit that would delight the children. She'd probably have a bow tie or some silly pet costume in her purse ready to give away to my mother's chihuahua. She'd be a ray of sunshine that made me feel warm and at home, when I've always felt slightly apart from everyone else.

Then I shake my head to clear the thought, grab a beer, and go join my brothers.

Penny isn't here. She isn't *supposed* to be here. Better not to entertain those kinds of thoughts at all.

19

PENNY

Iᴛ's strange to walk into Marcus's house on Monday morning. My heart races, my palms sweat, and I wonder for the millionth time since Saturday night if I made a colossal mistake on Bonnie's balcony.

I've been living a life of strict routine for a long time. The past year has been rigid. Bear's two-a-day walks were like tentpoles I used to structure the rest of my days. From when I'd eat to when I took my birth control pill to when I sat down at the sewing machine, everything happened on a schedule. Day in, day out, it didn't change.

Now it's all messed up. I wake up at the same time, but my meals are all over the place. I'm never home, and even though I get more sewing done, it feels like I'm always trying to catch up. Then I went and hooked up with my boss at a Halloween party, screwing things up even more.

My worries melt away when Bear tackles me to the ground and slobbers over my face and neck with doggie kisses. I screech and laugh and try to push him off me, and the world rights itself again. I take him out for a walk, feed him, freshen up his water, and feel almost normal.

Then, it's time to get to work. My sewing machine whirrs, my lips curl into a smile, and I let myself fall into that state of flow that only comes when I'm sewing.

Until.

Until the garage door opens, and I know I'm no longer alone. As I press the seams of my latest project flat, my hands tremble. The interior door to the garage just opened. Heavy, familiar footsteps enter. I run the iron over my project and keep my eyes on my work, trimming stray threads with all the focus I can muster.

The footsteps grow closer.

I turn the sweater right side out and check it, satisfied. Movement happens in the corner of my vision, but I ignore it as my heart thumps hard against my ribs.

Marcus enters the room, and all the air is sucked out of it. Unable to breathe, I turn to face him.

"Hello, Penny," he says quietly, his green eyes dark as a shady forest.

The sound of my name makes my whole body clench, but I manage to hold his gaze. "Marcus. You're home."

He steps closer, until there's only a scant few inches of space between us. Beside me, the iron gasps out a breath of steam, gurgling where it stands. I should turn it off, but I'm frozen in place.

Marcus's eyes are intent on mine. It's the same look he gave me when I left the party, the one that said whatever happened between us wasn't over.

I spent all weekend thinking about the balcony. Wondering how I could be so impulsive, so stupid. I lambasted myself about what I did, because surely I ruined what I had going here. The workshop, the steady paycheck, my time with Bear.

I resolved to keep things professional from now on. I told myself it was an aberration, a mistake. It wouldn't happen again.

But when Marcus takes a step closer, crowding into my space, I know I was wrong.

It'll happen again, and it'll happen right now. His broad hand sweeps up my neck to cup the side of my jaw, thumb coasting over my cheek, eyes never leaving mine.

"I haven't been able to work all day, knowing you were here," he says in a low rumble.

"Oh?" I answer, trying to ignore the bird flapping its wings in my chest.

His other hand sweeps around my lower back, pulling me tight to his body. "I'm supposed to be reviewing contracts and preparing for the biggest deal in my company's history. But all I've been able to think about is you, here, in my home."

My body is a bowstring, taut and tense. My breasts press against his chest, and I wonder if he can feel the pebbled nipples, the rioting of my heart, the trembling of my belly.

Probably. He can probably feel every bit of my need. His hand slides down my back to cup my bottom, pulling me tight to his body as his lips descend on mine.

And oh, I missed this. It's only been a day and a half, but I missed feeling him pressed up against me, I missed his mouth exploring mine, his breath mingling with my own. I missed those broad hands claiming me, like he already knows all the ways I want to be touched.

Ever since Billy, I've been afraid. Cautious. Nervous. But

when I'm with Marcus, all I want to do is let go. I want him to bend my body to his will, to do whatever he wants with me. I want to *let go*. Let go of the fear and anxiety, the overcautiousness. I want to give myself to him, because deep down, I know he'll keep me safe.

It doesn't make sense. I shouldn't feel this way. I should still be afraid.

But I can't help it.

As if he can hear my thoughts, Marcus deepens the kiss, then wraps both hands around my waist and lifts me onto the edge of the table. He fits his thighs between my knees and groans into my mouth when I wrap my ankles behind his back. Leaning against me, he pushes me down onto my elbows and angles his broad body over mine. His big hand slides up my thighs and under my floral, knee-length dress.

And then he freezes.

"Penny," he growls against my lips, his hand stone-still on my hip. "You're not wearing underwear." His fingers slide across my front, teasing my belly, then move down to cover my aching, empty core.

My breaths heave. "Um. I—uh..." I trail off and bite my lip, leaning back until I'm lying flat on the table. "No," I answer. "I'm not."

Marcus's fingers start delving between my legs, where I'm already hot and wet. He closes his eyes and lets out a shudder. "Why not? You've just been sitting here all morning, in my house, and—"

He kisses me just as his fingers surge inside me. I moan at the intrusion, knees falling wide as my ankles come apart at his back. Then Marcus moves quickly, yanking me to the edge of the table and kneeling before me. He spreads my legs wide, pushing my skirt up, and laves my core with his tongue.

I squeak. It's not a great noise, but it's what happens. My hands scrabble for purchase on the smooth table, finding the edge, while his hands hold my thighs wide and his mouth works me to a fever pitch. I find the strength to lift my head up to look at him, only to see his eyes closed in concentration while he makes noises of absolute pleasure.

Pleasure. At the taste of me on his tongue.

I let my head fall back. Everything from my navel to my knees is a knot of heat. I cling to the edge of the table, bucking at every nibble, every kiss. And when he adds his hand to the mix, I lose all sense of reality.

Ten minutes ago, I was ironing a dog sweater. Now I'm laid out on my worktable seconds from a mind-bending orgasm. As if he can sense how close I am, Marcus does something incredible with his tongue, moves his fingers in a special kind of way, touches me at just the right place...

And I explode. I think I lose consciousness for a second. It's that intense.

When I come back to myself, Marcus is kissing my inner thigh, watching me with gleaming eyes.

"Nnghh," I say.

What the heck is happening to me? Is this my life?

He chuckles, laying a kiss on my curls before standing.

Through the haze in my vision, I notice the bulge at his crotch, and I realize that's twice he's been selfless with me. Twice he's given without asking anything in return.

And suddenly, I want to give. I think of the way he went down on me, groaning as if he enjoyed it as much as I did, and I wonder if it could feel that way to reciprocate.

I've always been vaguely prudish about blowjobs. It felt wrong and degrading to do that with Billy. He always made me feel like I owed him my mouth, then when it was over, like I should be embarrassed about it.

But that was before. I'm feeling all kinds of things I haven't felt in a long time. I'm letting a man touch me—no, I'm *enjoying* a man's touch. I'm *craving* Marcus's hands. I'm twisting in my sheets at night at the memory of my boss's hands and lips on me.

I want Marcus to feel as good as I do. Whatever's happening between us—even if it's just lust, if it's just temporary—I don't want it to be one-sided.

He's a billionaire, a boss, the best-looking man I've ever seen. We'll never have ever-lasting love. I'm not stupid. I know I'll probably get hurt, because I already feel like I'm falling for him.

But what if I could use this lust to crawl out of my shell? Maybe this can be a new beginning for me, even if there's no chance of me and Marcus ever being anything more than bed partners.

As Marcus gathers me in his arms and kisses me deeply, I know I'm not ready for this to be over. For the first time in many, many years, I feel safe with a man. I had *orgasms* with a man. I've been vulnerable, with my legs spread, and I don't regret it. Not even a little bit.

In a way, I feel like the old me. A little reckless, a little adventurous, a little brave. The feeling stretches inside me like a balloon filling up all the corners that have shrunk down over the past eight years. I've lived a small, scared life.

I don't want that anymore.

While he kisses me slow and deep, my hands reach for

his belt buckle. I'm sitting up on the worktable while he cups my face, and he pulls back to watch me fumble with his pants.

Then his gaze meets mine. "You don't have to do that, Penny. You told me you wanted to take things slow."

My heart grows another three sizes, and I realize *this* is why I feel safe with Marcus. Yes, he's slightly overbearing and arrogant and annoying. He's grumpy and growly. But he *listens*. He respects me. Me! The woman who walks his dog, who makes canine clothing for a living. Who wears home-made clothes.

Even though he walked in here and it was obvious what he wanted, it never felt like he was using me. It felt like he was *giving*.

"I know I don't have to do anything," I answer, tugging his zipper down. I flick my gaze up to his. "But what if I want to?"

A long, slow breath escapes his lips, and he closes his eyes. As if he can't find the words to say what he wants. As if the words I spoke were exactly what he wanted to hear.

And in that moment I wonder if Marcus and I have something in common. Have we both been living a life with high, thick walls surrounding us? Have we both been too safe? Too guarded?

I slide off the table and lower myself to my knees.

"Penny." It comes out as a choked groan.

I ignore it. I push his pants and underwear down to his ankles and grip the hard, hot length of him, my heart turning over at his size. I know it's been a long time, but it seems awfully big. That's supposed to fit...down *there*?

A jolt of fear and desire makes me want to climb on top of him and try. But first—

The tip glistens, and I lick my lip. That draws another strangled noise from above me, which I also ignore.

If I hesitate much longer, I might lose my nerve. But even though I'm nervous about this, about what it means, I still want it. I want to be a sexual, desirable, desired woman. I want to open my life up to companionship, to sex. I want to stop living smaller than I need to.

So I take his cock in my mouth, and I suck. Lust surges inside me as Marcus gathers my hair in his hand, holding it out of the way in a clumsy tail. I splay one hand over his thigh for balance and wrap the other around his girth, and I take him as deep as I can.

And the sounds he makes—my goodness. I've never been so turned on in my life. He pushes my head gently, guiding me as I take him deeper, and I let instinct take over. There's little technique, but I make up for it with enthusiasm. And Marcus doesn't seem to mind. He moans my name and tightens his hand on my hair, hips moving in jerky little movements that seem out of his control.

I feel...*powerful*. I feel strong. I feel in control.

Sex has terrified me for so long. *Men* have terrified me. How is it that in less than a week, a couple of irresponsible and spontaneous sexual encounters can make me feel like a new woman?

Before I know what I'm doing, my hand is clawing at my skirt and reaching for the throbbing bud between my legs. It feels too good to be making a powerful man like Marcus Walsh moan my name, jerk uncontrollably, tug my hair. It feels too good to be *free*. I need to touch myself, to sate this need rising inside me.

"Oh, fuck," Marcus says when I moan, my hand moving

frantically between my legs while I take him in my mouth. "Oh, Penny. That's it." His voice is a low growl. "Make yourself come while you suck my cock. That's a good girl. Come for me, come with my cock between your lips."

Oi. *Dirty*. So fucking dirty, but in my lust-addled brain, it's the hottest thing I've ever heard. Power shifts between us again, and now Marcus is in control. Now he's the one commanding me to come, and I'm the one who wants to obey.

And I do. I moan, an orgasm rippling through me in tight, hot waves. Vaguely, I hear Marcus answer with a moan, I feel his cock throb against my tongue. His fingers tighten in my hair, and in some part of my brain, I register that he's telling me he's going to come.

But as my body bucks and pleasure floods me, I don't want to stop. I don't want to let go. Not until he's jerking against my tongue and I taste the salty heat of his orgasm sliding down my throat.

I collapse on the floor, and Marcus joins me. We lie beside each other, breathing heavily, clothes askew, saying nothing for a long time until Marcus throws a hand across my stomach and pulls me close to his hammering heart.

"Why," he growls between breaths, "didn't you wear underwear this morning?"

20

MARCUS

Between one heartbeat and the next, Penny's face turns beet red. And I have to laugh, because after everything we just did, *that's* what makes her blush?

"Well," she starts. "Here's the thing."

"Mm," I answer, curling my body around hers. We're lying on the floor, limbs intertwined, in a little bubble of post-coital bliss. In an hour, I'll probably regret what just happened. Logic will re-enter my mind. Right now, though, it's heaven.

"You remember Nikita? My friend? She sang karaoke with me at Bonnie's party."

"Vampire dominatrix nun," I murmur into Penny's hair.

She lets out a little giggle that makes something twist in my chest. She laughs so easily, but it always feels like a gift.

"Yeah, her," Penny says. "Well, she came over to my place to get ready before we went to Bonnie's, and she saw my underwear drawer."

My brows tug together. "Okay…"

Penny clears her throat, and her butt wiggles at the same

time, nestling against my crotch. I shift my arm so she can use it as a pillow and pull her tight to my body. Perfect.

"I think the only word I can use for Nikki's reaction is 'horrified,'" Penny continues. "She went to the kitchen and grabbed tongs to take my underwear out of the drawer and demanded that I explain."

If Penny weren't laughing so hard, I'd be demanding where this Nikita chick lives so I could go ask her what the hell her problem is.

"What the hell is her problem?"

"Um, well, you see..." Penny clears her throat. "I hadn't really bought any new underwear in a while. Like, a *long* while. Over eight years. So she was right, really. My underwear was a disgrace."

The tips of Penny's ears, which are the only bit of skin I can see on her head from this angle, are bright red. My lips curl. "Oh? I didn't mind the look of your underwear on Saturday night."

I didn't think it was possible for Penny's ears to get redder, but they do. It makes me smile.

"Those were new," she says. "We had to go out and buy them. She paid for them, actually. Said she was making a donation to a good cause."

"It was a good cause, in the end," I say, kissing Penny's neck. "But you still haven't told me why you weren't wearing undies *today*."

"Well." Penny giggles once more, and incomprehensibly, it makes me smile in response again. I don't smile at giggles. I don't even smile when babies giggle! Giggling is not something I enjoy. Unless Penny Littleton is doing it, apparently. "We sort of ritually disposed of all my old underwear, bought those things I was wearing at the party from a nearby sex shop, and I said I'd go buy all-new undies on my own. But then it was Sunday and I didn't want to go out, so I figured I'd go buy some after work today."

"So you went commando."

"So I went commando," she repeats.

I let out a low growl. "I guess I can accept that explanation."

"It worked out in the end," she says, turning her head to give me the most brilliant, beaming smile I've ever seen. It strikes me right in the chest. And lying on the floor with my pants undone, my arms around a beautiful woman made of sunlight and strawberries, I feel like the sun's shining down on me and only me.

So I kiss her. Stopping myself from pressing a gentle kiss to Penny's lips would be impossible right now. We're like two magnets, drawn to each other.

There'll be hell to pay when the reckoning time comes. I already know it. I don't get to act out my desires and urges without paying for it later. I don't get to *feel* anything for a woman without knowing it'll blow up in my face.

But right now I can kiss her, tell myself everything will work out. I can tell myself it's just sex. It's just fucking. It's lust, pure and simple.

We pull apart, and Penny rests her head in the crook of my shoulder and my chest. I run my fingers through fine, straight, red strands of her hair, marveling at its silkiness.

"Why hadn't you bought any underwear in so long?" I ask. "Not that I mind the result. If you came here every day and never wore underwear again, I wouldn't complain."

She huffs, giving me a playful smack. Then she goes quiet.

"Penny?" I pull back, trying to see her face. She keeps her head curved down toward her chest, and all I can see is her forehead and the fan of her lashes on her cheeks.

Her lips purse slightly, and she lets out a small breath. "Okay. I'm going to tell you something, but you should know that it's private. Okay? So I don't want you to tell anyone else."

A shift occurs in my chest, some deep, seismic clashing of tectonic plates inside me. This woman, who gave me her body, who gave me her smiles and her joy, wants to give me more of herself. I don't deserve it.

"You don't have to tell me anything you don't want to," I hear myself say, but it's a lie. A dam has broken between us, and now I want it all. I've tasted her, I've kissed her, I've felt her skin against mine, I've heard her laugh and seen her smile. I want everything else. The good, the bad. I want her wrapped up around me like this every night, in my bed—in *our* bed. I hadn't even realized I was missing something until Penny gave it to me.

It's not sex. Well, it's not *only* sex. It's more than that. It's the sun breaking through dense, gray clouds.

No. I inhale sharply and remind myself—this is physical. We're attracted to each other, and we're scratching an itch.

Right?

"I know I don't have to tell you," she responds. "But in a way, it kind of helps to say it out loud. The more I talk about it, the easier it seems to get." She lifts her head up and meets my eyes. "And I kind of want you to know." Bunching her lips to the side, she shakes her head. "Maybe that makes me stupid."

"Why would that make you stupid?"

"Because you're my boss! You're a big-shot billionaire, and I'm just a little insect who walks your dog." Her face is drawn, serious.

My brows shoot down low over my eyes. "Don't say that." An insect? I want to crush whoever made her feel that way about herself. I kiss the tip of Penny's nose. "Tell me about your underwear."

The seriousness of her expression breaks, and a smile stretches over her lips. "If I had a nickel…"

I huff a laugh, then haul her up on top of me. She straddles my hips like her body was made to fit there, sitting up so the weight of her is pressed on my lap. I'd be lying if I said the weight of her on top of me like this didn't make my body come alive. I can feel the heat of her against the thin barrier of my boxer-briefs, and I start thickening in response.

Penny fusses with one of the buttons of my shirt. "Okay." She takes a deep breath, and I try to think chaste thoughts.

"Okay," she repeats, eyes still on the button of my shirt. I put my hands on her thighs, just below the hem of her skirt. She lets out another deep breath and nods. "I had this boyfriend, back in college. His name was Billy."

She undoes the button, runs a little, soft finger between my pecs, feeling the coarseness of my hair, then does the button back up again. I let my thumbs stroke her thighs in long, slow movements. There's an intimacy to this moment that has nothing to do with sex, no matter how much I want to tell myself the opposite.

"Billy seemed like a good guy, but then he got really controlling. It happened slowly. First, it was the clothing I wore. He didn't like when I wore short skirts and dresses.

Then it was all skirts and dresses. Then it was anything tight. Then it was makeup. If he saw me talking to a guy—no matter who that guy was—he'd blow up on me. He'd read my messages and emails, he demanded to know all my passwords, he turned my friends against me. He'd call in sick to work until he got me fired, and then he convinced me to move in with him. He pretended to be me when he emailed professors and bosses. Got me in a lot of trouble in my classes, then lied about doing it. He was way better at computers than I was, so he was able to cover his tracks pretty easily."

She toys with the button again, and I stay silent.

"You know that saying about boiling a frog? How if you throw a frog in a pot of boiling water, it'll jump right out? If you put it in *cold* water and slowly heat it, the frog doesn't notice, and it allows itself to be boiled alive." Penny lets out a breath. "I was the frog. I let myself be boiled to death." She closes her eyes and gives her head a sharp, violent shake. "No. I take that back. *He* did it to me. I didn't do it to myself. It was his fault, not mine."

My hands squeeze on her thighs.

Penny straightens her shoulders and puts a palm flat on my chest. "It's okay," she says, as if she can sense the tension mounting inside me. I want to find this Billy asshole and rip his fucking head off. But Penny just moves to the next button on my shirt and starts playing with that one.

"It got worse, and before I knew it, I was completely isolated. And then I tried to break up with him." Penny gulps, her slim throat working hard, as if there's a rock lodged inside it. "He didn't take it well. He..." She takes a deep breath. "He stalked me."

She lets out a little laugh, and finally lifts her eyes to meet mine. I don't know what she sees there, but her expression softens. Maybe I'm hiding the incandescent rage erupting inside me better than I think I am.

"You have no idea how many years it took me to actually admit that to myself, let alone other people. That my ex-boyfriend turned into an abusive stalker and ruined my life. But I just told you."

My throat is full of gravel when I say, "What happened next?"

She shrugs, eyes returning to my shirt, to the buttons that seem to fascinate and distract her. "I ran away. Dropped out of college and enrolled in a community college. Changed my number, started documenting everything, cut everyone out of my life. Moved from Long Island to the city. Became a hermit."

"Started your business?" I guess.

She smiles a little, as if to herself. "Yeah. Well, first I started walking dogs. They understood me, you know?"

I nod. "Yeah. I know."

"And I was spending so much time by myself, locked up in my apartment, so I started sewing a lot and walking dogs to pay the bills. I met Brian at the park near my house. He'd walk his dog at the same time as a couple of my old clients. He commented on the bow ties and encouraged me to sell them. Then the business just sort of grew from there." Her tongue darts out to lick her lips, and she gives me a little shrug. "And this year, I finally feel like I'm moving on from all that pain. It feels good."

I'm afraid to move. This moment is crystalline, humming between us. Penny Littleton sits astride me, a five-foot-nothing redhead who walked through hell on bare feet and made it out the other side with her soul intact. I can't even put into words how that makes me feel. It's a gift. A privilege. To know that she shared her past with me—just like she shared her body.

It scares the absolute daylights out of me. I'm not worthy of that kind of gift, of that kind of intimacy. Ever since the balcony, I've been wondering how long it'll last, or how best to keep my distance. I've been building my walls up thicker and stronger ever since I met her, and she's been tearing hers down.

I'm not worthy of her. Not by a long shot.

"And you never bought new underwear?" I finally ask, trying to bring my swirling thoughts back to earth. It's supposed to come out as a joke, but my voice is lower and rougher than I intended.

Penny laughs that beautiful, glorious laugh. "I never bought new underwear. There was no point. I didn't want or need to be sexy. For eight years, since I ran away from Billy, I kind of turned that part of me off. The part that wants sex and intimacy. I decided that men were bad, and I should stay away from them."

Her eyes climb up to mine, and my carefully erected defenses shatter.

"Until we kissed," I rasp.

A small smile. "Until we kissed."

We say those words, but we both know what they really mean: *Until you.*

Our gazes hold for a moment, then Penny blows out a breath and sits back on my hips. My body reacts as you'd expect to direct contact between her bare pussy and my underwear-covered cock. My violent throbbing makes her eyes twinkle.

"I have no control over what he does," I say, glancing down at my crotch.

"Mm-hmm," she answers, rocking her hips slightly.

My vision goes white. "Penny." It comes out as a choked gasp.

"You know, one thing about my self-imposed celibacy is that I forgot sex is fun. And I forgot it feels good." Her hips rock, angling just right, and my hands squeeze on her thighs. Her breath hitches, lush mouth falling open.

"You told me you wanted to take things slow," I grate, trying to regain control over my body. "This doesn't feel slow, Penny."

"Maybe I was wrong," she says breathlessly. "Maybe I've been taking things slow for eight years, and it's time for me to move fast. Strike...while the iron is...hot."

I close my eyes at the feel of her core against the fabric of my underwear. The heat of her feels too good for words. "What are you saying?" I finally ask.

She meets my gaze, big blue eyes clear. Her tongue darts out to lick her lower lip. "I'm saying I'm ready. I want you, Marcus." Another hitched breath. Another rock of her needy clit against my cock. "Right now."

21

PENNY

RECKLESS. Impulsive. Horny.

Three words I never thought I'd use to describe myself.

After telling Marcus about my past, it feels like something snapped inside me.

I've been holding myself back for so long. I've been afraid for So. Damn. Long.

Why?

Whatever's happening between me and Marcus, it probably won't last. As soon as he no longer needs me to watch Mackenzie and I move out of this workshop, things will fizzle out. Even though that makes pain slice through my chest, I push it aside.

Maybe I can use this moment, this connection. Running into Nikita was the first step toward the new me. Agreeing to move my workshop here was the next one. Going to Bonnie's party was another step.

Hooking up with Marcus on the balcony was a leap into the unknown.

I'm afraid of the consequences. Afraid I'll get hurt. Afraid another man will use his power and influence to terrorize me.

But I can't let that fear control me. Not anymore. Not for the rest of my life.

There's so much living to be done. I've missed out on so many parties and friends and lovers. I've shut myself away because I was terrified of being hurt again. Terrified of being stalked and harassed.

But this...this is different. I'm in control here. As long as I keep my heart insulated, maybe I can use this as another step toward the new me.

I *like* kissing Marcus. Touching him. Having his hands on my body, feeling the heat of his skin against mine. His cock is hard beneath me, and I *crave* it. I want to feel it inside me so badly, I can hardly put it into words.

He listened to my story without judgment, and he didn't blame me for what Billy did. He seemed angry, protective. Isn't that as good a reason as any to trust him with my body? It doesn't mean I have to give him my heart.

I'm young, and healthy, and fit. I want sex. Is that so bad? Can I not be irresponsible, for once? Do something wild?

My hips rock against him.

"Penny." He says my name like it means something, like it's been ripped from his throat by force. His fingers dig into the flesh of my thighs, and I wonder if they'll leave marks. I hope they do. I want to have proof that this happened, that I was here, that a man touched me and I enjoyed it.

"You feel so good," I hear myself say as my hips jerk, pleasure winding through my lower half.

I'll never date him—the sexy, billionaire CEO-slash-entrepreneur and his dog walker? Please. I'm attracted to him, I have a silly crush on him, but Marcus Walsh and I aren't on the same level.

But maybe he can help me out of this hole I've dug around myself. Maybe sleeping with him can be another leap in my new beginning.

As long as I don't let him get too close, I'll be safe. As long as I keep my heart as protected as I can—but that should be easy. Marcus Walsh doesn't want to date me. I'm a curiosity, I'm convenient. I'm the woman who moved into his spare room for a short amount of time.

Might as well make the most of it.

He lets out a tortured noise, hips bucking beneath me. I gasp as the movement hits me just right, pleasure shattering through me. *Yes*. That's what I want. More. All of it.

Reaching between us, I feel his length over the fabric of his underwear, stroking my palm over him. He lets out another strangled grunt. His eyes open, meeting mine. They're dark, dangerous.

"You're sure?" he says, and his voice sounds almost alien, it's so rough. It turns me on another notch. I did that to his voice. My hand and my hips and my body turned his voice into a wild rasp.

I nod. "Yes."

The next few moments happen quickly. He levers himself up, pulling my dress up with him. Before I know it, it's off my body and tossed across the room, and Marcus's hands are braced along my ribs. I'm naked. His mouth comes down on my breast and I fall back, arching into the feeling.

I lose myself in him, in his touch. He bites my nipple and strokes my side. He clamps a hand on my hip and grinds my hips into his, drawing choked little gasps from me.

Then I'm on my back. I don't know how it happens. One moment, I'm straddled across his lap, and the next, I'm on the floor with my legs spread wide. Marcus's hands shake as he reaches for his pockets, pawing for his wallet. He flips through it, then swears.

"I don't have a condom. Do you?" His hair is mussed. I've never seen him look this undone. His eyes are hazy, meeting mine for a moment before dropping down to my lips, my breasts, my core.

His gaze feels like a physical touch. Heat flows where he looks, and I never want him to stop. "Um. No." I let out a little laugh. "I don't have a condom." Why would I have a condom? I haven't had sex for years. The only reason I'm still on the pill is because I get hormonal acne.

My head is spinning. I can see the outline of his cock, and I can hardly think of anything else. He's kneeling between my spread legs, both of us breathing heavily. I'm cold without his hands on me. My nipples are hard and wet from his mouth.

I need him. It's like a monster inside me, this desire. Eight years—longer—of suppressed wants, of ignored urges. My hand slides between my legs to try to ease some of the ache.

In a distant part of my brain, I wonder if I should be embarrassed at the brazenness of my movements. I've never touched myself like this in front of a man. I've never wanted to. But right now, it feels like I'll die if I don't get some relief. I feel empty, achy, needy.

"Christ," he swears, hands landing on my knees. His eyes are completely dark as they watch me touch myself. His own hand slides inside his clothes, pulling out the hard length of his cock. I gulp down a hard breath at the sight of that big fist moving up and down his shaft in rough, jerky movements.

I'm not myself. I'm a creature of lust. I'll pay the consequences later.

"I'm on the pill," I tell him, watching him work his cock in increasingly fast movements. "Please, Marcus."

He inhales sharply, one hand sliding down to join mine at the apex of my thighs. "I'm clean," he grates in that deep voice. "I swear." His fingers thrust inside me while I touch myself.

I nearly come apart, arching off the floor with a cry. "I believe you." I roll my hips. I've lost control.

"You're sure?" His eyes don't move from my center, watching us both pleasure me together. His other hand pauses, squeezing the base of his shaft as he closes his eyes and inhales deeply, like he's trying to get himself under control.

I did that to him. Me. "Fuck, yes, I'm sure," I answer.

A long exhale, and then he's on his feet, shucking his pants off in a quick, unceremonious movement. His knees thump on the floor as he comes back down to me, both hands landing above my shoulders.

"Put it in," he commands in a tone that brooks no argument.

So I reach between us and do as he says. And when he pushes deep, I lose my ever-loving mind.

It feels so good to be stretched, invaded, claimed. My knees fall open as a whimper escapes my lips, my hands moving to his hips to urge him deeper. Slow, inexorable thrusts tear at the fabric of my reality.

I'd forgotten.

I'd forgotten how good it feels. Maybe I never knew. Maybe it's never felt this good. Marcus groans, his head buried in the crook of my neck, one hand sliding down to squeeze my breast for a moment before continuing down to my thigh.

He hooks my knee over his elbow and thrusts hard. I see stars.

"You feel me inside you?" His voice is dark, smoky. "Feel me deep, right where I'm supposed to be?"

I nod.

"You came to my house with no panties on. Sat here all day with your bare pussy on my chair. Didn't you?" Another rough thrust.

I make an unintelligible noise that might be acknowledgment.

"But you knew what you were doing. You wanted this all along. Didn't you, Penny? Wanted me inside you. Wanted my cock."

"Yes," I whine. "Yes, I wanted you."

"Ever since the party. You been thinking about my cock, haven't you? Been dying to suck it, dying to feel it inside you. You've been greedy for it."

I nod, gasping. It's true.

At some point, my orgasm overtakes me. I don't know when. I don't know how. All I know is that I'm completely consumed by this moment, by Marcus. My nails dig into his skin and my mouth falls open as I cry his name. Sweat slicks my skin and his. His lips find mine for a kiss, until I bite his lower lip.

That seems to do something, break something inside him, some final restraint. He grunts, then sits back on his knees, his hands moving to my waist. His hands almost span the whole way around me, holding me in place. He pulls me up so my back is arched and the only parts of me touching the ground are my heels and my upper shoulders and head. He holds me there, driving in and out of me so deep and hard I can't think. I can barely breathe.

"Touch yourself," he grates, eyes on the space where we're joined. "Just like before, Penny. I want you to touch yourself while I fuck you."

Oh, God. I should have known he'd be like this. I should have known he'd be merciless, he'd break me apart and put me back together again.

What else can I do but listen to him? With my body arched and in his control, his hands still clamped around my waist, I reach one hand between my legs and use the other to play with my breast. I let go of all inhibitions. I forget about all the things that scare me. Years of restraint and fear are annihilated by the desire Marcus creates in me. Nothing matters but this moment, on the floor of his spare room.

He finds his release a moment after I do. I feel it, deep inside me. It sends another bolt of pure desire through me. We both cry out, bodies bucking, arching, collapsing. It takes me a long, long while to catch my breath, to come back to myself.

Marcus rolls off me, throwing an arm over his face. He exhales. "Damn, Penny," he whispers.

"Nnghhfff," I answer, body still twitching.

Time stops. I lie on the floor, naked, thoroughly fucked, unable to do anything but breathe.

I finally come back to myself when Marcus props himself on an elbow and brushes my hair off my forehead. His eyes have returned to their usual stunning shade of green, and his face looks more relaxed than I've ever seen it.

"Hey," he says.

"Hi." My heart squeezes. Now that the haze of lust is starting to clear, I wonder if I just made a mistake. He's so beautiful like this, when he isn't scowling. I take a finger and stroke his brow, tracing his eyebrows.

Why would a man like him want a woman like me? When he decides he's done with me, it'll hurt. A lot.

But maybe... Maybe, it'll be worth it. After all, I just had sex for the first time in years, and I loved it. I feel beautifully achy. Sated. Once this is over, dealing with bruised emotions might be a fair price to pay for me to emerge from my self-imposed life as a recluse.

Maybe, once I recover from him, I'll be able to live life to its fullest.

Or maybe, he'll toss me aside and I'll end up more broken than I was before.

"I'd like to take you out," he tells me in the silence of the room.

I blink. I was expecting him to say something about work, about having to leave. I was expecting him to retreat and make me feel used and discarded. "Take me out?"

He nods.

My brows tug together. "Like...a date?"

A glimmer in his eyes, another stroke of his hand over my hair. "Like a date."

"Oh." I blink.

Marcus frowns. "Is that a no?"

"What? No. No, it's not a no. I just thought..." I shake my head and hear myself let out a nervous snort. "No, I just didn't think..."

"Didn't think I'd want to take you out?"

Heat rises up my neck and over my cheeks. "I don't know. I figured this was kind of like...a one-and-done situation."

There's a tiny movement of his head, almost like a flinch.

"Like why would *you* want to date *me*, you know?" I slide my gaze away from his. It's important that I keep my distance from him. He might be the first man I've slept with in nearly a decade, and that makes him special. But it doesn't mean *I'm* special to *him*.

If I'm going to recover from this when it's over, I need to try to stay on solid ground.

Marcus lets out a low rumble. "Why wouldn't I want to date you?"

That makes my mouth snap shut, and Marcus leans down to kiss it. Then his mouth moves to my breast, and he spends a few moments kissing that, too. Thoughts flee from my mind again.

Before I can get too distracted, he jumps up to his feet and extends a hand to help me up. "I have to go. Are you free tomorrow night?"

"Um. Yeah," I answer. "Sure."

A devastating smile. An arm around my waist, pulling me close. Another kiss.

When he lets me go, I nearly fall over.

He grabs his pants and slides them on in a quick movement, tucking in the shirt he's still wearing before grabbing his shoes. With jerky movements, I follow his lead and get dressed. Once I have my dress over my shoulders, he comes over to tuck a strand of hair behind my ear before kissing my forehead. "I'll pick you up at seven. Wear something nice."

22

PENNY

I LET OUT a screech and kick the mountain of clothing on my bedroom floor. "'Something nice?' What the hell is 'something nice?' What does that even *mean*?"

Nikita smashes a pillow over her head and starts laughing into it.

"Stop it." I shove my finger in her direction. "Stop that."

She lifts the pillow and laughs in my face.

"You are the worst girlfriend in the history of girlfriends," I announce. "No help whatsoever." The buzzer sounds, so I stomp across to the front door to answer it. "Yeah?"

"It's Bonnie," she says over the speaker. "Let me in. I have wine and accessories."

I buzz her up and turn to see Nikita hunting through my cabinets.

"Wine glasses are above the sink," I grumble, falling onto my couch with a low *oof*. I throw my arm over my eyes like the dramatic ball of nerves I am. I don't move when I hear the click of high heels in the hallway outside, or the door opening and my two newest friends greeting each other.

I don't move until someone takes my hand and wraps it around a wine glass.

Bonnie arches a fine, golden eyebrow at me. "I see we've entered the stage of despair."

"I have nothing to wear on a date with a billionaire," I say, burying my nose in my glass of wine. It's delicious, which, of course it is. Bonnie probably has fancy friends with degrees in wine tasting. Or whatever. *She* would have a million outfits for dates with billionaires where she's supposed to wear something nice. She wouldn't be in over her head at all. She wouldn't still be reeling from the body-shattering sex she had yesterday.

"What are you going to do with him?" Bonnie takes a seat beside me and glances at Nikita, then at me.

"Hell if I know. I'm just supposed to 'wear something nice.'" I sound like an overtired, grumpy toddler.

Bonnie hums. "That's not overly specific. What are our options?"

"Nothing." I huff. "No options. I have nothing to wear."

Nikita starts laughing again. Damn her. "I missed you, Penny," she says fondly.

And how can I stay mad at *that*? I missed her too. The jerk. I glare at her to let her know I care.

My phone rings, and my heart takes off.

"Is that him?" Bonnie asks, eyes wide.

I grab my phone from its charger in the corner of the room and look at the tiny, pixelated screen. "It's Brian," I answer. I stick my thumbnail in my mouth and start chewing as the phone keeps ringing. I glance at the two women and arch my brows. "Would it be terrible if I didn't answer?"

They exchange a glance, and Nikki shrugs a shoulder. "You're busy," she notes.

Bonnie nods. "You can call him tomorrow."

"What if it's about the business?" I ask, letting my gaze slide back to the chipped, dented flip phone in my hand.

"There's nothing he can tell you tonight that will collapse your business that can't be dealt with tomorrow," Bonnie says sagely.

I bunch my lips to the side, let out a sigh, and set my phone down. It makes me feel horribly guilty to ignore Brian like that. He was my only friend for a long time. He's my business partner. I shouldn't be blanking his calls.

But with how we left things after Bonnie's party, I'm not sure I want to talk to him right now. How would he react if he knew I'm going out with Marcus tonight? Do I really want to deal with another sanctimonious lecture?

"Okay," Bonnie says, setting her wine glass down like she means business. "I've known Marcus a couple of years, and he doesn't strike me as the kind of guy who will take you somewhere overly fancy. He's not that kind of man."

I stare at her, nodding. "Okay..."

"What do you mean?" Nikita asks, crossing her long legs and leaning back as she sits on my armchair. I remember her sitting just like that in a similar armchair in our shared apartment, nearly ten years ago, and some of my bad mood ebbs.

"Well," Bonnie replies, "Marcus is kind of a dark horse. After Emil and Dani had their baby, he bought the family—all five of them, including Emil's two kids—a trip to Disney World. Except he somehow wrangled a tour of the inner workings of some of the rides. Dani thought it was the coolest thing ever, all that engineering." She shakes her head. "It was beyond me, really, but Emil and Dani are into that kind of technical thing. They fell in love over car engines, for crying out loud. And the kids learned a lot. Don't ask me how he got that kind of backstage access. I have no idea."

I frown. "So what does that mean for tonight?"

Bonnie's eyes glimmer as a slow smile spreads over her lips. "It means he's going to be *thoughtful*."

My stomach does a flip and a twist and sticks the landing. I put a hand over my middle. "That's somehow worse."

Nikita laughs. "Oh, come on, Penny. Poor you! You have to go on a date with a handsome, thoughtful billionaire who loves eating your pussy. Must be hard."

My face explodes. Or at least, that's how it feels with how hot it gets between one second and the next. "Nikki," I chide.

"Come on." She stands. "You like dresses. I saw a pleated silk midi skirt in your pile of clothes that would look cute."

"It would also provide easy access," Bonnie adds, topping up her wine.

I glare at the two of them. "Easy access for *what*?"

The two women exchange a glance, then start giggling. Nikki winks. "You know what, Penny."

WHEN MY PHONE rings and Marcus's name appears on the little screen, I'm dressed and made up and I've had three quarters of a glass of wine—enough to take the edge off of my nerves, not enough to feel drunk. Nikki and Bonnie send me off like proud grandmothers, sneaking out through the back door of my apartment building while I head toward the front.

I'm wearing my silk midi skirt, which hits me right at mid-calf. It's black, so I've paired it with black booties and sheer tights. Nikita lamented the lack of easy access with the tights, but I reminded her it was November and I wasn't really wanting to freeze my tush off for the sake of sexual satisfaction.

Up top, I'm wearing a malachite-green camisole with a dipping neckline and a blazer I made myself. It's a black-and-white houndstooth pattern, and it hits me exactly at my hip. My tailoring skills aren't incredible, but this blazer fits me perfectly and I'm fairly proud of it.

I'm hoping my outfit is classy enough to allow me entrance to whatever fancy restaurant Marcus might have reserved, while being casual enough not to stand out if we go somewhere "thoughtful." I feel like I've run a marathon, and all I've done is get dressed.

"Penny," Marcus says, standing next to the waiting car. His eyes are low and dark as he takes me in, and before I know it, his arms are around me and he's kissing me.

How did this happen? A couple of days ago, I never would have imagined I'd be kissing Marcus outside my apartment.

He pulls away. "You look beautiful." His finger trails over the lapel of my blazer, down to the neckline of my top. His skin feels warm against mine, drugging.

I take a quick look at his outfit. Dark jeans, a navy cashmere sweater, and a black peacoat. Not too fancy. Maybe my outfit will be okay.

"Not bad yourself," I answer. He smiles, then guides me to the car. I slide into the back seat and clip myself in, heart fluttering.

I'm on a date. I haven't been on a date in years! How do I act? What do I say? What do I do with my hands?

Deep breaths, Penny. Try not to think about the fact that the man sitting next to you screwed your brains out on the floor of his spare bedroom.

"Where are we going?" I ask once we get going, my voice only squeaking a little.

Marcus just smiles. "It's a surprise."

"I hate surprises," I lie. My heart does a backflip.

He glances at me and arches a brow. "I don't believe you."

I stick out my tongue at that, because I'm a grown, sophisticated woman. Marcus laughs in response, which makes a delicious, tingling heat explode all over my skin.

He reaches over and takes one of my clammy hands in his, threading his fingers through mine. It feels normal, somehow, which sends my mind scurrying in a thousand different directions.

We drive for an eternity, for the blink of an eye, into the heart of Midtown. The Garment District.

Will jumps out and opens the door, allowing Marcus and me to exit the back seat. Marcus puts his hand on my lower back and leads me to the front door of a tall, stone building. In the fading light of the chilly evening, the building looks stately and imposing, if a bit rough around the edges. It must have been beautiful in its heyday nearly a hundred years ago, with square, geometric columns set into the front of the building with Art Deco details.

"In here," Marcus says, and leads me to a set of revolving glass doors. We enter onto echoing stone floors and walk across to a bank of elevators. Once inside, Marcus presses the button for the seventeenth floor, then stands beside me, his hand still on my back.

Being this close to him is comfortable and stressful all at once. I want to rip his clothes off and pick up where we left off yesterday, but I also want to run away screaming at how new and uncomfortable this is. I'm in a small space with a man—with my boss—and I don't feel any of the usual panic I normally feel. I should be protecting myself. Should be keeping a distance.

But it's addictive, this feeling of comfort, security, illicit thrill. The feel of his hand on my back. The smell of his cologne in the small space of the elevator. The taste of his lips on mine.

I want more.

The doors open, and a tall man greets us on the other side. He's wearing a black turtleneck and little round glasses, and his bald pate shines under the fluorescent lights above.

"Marcus," he says, smiling. "Welcome. And you must be Penny. My name is Raphael. Come in."

I step into a wonderland of fabric and sewing. Vast tables are set up in the middle of the room, with sewing machines set up at one end. The far side of the room has mannequins in various states of undress, with gowns and pants and beautifully draped garments in the process of being created.

Then the penny drops. "You're Raphael Garcia," I say, eyes as wide as Bear's when he sees the treat bag come out of the pantry.

Raphael smiles. "The one and only, lovely. Come in. Marcus said you were a designer yourself."

I nearly choke. He told an *actual* designer of *human fashion* that I'm a clothing designer. The man must be out of his mind. I whirl my head around to glare at Marcus, but his face is impassive.

He meets my gaze, and I swear I see him wink. He presses his hand over the small of my back to get me moving to follow Raphael into the space.

"We moved into this building just over a year ago," he tells us. "This history of the Garment District is inspiring to me. Being here, knowing we're in the same space as so many textile manufacturers from times past, it helps me create." Raphael walks to one of the mannequins and unpins a pleat, readjusting it a fraction of an inch. He sweeps his arm around. "This is where we bring designs to life, but I have a feeling you'll be more interested in the next room." Raphael smiles at me. "The textiles."

We walk into a dream. I'm no longer in the lead in the She Who Dies With The Most Fabric Wins competition, and I don't even care. Rolls and swags and stacks of it surround me on all sides, as far as the eye can see. Prints and patterns, sequins, metallics, scraps and samples.

I suck in a hard breath and let it out slowly. "Wow."

"Marcus said you'd be interested in designing your own print," he says, leading me to a computer on the far end of the room. "We are known for our prints and colors here, so it became important to be able to hand-draw ideas and have them come to life right here in the studio." He jiggles a mouse to bring the computer to life. "Marcus tells me you have a similar design philosophy."

"Um," I say, wondering if I should admit that yes, I enjoy prints and patterns and color—for *dog clothes*.

I'm going to kill Marcus. This is the most embarrassing moment of my life.

But it'll be worse if I don't say anything. I square my shoulders and face the world-renowned fashion designer offering to let me design a custom fabric on his machine. "Mr. Garcia, I'm not sure how much Marcus told you, but I'm not actually a fashion designer. I, um..." I clear my throat. "You see, I design clothes, but they're not..." *Gah! Why is this so hard?* I take a deep breath. "I make dog clothes," I finally blurt.

Raphael freezes, his thick brows drawing together. The light shines on his head as he tilts his head. "Dog...clothes?"

I nod. "Mm-hmm." I smile, and I think it might look a bit deranged. "Clothes for dogs. Custom outfits and some costumes as well, but mostly bow ties, rain jackets, and sweaters."

"Dog clothes," Raphael repeats, glancing at Marcus with an indecipherable expression on his face.

I'm flushing so hard I feel lightheaded. "I'm not sure I should use your computer. It's not... I'm not... I'm not a designer. Not like you. And computers and I just don't mix."

Marcus shifts beside me and pulls out his phone. "Here, Raph," he says. "Look."

Raphael takes the phone and starts flicking his finger over the screen. I want the floor to open up and swallow me.

Thoughtful? This is supposed to be *thoughtful* of Marcus? This is the most horrifyingly embarrassing moment of my life. I would prefer an endless engineering lecture on the inner workings of Disney World rides to *this*.

"Wow," Raphael says, frowning, then starts laughing. "Oh, this one is great. And on trend for this year, too." He flips the phone around to show me the dog tuxedo I made on a whim a couple of weeks ago. "Wide lapels. Very good."

He's laughing at me. I close my eyes. "I'm sorry to waste your time, Mr. Garcia. Thank you for showing me your workshop. It's beautiful. And I'm very jealous of your fabric collection." I turn to Marcus. "Let's go."

"But you haven't made a print yet," Raphael says, handing the phone back to Marcus. He frowns at me. "Did you not want to make a custom fabric? From what I can tell, you're very talented." His eyes coast over my outfit. "You made that jacket, didn't you?"

My breath hitches. I nod.

Just then, a little dog comes trotting over from the corner of the room. I hadn't noticed the dog bed in an alcove, but now I see it's upholstered in one of Raphael Garcia's own fabrics. The designer bends over to pick up the scrawny Italian greyhound, kissing the dog's head.

"What do you think, Bert? Would you like a new outfit to wear for our next show? You want Penny to design something for you?"

Ho...lee...shit. Raphael Garcia isn't serious about that... Is he?

Bert yawns, tail wagging as he snuffles against Raphael's face.

Raphael laughs. "Yes you do." He glances at me. "Well, come on. I'll show you how the software works. I'm curious to see what you come up with."

Marcus's hand slides up my back to rest on my shoulder. "What do you think, Penny?" His eyes are smiling even though his lips are still.

"Gnnfff," I reply.

"You'll do great." This time his lips smile too.

So I nod, sit down at the computer, and design my very

first custom fabric, right here in the New York City Garment District, under the watchful eye of a real fashion designer.

And I think I might have just fallen in head-over-heels, scream-it-from-the-rooftops, never-coming-back-from-this love with Marcus Walsh.

23

MARCUS

PENNY'S CHEEKS are flushed and red as she clicks away on the computer, jumping every time the machine makes a noise. She's so damn cute. I can't stop staring at her. I no longer hate her cuteness. It was a lie, anyway. I've always loved how adorable she is.

Raphael is besotted with her, of course. He's pulled up a chair and is intermittently helping her work the computer, kissing his dog, and scrolling through her online store to see her creations.

"Smaller prints work better for dogs," she tells Raph, "because you have less area to work with. Larger-scale prints tend to get lost, unless you're dressing a St. Bernard or a Great Dane or something."

"Mm," the designer says, nodding. He points something out on the screen, and Penny makes a change. She reaches over and gives Bert a little scratch on the head, and the dog crawls over to rest his front paws and head on her thighs.

There's a feeling in my chest that's unfamiliar—a twisting, jumping warmth. Every time I look at that wrinkle in

Penny's nose when she's trying to figure something out on the computer, followed by the triumphant little smile, it makes me feel like I've just seen one of the wonders of the world. Her cheeks are flushed, her freckles are numerous, and I'm too far gone to care.

My phone buzzes in my pocket for the thousandth time. Probably work. I haven't wanted to check it, because I've been enjoying seeing Penny laugh, seeing her create. But I pull the phone out, ready to chew Todd's ear off for bothering me when I told him I wasn't to be contacted tonight.

But it's not Todd, or anyone from work. It's my mother.

And she's called me twelve times already in the space of three minutes. I take a few steps back and put the phone to my ear. "Mom? What's wrong?"

"Finally," she cries. "Marcus, there's a problem with the kitchen sink. It's spraying everywhere!"

I glance at Penny. "Have you called a plumber?"

"Of course I've called a plumber! No one can make it here in time. We had to turn the water off to the whole building. Now the neighbors are knocking my door down, because they need water for dinner and showers and laundry." A screech in the background, and my mother pulls her head away to yell, "*Anna! Stop it! Leave your brother alone.*" Then her voice gets louder again: "You know plumbers, don't you? You can get someone to come over? *Oliver, no. Both of you. I'm going to count to three!* Marcus? Are you there?"

"I'll make some calls."

There's a crash. My mother lets out a low curse, then shouts to the kids in the background again. "I'm losing it, Marcus. Ollie isn't back for a few hours, and the kids are

going crazy. Can you come over? I need help. Oh, no, no, no...
The water! It's spraying again! Someone turned it back on—"

The line cuts.

I close my eyes, pinching the bridge of my nose. I had the evening all planned out. After touring Raphael's workshop and getting Penny to design a fabric, I was going to take her out to dinner, then go for a midnight tour of the Metropolitan Museum of Art to check out their newest Costume Institute collection.

My plans did *not* include saving my mother from the terror of her misbehaving grandchildren and a plumbing emergency.

I wish I could say my mother can manage. She's Superwoman, but I could hear the strain in her voice, the edge of panic.

I'm the one who's supposed to take care of her. I'm the only one who can. I'm the one propping up this family, the last line of defense against everything that tries to make our lives difficult.

I should be there, instead of going out on a date with my employee. What was I thinking? This is why I don't date. This is why I don't get involved with women. I have enough on my plate as it is. I can't support yet another person, because every time I turn around there's a fire to put out in some yet undiscovered area of my life. I don't have the time, energy, or mental bandwidth to take care of a woman too.

Plus, what happens when Penny starts demanding to be the ultimate priority? What happens when she starts inserting herself between me and my family? Isn't that what's bound to happen? I'll put her first, ignore my family, and then everything will go to shit, exactly like it did before.

What am I even *talking* about? Penny isn't my girlfriend. We fucked once. Kissed a couple of times. I took her out because of some misplaced sense of obligation, because she doesn't strike me as the type of girl who would be okay with casual sex. I'm the asshole who shat where he ate, so I was trying to do some damage control by taking her out on a date. That's all.

Yeah, right. Keep telling yourself that, buddy.

I find Todd's number. Before I can put the phone to my ear, a small hand touches my shoulder. I turn to see Penny looking at me with big, blue eyes.

"Is everything okay?"

I glance back at my phone and speak through a tight jaw. "My mom's having some plumbing issues. I'm going to call Todd and get him to send someone over. She's watching a few of my nieces and nephews, and she sounds overwhelmed." My voice is tense, and I can't meet Penny's eyes.

This is why I don't date. There's always someone who needs me. Penny will probably resent this interruption. She'll think I'm an asshole for not putting her first—because that's how women always react to these situations. They look at me like I'm crazy for being close to my family. They tell me I need to cut the apron strings, but what they don't understand is that my family is *everything* to me. My mother has no one to rely on but me. My brothers and sisters and nieces and nephews would be struggling through life without my help. What kind of asshole would I be if I let that happen? All for what? For that bit of warmth and ecstasy between a woman's legs? Please.

Penny grabs her purse from the desk. "You want to go over there and make sure she's okay?"

248

I shake my head. "It's fine. I'll just call Todd and get the plumber sorted out."

"Okay," Penny says. She smiles kindly at me. "Raphael said my print would be ready to pick up tomorrow, and I don't mind going home if you need to see to your family. Is there anything I can do to help?"

Her words hit me hard, even though she speaks them softly. I don't remember the last time someone asked me if I needed help. Don't remember the last time I could lean on another person, instead of them leaning on me. I'm speechless for a moment.

Penny squeezes my arm. "Go see your mom. There's a subway station nearby, so you don't even need to drop me anywhere." Her smile is bright, blinding. "I got to do something incredibly cool tonight, so it wasn't a total bust. Even though we didn't get to spend much time together."

My world tilts on its axis, and the only thing that makes sense is the smile on Penny's lips. My chest aches so much it's hard to speak, but I manage to shake my head. Then words tumble out of my mouth, unbidden, coming from some place in my heart I've been too afraid to explore. "I don't want to drop you off at home. I want you to come with me."

24

PENNY

As far as first dates go, this one started pretty well. Exploring the inner sanctum of a real fashion designer? Amazing.

Getting to design a custom print with Raphael freaking Garcia sitting beside me? Unbelievable.

But—

Meeting Marcus's mother? *Terrifying.*

This is the first date I've been on in over eight years. The first time I've felt comfortable being in the presence of a man other than Brian. The first man I've *kissed,* let alone done everything else with.

But meeting the parents is a whole other universe of stress. I wring my hands on my lap as we drive to Washington Heights until Marcus reaches over and takes one of my hands in his again. He brings my knuckles to his lips and kisses them one by one.

It does nothing to calm me down. For his part, Marcus looks almost...resigned. Or shellshocked. Or dazed.

"Marcus, what if she hates me?"

"She won't hate you."

"Was this your plan all along? Butter me up with a fancy fashion designer, then *bam*! Going to meet your mother."

"My plan was to take you out to dinner, then go to a private midnight tour of the Met's Costume Institute exhibit. Fixing my mother's kitchen sink while my niece and nephew act like terrors was most definitely *not* the plan." His voice is wry, amused.

"Oh." I say. "Dinner and the Met sounds nice. How did you organize that so quickly?"

He gives me that crinkly-eyed smile of his, just a slight curve of his lips. "I have my ways."

"Although," I say, leaning back in my seat, "you could tell me anything right now. You could say you'd booked a spot on a spaceship to go into orbit for a minute or two, and I wouldn't be able to prove you wrong."

"After we check on my mom, if we have time, we'll head to the Met. The spaceship is being prepared for our second date."

He wants a second date! Eek!

My lips twitch. "Fine." My hand is still in his, and I don't want to remove it. I turn to look at him, watching the street-lights cast him in alternating light and shadow as we drive. "And Marcus?"

"Mm?"

"Thank you. I had fun at Raphael's workshop. I've never done anything like that before."

All he does is squeeze my hand in response.

For the rest of the drive, I wonder if this is going too fast. Within a couple of weeks, my safe, ordered little life has been turned upside down. I mean, I'm sitting here with my body buzzing, wanting to climb over onto my billionaire boss's lap.

I want to do every dirty thing I've ever thought of, and then I want to snuggle up to him and fall asleep on his chest. Me! The near-asexual creature who vowed to never get close to a man again. I'm *holding hands* with him. Meeting his mother.

It's too fast, isn't it? I'll get hurt. I'm tumbling through the void, with no idea when I'm going to hit the ground with a wet splat.

Marcus blew a hole through my defenses with a bazooka, and I'm thanking him for the damage, asking for more. What happens when he gets bored of me? What happens after he no longer needs me to watch Mackenzie and I move my little workshop out of his spare room?

For me, Marcus is a life-altering experience. He's crashing into my heart and bringing me back to life.

But for him, what am I? The flavor of the week? A curiosity? An itch that he'll scratch, then forget about? A convenient piece of ass?

I'm opening myself up to a world of hurt. I'm *trusting* him. Why? How can I trust a man I barely know? One who already has so much more power than I have, being rich, my boss, and well-connected? If this all goes sideways, I'll end up hurt.

His thumb sweeps over the inside of my wrist, soothing. Over and back, he strokes the soft skin there, and it feels almost hypnotic. My worries fade as my body comes alive.

And that's dangerous too, isn't it? All it takes is the touch of his finger on my pulse point, and I'm ready to let him in again.

"We're here," he says a moment before the car comes to a smooth stop. There's a plumber's van parked outside the door, so we double-park long enough for Will to let us out. Marcus puts his hand around my shoulders and leads me to the front door, using a key fob to let us inside. We walk to the elevator, and my stomach twists itself into a pretzel.

I pull away. "I'm not sure about this, Marcus. I mean, a date is one thing. What we did yesterday...that was... That was..."

He arches a brow. "It was what?"

"It was *something*," I say, "but meeting your mom? I haven't been on a date in eight years, and now I'm here?" I shake my head. "What... What's going on? What is this between us? A date, I understand. Sex, yes, okay. But this?" I blink at him, searching his face. "I walk your dog, Marcus. I'm not—"

The elevator door opens, and Marcus herds me inside. Words die on my lips when he presses the button for the third floor, lets the doors slide shut behind him, then cups my face in his hands and kisses me.

I'm wobbling on my feet by the time we step into a tired old hallway. Screams echo from a door to our left, and Marcus leads me there. I'm a zombie. I'm so nervous I could puke.

We enter into a bomb site. Water gushes over the kitchen tiles and onto the living room floor. A small, black-haired girl with a bright-pink cast is throwing crayons at a slightly bigger boy, who looks angry enough to scream. A chihuahua chases the projectiles and pounces on them as they hit the ground. A baby screams in the next room, and an older woman argues with a chubby, short, gray-haired man.

"Mom. Jared." Marcus strides in, and all the action stops all at once.

"Marcus!" the woman cries. "Thank goodness. Jared won't give the plumber access to the utility room."

"He's not on the approved list of contractors," the man says, his face growing redder by the second. "Our plumber can't make it until morning."

"You expect my mother to have no water in her place all night?" Marcus's voice is low and dangerous.

I edge to the side, glancing at the two children in the living room. They're glaring at each other. The dog chews a lime-green crayon like it personally insulted him.

"We can't let non-approved contractors into the building's utility room," Jared replies in a voice that tells me he's repeated that sentence a million times already. "Can't you just turn the water off at the sink?"

A large, potbellied man looms in the kitchen doorway. "The leak's in the wall. I need to turn off the water to the apartment." He glances at Marcus, nods, then starts gathering his tools.

"Wait. Don't leave." Marcus's mother holds up a hand to the plumber, then turns to the building's super. "Jared. Please."

"Jared, can I speak to you outside?" Marcus says, and it would be a brave person who refused him when he's using *that* tone of voice while wearing *that* expression. He looks at the plumber. "You too."

The super and plumber follow him outside, and the door snicks shut.

Marcus's mother's gaze lands on me. Her brows furrow. "Hello," she says.

"Hi." I wave a hand awkwardly. "I'm Penny."

Her eyes take in my outfit, then slide to the door, then back to me. "You and my son..." She frowns. "You work for Marcus?"

LILIAN MONROE

"Um," I answer. "Sort of. I'm his dog walker."

The woman's face breaks into a smile. "The bow ties!" She hurries to a sideboard and pulls open a drawer. Her little brown dog comes trotting over to investigate, and I'm guessing that's where she keeps his leash. She pulls out one of my older designs, a blue-and-orange chevron bow tie.

Something lurches in my chest. I'd left a box of six bow ties as a present in my first week as Bear's walker. The thought of Marcus bringing one of them to his mother...it makes me vaguely embarrassed and flattered, somehow. I had assumed he stuck them all in that Tupperware container beside Bear's dog food in the pantry, where I saw the rest of them.

Her dog sits patiently while she clips it on. "Frodo loves this thing," she says as the dog spins in a circle and prances back to the pile of crayons near the living room wall. She extends a hand to me. "I'm Martha."

"Penny."

The baby in the other room cries again, and Martha lets out a sigh. "Excuse me." She hurries away, and the little girl starts pinging crayons at the boy again. He growls in response, batting the crayons out of the air.

"Hey," I say, planting my hands on my hips.

Both kids look at me. The girl glares.

"What are you doing?"

"Anna is a big pile of poo," the boy proclaims. "She's the worst sister ever. Everrr!"

"You stink, Ollie," the girl says, sticking her tongue out. "Stinky poo-poo bonehead." She whips a crayon at him.

He ducks out of the way, picks up a teal crayon from the floor, winds back, and fires it at his sister.

In some sort of ninja move I didn't know I was capable of, I reach out and grab the crayon out of the air. Both kids freeze. Even Frodo the dog stops his investigation of the graveyard of crayons to look at me.

I inspect the crayon, then look at the two kids. They look back at me. I arch a brow. They duck their heads and stare at their shoes.

"Come on," I say with a sigh. "Help me clean up. Then maybe we can use these crayons for drawing like we're supposed to."

"Anna said my drawing was ugly," Ollie grumbles. "She said my dad would hate it." He reaches down to gather broken bits of crayons.

"That wasn't very nice," I note, pulling the box of crayons over so we can all dump the projectiles into it. I glance at Anna. "Why did you say that?"

Anna's face is pinched. Her cheeks are bright red, and her eyes are glassy. "I didn't mean it. I was mad that he ripped my drawing."

"I was just trying to look at it," Ollie protests. "You pulled the other side of the paper."

"And then you ripped it up in little pieces!" Anna cries, lip wobbling. She points her hand at a pile of ripped paper.

Ollie's eyes are as watery as hers. He drops his head and picks up the last of the crayons. "I'm sorry," he says.

I'm kneeling on the ground, so I sit back on my heels while I gather up the pieces of ripped paper. Anna and Ollie watch me quietly as I flip them all over onto the coffee table, reassembling them like a jigsaw puzzle. Anna had drawn Frodo the dog, and it's not bad. A bit wonky looking, but she looks like she's about six years old, so I'll give her a pass.

"It's ruined," Anna says sadly.

I chew my lip, and an idea springs to life in my mind. "Have you ever heard the word *kintsugi*?" I ask.

Both Anna and Ollie stare. They shake their heads in unison.

"It's a Japanese art of repairing broken pottery. They use gold to mend all the cracks, and it makes a new piece of pottery that's more beautiful than the original." I smile at Anna. "I think we can do something similar here. We can make new art from all these broken pieces."

Anna's little dark brows tug together. "How?"

I pull a piece of blue construction paper from a stack of art supplies on the coffee table. I arrange the drawing of Frodo on the blue background, then explain to Anna that we can glue the pieces down, so a little bit of blue shows through between every piece. Excitement sparks in her eyes.

Then Ollie takes his own discarded drawing, looks at it, and hands it to Anna. "Rip it up, Anna," he says. "I want to make one too."

The little girl smiles at her brother, throws one arm around him while keeping her pink cast clear, then starts ripping the drawing. I scratch Frodo's ears and smile at the kids, then stand up and turn around.

Marcus and his mother are standing there, watching me. I jump and put a hand to my chest.

Martha's bouncing a baby, eyes flicking between me and her son with a curious, knowing expression on her face. Marcus looks dumbstruck. He tugs at his collar, glances at his niece and nephew, then runs a hand through his hair.

"Well done," Martha says conspiratorially, tugging me away from the two kids. "They've been at each other's throat all evening. It would have been fine if not for the leak flooding my kitchen."

I shrug, blushing. "It's fine. I learned how to be creative with scraps of fabric a long time ago, so I know how to fix mistakes in art projects."

"You..." Marcus clears his throat. He blinks, glancing at Anna and Ollie and then back at me.

"Are you hungry?" Martha asks brightly.

My stomach grumbles in response. Everyone stares at it, and I laugh. "I guess that's a yes."

Marcus checks the time. "I'll call the restaurant. The reservation is past, but they might be able to get us a table."

"Nonsense," Martha says. "I have food here. I want to talk to Penny. I have a feeling there's a lot about you I'll want to find out." She winks at me. "And you'll eat too," she calls out to the plumber, half in question and half in command.

The man lifts his head from under the sink and nods. "Sure. Don't tell my wife, though."

Martha nods once, then thrusts the cooing baby in Marcus's arms. He doesn't even blink as he takes the baby, which makes me think that kind of hand-off happens regularly in this house.

He sits down on an old sofa on the edge of the living room, keeping the baby cradled in his arms, and arches his brows at me. "I'm sorry, Penny."

I plop down beside him. "Don't be."

"You sure you're okay staying here?" Marcus bounces the baby like he knows what he's doing, bringing one long finger up so the infant can wrap their tiny fist around it. He isn't even looking at what he's doing. It's all automatic.

And my ovaries wave a white flag of surrender.

I've thought about kids, a family. Sometimes I'll see parents with a baby at the park or at a coffee shop, and I'll get an odd sense of yearning inside me. But I always assumed I could never have that. How could I even dream of a family when I was terrified of men? How could I ever entertain the idea of marriage, partnership, and kids when I lived the sad life of a frightened hermit?

Now, after what's happened over the past two weeks, seeing Marcus holding a baby in his arms like it's the most natural thing in the world makes my heart take a sharp dive into the pit of my stomach.

"Penny?" He frowns at me, still jiggling that tiny, fist-wrapped finger while the baby tries to eat it.

"Of course it's okay to stay here," I answer. "I think your mom will appreciate the help anyway." I nod to the baby and the kids.

Frodo the dog jumps up onto my lap and demands scratches. I smile and greet the dog properly, straightening his bow tie.

Martha reappears with a plate full of sliced carrots, cucumbers, and red peppers, along with a bowl of vinaigrette for dipping. She places it down on the coffee table next to the kids and gestures for us to have some. Anna and Ollie grab a few sticks of veg with a mumbled, *Thank you,* while they work on their kintsugi'd drawings. The next trip from the kitchen brings a warmed bottle for the baby, which Marcus takes with a nod and starts feeding the now-happy infant.

I can't even look at him directly now. It's making me feel like my heart is about to explode. All of a sudden, I want to see this every single day of my life. I want that to be *my* baby in his arms. I want to be in our living room, feeding our baby, knowing our shared bed is just a few steps away.

I close my eyes. Those thoughts are dangerous. If I start imagining a fairy-tale ending to this tryst between us, I'll only be all the more heartbroken when it inevitably ends.

Marcus isn't the future father of my children. He's the man who is helping me out of the rut I've been in. I can't cling to some ridiculous fantasy just because I've been starved of intimacy for years. I have to protect myself.

"Penny, look!" Anna holds up her fixed drawing and I have to admit, it looks pretty cool.

Proud of myself—and of her—I smile. "Looks awesome, Anna."

"I'm going to make another one! What about you?"

The heat of Marcus's body is soaking into my side, and every time I look at him taking care of that baby, I feel like my womb is banging a drum, trying to make itself heard. So I slide off the couch to get some distance, crunch on a carrot stick, and pull a fresh piece of paper from the pile. "Sure. I'll make one too."

25

___

MARCUS

MY MOTHER ADORES PENNY. Utterly, completely adores her—and I know there's no coming back from this. They treat each other like long-lost friends, talking and laughing through dinner. The sink has been fixed, the water's been turned back on, and the plumber has gone home.

When dinner's over, I'm shocked to see that my mother actually lets Penny help her clear up. Normally, she'd banish us all out of the kitchen upon threat of evisceration.

Not Penny. She helps with the dishes, puts leftovers in containers, and accepts my mother's offer of decaf coffee and cake for dessert.

Ever since I walked in to see Penny mending the fight between Oliver and Anna, I've felt thunderstruck. Now I feel numb.

I thought we'd be here to help with my mother's emergency, then we'd continue our date. Instead, we stay at my mother's place until my brother and his wife come by to pick up their kids. They're surprised to see Penny in the kitchen while I watch the kids in the living room, but they quickly start laughing with her like they've known her for years. When they find out she's the one who made Frodo's bow tie —and Penny finally tells everyone about her online store—I think my brother, sister-in-law, mother, and nieces and nephews fall completely in love with her.

They're not the only ones.

We eat cake and drink coffee until the kids are dozing on the couch and Penny gives a great big yawn.

"We should go," I say, standing. "Thanks for dinner, Mom."

"Anytime." She looks at Penny. "You'll come to family dinner on Sunday?"

Penny starts. She glances at me. "Oh, I..."

"We'll see, Mom," I grumble.

"Any time after four o'clock," my mother says. "Don't bring anything except yourself." She pats Penny's hand, then surprises me by giving her a tight hug. "Thanks for helping with the kids."

Penny gives one of her brilliant smiles, and I finally succeed in herding her to the door. My heart thumps as I lead her to the elevator, and then I can't resist. I push her up against the wall and crush my lips to hers. I kiss her until the doors slide open on the ground floor, then close again without us having time to fall apart.

Penny laughs, breathless, and sticks her foot out to stop the door from sliding shut. Her lips are swollen with my kiss, but I want more. I want her in my bed.

"Mackenzie's at a friend's house tonight," I say while the door starts buzzing, wedged open with Penny's foot. "Come back with me."

She gulps in a little breath of air, eyes wide and bright. "I..."

"Don't say no, Penny. Please." I'm begging, and I don't care. I kiss her neck. The elevator yells at us some more.

"Okay," she finally says. "It'll save me the commute in the morning."

Grinning, I tug her out to the waiting car and take her home. As soon as we enter the house, I can't keep my hands off her. I strip her down before we make it to the hallway, kissing her breasts and her neck and her stomach while she leans against the back of the sofa. She moans my name and tangles her fingers in my hair, and I lose my fucking mind.

This woman is perfect. Right now, I don't care about all the reasons I shouldn't get involved with someone. I'll deal with the consequences later. I need her in my bed, under my skin.

I give Penny her first orgasm right there up against the couch using my fingers and tongue, then I carry her limp and sated body to the bedroom. She opens up for me, spreading those gorgeous legs as soon as she's on my sheets. I can't get out of my clothes fast enough.

My thoughts are jagged, sharp. All I can see is her beautiful, freckled skin. Her red hair. Her blue, blue eyes. The laughter always teasing the corner of her lips, and the kindness that permeates her entire being.

Tonight, she was perfect. She fit into every part of my life like she was made for it. She didn't shy away from the chaos and noise of my family. She didn't act standoffish or awkward. She didn't make me feel like I was doing wrong by her by bringing her to my mother's house, or like she deserved more for a first date. She didn't make me *choose*.

She made me feel like I was worthy of her smiles, her attention.

She is mine. She was made for me, and I was made for her. I don't have time to doubt those thoughts, to disagree with them. Her body calls to me, and all I can do is answer its summons.

I thrust into her, relishing the rake of her nails across my back, drinking in her cries. She's the most perfect woman I've ever had, ever will have. She comes apart around me, body flushing, and it feels like a gift. We chase ecstasy together there in my bed, and when it's over, I tuck her against my body and watch her fall asleep.

WHEN DAWN COMES, Penny's ass wiggles against my lap in the best wake-up call of my entire life. Lying on my side with her back to my front, I feel every inch of her short, curvy body pressed against my skin. I curl my hand around her hip and pull her flush to me, growing hard as stone at the sound of her sleepy, lustful moans.

"Morning," she mumbles, pushing back against me.

I slide my hand through the little thatch of copper curls between her legs to find her wet and ready. We make love once more, my body curled around hers, my fingers on her clit, my cock buried deep in the perfect wet heat of her.

She's never leaving my bed again.

AFTER WE SHOWER, I watch Penny get dressed. I can't help kissing the nape of her neck, her shoulder, her hair. She flushes, glancing at me through her lashes.

"What happens now?" she asks.

"I go to work. You stay here and work. Mackenzie comes home. The three of us have dinner."

"Oh, you have it all figured out, do you?" Her smile is teasing while her cheeks grow pink.

I tuck a strand of hair behind her ear. "You okay with that plan?"

She blinks at me, then nods. "Yeah. I am. But—" A deep breath. "Mackenzie...?"

I understand immediately. "You don't want to make her feel uncomfortable."

Penny's shoulders drop. "She's made a few comments about being kicked out. About feeling uncomfortable at her mom's house. I think... I would just feel terrible if I made her feel uncomfortable here." Pools of sapphire blue stare up at me, worried.

My heart grows three sizes. I'm in too deep already. "You're right. My niece needs stability. I'll talk to her, make sure she's okay with us seeing each other."

She clears her throat. "Are we? You know...seeing each other." She nudges her toe on the carpet and doesn't meet my eye. "I know you have, um, other women." She looks at my phone on the nightstand, and I remember that stupid picture she saw. "I'm not asking to be...exclusive...or anything. But I'd just like to know."

Penny doesn't want to be exclusive. She met my *mother*, and she's not sure if we're seeing each other. An emotion rises up inside me, and without looking at it too closely, all I can tell is that it feels a lot like panic. And jealousy.

"We're seeing each other," I growl, "and we're exclusive."

Penny finally meets my gaze. I can't take that look in her

eyes—confusion and fear and hope—so I kiss her until she softens.

"Oh," she says when we finally pull apart. "Okay." Penny has that low-lidded, dazed look on her face that drives me wild.

"Turn around, Penny," I say darkly. "Put your hands on the bed."

"Uh-huh," she says in a faraway voice. "Great idea."

She does as I say, placing her palms flat on the bed. I flip up her skirt, tear her sheer tights down to her ankles, and use my mouth to show her just how serious I am about her.

I'm late for work in the end, but I'm the boss, so no one says anything. Todd does give me a long, blank look, though.

26

PENNY

I BLINK, and it's Thanksgiving.

Just like that, three weeks have passed in bliss. Marcus and I have fallen into a routine of covert kisses when we're at his house, lunchtime romps when he has time to come back from work, dinner dates a couple of times per week, and Sunday dinners at his mother's apartment.

I don't sleep over at his place, because I don't want to make Mackenzie uncomfortable. She seems happy that Marcus and I are seeing each other, but I know Marcus's house is her home. If things work out between him and me, there will be plenty of time for overnight visits once she's back with her mom.

Also, the thought of taking that next step in this relationship terrifies me, so there's that. Having that little bit of distance helps me keep the freakouts at bay.

Brian and I patch things up for the sake of the business, but he still mostly gives me the cold shoulder. At one point a week or two ago, he told me that he didn't "approve" of me working from Marcus's house, but he'd accept it for the time being since we both knew it was temporary.

The words felt barbed, dipped in acid. It hurt, and he knew it.

As I roll out pie dough on my microscopic kitchen counter, my muscles strain, and my mind wanders. This afternoon, I'll head to Martha's house and be welcomed into the warm embrace of her gigantic family. Nikki and I have plans to go for a long walk tomorrow, and the two of us are meeting Bonnie for a late lunch on Sunday.

For the first time in nearly a decade, I have *friends*. I have a *boyfriend*. I have a community.

Brian will come around. Maybe he got too used to being the center of my social universe. He was able to come over to my place whenever, make plans on the fly, have all my attention. Maybe our spat is just a temporary wrinkle in our long friendship and partnership.

While the pie dough is blind baking, I work on sketching some new designs. Ever since Raphael Garcia shared a picture of his dog in one of my bow ties—which I hadn't even realized he bought—more and more orders have started pouring in. There are lots of custom requests coming in through social media, which Mackenzie keeps track of like a champ.

The custom fabric I made on my first date with Marcus is gorgeous. It's an abstract, paint-splatter design, and I'm working on a limited-edition collection that should be ready by next summer. After Raphael shared my bow ties, I reached out to thank him, dropped off a bow tie for his dog with the new fabric, and nearly died when he mentioned we should collaborate.

That hasn't happened yet, but even the thought of a collaboration with an actual designer makes me feverish and jittery.

In other words, my life is busy and vibrant and full of new relationships that I cherish more than I thought possible.

I'm also exhausted and achy—and whether that's to do with the business, with all my new relationships, or with the stress of my tiff with Brian, I'm not sure. But the past two weeks have been rough. Maybe I picked up a virus of some kind and my body's busy fighting it off. Maybe it's all the sex. Maybe it's all the smiling and laughing I've been doing.

I finish the pumpkin pie, get dressed in an autumnal-colored plaid dress and a burnt-orange top (to match the pie, of course), and head out the door. I make it to Martha's house early, while only she and Tara—Marcus's eldest sister—are there with Tara's husband and kids.

"Penny!" Tara gives me a big squeeze. She smiles at me. "You brought pie!"

And an hour later, when Marcus arrives straight from the office where he'd been finishing up a few things before the weekend, my heart does a happy pitter-patter. He crosses the room toward me and—right in front of his mother, sister, brother-in-law, and all their kids—plants a big, wet kiss on my lips.

Head spinning, I laugh. "Hello to you too."

"You look beautiful." His thumb coasts over my cheek and he holds my gaze for a moment before pulling away to greet his mother, who inexplicably has tears in her eyes.

More family members arrive. They greet me like one of their own.

When it comes time to eat, Martha calls for attention and

raises her glass. "I'm thankful for all my children and grand-children. I wish Stephanie were here with us today, but I'm glad she's getting herself better. Hopefully, in a month's time, we'll all be together for Christmas, celebrating her healthy return."

I catch Mackenzie ducking her head and blinking rapidly. Marcus shifts in his chair next to me, his jaw clenched so hard it could be made of stone. Everyone lifts their glasses and we toast the only missing sibling, then we eat and drink and are merry.

It's when people are digging into my pie and compli-menting it that I realize I'm happy. Truly, down to the marrow of my bones, all the way out to my skin and every little freckle and follicle dotted over it, happy. I've spent eight years hiding away, living small, embracing fear. It leaves me reeling to think that things have changed so quickly.

"So, Penny." Terry—Marcus's younger brother—points his fork at me. "You must come from a big family. No one else can handle us wildlings unless they also grew up in chaos and cramped quarters."

I smile, dabbing my lips with my napkin. "Actually no," I tell him. "My mother passed away in childbirth, and for a long time it was just me and my dad. He remarried when I was eleven, and he and my stepmom had my little brother. My stepmom has a sister, but she lives across the country, so we never got to see her. No other aunts or uncles." I don't tell them that my home life was fraught, that I often felt like a stranger in my own home. That my father constantly chose his new wife and son over me, and I spent my teenage years feeling like I was watching him live out his second chance while leaving me behind. I moved out as soon as I turned eighteen, and I met Billy not long after. "I always dreamed about having a big family, though." I blush, shrugging. "Never had the full experience until I met all of you."

"And you're not running away screaming?" Tara winks at me.

"Not yet," I say, glancing at Marcus.

His eyes are softer than I've ever seen them. If I didn't know any better, I'd think they were full of affection—or love. But it's probably just sleepiness from all the food we just consumed. He slings his arm around the back of my chair and lets his thumb brush the edge of my shoulder.

"Well, we're glad you're here," Martha says with a decisive nod. "Aren't we? About time my son found a good woman."

"Mom," Marcus cuts in, glaring.

"Oh, no. I'm just the dog walker," I say, and everyone laughs.

Later, Marcus threads his fingers through mine while we stand on the balcony and overlook the courtyard below. "Come home with me tonight," he says.

I look up at him, the moonlight silver over the harsh angles of his face. "Mackenzie?"

"She'll be fine."

My heart thumps. My mouth turns dry—but I nod. "Okay." And with that one word, I take another step toward the cliff's edge. Another step toward a new life. Another step toward risk and possible reward—or heartbreak and disaster.

We stand in silence for a while, until I say, "She seemed upset when your mom made the toast about Stephanie."

Marcus says nothing, but I know he's listening.

"You seemed upset too," I continue.

"Things between Steph and me have been tough for a

long time." His voice is raspy, full of old, cauterized wounds that never healed quite right.

"What happened?" I send the question out into the air between us and watch it shimmer there, waiting for him to bat it down or answer it.

It takes a while for him to react. We stand in the chill of the late-November evening, our breath making white puffs of air in front of our faces, our stomachs full, until Marcus finally drops his shoulders.

"I fucked up," he finally tells me. "I was supposed to be there for her, and I let her down."

I squeeze his hand.

Lips curling in a bitter smile, he lets out a long breath and stares at the courtyard, leaning his free hand on the old railing. "I had a girlfriend," he starts. "And I loved her more than anything. I thought I did, anyway." His fingers tighten on the railing, and his eyes take on a faraway look.

Stupidly, I feel jealous of this woman—jealous that he loved her, that she was so important to him that he still feels the pain of their breakup. I'm not a total idiot, though, so I keep those thoughts far away from my face.

"She never got along with my family," he continues. "She said they asked too much of me, and I—being the idiot I was in my early twenties—listened to her." He lets out a bitter snort. "Sellzy was new. I had just quit my job and committed to the business full-time. I had more money than I knew what to do with, which wasn't even that much in the grand scheme of things. But this girl convinced me that my family was trying to take advantage of me. The irony of that statement, with her being who she was, is not lost on me now."

"Stephanie didn't like her?" I guess.

"Stephanie and I were close," he says. "And no, she didn't like my ex."

When he pauses, I give his hand another squeeze. "We don't have to talk about this if it's too painful," I say.

"No," Marcus replies. "I want to. I wanted to tell you all this when you told me about your ex-boyfriend, but I'm just... scared, I guess." He gives me a wry smile, then tugs me close. "You're the first woman I've dated since my ex."

"Well, that's something we have in common."

"We have a lot in common." He smiles, lacing his arms behind my back. Here, in his arms, I feel like everything in the world is okay. I feel protected and cherished and safe, which are things I never thought I would feel unless I was locked in my own apartment with the deadbolt turned and the phone off.

"I was with my ex when my father died," Marcus finally admits, his eyes tracing the contours of my face. "I was supposed to pick Stephanie up from a swim meet she had in Jersey, but I bailed. My girlfriend had some emergency and she needed me—I don't even remember what, there was always something—and I picked her over my own sister. My dad went to pick Stephanie up instead. A truck ran a red light and hit his car, right outside the pool where my sister was waiting. She saw the whole thing happen, and she never forgave me." His hands are warm against my face as he runs a finger over my hairline, over my lips.

My throat is choked tight, my eyes blurry. "Marcus," I breathe.

He gives me a bitter smile. "Steph started drinking not long after. Got pregnant, decided she needed to clean herself up. That lasted until Kenzie was six months old, and she had her first relapse. It's been a battle ever since. I hope she kicks the alcohol this time around, but..." He exhales, eyes not meeting mine. "Anyway, I broke up with the ex. I realized that my family was everything to me, and I'd let them down. With my dad gone, we almost lost everything. So I made sure my business was a success and that my family were taken care of. It was the least I could do after Dad died."

His voice is flat, and it breaks my heart. Folded beneath the words, I can hear years of guilt and shame and pain.

"You know your father's death wasn't your fault, right?" My hands climb up to his shoulders and wrap around the back of his neck. "You know that, don't you?"

"It was," he says, and he sounds so resigned, so empty, that my heart bleeds for him. "If I'd gone to get Stephanie, my father would be alive." The words sound like a mantra, like something that's been repeated so often that he no longer questions whether or not it's true.

"And maybe you wouldn't have poured your grief into your business," I say gently. "You wouldn't be able to help them as much as you do. You might even still be with that horrible woman."

He ignores me and tightens his arms around my waist. "Mackenzie looked emotional at dinner because we've been through this before. Stephanie gets clean, everything's great for a week or a month or a year, then she relapses. And I got emotional because I know I'm the one who caused it."

I know there's nothing I can do to change his mind, so I just pull him down and press my lips against his.

It took me a long time to realize that what Billy did to me wasn't my fault. I was so deep in my self-loathing that I couldn't assign blame where it was due—on my stalker's shoulders.

Marcus doesn't have someone to blame, except maybe that truck driver. He's so busy protecting his family and taking care of them all that he doesn't realize he's not taking care of himself. It hurts me to think that he's in pain. I want to suck the poison out of that wound and bandage it up. I want to wrap him in my arms and let him weep on my shoulder until everything's okay.

But Marcus is closed off. His wounds are his own. He pulls away with one last gentle kiss on my lips and gives me a soft smile. "Let's go home," he tells me, the words echoing between us, their meaning clear.

Home is with him. *Home* is together.

27

MARCUS

LONG AFTER I make love to Penny and watch her fall asleep, I find myself wide awake, staring at the ceiling. I slip out of bed and pad out to the front room, giving Bear a quick pat before opening the fridge to grab a bottle of sparkling water.

"Can't sleep?" Kenzie leans against the hallway wall, rubbing her eyes. She gives me a half-smile. "Me neither."

"Want a glass?" I lift the bottle of fizzy water.

She shrugs. "Okay."

We lean on opposite counters facing each other and sip our drink until I nudge her calf with my toes. "You okay? Does it bother you that Penny's here?"

"No, of course not," Mackenzie says. "I just... I missed Mom today, is all. I can't stop thinking about her. She's in some beige medical facility, eating dry turkey and canned cranberry sauce all by herself."

"She's getting herself right so she can be your mom again."

"I know that. Just...how many times will we have to do this? When is rehab actually going to work?"

I scrub my scalp and shrug. "I don't know. That probably depends on Steph. But she'll be back in a month, and she'll be herself again."

"I don't even know what being herself is anymore. Sometimes I think the drunk version of her is the real version. The honest version."

I put my glass down. "It's not. Your mom is funny and silly and kind. She'll come back to us." *She'll come back to you*, more accurately. My sister and I are beyond repair.

Mackenzie grimaces and rubs her hand over her biceps to warm herself up. "Yeah." She blinks a few times, then glances at me. "What if she doesn't?"

I let out a slow breath. "Then you'll stick around here, keep your grades up, and figure out what you want to do after you graduate."

"You won't kick me out?" She says it like a joke, but it's the same old worry that must swirl around and around in her mind.

"I'm not kicking you out, Kenzie. Not ever. Got it?"

That half-smile returns, and she gives me a nod. "'Kay." She heads for the hallway again, then turns. "And Marcus?"

I'm at the dishwasher putting our glasses away. I arch my brows. "Yeah?"

"I like Penny a lot. I'm happy for you and her. I think you're good together. You seem..." She swirls her hands in front of her body like she's waxing Mr. Miyagi's car.

"I seem what?"

"You seem...like you are when you're horsing around with the kids. Except all the time." She grins. "It's good. You're less moody."

"A fourteen-year-old girl is telling me that *I'm* moody," I deadpan.

She shrugs. "I only speak the truth."

"Of course you do, oh wise one."

She grins. "All I'm saying is you should hang on to Penny. She's good for you."

"What would you know about any of that?"

She rolls her eyes so hard it must hurt. "Serves me right for trying to say something nice."

I snort, then hook my arm around her shoulder. She hugs me tight, then says goodnight. I head for my own bedroom and crawl in beside a lightly snoring Penny.

In the darkness of the bedroom, her hair looks darker. Her freckles are washed out, and her lips are berry red. I run a finger along her brow, tracing the shell of her ear.

You know your father's death wasn't your fault, right?

No one has said those words to me in a long, long time. My mother said it to me at the funeral, and I brushed her off. Instead of sinking down into self-pity and grief, I worked. And worked. And worked. I built an empire and then doubled it. I hired my family members, supported the ones who needed it, made sure I was always the one they could call.

How much of my motivation to take care of my family is a misplaced sense of responsibility for my father's death? Have I just been atoning for my sins all these years? Trying to prove that I'm worthy of my family's love despite the fact that my father would be alive if I'd been there for Stephanie that day?

A sleepy mumble, and Penny turns into me. "Love you," she says, then curls up against me like a sleepy kitten and starts snoring again.

My heart pounds. I hold her in my arms and listen to her breaths, feeling the steady beat of her heart. Then I whisper, "I love you too."

28

PENNY

THE STREETS ARE COVERED in day-old slush, the sky is a dull dome of gray, and my socks are wet—but I have a smile on my face. It's the first week of December, I've just finished doing my profit calculations for the business, and last month was very, very good.

I hike my purse higher on my shoulder and hurry to the diner near my house, pushing the door open to feel the gust of warm, bacon-scented air hit my face.

Brian's in the corner booth, on his phone. He glances up when I reach the table and lets out a strangled little yelp when I throw my arms around his neck.

"I have good news," I say, pulling away to slide into the booth across from him.

He takes a sip of coffee and watches me over the rim of the mug. "Don't tell me you're getting married unless I'm your Man of Honor."

My stupid cheeks flush. I shake my head. "Of course not." I pass him a piece of paper which I just printed from the printer in Marcus's home office this morning.

His brows draw together. "What's this?"

"An itemized list of our sales, and at the bottom, your share of last month's profits." I can't keep the pride from my voice.

A very round waitress with hair big enough to admit her into the Texas Hair Hall of Fame walks up to our table, flips over the white mug in front of me, and fills it with coffee. "Something to eat?"

"Two scrambled eggs on whole wheat toast," I say, beaming.

Brian just shakes his head and waves her off, eyes still on the sheet of paper. When the waitress walks away, he lifts his gaze to mine. "This is way more than what we sold on Sellzy."

Impossibly, my smile widens. I think the edges of my face are creaking with the effort, but I can't stop myself. "I know. I've been getting orders direct from social media. Isn't it amazing? Nearly double what we made in October."

Brian doesn't look like he thinks it's amazing. He looks like he wants to tear the paper to shreds.

Instead, he places it down very carefully between us and stirs the coffee the waitress just warmed for him. His voice is oddly flat when he speaks. "Social media? Since when do we have social media?"

I huff impatiently. "Brian."

"We spoke about this months ago."

"I know, but—"

"Is this Marcus fucking Walsh's doing?" His words lash across my face like a whip, stinging so much I can almost feel the dribble of blood from the wounds.

"Brian," I say softly, not knowing what else to add.

He takes a long breath, combing his fingers through his curly blond hair. "Sorry. I just—I miss you, Penny. I went from seeing you nearly every day to being lucky if I get your voicemail."

Guilt churns in my stomach. I spin my mug around between my hands, staring at the strong-smelling coffee. "I know. I'm sorry. I've been busy. I thought..." I lift my gaze to his. "I thought you'd be happy about the extra money."

"I'd be happier if we were making business decisions together, Penny. You know how I feel about social media."

I point at the sheet of paper. "Even if this is the result? I was always planning on telling you, but I wanted to show you just how much we could make first."

He scowls. "How did you even figure this out? You suck at computers."

My spine snaps straight. He's right, of course, but why does it hurt to hear those words? I take a slow breath and let it out, then say, "Marcus's niece helped me set everything up. Remember when I met Raphael Garcia? Well, he ended up buying one of our bow ties and posting about it. I've been getting lots of custom orders ever since, straight from the social media accounts. It's all new—just a couple of weeks old. I thought... I thought you'd be happy. It was supposed to be a surprise."

There's a long, empty pause. Brian's face remains horribly blank as he stares at the paper. Finally, he lifts his gaze and forces a smile onto his lips while his eyes remain dead. "That's great, Penny."

My food arrives, but I'm no longer hungry.

.   .   .

"Everything okay?"

I look up from my handwritten ledger to see Marcus leaning against the doorframe. Leaning back in my chair, I give him a smile. "Yeah. I'm good."

"You were frowning."

"Math is hard."

He pushes himself off the frame and stalks inside. "That's not exactly true, is it?" His hands land on my shoulders and start kneading. "You have no problem with sums."

I let out an orgasmic groan. "Fine. No. I'm pretty good at math."

"So what's wrong?"

My head falls forward as his thumbs dig into the flesh at the side of my neck. Another moan falls from my lips. "I just met up with Brian," I finally admit.

His hands freeze for a moment, then restart. "And? How is he?"

"He didn't seem so happy about the social media sales."

Marcus hums. "Why not? You said he'd be happy, didn't you?"

"I thought he would," I say. "He's always talking about expanding the business. But I dunno. He seemed upset and kind of...blank. Like he was trying to hide his feelings from me." What I don't add is that things have changed between Brian and me, and it started when I started seeing Marcus. If I didn't know any better, I'd say Brian was jealous.

But Brian and I have never been romantically involved. Our relationship is platonic—always has been. So maybe my friend is jealous of the time I'm spending with Marcus. Brian no longer has me to himself, and he's upset.

God, I sound conceited, don't I? All these men begging for my attention and getting upset when they don't get it.

Psh. Right. Maybe I need to get over myself.

"How do you two usually manage the finances in the business?" Marcus asks. "Maybe he dislikes surprises."

"There's that too," I say. His hands lie flat on my shoulders, squeezing gently. I sigh. "Usually, the money from Sellzy goes to my account. I keep track"—I put my hand on the ledger—"subtract my expenses and whatever things Brian has bought—subscriptions and software and the like—and then we divvy the profits fifty-fifty. Every month, I cut him a check and give him a receipt." I spin in my chair and look up at Marcus's gorgeous green eyes. "I don't get it. Our profits were nearly double what they were the previous month. He should have been happy."

Marcus is holding back; I can tell. He wants to say something, but he's zipping his lips shut and keeping it inside.

"Say it," I grumble. "Just tell me what you think."

"You're not going to like it."

"Marcus, please. I'm a big girl. I can handle it."

"Brian is jealous," he finally says, and my stomach sinks. "For years, he had you to himself. You were at his beck and call. You asked him for advice about the business and didn't do anything without his approval. Things have changed."

"You think he's afraid of getting pushed out of the business?"

Marcus lets his thumb coast along my cheek, then leans down to kiss the tip of my nose. It warms me down to my toes. "I think he doesn't like seeing you grow."

I pull back, shake my head. "No. Brian's a good friend. He's happy for me." He said he wanted to be my Man of

Honor. It was a joke, but he's not upset about me being in a relationship.

Is he?

Marcus's eyes are steady on mine, until he finally nods. "You hungry?"

Sighing, I close the ledger and stand. "Yeah."

29

MARCUS

PENNY GOES BACK to her apartment after eating dinner with me and Mackenzie, which is the first night we've spent apart since Thanksgiving. I don't like the way her lips turn down or the pallor of her skin. But I kiss her goodbye and bundle her in my car so Will can drive her home.

Mackenzie is watching me when I turn away from the front door. Bear comes padding closer, shoving his head under my hand for rubs. I scratch him behind his big, floppy ears while I squint at my niece.

"What?"

"Everything okay between the two of you?"

"Stop it, Kenzie. I don't need a teenager to act as my couples therapist."

She throws her hands up, brows climbing up to her hairline. "Fine. Fine. Forget I said anything."

Silence stretches between us, until Bear leaves me to go rub against her legs. She bends down from her spot at the island barstool to give him his fair share of rubs.

"So, Marcus," she starts, then stops.

"Yeah?" I pull out a bottle of wine and pour myself a glass. The house echoes oddly without Penny in it.

"My mom gets out of rehab a few days before Christmas."

I dab a napkin on the edge of the bottle to catch a stray drip, then meet my niece's eyes. "You want to know the plan for when she's back?"

Mackenzie nods, a single sharp dip of her chin.

I take a sip of the rich Bordeaux and put my glass back down. "What would you like to happen?"

She bites her lip, thumb tracing one of the veins of the marble countertop. "Well... I don't know." She's silent for a while, then says, "I really like living here, but..."

"It's not home," I finish.

Her eyes are glassy when she lifts them to mine. "Your house is way nicer than Mom's apartment, but it's just... I don't know... I'm sorry, Marcus."

I circle around the island and wrap her in a hug. Bear presses closer to her, his bulk between my legs and my niece's. "You don't need to apologize. What did your mom say when you spoke to her last?"

"She said we could redecorate my room together. That she'd saved a bit of money before and she wanted to spend it on me."

My lips curl as I kiss Mackenzie's hair. That sounds like my sister.

"You don't need to apologize for wanting to go home, Kenzie," I say, pulling back. "Your home is with your mom. But you'll always have your room here too, okay?"

A gently wobbling lip is the only indication I get that a sob is coming. It convulses through Mackenzie, and she wraps her surprisingly strong arms around my waist while she lets it all out.

It's been a learning experience to share my space with a teenage girl—but it's been great. I thought I got my fix of kids and teens when I went to family events, but living with Mackenzie has made me realize that I might be missing out on a lot more. The normal moments, when Mackenzie tells me about the petty dramas at school. The ruined kitchens. The pounding music. The laughter. The hugs. The eye rolls. The crusted Cheerios.

For the first time in my life, I find myself wanting kids of my own.

I'm not in denial—I know that being with Penny has something to do with that desire too.

But I pull away from my niece, wipe her tears, and smile. "Your mom has great interior design taste. I bet she has a ton of ideas already."

Mackenzie nods, grinning. "She told me she'd get me a new screen and a desk, and even a mini fridge so I could have cold drinks for when I study. And a real vanity for my makeup."

"Sounds awesome," I say, ruffling her hair.

She pulls away and glares at me, patting her head to fix the mess. "*Anyway*," she says pointedly. "I guess I'm saying thanks, Uncle Marcus. Even if my mom won't."

A familiar pain stabs my chest, but I let it pass. "Anytime, munchkin."

I'm rewarded for that pet name with a vitriolic glare. Got to love teenagers.

· · ·

Mackenzie's upcoming departure brings up another question—one that Penny and I skirt around like planets around a sun. What happens to Penny's workshop when she no longer needs to be here after Mackenzie's school is out? What happens to *us*?

"What happens to us when Mackenzie leaves?" Penny spins around in her chair to look at me leaning against her workshop doorway. "What happens to this room?"

I guess I'm a cowardly planet; she's a self-destructing asteroid heading right for the heart of the matter.

Clearing my throat doesn't order my thoughts, but I do it anyway. "What would you like to happen?"

She gives me a flat stare. It's lunchtime, and I ducked away from work to come here and see her. I've been doing that a lot lately.

"I'm serious," I say, entering the space. "This room is yours, Penny. You can keep it as long as you like."

"You just want me here so you can carry me off to bed whenever you feel like it."

"I'm a selfish man," I concede.

Her coppery brows knit. "None of this was supposed to happen."

I tug her up off the chair and wrap her in my arms. There. That's better. "But it did."

She tilts her head up, resting the point of her chin on the center of my chest. "It did, didn't it?"

I kiss her. Then I cart her off to bed.

Later, I kiss her forehead and tell her that I want her to stay.

She blinks those big, blue eyes at me and says the sweetest word I've ever heard: "Okay."

. . .

WE'RE PROBABLY MOVING TOO FAST. I'm doing what I've done before—putting a woman first when I should be prioritizing the other people that rely on me. But hope buds in my heart that maybe I can have it all.

The next week is spent catching up on work. Now that I know Penny's staying at my place, I can focus. I comb through the acquisition contract and sign off on it, right in time for the winter holidays.

Then I come home to the smell of fresh-baked soft gingerbread cookies, with Mackenzie leaning over the counter and Penny slapping her hand away from the piping-hot cookie sheet. Mackenzie laughs, Penny grins, and I feel like my life is complete.

"I have to meet Brian tonight," Penny tells me once Mackenzie's stolen a gingerbread treat and carted it off to her room. "We have to discuss the next few weeks and come up with a plan for January, post-holidays."

Bitterness coats the back of my throat. I dislike her business partner more than I can say, for reasons I can't quite explain—but I just nod. "Sure." Then, because I want to prove to Penny—to myself—that I'm the bigger man, and I'm not so insecure as to care about some curly-haired, Converse-wearing chump, I say, "Does Brian have family in the city? Would he like to come to my mother's house for Christmas Eve dinner tomorrow?"

The words taste acrid as they come out, but Penny's face splits into a smile. She throws her arms around my neck and kisses me deeply. "I'll ask him," she says when we come up for air. "Thank you, Marcus."

I guess being the bigger man is worth it sometimes.

I watch her go, and it's like all the light leaves my home at once. Night falls with a crash, and I'm standing alone. Bear's snoozing on his bed; Mackenzie's locked in her room. How did I live like this before? What did I do? I find myself grabbing a soft, warmly spiced cookie that I'm technically not supposed to touch until tomorrow. My feet carry me down the hall to the last door. In Penny's workshop, my shoulders relax.

The fabrics are a riot of colors and chaos. The sewing machine sits patiently waiting for its mistress. The curtains are open, and gloomy light from the street spills in with sickly yellow rays—right onto the ledger placed on the corner of the table.

If you were to ask me what possesses me to open it, I couldn't tell you. All I know is, missing Penny by my side and hating the fact that she's going to see her sniveling, snot-nosed business partner, my feet carry me deeper into her space and my hand opens that book.

And I notice something.

A sandy, bone-dry texture coats my tongue. My pulse pounds in my ears, and I fumble with my phone to double-check if I was right—and I am.

Then it's the work of moments to rush to my home office, fire up my computer, and confirm my suspicions. I lean back in my chair, staring at my screen, and horror dawns on me like the darkness of an eclipse.

30

PENNY

MARCUS SEEMS DISTRACTED, but that's to be expected with the absolute bedlam that surrounds us. Apparently, it's tradition that his mother hosts a dinner on Christmas Eve, even though the family has grown so much that the small, three-bedroom apartment is absolutely bursting at the seams.

I'm sweaty and laughing as I bustle around the kitchen with Martha and Tara for an hour or so, then am banished to go enjoy myself with the rest of the family. Being here, surrounded by all these people, all this love—it almost feels fake. I thought families like this only existed in sitcoms. I thought billionaires lived in lonely, marble-covered mansions and counted their money for fun. I thought I was destined to end up alone.

Being wrong never felt so good.

The door opens again, and Brian appears. He's wearing a white button-down with a faint blue checkered pattern, dark jeans, and clean sneakers. His hair is gelled back. I smile, going to him and giving him a big holiday hug.

"Hey, Penny," he says, eyes darting around the room. "Wow. I wasn't expecting..."

I laugh. "I know. Come in. I'll introduce you to everyone."

Introductions take a while, and I settle Brian in between Marcus and his brother-in-law, giving him a cold drink and a wink. Then my legs are assaulted by half a dozen small children, and I'm carted off to another area of the living room to play a game I only vaguely understand. I can't stop laughing when I fall over and am pounced on by Frodo the dog, who seems to understand the rules of the game significantly better than I do.

I meet Marcus's gaze across the room. His smile looks different from usual. More...forced. He looks almost sad when he lifts his untouched beer in my direction in a sorry excuse for a salute.

Am I making a fool of myself? Is he angry I'm here? Is he upset I brought Brian? Does he not want me to stay at his place after Mackenzie leaves?

There's a knock on the door a moment before it opens. Mackenzie is there, beaming, dragging her mother inside. Cheers erupt around the room, and Stephanie's cheeks grow red. She rolls her eyes but accepts hugs and kisses from her siblings, mother, and nieces and nephews.

When she's free of the hubbub, I'm surprised to find her in front of me.

"Penny, right?" she asks, tugging the hem of her shirt down in a sharp, jerky movement.

"Yeah," I answer. "You're Stephanie?"

She nods. "Look." Her eyes drop, and she clears her throat. "I wanted to apologize for how I spoke to you the last time we met. I...wasn't in a good place. Mackenzie told me everything you've done for her, and—"

Her voice cuts off, as if the shame of apologizing to me becomes too much.

My own embarrassment makes it hard to think of the right thing to say. I settle on, "Mackenzie's a good kid."

Stephanie nods, eyes luminous. "The absolute best."

I smile, and something hard dissolves between us. She reaches over and awkwardly squeezes my forearm, then drifts toward the sanctity of the kitchen.

"What did she say?" Marcus says from behind my shoulder. His eyes are dark green—the forest at dusk.

I scowl. "None of your beeswax, mister."

He grins, but it fades quickly. "You okay?"

"I'm great."

When he kisses me gently, I flush all the way from my scalp to my toes. My eyes dart around the room, but no one seems to be watching us or caring about our PDA—apart from Brian, who quickly looks away.

When it's time for dinner, I watch the choreographed precision of a table being created from the kitchen all the way to the end of the living room, cobbled together from various different folding tables and tablecloths, along with mismatched chairs. Centerpieces appear from the bedrooms where they were stored, and candles are lit at equal intervals.

It's beautiful. I glance at Marcus, who still has that strange, solemn expression on his face. I wonder if he'd prefer to have rented some venue, to have waiters and chefs preparing this meal instead of this cramped, chaotic experience. He could afford anything, after all.

But his mother comes up behind him and he hooks an

arm around her shoulders, planting a kiss in her graying hair—and I know this is as special to him as it is to me. I know he provided all the food, drinks, and decorations for this dinner, and he made sure his mother had hired help for the prep work beforehand and the cleanup afterward, but the core of this holiday still feels homey and beautiful. It's a dry meal, since Stephanie is just back from her stay in the treatment facility. No one seems to mind the lack of alcohol, and I'm reminded of how much these people care for each other.

I end up seated between him and Mackenzie. Brian is directly across from me, looking gangly and out of place and slightly nauseated by all the noise. I wink at him, and he arches a brow in response.

It's nice to have him here, like all the disparate pieces of my life might end up unified in the end. I want him and Marcus to get along—I'd love for us all to be friends.

There's the sound of a fork on a glass, and the chatter around the table quiets down. Even the kids grow silent, staring at the head of the table.

Martha stands holding her glass of bubbly, non-alcoholic grape juice, smiling beatifically. "My wonderful family together again," she starts, eyes scanning the table and coming to rest on Stephanie, who sits to her left. "I know we're all hungry, so I'll make this quick. I love each and every one of you and I'm so happy to see us reunited and happy for this holiday. Maybe next year"—her eyes touch mine briefly —"I'll have new grandchildren to dote on."

"Mom," Marcus protests, sounding so much like an angsty teenager and so *not* like a wealthy CEO that it makes me snort.

Martha's brows arch. "What? I was talking about Ollie, of course."

"Sure you were," Tara says with a grin.

"Who's pregnant?" one of the nieces—Clarissa, I think— calls out from the kids' end of the table.

"No one," Marcus says emphatically. He lifts a finger in his mother's direction. "If you start quoting *Hamlet* at me, I'll leave."

Martha laughs, then simply says, "Let's eat."

I nudge Marcus with my shoulder. "What was that about?"

He shakes his head and stabs a green bean. "My mother is insane. And baby crazy. She's been wanting me to procreate for years."

"I heard that!" Martha says, before returning directly to her conversation with Stephanie.

"I thought you were fully committed to Penny," Brian says from across the table, slicing a piece of ham with precise movements. He lifts his eyes to Marcus. "Are you so opposed to having a family with her?"

"Brian," I chide, eyes widening.

He ignores me. Marcus sets down his fork and knife and meets my business partner's eyes across the table. "You. Do *not*. Speak about Penny and me," he says in a low, dangerous tone.

The sound of conversation dies in a slow wave rippling out from the three of us.

I reach under the table and squeeze Marcus's granite thigh in a futile attempt to defuse the situation.

"It was a simple question," Brian says, picking up his glass of water and dangling it in front of his lips. "You're willing to move Penny into your apartment, sequester her there, introduce her to all your fancy designer friends—but you don't see a future with her?"

"Brian, stop," I hiss, feeling the eyes of the Walsh clan on my skin like a thousand marching ants.

"It's a simple question, Penny. You're my best friend; I want to know his intentions."

"Best friend." Marcus lets out a humorless laugh before I can answer. "My *intentions* are none of your business." His jaw is diamond-hard, his eyes dark as a starless night.

"I beg to differ," Brian says casually, leaning back in his chair. He arches an insolent eyebrow, challenging. I've never seen him like this. I never want to see him like this again.

"Both of you, stop," I cut in. "This isn't the time or the place."

"No," Marcus grates. "You're wrong. This is exactly the time and the place. I want to hear more from your *business partner*." He emphasizes the words strangely. "Tell me, Brian. What would you possibly know about good intentions?"

Brian blinks. I start. We both stare at Marcus.

"What are you talking about?" I whisper.

"Marcus," Martha calls. "Can we just eat in peace? We're celebrating your sister. It's Christmas..." Her voice trails off when Marcus doesn't turn to look at her. His stare is glued across the table.

I feel it coming—the disaster. The vibrations start in the marrow of my bones, warning me of impending doom. I know, in those few moments, that something is about to go horribly wrong.

"I'm just trying to look after Penny's best interests," Brian blusters, color rising high on his cheeks.

"By *stealing from her*?" Marcus's voice grows louder with every word, as if he can't contain the fury burning inside. He pounds his fist on the table, jangling the cutlery and Martha's nicest dishes.

Brian stares. "What?"

I rear back. "*What?*"

"Is that why you were so opposed to her moving her workspace?" Marcus continues, ignoring us both. His eyes are burning coals. His muscles are marble, pressing against the soft cashmere of his sweater. "Is that why you're so quick to tell her she shouldn't be anywhere near me? Afraid someone would find out what a piece of shit you are?"

"Marcus," Martha tries again, her voice high and thin.

"Mom, stop." Marcus slices a hand through the air. "I'm trying to understand from this despicable dickhead, this wriggling worm, why he thinks it's acceptable to steal from the woman who pays his rent."

My thoughts congeal like day-old gravy. I blink slowly, listening to this conversation like I'm underwater, at a distance. My head swivels from Marcus to Brian, and then I see.

I see the hardness in Brian's eyes. The snarl on his lips.

And I know Marcus is telling the truth.

"Brian?" I hear myself say, as if my voice is coming from some foreign body.

Brian doesn't even look at me. His rage is directed at the man beside me, the man who takes that anger and throws it right back across the beautifully appointed table.

"You been checking up on me?" Brian asks in a cold, hollow voice. "Is that what you think Penny needs? After being stalked and harassed for years, you think she needs some macho man to look into her business and tell her how to run things? You think she'll appreciate you digging into her private accounts, when the first guy who did that ruined her so completely?"

Ruined me—

I can't speak. My throat closes up so tight it's hard to breathe. In front of all these people, in front of Marcus's *mother*, Brian has the gall to bring up my past? To talk about it so casually? To speak about me so contemptuously? To lay out the pieces of my trauma like a broken Christmas bauble?

I'm shaking. I don't know the man across the table. He— *Stealing* from me? Since when? How? Why?

Marcus's hands ball into fists beside me. "I think she deserves a hell of a lot more than you."

Brian pushes his chair back so fast it topples over and knocks the wall behind him. The multitude of family pictures on the wall tremble. My—former?—best friend and business partner turns those icy, cruel eyes to me. "Is this what you want, Penny?"

I don't know what to say to that. Is *what* what I want? To be stabbed in the back by the one man I thought I could trust? To have the man I thought I loved snooping in my private business? To have my past exposed in front of all these people? To be *humiliated*, like—

"Get out," Martha says in a quiet, deadly voice. She crosses to the door and opens it, inexorable.

The rest of the family stands, staring at Brian, circling the wagons around me and Marcus like I belong here with him. But I—

How could—

It's not—

I'm—

Brian marches through the door and disappears, dragging his winter jacket along the ground beside him. When he's gone everyone takes their seat again, sipping their water, clearing throats like nothing significant happened. Martha's gaze is heavy on my skin, my face, and I want to rub it off. I want to wash her attention off of me like I'd scrub a coffee stain from my shirt.

"Penny," she says gently.

I snap back to myself. My eyes find Marcus's, and he looks...ashamed.

He looks into my eyes, and he knows what I'm asking without me having to say a word. It would be a beautiful testament to our connection if it weren't so fucking tragic. "I saw your ledger yesterday," he starts. "I noticed that the unit price you were getting for your orders looked low, based on the list price on your online store. I know the fees we charge at Sellzy, and I've shown enough people your storefront that I knew what you charge for your products. It didn't add up." His eyes are green again, like soft summer grass. I don't trust them. I want to cry. "I logged into the Sellzy back end and investigated—"

"You *what*?" It comes out as a low, burning whisper.

Maybe I shouldn't be mad at Marcus. I should probably thank him for noticing something I never would have found out otherwise. He did this because he cares about me, because he wanted to protect me.

But he *logged in* to my accounts and—

Suddenly, I'm eight years younger. I'm noticing that my email trash bin has been emptied. I'm getting strange email responses to messages I never sent. I'm worried someone's reading my text messages. My social media is strange; notifications are disappearing. Every man in a hoodie makes me flinch. Every car engine makes me check the deadbolt on my door, the locks on my windows. I can't sleep. I can't eat. I can't think.

"I'm *sorry,* Penny," Marcus says, those soft, tender eyes tortured.

I want to take my fork and stab him right in the iris. I want to explode, spraying blood and gore all over this beautiful Christmas tableau. I want to curl up in a ball and sink to the bottom of the ocean.

Marcus continues, as if my world isn't imploding. "He had an intermediary bank linked to the Sellzy account. I'm guessing that instead of you getting all the money directly, he skimmed some before sending you the rest. He'd take about twenty percent," he adds, almost like an afterthought. "Then you'd do the bookkeeping and send him his share of the profits. Fifty-fifty, like you'd agreed, except he'd already taken an extra cut off the top."

My heart beats so hard I feel dizzy. I look at this man, and I see Billy. Instead of speaking to me, of treating me like an equal, he went behind my back. He snooped into my private business without telling me.

Marcus betrayed me.

Brian betrayed me.

Billy betrayed me.

And as I stand up, numb all the way down to the bottom of my feet, I know that I can't trust anyone. I was a fool to think I could, to think this beautiful, shimmering life was real. I was a gasping, dying woman in a desert of my own pathetic loneliness, and I believed a mirage.

My empty, sightless gaze drifts up to meet Martha's. "Thank you for a beautiful dinner," I say mechanically.

"*Penny*," Marcus says, standing beside me.

"I have to go." I don't meet his eyes. I dodge the hand he extends. The thought of touching him right now—of having those warm, loving hands on my body—

The next thing I know, I'm outside, gulping down big, cold breaths. When I get back to my apartment a second later, an eternity later, I collapse in my empty living room and die in the oasis that never existed.

31

MARCUS

THE THREE WORST days of my life follow.

Penny won't talk to me, Mackenzie moves out, and I end up alone in my house, wondering what the hell went wrong. I've barely managed to get myself fed and showered and take care of Bear. There isn't even any work to bury myself in, since this whole debacle happened during the stupid holidays.

Tomorrow, I'll be able to go back to normal, go to the office, and figure something out to fix this mess.

I should have talked to Penny when I opened her ledger and suspected something was wrong. She told me how sensitive she was about her privacy, and I violated that.

But—

I shove my hand through my hair and lean back on my couch, staring at the ceiling.

Penny will come back. She has to. All her stuff is here. We'll talk, and she'll understand that I was just looking out for her. We'll make up. She'll sleep over. I'll give her a million orgasms, and she'll forgive me. Everything will be fine.

My phone rings.

I slide sideways on the sofa and grab my phone from where it was resting on its arm, my heart jumping when I see Penny's name on the screen.

"Penny," I say on an exhale, relieved. "Hey."

"Hi." The strain in her voice makes my chest ache. She takes a deep breath. "I was hoping to come over tomorrow to pick up my stuff. Is that okay?"

I sit up, ice jetting through my veins. "Pick up your stuff? What do you mean, pick up your stuff?"

"I'm moving my workspace back to my apartment," she informs me.

"But—we talked—"

"I'm moving my workspace back to my apartment." The repeated words come out robotic, as if it's taking all of Penny's effort to keep her voice steady.

"Penny, talk to me." I lean my elbows against my knees, staring at the rug poking through between my feet. My heart pounds.

"I think it would be best if you weren't home while I was there, but I understand if you're not comfortable with that."

Bear, who had been lying on the couch next to me, lifts his head.

"What about Bear?" I ask, desperate. "Are you still going to walk him?"

There's an excruciating pause. Then, "Marcus." Her voice is thin, broken. "You know I'm not going to be walking Bear anymore."

"Penny." It comes out rough. "Please, Penny. Let me come over and we can talk about this."

"I have to go."

There's a click, and the line goes dead.

AFTER A SLEEPLESS NIGHT, I'm up with the pale, gray dawn. I do a workout, drink too much coffee, feed and walk Bear, then pace my living room for so long the soles of my feet get sore. I send a message to my team letting them know I won't be in, then check the time every two minutes until it's past nine o'clock.

Then a moving truck pulls up outside. Penny slides out of the passenger side, her hair pulled back in a ponytail, wearing a faded purple puffer jacket. From the driver's side, her friend—the dominatrix vampire nun, can't remember her name right now—exits and comes around the front of the truck wearing a bulldog expression and knee-high boots.

I open the door before they get to it, and Penny freezes. The friend edges around to stand just in front of her, as if she's trying to protect her from me. As if she *needs* to protect her from me.

"I thought you said he wasn't going to be here?" the friend —Nikki, her name is Nikki—says.

"You don't need to do this, Penny," I say, ignoring the other woman.

"Oh, I think she does, buddy," Nikki interjects. "Now move aside and let her get her stuff."

Penny puts a hand on Nikita's forearm before taking a step forward. She looks like she hasn't slept in days. Her eyes are puffy, with big, purple smudges underneath. Her skin looks sallow and pale. Her mouth is turned down.

I hate it. I hate that she's unhappy—that it's my fault. I want to shake her, make her talk to me. I want to cry.

"I need some space, Marcus," she says quietly. "I'm sorry I didn't give you notice about Bear."

"I'm sorry, Penny," I say. "I'm sorry I looked at your account. I just—I didn't want that asshole stealing from you."

Her eyes slide away from mine, focusing on the façade of my house. "Please," she says, lip wobbling.

And what am I supposed to say to that? How can I refuse? I step aside and let them in, ignoring Nikki's glare, and let them head into the spare room. I want to help, but I know I'll just make things worse.

Bear trots after them, and when they're bringing the first load of boxes out to the car, he sits down beside me and glances up, confused. I put my hand on his head.

The women refuse all my offers to help and glare when I try to pack some of the boxes into the moving van, so I end up sitting at the kitchen island, watching them go back and forth to the back room, feeling like my world is ending.

A while later, Penny comes out of the back room and gives me a curt nod. "That's the last of it."

I swallow past the lump in my throat. This feels like a goodbye. A real one. "Can I call you?"

Her gaze drops, and redness sweeps over her cheeks. Even exhausted, she's gorgeous. I don't know if I'll be able to stand not having her near me, knowing she's not working from my house, keeping my dog company, getting under my skin.

Finally, Penny squares her shoulders and meets my gaze. "I'd rather you didn't," she says, then continues out the door, closing it gently behind her.

My world crumbles. All the color drains from the room, like melting wax dripping down the walls and furniture. My heart withers a moment before anger sweeps through me. Strong, bracing anger. Righteous anger. I cling onto it with both hands, letting the emotion drag me out of the bleak despair that tries to pull me down.

She's dropping me like a sack of garbage after I tried to *help* her? She's turning her back on me when all I did was take care of her? She's blaming *me* for her business partner's betrayal? What the actual fuck?

All I did was take care of her—just like I always do. I protected her—just like I always do. I used my resources to try to make her life better—just like I always fucking do.

My whole life has been an exercise in doing the right thing, in making things right, in fixing mistakes before the people I care about get hurt. And how do I get repaid? With the only woman who ever mattered to me walking out without looking back.

I want to trash my own goddamn house. I want to break every window, rip up every canvas, toss my rooms like I'm trying to rob the place. I want to scream.

Instead, I stand in the middle of the room, fuming, impotent.

And someone rings my doorbell.

Hope and anger war within me, and before I can stop myself, I'm tearing the door off its hinges to open it.

But it's not Penny. It's my sister.

"Steph," I grate, chest heaving.

She arches a brow. "Bad time?"

It's a terrible time, but I open the door wider and stalk back toward the couch. Stephanie follows, shedding her jacket and boots before flopping down on the armchair to my left. I feel raw, stripped bare. Furious.

A deep breath, and I claw back some control over myself. I still can't look at my sister.

In my peripheral vision, I watch her lean her chin on her palm and look at me for a long second. "You look like shit."

I close my eyes. "Please don't, Steph."

"Penny hasn't come around?"

I grimace.

She's quiet long enough for me to crack an eyelid. My sister's still watching me, and she gives me a sad smile. "Sorry, Marcus. I liked her."

I hate the past tense. Penny isn't in the past. Not yet. This is just a fight—a misunderstanding. Except for the way she said, *I'd rather you didn't*, and then walked out without looking back.

Desperate to change the subject, I say, "How's Mackenzie?"

A smile blooms on my sister's face. She suddenly looks ten years younger. "She's really good. We set up her new room. Built her new bed"—she gives me a rueful smile—"and by that I mean, the bed is put together and I only ended up with four extra screws that I'm pretty sure weren't supposed to be extras."

I snort, the closest I can get to a laugh. Everything aches. My skin, my eyes, my muscles. My heart.

Stephanie's quiet for a while, until I wave a hand at the kitchen. "You want a glass of water or something?"

She shakes her head. "No. I'm good. I'm here because..." A deep breath. "I wanted to talk to you. Wanted to apologize, I mean."

"No need," I say. "You have nothing to apologize for."

Stephanie laughs. A real, head-thrown-back cackle.

"That's a lie," she finally answers. "I have plenty to apologize for."

"We both do." The pain of the day strips me bare, and I can feel that old, pulsing wound from years ago. The guilt, shame, embarrassment. The look in Stephanie's eyes when our father passed away on a hospital bed with a thousand tubes sticking out of him. The sound my mother made when she finally let out a sob.

If I hadn't been so selfish, so wrapped up in a woman, my dad would be alive.

What have I ignored since Penny's been in my life? Am I making the same mistakes all over again?

I don't have the strength for this. I'm a fraud. I'm not a protector, a provider, or a man worthy of what I have. I don't deserve any of this. The money, the staff, the house, my family. Penny. It's built on a bad foundation.

"I'll go first," my sister says. "I'm sorry for how I've treated you since Dad died."

I blink, startled.

Stephanie smiles sadly. "I know. I'm as surprised as you are."

"No, it's not that, it's just..."

What is it? Why does this feel so sharp? To her my sister say those words, absolving me—

"You know, I've been through detox six times already," she continues, as if I hadn't spoken. Her eyes are focused on a huge canvas on the opposite wall, tracing the abstract lines of the painting. "Every time, I went in there knowing it would fail. The first three times, I didn't even start the rehab program after detox, let alone finish it. But this time... This time, it was different, because I knew

Mackenzie wouldn't come back if I messed it up again." My sister pauses, swallowing. "I saw it in her eyes, before Mom drove me to the facility. I've been hurting my little girl this whole time, and I don't want to do that anymore. I kicked her out of her home because I was so deep in my addiction."

The last sentence comes out flat, like Steph can't quite get past the shame. I know how that feels.

I think of the loud music, the sass, and the fear in Mackenzie's eyes when she thought I'd kick her out of here. No kid should go through that, and we both know those wounds will linger.

"There was this therapist there," Stephanie says, her voice far away, her gaze in the past. "I don't know what it was about her, but the way she asked questions... She just made me think. She asked me about Dad's death, and about you."

There's a long pause, so I say, "Yeah?"

"At one point near the end of my stay, she made me realize that I took all the hatred I have for myself—all the ways I've blamed myself for what happened, for fucking up my life, for hurting Mackenzie—and I put that all on you. On some level, I felt like you could take it. I hated you so much, Marcus. I couldn't stand looking at your face." Her voice grows thick, and she finally slides her gaze over to mine. "But the truth is, I don't hate you at all."

I can't speak, so I just nod.

"I'm sorry, Marcus," she says. "I'm sorry I sent all that pain your way. I'm sorry I blamed you for what happened to Dad. I'm sorry I blamed you for what I did to myself. You've done nothing but try to keep our family together, and I resented you for it. That wasn't fair." Her voice catches.

"Steph," I whisper, because my throat is so hoarse I can't manage anything more. "It's okay."

"It's not." The words are vehement, her face set. "It's not okay. I've been awful to you, and all you've done is be there for my daughter, for Mom, for everyone. You didn't cause Dad's accident any more than I did. It was a shitty thing to happen. Just a shitty, horrible thing."

My throat is too tight to speak, and we both sit there with those words unfurling between us.

Then my sister takes a deep breath. "I've always thought of myself as weak, you know. And I hated that. I hated that I went back to drinking every time life hurt too much to handle. But I'm trying, Marcus. I'm really trying. I think getting up every day and *trying* might mean I'm strong." She gives me a slight smile. "Like you."

There's wetness on my cheeks. I brush it away impatiently and shake my head. No words come out. The emotions inside me are too big to wrestle with. I don't know what to think, what to feel.

My sister is building a thin, tentative bridge between us. I want to grab on to it, shore it up, secure it so it never collapses. But then I think about Penny leaving, about all the years of work and sacrifice, about how fucking empty my life feels now that she and Mackenzie are gone, how pointless everything is without them.

All I ever wanted was my sister's forgiveness. All I wanted was for her to look at me and tell me, *It wasn't your fault.* I thought being absolved of that sin would make everything make sense.

Now that I have it, it's hollow. The space where my guilt germinated and grew is filled with nothing. Even if I were to let it go, to forgive myself the way Steph is forgiving me, I'm not sure it would change anything. Because what's the point? For years, I've been letting guilt and atonement drive me onward. And in the past couple of months, there's been something new.

There's been love. Companionship. Happiness.

For the first time in my life, I felt a different kind of fire beneath me. A new reason for being.

And now I've lost it all. I can't even cling to the guilt anymore, or the hatred that Steph fed me. The anger that filled me when Penny walked away slips through my fingers, and I'm bereft.

"Hey," my sister says, crossing to sit next to me on the couch. Bear jumps up on the other side of me, resting his head on my thighs.

"Penny's gone," I choke out. "She left, and she's not coming back."

Arms wrap around my shoulders, and for the first time in over a decade, my sister hugs me—but that's not the reason tears start running down my cheeks.

32

PENNY

I FIND out I'm pregnant halfway through January. I've been in a daze, spending all my time sewing, crying, and trying to ignore the black abyss that is my future. Nikita's been a rock, making sure I eat and sleep and don't dissolve into a puddle of my own tears.

Now I stare at the pregnancy test while Nikki knocks on my bathroom door. "Penny?" she calls out. "I heard the timer go off. What does it say?"

I open the door and lift my gaze to hers. "It's positive."

Her face goes through a few rapid emotions—shock, horror, fear, anger—and finally settles on a vaguely concerned, neutral mask. "Are you sure?"

I grab the test from the bathroom counter and show her. "Yeah."

"You should go to the doctor to make sure. Aren't you on the pill?"

I nod. "Yeah. I don't know what happened."

"Maybe it's a false positive."

I shrug a shoulder, but I know. I *know*. All the things I've been feeling—fatigue, mostly, but also pain in my breasts and nausea—it all points to this at-home pregnancy test being accurate.

"I didn't always take my pill at the same time," I admit. "When I moved my workshop to Mar—to his house—my routine got all messed up. There were a few times I forgot to take it and had to take two pills the next day."

Nikki's face screws up, then she tugs me out of the bathroom doorway and gets me to sit down on the couch. I stare blankly at my sewing machine and the piles of fabric in my living room. Instead of being comforting, the fabrics tower over me, looming. The space feels small—too small. I want to scream.

Maybe all those feelings I had for Marcus were false. Maybe this whole time, I've been pregnant, my body flooded with new hormones, and I mistook that for love. That's why it blindsided me so much when he went through my private business behind my back.

A mug of tea appears in front of me, and Nikki takes a seat beside me. "So," she says.

I blink, watching the steam curl from my cup.

"It's his?" she asks carefully.

I nod, just a slight dip of my chin.

"Okay." Nikki rubs her hands over her thighs. "Okay." She blows out a breath. "Well, at least you have your business back. You haven't heard from Brian?"

I shake my head. "I got an email from Sellzy that payments from my store were suspended until I could verify a new bank account. I'm assuming it was—" I can't even say Marcus's name out loud, so I try again. "I'm assuming he put a block on my account when—" I stumble on the words and fall silent.

Nikki takes a bracing deep breath. "Right. Well, that's good. You'll still have some income coming in once you fix up the Sellzy store. Have you done that already?"

"No." It comes out as a croak. I've been on autopilot, using my old clunky laptop to sign in to the Sellzy account to fulfill orders over the past three weeks. I've barely touched the social media accounts Mackenzie set up for me, because honestly I can't be bothered and looking at them makes me cry.

But no, I haven't changed the bank account on the Sellzy interface. It's too confusing. Every time I log on, there are alerts and notifications, and they ask me for all kinds of numbers and identification and tax information and my head is a mess and I just don't know. I've never had to deal with any of this before. I had Brian, but apparently he was embezzling from our company and...and...and... Everything is so *hard*.

And now I'm pregnant with Marcus Walsh's baby.

A wave of emotion crashes into me, and it takes all my strength not to break down. I suck in a long breath, close my eyes, and let it out. Then I open my eyes and whisper, "How do I tell him?"

Nikki wraps her arms around me. "Don't think about that right now, okay? Let's just get you on solid footing. Step One is determining whether or not that was a false positive, so you need a doctor's appointment. Step Two is deciding what you want to do with—with the baby." She pauses, to let that sink in. "Step Three is way, *way* down the list, and that's deciding what and how you'll tell that scumbag of an ex-boyfriend of yours."

I nod, even though I want to protest the word "ex-boyfriend." Billy was an ex-boyfriend. Marcus was something entirely different. Something more. Being with him was like tasting sweetness for the first time, when all I'd known before was sour and bitter.

"So. Step One. Who's your doctor? Let's make an appointment."

IT'S NOT A FALSE POSITIVE. I sit on the chair in the doctor's office a few days later while she tells me that I'm definitely, one-hundred-percent pregnant. I'm nearly done with my first trimester, in fact, so then I have to try not to have a panic attack about the fact that I've been pregnant for eleven weeks and I didn't even know.

When I phone Nikita to report back, she calls in sick to work and hurries over to my apartment. She finds me on the couch, curled up on my side, taking in big, gulping breaths as I try not to give in to the urge to break down.

I can tell Nikki doesn't know what to say, but I appreciate her sitting on my slipcover-clad couch with my feet on her lap, being there for me. There have been so few people in my life that have been in my corner. The fact that she's here at all helps me gather myself together and sit up.

We stay like that in silence for a while, sitting side by side.

"Are you ready to talk about Step Two?" she finally asks.

"I'm keeping the baby," I blurt, before I even have time to process the question. Then I blink, frown, and meet Nikki's eyes.

She gives me a slow nod. "Okay. I support you, Penny,

whatever you decide. But you've thought of all the options? Adoption, termination...?"

A sick, squelching feeling passes through my middle. "I— can't." A breath. "It's mine." I put a hand over my lower abdomen, eyes wide, meeting my friend's gaze. "I know it's crazy. I know I'm alone—"

"You're not alone," she says automatically.

That's when the waterworks start. It takes a while and almost a whole roll of toilet paper (I ran out of tissues days ago) to get us both to stop blubbering.

Finally, when my nose is raw from rubbing it and my eyes are nearly swollen shut, I stand in my living room and touch the top of my sewing machine. "I'm going to have a baby. I'm going to be the best mom in the world. My baby will be able to look at me and see a business owner and a badass mom."

Nikki smiles, blows her nose once more, then gives me a sharp nod. "Damn right they will."

"I don't want to talk about Step Three yet," I tell her, eyes on my silent sewing machine. "I just want to talk about Step Two."

My friend's face softens. "Of course."

"And if I'm keeping this baby, I need to figure my crap out." I glance at the old relic of a laptop halfway shoved under the couch. "I need to get that bank account changed on my Sellzy account, figure out the whole social media thing, and get my business up and running again. And for that I'm going to need a new laptop and a smartphone."

Nikki inhales sharply and puts her hands to her chest. "Who are you and what have you done with Penny?"

I roll my eyes, but for the first time in many weeks, a hint of a smile tugs at my lips.

I won't pretend I'm not terrified. My life is upside down. I'm heartbroken, reeling, and pregnant. But I'm *pregnant*, which means in not very many weeks, there's going to be a squishy little human relying entirely on me for survival.

And I damn well better be ready.

Brian betrayed me and hasn't even tried to reach out. He stole from me, lied to me, and kept the tech-related parts of the business hidden from me.

Marcus lied to me, snooped on me, and made me feel violated.

Billy broke me. My father ignored my pleas for help. All my life, men have made me feel small and incapable and alone.

But I'm stronger than all that. I have a human growing in my womb. I can't rely on unreliable men. I can't keep letting others push me around. I can't keep living small.

"I need to get over my fear of technology," I tell Nikki, pulling out my old laptop and staring at the dented and scratched surface of it. "I need to learn how to do everything Brian was doing."

"Except you're going to do it better," Nikki says.

My lips twitch, defiant, as I meet my friend's gaze. "Except I'm going to do it better."

33

PENNY

I MAY HAVE UNDERESTIMATED HOW difficult this plan would be. With Nikki here to bolster me, it seemed so easy—get new electronics, figure them out, become a dog clothing queen, give birth painlessly and quickly, then skip off into the sunset with my new baby.

Ha. Right.

My body is sore, and my exhaustion hasn't let up. I can't freaking think properly. I'm distracted all the time, short of breath, and I have weird aches and pains all over.

Oh—and anytime I feel like I'm on a roll, I have to go pee. Seriously, I even have to pee right now, and I literally *just* peed.

I'm sitting in my living room fighting with a computer— and the computer's winning. But I can't tell if I'm just being a hormonal, pregnant idiot (likely) or if the computer is malfunctioning somehow. Then my new phone beeps, and I try to get it to scan my face so it'll unlock, but it keeps shaking and buzzing and saying "error." There's a text message from

Bonnie, but I can't get the stupid phone to show me what it says.

I toss the ridiculously expensive smartphone on the couch cushions and turn my frustration back to the laptop on my knees. A big red notification tells me I entered the wrong password on the Sellzy account, and I only have one try to get it right before I'm locked out.

Maybe if I smashed it with a hammer it would help.

It's been a week since I decided on a game plan, and I've had my new computer and phone for six days. Six excruciating days when I've done nothing but sew, fight with technology, and sleep.

Look at me, I'm supermom. Not.

Marcus called me once, four days ago. He sent me a text immediately after. I deleted it without reading it. I had this deep, irrational fear that he'd somehow found out about the pregnancy and was going to take my baby away. So I've just been ghosting him, like a responsible, rational human being.

He hasn't contacted me since. I can't decide if that makes me feel better or worse.

I heave myself up and go to the bathroom again. I'm not even showing yet, and I have to heave myself up to stand. The next twenty-eight weeks will be rough.

When I walk back to the living room and glare at my computer, my phone rings, saving my computer from a hammer-induced death. I don't recognize the number.

"Hello?"

"Hi," a bright, female voice replies. "I'm Amanda, calling from Sellzy. May I speak to Penny Littleton?"

I sit back down, frowning. "Speaking." My throat clenches. Why is Sellzy calling? Did Marcus set this up? Am I going to get kicked off the platform? Are they locking me out of the account? Did Brian do something?

"Hi, Penny," the woman says. "The team at Sellzy wanted to congratulate you. Your store has gone through fantastic growth over the last year, and we wanted to extend some of our concierge services to you. I'm your account manager, so I can help you with any problems you might be having with the platform."

I blink. Open my mouth. Close it again. "Oh."

"Have you been having any problems?"

"Well, right now I'm having problems logging in, even though I'm *sure* I'm putting the right password in."

"No problem," the woman says, her voice still bright and bubbly. "I can go ahead and send a reset link to your email and walk you through the process of setting a new password."

With Amanda in my ear, we do just that. When my sales dashboard pops up, I let out a little sigh. Thank goodness.

"I've been trying to change the bank account associated with my profile," I say.

"Oh, yes, I see we've put a freeze on it. Did you want me to assist you with that?"

Relief crashes through me. "Yes. Yes, please. I'd love that."

She laughs, and something in the back of my mind tells me I've heard that laugh before. "No problem, Penny. Okay, if you go to the top right corner of your screen, you can click on your store's logo and select, 'Account Details.'"

For the next half hour, the woman on the other side of the phone helps me navigate the Sellzy interface, shows me things I never knew about, and even gives me a handy break-down of competitors' pricing on the platform and where I sit compared to them. I'm pricing too low, according to Amanda.

By the time we hang up, I'm bursting for a pee and almost giddy with excitement. Nothing she showed me was terribly difficult—I just had to know where to click. The computer didn't go up in flames, and nothing froze and started beeping menacingly.

When I get out of the bathroom for the twelfth time today, I have a notification email about our next call, scheduled for one week from now. I read the email over half a dozen times, then mark the call in my calendar. Whatever happens between now and then, I know I'll be able to make a list of questions and get Amanda to help me out with it. I'm not alone.

I'm not made of magnets and destined to make all electronics malfunction.

Maybe I can do this. My plan of being Supermom, Queen of Dog Clothes might not be so far-fetched, after all.

LATER THAT DAY, when I've finally shut down my new laptop and made a list of all the sewing projects I need to complete tomorrow, I decide to head out for some groceries. There's also an extremely overpriced baby store a few blocks away, and I might give in to temptation and go look at all the adorable, teeny tiny shoes and outfits for sale.

It feels scary to be excited about the baby, about the future. I've spent over eight years terrified of my own shadow, content to live my life on an endless, lonely loop. But now, there's more. There's a reason for me to live, to thrive.

An image pops into my mind: Marcus, on the couch at his mother's house, holding his nephew in his arm and giving him a bottle. I have to grip the doorframe in my apartment's lobby as a sharp pain passes through my chest.

I want that.

Marcus and me, our baby, together. I want him to look at me the way he always did, like he can't quite believe or understand how I ended up in his bed.

But how can I trust him? How can I go back to him when he did the one thing that he knew would hurt me? It terrifies me to think that I could slide back into a situation like me and Billy—except worse, because I'd have a baby. Sure, Marcus meant well by logging into my Sellzy store—but what next? Would he mean well if he wanted to take a peek at my text messages? Would he mean well when he asks me where I'm going, who I'm with, why I didn't ask for permission? Would he mean well when he called to check up on me over and over again?

His betrayal might seem like something small compared to what Brian or Billy did. But it's not small at all. It's the first step in an unbalanced relationship, and it terrifies me.

I take a deep breath and step outside. I can do this on my own. I know I can.

"Penny?" A man jogs toward me through the slush and old snow.

I freeze. "Brian." My voice falls flat between us, deadened by the big, wet snowflakes falling down from the gray sky above. I grip the door behind me, wanting to run.

He comes to a stop three feet away from me, pushing the hood off his head and meeting my gaze. "Hey."

Hey? He steals from me, lies to me, betrays me, and all he can say is *hey*?

"I have nothing to say to you," I grit out, turning my head to look down the street in dismissal.

"Penny, please. Hear me out."

"Hear you out?" My voice is colder than the winter chill that seeps into my bones. "You don't deserve to be heard out, Brian. You should be paying me back the thousands of dollars you stole from me."

He grimaces, looks down at his shoes. "It wasn't supposed to happen like that."

"I'm sure it wasn't."

"I was just worried about you dating that asshole!" he says, throwing his arms out to the sides.

I frown. "You've been stealing from me for months, Brian. Long before I ever got involved with Marcus Walsh."

"Oh, so you're involved? What does that mean?" His face twists, and he takes a step toward me.

I have my back to the building's entrance, and suddenly my heart starts to thump. I don't like this. I don't like him. I don't like feeling like I'm unsafe. "It doesn't mean anything," I say in a voice that only trembles a little. "I'm not seeing him anymore."

Something like hope blooms on Brian's face, and I get an awful, acidic feeling in my stomach. "You aren't?"

I shake my head, slowly reaching into my purse for my keys. I want to put this door between us. I want him to leave and never come back.

"Penny, I wasn't stealing from the business." He stares at me, imploring. "I swear. I was saving the money."

"Okay," I answer, finally finding my keys in my purse. I feel for the fob that'll open the lobby door and grip it tight. "I believe you."

"No, Penny." He shoves a hand through his hair. "You look scared. Don't be scared. It's me, Penny! Brian. We're besties." He reaches into his pocket and pulls out a little velvet box, flipping it open to show me a diamond ring. "I was saving the money for this, Penny. For you—for us."

In the fading light of the January afternoon, the diamond twinkles merrily. I stare at the rock, then at the man holding it.

I don't know this man. I probably never knew him. I think of all the ways he made me feel strange over the past few months, from demanding to know where I went when I met up with Nikki, to being oddly hostile and wanting to drag me from the Halloween party, to sulking when I moved the workshop. In isolation, I could have explained any one of those instances away. I even understood them.

But taken together? They tell me a story about a Brian I never truly knew. One who stole from me for months and doesn't understand why that's wrong. One who thought our relationship was something very, very different than it was.

I treasured our friendship. I thought I could trust him. But all this time...

My muscles lock in place, because I'm afraid of him. He's the one man I thought was safe, but he's just like Billy. I want to tear through the lobby door and lock it behind me. I want to bury myself under my blankets and never come out.

But that was the old me.

The new me—the mother, the business owner—squares her shoulders and looks Brian in the eyes. "Brian, I'm not going to marry you. You were my friend, and I will forever appreciate the time we had together, but I can't forgive you for lying and stealing from me."

"Penny—"

"Thank you for your friendship. Please don't contact me again." I'm still gripping the key fob tight, ready to open the door and lock myself inside. My heart is beating so hard I can hardly hear anything but my own pulse.

Brian's eyes fill with tears, and I feel absolutely nothing. It's like I'm staring at a stranger. He thrusts the ring toward me. "I know our relationship wasn't like that, but... But it makes sense, Pen. You and me. I mean, who else are you going to marry?" He sees my face and adds, "No, I didn't mean it like that! I mean—"

"It doesn't matter what you mean, Brian." My voice sounds stronger than I feel. "Please leave me alone."

His shoulders drop as he searches my face. "You're serious."

I just stare back.

He snaps the ring box closed and slides it into his pocket. His mouth opens, then closes. He gives me one last, pathetic glance. "If you change your mind..."

"I won't," I say.

As soon as his back is turned, I slip back inside my apartment and hurry up the stairs and out of view. My phone is in my hand—how did it get there? I pull my mittens off and dial Nikki's number, even though she's not the person I really want to see.

34

MARCUS

"He's alive!" Leif calls out, throwing his hands in the air.

I roll my eyes and take a seat at the bar next to him.

Emil gives me a fist bump behind Leif's back. "Didn't think you'd make it," he says.

"First time we've met up for drinks in months," I answer. I nod to the bartender and order a beer, then turn to my friends. "What's up?"

Emil arches a dark eyebrow. Leif does the same with a blond one.

I take a sip of mostly froth. "What?"

"Bonnie told Dani that you and Penny aren't together anymore," Emil says.

"Yet we haven't heard a peep from you," Leif adds.

I shrug. "It's nothing."

"Hmm," Leif answers, which is a completely useless thing for him to say. It doesn't even mean anything.

"She seemed nice," Emil says casually, and it takes me a minute to remember that he was at Bonnie's Halloween party. Was that really less than three months ago?

"What happened?" Leif takes a gulp of his drink and puts it down on the coaster before turning to me.

I shrug. "Didn't work out."

The two men stare at me.

Leif lets out a sigh. "What a surprise. The man who told me to drop Layla like a sack of garbage before I even knew her didn't want to fight for the only woman he's ever cared about."

I bristle. "It's not like that."

"So what's it like?" My friend narrows his eyes at me, and I have the urge to punch him in his stupid face.

"Not like you and Layla," I answer pathetically. I drink the rest of my beer in one gulp and order another. I shouldn't have come here. They've been hassling me to meet up for weeks, but I should have kept pushing it off. I'm not in the mood to talk about Penny or be reminded of how badly I screwed up.

The past weeks have been excruciating. I don't need two assholes to highlight that and make me admit it out loud.

Emil clears his throat. "So... Dani's pregnant again."

Leif turns around, eyes wide. "What?"

Emil can't keep the smile from his face. "Yeah. Number four. Can't believe it."

Leif lets out a whoop and claps Emil on the back so hard Emil nearly spills his beer. They both laugh, and I join in to congratulate my friend. I give him a hug and a hard slap on the back, then pull away and sit back down on my stool.

My smile feels false, though, and I can't quite shake the feeling that something is wrong for the rest of the night. It's not until later, when I'm back in my silent home, brushing my teeth and staring at myself in the mirror that I realize I'm jealous.

Jealous of Emil's happiness, of his growing family. Jealous of Leif, and the way he fought for Layla even when things looked like they'd never work out.

I'm jealous of my two best friends, because for them, things worked out. They got the girl, the family, and the happily-ever-after.

In a moment of weakness, I send Penny a text message. I just want to know how she's doing, make sure she's okay. I'm surprised when I see the color of the text bubble change from green to blue—she got a new phone. Excitement blooms and then dies in my chest when my text goes unanswered.

It takes me a long time to fall asleep, waiting for a response that isn't going to come.

35

PENNY

BONNIE LOUNGES on my sofa like she's a blond Cleopatra, waiting for a buff man to feed her grapes. She looks at her cuticles and says, "I saw Marcus last week."

I only pause for a second while putting a pot of coffee on for her and Nikki, but I know they both notice. "Oh?"

It's Wednesday, seven days since I saw Brian and jettisoned him out of my life—then buried myself in ice cream to recover. Both Bonnie and Nikki got the full debrief of what happened and have been checking up on me every day since. It feels good to have girlfriends on my side. Their friendship makes me realize that Brian was a bit too possessive, a bit too suffocating. It was the only friendship I had, so I didn't realize how toxic it'd become.

"Yeah," Bonnie says. "Marcus looks like garbage."

I snort. "I highly doubt that." I bring her and Nikki their coffee, inhaling the scent and mourning the fact that I can only have one cup per day.

Bonnie and Nikita exchange a loaded glance. I ignore it.

Nikki says, "Has he texted you since the last time?"

They see me bite my lip and lean in. Damn it. I need to come up with a better poker face. I nod, then grab my phone from its charging cradle, unlock it (I'm getting pretty good at that), and hand it over. They crowd around excitedly, then pull back a second later.

Bonnie frowns. "That's it?"

I know exactly what the screen is telling them. There's one text from Marcus, six days ago. It says, *Hi Penny. How are you?*

I saw it the morning after he sent it, agonized over how to answer, then decided he'd probably sent it when he was drunk or suffering from insomnia, since it was sent after midnight, and figured it was best not to answer.

But it felt bad. Everything about the text, my mental battle, and my lack of response felt awful.

"He sent this nearly a week ago," Nikki says, blinking. "Why didn't you answer? Or block him? One or the other is better than ghosting, surely."

I slump down against the kitchen counter, groaning. "I'm a coward."

"False," Bonnie says, pointing at me. "You're brave and strong and beautiful."

I give her a half-smile. Then I say, "So where did you see him?"

"Dani's pregnant again," she tells us. "We all went over to their penthouse to celebrate the announcement."

"I also have friends with NYC penthouses," Nikita says. "Lots of them. Just saying."

Bonnie giggles. "I'm sure you do. Will I get to meet them one day?"

"Dani's pregnant?" I ask, cutting through their byplay.

Bonnie nods. "Yeah. Emil's fourth. He's so thrilled; it's cute."

My heart twists. I manage a sad excuse for a smile, then nod. "That's good. Give her my congratulations."

Bonnie moves her legs so I can sit on the sofa, then gives me a serious look. "Marcus misses you, Penny. And he has a right to know about you-know-what." She points at my abdomen. "I didn't like keeping a secret from him."

I let out a sigh. "I know."

"Have you thought about how you're going to do it?" Nikki asks, passing my phone back.

I stare at the blank screen. "Um. Text message?"

"No," Bonnie says at the same time as Nikki shouts, "Absolutely not."

They both pause, then Bonnie puts a hand on my forearm. "This is a phone call, at least. Marcus deserves that. Don't you think?"

"Ugh," I say. I pick at a loose thread on my slipcover and decide I hate the color of it. I should make a new one. It's when I'm planning out exactly how I'll cut the pattern that I realize I'm avoiding the topic at hand, even in my own mind.

I let out a long breath. "I'll tell him. I just need to get through the Valentine's Day orders from the shop, then I'll set up a time to speak to him. I promise."

Judging by the look on my friends' faces, they don't believe a word coming out of my mouth. I'm not sure I do, either.

LATER, when the girls are gone, I sit down at my computer for my weekly phone call with Amanda. She's helped me so much over the past weeks, and now I'm at a point where I can pretty much manage the online store myself. I've had to ask neighbors to let me use their dogs as models for new products, along with photos that customers have posted on social media, but I've almost got everything in hand.

Except today, I'm trying to set up a special section on my store for Valentine's Day, and it's not working. Amanda's voice is in my ear, but I've somehow managed to not hear anything she just said.

"I'm sorry," I say. "Can you repeat that last part? I click on 'Create New Page?'"

"Select 'Create New Display,'" she corrects. There's a pause, then, "Is everything okay? You seem distracted."

"Pregnancy brain," I blurt. "I swear I'm dumber than a bag of rocks right now."

"Oh!" She sucks in a breath. "You—you're— Congratulations!"

I wait for the dart of fear that usually comes with thoughts of my pregnancy, but instead I just feel the warm tingle of pride and excitement. "Thank you," I say through my smile.

"How impressive. Pregnant and running a doggie clothes empire. You're an inspiration," she says, and it actually sounds like she means it.

I lean back in my chair and stare out the window. The sky is blue today, and I know it's bitterly cold outside. "Do you have any kids?"

"Just the one." Amanda laughs. "To my mother's eternal dissatisfaction. She's been asking me for more grandkids since before I got married."

I huff a laugh. "I think my mom would've been happy

too." There's a pause, and to spare Amanda having to ask, I say, "She died when I was born."

"I'm sorry to hear that." Again, Amanda actually sounds like she means it. I find myself telling her about the pregnancy, how far along I am, how excited and terrified I feel. I don't mention the baby's father, and she very tactfully doesn't ask. Before I know it, she's letting out a little surprised, "Oh!" and I realize we've been talking for half an hour.

"I'm so sorry, Penny, but I have to interrupt you. We're about to go over our allotted time, and I really want to help you get your Valentine's Day storefront set up."

"My fault," I say. "Thanks for listening to me babble."

"Anytime. Should we get back to this website?"

I nod, bolstered by the conversation. "Let's do it."

Thirty minutes later, all my Valentine's bow ties and outfits are live on the Sellzy storefront, and I'm able to post about them on social media with working links to purchase. I get my first sale two minutes later.

Pride burns through my chest. Even after all this time, I can still hardly believe that people pay real money for my creations. And now, I can say that I've done it from start to finish—including the terrifying technological mumbo jumbo that would have previously been impossible to figure out.

If I can do this—the online store, the photos, the social media, the links, all of it—I know I'll be able to do motherhood. A few months ago, I would have been lost. Without Brian to take care of all these responsibilities, I probably would have let the online store languish, and my business would have collapsed.

Not anymore.

I'm a new woman. I've changed.

There's strength flowing through my veins, power that I've never tapped into before. I'm not a scared, small woman who flinches when men look her way. I'm not reliant on a lying thief for all my tech needs. I'm standing on my own two feet, and I'm succeeding.

"Well, that should be it for today," Amanda says brightly. "Any more questions?"

"No. Thank you," I say, hoping she can hear how sincere I am. Without her coaching me through the Sellzy interface over the past weeks, I probably would have given up by now —or at the very least, I would've taken a hammer to my laptop a dozen times over.

"Anytime. Talk to you next week! And congratulations again. Hopefully your baby will get your beautiful copper hair! Ta-ta!"

The phone clicks. I lean back with a sigh, putting a hand over my stomach.

Life is good. Step Three of my plan is looming, but for now, I want to bask in the pleasure of being proud of myself. Of feeling empowered and strong and capable.

I haven't felt this good in a long, long time.

It's three full days later, on Saturday morning, when I'm shampooing my head in the shower, that a question smacks me right in the face:

How did Amanda know the color of my hair?

36

PENNY

MY HAIR IS STILL WET, stuffed under a woolly winter hat with a gigantic pompom, when I get off the subway in SoHo. I blink at the bright winter sun as I emerge on the street, letting streams of people pass me.

What am I doing here?

The thought comes and goes in my mind, dissipating like the white puffs of breath floating from everyone's lips. I shuffle down the sidewalk like a robot, body hot and cold at once.

When I make the final turn and trudge down the street to stand in front of a familiar refurbished factory, I stare at the warm glow of the windows and pause.

I shouldn't be here. This is silly. I'm going to look like a crazy person, showing up at Marcus's door out of the blue. He's going to slam the door in my face.

But—

It was *Amanda*. This whole time, the woman on the other side of the phone was lipstick-pink, bodycon-dress-wearing Amanda. The one from head office, who works closely with

Marcus. No wonder I recognized her voice, her laugh. I'd *met* her.

Her calls weren't some concierge service they offer to successful Sellzy stores. I didn't qualify for it because I sold a zillion dog bow ties.

Marcus organized the whole thing.

I considered being mad about it as I rinsed the shampoo out of my hair. I indulged in that emotion while I conditioned, but I got over it by the time I turned the water off.

Sure, he kind of went behind my back to organize Amanda's calls—but he did it for *me*. Without Amanda's help, I don't know that I would have believed in myself enough to figure out the online store. I would have given up and gone back to farmers' markets and dog walking. She spent hours on the phone, explaining the website to me step-by-step, coaching me through every single click and notification and error message.

Marcus did that for me.

He didn't take over. When he exposed Brian, he didn't demand that he be the one to manage things. He made it so *I* could take care of my own business. He empowered me to face my fear of technology, helped me upskill myself so I could actually reach my full potential with my own business.

He stepped back and gave me the support I needed.

Has anyone ever done that for me? Anyone, ever?

Billy didn't. My father didn't. Brian sure didn't—he locked me out of the technical parts of my business and convinced me it was for my own good.

Marcus is the first man in my life who has handed me the reins, and he didn't even tell me he was doing it.

That's why I take a step toward the front door. Because a

man like that—one who pushes me to be better—deserves to know about the baby. He deserves better than me running and hiding from him.

Yes, he scared me when he snooped behind my back. He reminded me of those early days with my ex-boyfriend. He made me feel like that same frog, willingly climbing into the pot that would boil me alive.

That's not me—and it's not him, either.

My finger only trembles a bit when I ring the doorbell. The seconds that follow are excruciating, and I jump when I hear Bear's low *woof* through the door.

Heart pounding against my ribs, I squeeze my eyes shut and will my feet to stay in place. I want to run away. I want to hide. I want to go back to my hermit ways and get away from this place, this man.

But that was the old me—the new me is strong enough to stand here and face him.

Then the door opens.

Gosh, he's gorgeous. His eyes widen slightly, bright green, uptilted, rimmed in thick, black lashes.

"Penny," he breathes, then frowns. "Your hair. It's wet—it's *frozen*." He reaches over and tugs my arm. "Get in here before you make yourself sick."

I stumble across the threshold and into the warmth of the house. It's familiar, comfortable—feels like home. I'm shivering violently, which I don't realize until Marcus takes my hands in his to warm them up.

"Why—" He cuts himself off, then tugs at my zipper. Then my jacket is off and on a hook. Bear is jumping up against my legs, greeting me excitedly while Marcus rushes toward the living area. I'm still scrubbing Bear's thick fur when a blanket is thrown around my shoulders.

"You're freezing, Penny," Marcus growls, wrapping me up like a burrito. "You'll give yourself pneumonia. Why did you go out with wet hair?" He tugs my soaked hat off and tosses it toward the front door.

Before I can stop him, his arms are wrapped around me. I sink into him, closing my eyes, and I realize that the tip of my nose is very, very cold. Actually, my entire face is cold, and my hair is thawing and dripping down my neck.

Whoops.

Maybe I stood on the street for longer than I realized, agonizing over whether or not I'd walk up to the door and ring the bell.

His hands rub at my arms, my back, and all I can do is enjoy his touch. This is *not* going to plan. I was supposed to be aloof and cool and sophisticated, not a human popsicle.

Finally, I pull back. "Thanks," I croak, moving to tug the blanket off my shoulders.

"Keep it," he says, wrapping it more tightly around me. Warmth that has nothing to do with the blanket spreads through my chest. His hands linger on the blanket, holding me close, until he forces himself to step back. Bear sits between us, his head moving from one to the other.

"Um," I say, staring at his chin. "Hi." My gaze climbs up to his eyes in time to see them soften.

"Hey," he replies. He jerks his head toward the kitchen. "You want a hot drink? Peppermint tea?"

Since when does Marcus drink peppermint tea? This has been a coffee household ever since I've known it. But I already had my twelve ounces of coffee when I woke up, so I dip my chin. "Sure."

We move to the kitchen, and Marcus starts boiling some water. I lean against the island, where an Allen key, a screwdriver, and two screws rest on the corner of the marble slab.

"Are you building something?" I ask, because I'm not quite ready to say, *Hey, by the way, I'm carrying your child*.

He turns to glance at me, then at the tools on the counter. "Uh, yeah," he says, then clears his throat.

There's a pause, and my body thaws a bit more. I let my gaze trace the hard lines of his face, his body, his hands. He's gripping the edge of the counter, swallowing thickly, as if he's trying to figure out what to say.

My heart just melts, along with the ice crystals in my hair. This man is nothing like my ex-boyfriend. I should never have run away.

"I know it was you who got Amanda to call me," I say.

His gaze flicks to mine, and a wry smile twists his lips. "Damn it. She wasn't supposed to tell you."

It takes all my effort not to smile. "She didn't. She just let something slip about the color of my hair, and I figured it out. Took me three days, but I did eventually clue in."

He lets out a little snort, green eyes still on mine. "Are you mad at me?"

"Um. I was, for two or three minutes. But I got over it."

That might be hope blooming in his gaze. "Yeah?"

"She helped me more than I can say. I'm no longer terrified of messing up my online store. For the first time in my life, I feel—I feel *capable*."

"Of course you're capable," he says, turning to pour hot water into a mug for me.

It's a throwaway comment—something he says on instinct. But it's *everything*. In that moment, Marcus doesn't even realize that something is clicking in place inside me. This man truly believes in me. He's not trying to keep me small and control me—he really does want the best for me. He wanted the best for me when he exposed Brian, when he offered the spare room, when he introduced me to Raphael Garcia.

From the very first moment he learned of my business, he's wanted to build me up. He respects me.

"Thank you," I say, throat tight.

He shrugs a strong shoulder, eyes on the cup as he dunks the teabag.

"I mean it, Marcus. And I'm sorry." I take a deep breath. "I was wrong to push you away when you told me what Brian was doing. I should have been thanking you back then, too."

That makes him look up at me. He searches my face, then lets out a shallow breath. "I went about it all wrong. I'm sorry. I know you felt violated by what I did. I should never have logged into the back end of your store. I should have come to you first. Especially knowing what you've been through and how important your privacy is."

Words won't squeeze past the boulder in my throat. I nod, clutching the blanket around my shoulders, and look down as Bear nudges my calves. Rubbing his fur gives me an excuse to duck my head away and hide the tears gathering in my eyes.

"So what are you building?" I ask, my voice only slightly croaky.

There's a long, long pause. Long enough for me to glance

up from Bear to see Marcus rubbing the back of his neck, looking positively uncomfortable.

"Marcus?"

"Ah," he says, not meeting my gaze. "Fuck it. I'll show you."

Leaving my cup of tea on the counter, we head down the hallway. Past the bedrooms, all the way to the room that was so special to me—my old workshop.

The door is open, and I can see the walls already have a fresh coat of pale yellow paint. A changing table is set up in the corner where my sewing machine used to be, right beside a gliding rocking chair. The pieces of a crib are strewn across the middle of the room, with crumpled instructions in the center of the disaster.

I freeze, eyes wide.

Marcus clears his throat.

With every bit of my willpower, I lift my head from the half-built crib to look at his face. "Is this...?"

His hair's sticking up in all directions, as if he just rubbed his hand through it while I looked around the room. His face is redder than I've ever seen it. Marcus—cool, aloof, grumpy Marcus—is *blushing*. "Amanda asked me when your baby shower was so she could get you something. I nearly had a heart attack."

I blink. Blink again. Stare at him, then at the crib, then the rocking chair. Then I blurt, "Don't billionaires have people to build things for them?"

He rolls his eyes and lets out a laugh, then spreads his arms. "I wanted to do the crib myself. It felt... I don't know. Like it was important." He kicks one of the pieces of wood on the floor. "It's stupid. I didn't even know if I'd ever see you again."

I drop the blanket from my shoulders, and it puddles at my feet. Then I close the distance between us, wrap my arms around Marcus's neck, and kiss him like my life depends on it. He lets out a noise, half moan, half pure relief, then wraps his strong arms around me and tugs me closer.

By the time we pull apart, his eyes are watery and his breathing is staggered. "Does this mean...?" His eyes flick between mine, searching, hoping.

"I love you," I say. "I'm so sorry I pushed you away. I'm so, so sorry, Marcus. I punished you for my ex-boyfriend's sins, and I was wrong. Please forgive me. I'm in love with you. I want—"

His lips are on mine, and his hands are lifting me up so I can wrap my legs around his waist. Then I'm pressed up against the wall and it's his turn to kiss me like he needs my lips to survive.

"I love you so much, Penny," he says, kissing my jaw, my neck. "I've been dying without you. Dead. I've been dead without you. You make life worth living, and you're everything to me. Let me be that baby's father. Let me be your man. Please. I'm sorry I hurt you. I was so stupid. I'll never do it again. I'll never violate your privacy, your boundaries. I'll never snoop. I'll never go behind your back—"

"Shut up and kiss me again, you idiot. I'm the one who's sorry."

He gives me a fierce grin, then obliges. Before I know it, he's carrying me down the hall to his bedroom and laying me down on the mattress. It feels so good to have his weight on me. I let out a sigh, content, turning my head as he kisses a line down my neck.

There's no coldness anywhere in my body now. I'm warmer than I've felt in weeks. That low-level fear that gripped me since I found out I was pregnant melts away, because I know this man will be there to support me. He won't keep me small. He won't stop me from being everything I want to be.

I open my eyes when Marcus lifts my shirt up, kissing around my belly button. And I freeze.

Frowning, I sit up and reach for the nightstand. "What..." I clear my throat. "What's this?"

A pair of earrings are on the nightstand. They're blue and gold, in the shape of flowers. My breath starts coming short and fast, and a chill sinks deep into my bones.

Did he have another woman here? He slept with someone—

My hands shake as I pick up an earring, horror making me move slowly. Again, I have no right to be mad. We weren't together. I have no right to be hurt, but...

Marcus sits back on his heels and puts his hands on my calves. "Those, ah..." He lets out a huff, scrubbing his hand through his hair before returning it to my calf. He clears his throat. "This is embarrassing."

I put the earring down, feeling cold all over. Numb. "It's okay," I hear myself say in a hollow voice. "You don't have to tell me. We weren't together, and I stormed out on Christmas Day, and—"

He lets out a strangled noise. "Oh, God, no—Penny. Those are *yours*."

LILIAN MONROE

My gaze snaps to his. He looks horrified, and his hands tighten on my legs.

"What?"

"They're yours."

"These are not my earrings, Marcus."

"No"—he takes a deep breath—"I mean I bought them for you. I...uh...I sort of kept them on my nightstand since you left because... God, I don't know. They made me think of you. This is stupid. I'm sorry. I bought them. They don't belong to anyone else." He leans forward, eyes intent. "There's been no one else in this bed but me. I promise, Penny. I haven't even looked at another woman—I can't. There's only you. There's only ever been you."

The roller coaster of my emotions goes through another loop and has me feeling like throwing up. I don't know what to say. I look at the earrings.

"Do you like them?" Marcus finally asks when I say nothing.

"They're beautiful," I breathe. "Thank you. I guess I never gave you your Christmas present, either. I got you one of those cashmere sweaters you like so much, but then I donated it after...you know. So...whoops."

"Oh, I bought those way before Christmas," he says, picking the other earring up off the nightstand. "I got these the day you helped Mackenzie shop for clothes."

I'm speechless again. Marcus notices after a moment and meets my gaze. I gape. "You bought these the day we *met*?"

"We met a year before that, when you couldn't work the front door," he tells me.

"You know what I mean."

He's blushing again, and it's honestly the cutest thing I've ever seen. He's blushing because of *me*. I love this man. I'm head over heels. I'm never going to recover from this.

"I love you," I say, even though it feels too small for what I feel.

He lets out a gust of breath, and finally smiles a bit shyly. "I love you so much, Penny. The only thing that kept me going this past month was watching old recordings of you waving at my security camera with Bear every day and imagining how you would've looked wearing these earrings."

"That's really creepy and I should hate it, but I don't."

He laughs, takes the earring from my hands, and places it on the nightstand. Then he leans over me and cups my face with his palm. "Stay here with me, Penny."

There's so much we need to talk about, but I know what my heart wants. I trace the line of his jaw with my fingertip and say the only thing I can. "Of course I'll stay. Now kiss me again and remind me what I've been missing."

EPILOGUE

PENNY

MY EYES HAVE ONLY BEEN CLOSED for a few seconds when my infant's cries wake me up. Then I check the time and am startled to realize it's been over an hour since I passed out on top of the blankets. The air conditioning blasts above me so powerfully that my body is covered in goosebumps.

A groan sounds beside me. "I'll do it," Marcus mumbles into his pillow. "It's my turn."

I pat his back weakly, then feel the mattress shift as he gets up. The crib is in the corner of our room, where we moved it when we decided we wanted the baby in our room for the first few weeks. In the shadowy darkness of our bedroom, I watch the man I love shuffle to the crib and pick up our son.

We chose to name Timothy after Marcus's father, and when Martha heard, she burst into tears. I quickly followed —but by that time, I was so pregnant and emotional that my tears were an almost hourly occurrence.

I'm not much better now, to be honest.

After another blink which turned out to be an hour and a half of sleep, I wake up to see dawn spreading its soft fingers into the bedroom.

Timothy is awake again, squalling, wanting more milk. I sigh. Marcus's arm and leg are thrown over my body, and it takes all my strength to gently extricate myself from his snoring form so I can attend to our baby.

Padding to the nursery, I arrange myself on the gliding rocking chair and start nursing. I run my fingers over my baby's soft infant hair and feel a rush of love.

Turns out, Timothy got Marcus's hair. When he first laid eyes on his son's black head, Marcus laughed and winked at me before saying, "Maybe the next one will be ginger, Penny. I guess we'll have to try again."

Having just given birth, I only had enough energy to give him a halfhearted glare.

The past few months have been intense. I moved out of my apartment and into Marcus's, found a real workshop space, hired a seamstress to help me, and nearly tripled the sales from my store.

Raphael Garcia graciously invited me to come design another print at his workshop, as long as I made three custom outfits for his dog. I was happy with the trade—and then he posted the outfits on his personal social media channels. Another explosion of custom orders happened, which Raphael celebrated with me over another fabric design session which included champagne for him and sparkling grape juice for me.

As I developed the business, new friendships, and a loving relationship, I realized that Brian wasn't helping me; he was holding me back. I got so used to telling myself—and

Brian repeating—that I was bad at technology, I never took the time to wonder if it was actually true. Turns out, I can learn things. I can become better at things. I can be a badass business owner who runs her own website, cultivates relationships with well-known designers, and celebrates new sales milestones every couple of weeks.

Brian did reach out to me a few times, and he even showed up at my door again once in the summertime. I told him in no uncertain terms that I didn't want to see him again. The fear of repeating what happened with Billy rose up in me, but Marcus was there to remind me I wasn't alone. Then Nikki and Bonnie (metaphorically) slapped me upside the head and told me the same thing.

Oh—and during all these months of changes and realizations, I was pregnant the whole time. Between the trips to the bathroom, the gestational diabetes that I unfortunately developed, and Marcus's incessant hovering, I was so ready to give birth, it wasn't even funny. That event in itself is a haze of pain and medical professionals and Marcus and more pain and the first cries of my newborn son.

As I watch him feed now, his eyes closed, my body exhausted, I can hardly believe how lucky I am.

Then Marcus appears in the doorway and places a cup of herbal tea on the table next to me. "I'll burp him once he's done," he says. He presses a hand to the side of my face and kisses my forehead. I lean into the touch with my eyes closed and our child between us, still not quite believing that this is my life.

Our nanny appears in the doorway for a moment, then slowly retreats until we've pulled apart, Tim's done feeding, and I've rearranged my shirt. She smiles. "Want me to take over burping so you two can get ready for the day?"

Marcus hangs on to his son for a moment, touching the baby's tiny fingers to his lips, then hands him over. He helps me up out of the chair and leads me back to the bedroom.

From there, he sits me down on the closed toilet seat and starts the shower, making sure it's just the right temperature for me. I smile tiredly at him and let him strip off my old jammies.

We shower together. It's not sexual in the least, but it's a kind of deep intimacy I've never experienced with anyone else. Marcus washes my hair and holds me under the warm spray of the water, kisses me tenderly, then finally backs away so we can finish washing.

When he squirts conditioner onto his palm and tells me to turn around, I do as he says. A deep scalp massage follows, and I feel like the luckiest woman in the world.

"I was thinking," Marcus says slowly.

"Uh-oh. That's never good."

His fingers make little circles over my scalp as a laugh rumbles through him. "I was *thinking*," he says, emphasizing the word, "about our wedding."

I freeze. Glance over my shoulder. Frown. "Our wedding?"

He nods.

"I wasn't aware we were having one."

"Turn around and tilt your head. I want to rinse this out."

"Marcus," I huff, then do as he says. My heart thunders, mind reeling. When the conditioner is rinsed out, I open my eyes and glare. "Did you just propose to me?"

His eyes glimmer. "I guess I did."

"In the *shower*?"

He laughs. "Yeah. In the shower."

"And you just assumed I'd say yes!"

He wraps his arms around me and pulls me close. "You are saying yes," he informs me.

"Oh?"

"Yep."

"How do you figure?"

"You haven't knocked my head against the tiles and beat me silly with the showerhead."

"You're insufferable."

He laughs, his hands coasting down my spine to rest on my ass. "What do you say, Penny? Will you marry me?"

"Of course I'll marry you. But I mean—the shower!"

Still laughing, he turns the water off and hands me a towel. I spend some time drying off before wrapping the gigantic bath sheet around my torso, then walk into the bedroom to find the father of my child down on one knee, holding a ring between his thumb and forefinger.

"Penny. Mother of my child, love of my life. Please marry me."

"Marcus, you're *naked*." I thrust my hand at his dingle-berries.

His shoulders shake, eyes gleaming, and I can't quite help the smile that tugs at my lips. He thrusts the ring toward me. The center stone is the same shimmering blue as my favorite earrings, with four oblong diamonds sprouting from it in the shape of—

"Is that supposed to look like a bow tie?" I ask, coming closer despite myself. Drips of water fall from my hair to the rug, and the air conditioner blasts cool air over my damp skin.

But warmth suffuses me from head to toe.

Marcus takes my hand in his and slides the ring where it belongs. "It's the shape of a bow tie," he confirms. "Because bow ties brought us together, and a bow tie will keep us that way forever."

The metal, warm from his fingers, feels solid against my finger. I lift my hand and watch the light play over the stone, my eyes turning misty. Marcus's arms come around me. When I tilt my head up, tears spill from my eyes. He kisses them away, then places his lips against mine.

"I love you, Penny," he says against my mouth.

"I still can't believe you proposed to me in the shower. And then again naked."

"I didn't want anything standing between us when I did it. You have all of me, just the way I am."

My heart does a tumble, and I laugh. "Only you could make a naked proposal romantic."

Then he kisses me hard, and I'm lost in him—just like I always am, always have been.

SIX MONTHS LATER, Marcus and I are married in a beautiful venue in Manhattan, in the lobby of a hotel I probably couldn't have afforded to look at before I met him. Our wedding date is exactly one year from the day I turned myself into a human popsicle and interrupted Marcus while he was building our baby's crib.

A procession of dogs starts the ceremony, with Bear as the ring bearer. Marcus's nieces and nephews follow, throwing flowers down the aisle with gusto. I have four bridesmaids— Nikki, Bonnie, Stephanie, and Tara—to match Marcus's four groomsmen. Leif and Emil accompany Stephanie and Tara, while Marcus's brothers, Terry and Ollie, walk down with Nikki and Bonnie. The bridesmaids are wearing a soft lavender to match the groomsmen's ties.

Martha walks down the aisle in front of me, carrying her newest grandson in her arms, looking like she's about to explode from happiness and pride.

Then it's my turn.

I wanted a simple dress, until I tried this one on. It's an elegant princess dress with a dramatic train and all kinds of pleating and lace details climbing up the skirt and over the cinched bodice. A matching veil hides my happy tears from the guests as my father walks me down the aisle toward my soon-to-be husband.

In planning the wedding, it took a lot for me to reach out to my father. Our relationship hasn't completely recovered, but I've forgiven him for what happened with Billy. I knew walking me down the aisle would mean a lot to my dad, even if my resentment made me want to deny him the privilege.

Now, as he dabs his eyes with a lavender handkerchief, I'm happy he's beside me. My life from now on won't be dragged down by old wounds and bitterness. I want to start this adventure with my husband from a happy place—and that includes having my father beside me. I'm saying goodbye to the old me, to all the chains that had been wrapped around my ankles, to the old thoughts and beliefs that held me back. I'm choosing love, happiness, and doggie bow ties.

Dad hands me off to Marcus, who lifts the veil off my face. His eyes are shimmery as he takes my hands in his. "You look like an angel," he whispers. "You're so beautiful."

"I love you," I whisper back.

"I love you too." He swipes at his cheek, then nods at the officiant.

A short ceremony later, we're husband and wife. And I know, without a doubt, that I'm the luckiest woman in the world.

~

EXTENDED EPILOGUE
MARCUS

PENNY'S HAIR is falling out of her bun. Her dress is askew, and there's a piece of decorative tissue paper stuck to her shoe. She rearranges a display of bow ties, bats her hair off her face, then looks around the small space with a frantic, drawn expression on her face.

I slide my hands over her shoulders. "Everything looks perfect, Penny."

She spins around and lifts her freckle-covered face toward mine. "What if no one shows up?"

I glance out the door as the city starts waking up, a few early risers glancing curiously at the sign above the door on their way to work. "People will come."

"I can't believe I agreed to this."

"Give me your phone," I say. "I'll take a picture for you to post online. Behind the scenes." I click my tongue and wave at Bear to come over.

Penny sighs, scooping her long copper hair into a fresh bun. She straightens her dress, then smiles at our dog. "Hey, boy."

Bear shoves his nose between her legs and makes her laugh. She drops to her knees and starts scrubbing his fur, laughing and flinching as Bear reaches over to lick her neck.

"There," I say, handing her back the phone. "Got some good ones."

She smiles at me and takes the phone back, flicking through the images. "Bear looks good."

I roll my eyes. "You both look good, Penny."

She gives me an impish grin and gets to work posting them on her various social media accounts, right in time for Mackenzie to enter the back door of our pop-up store with two of her friends. "We're here!"

My shoulders drop. "Finally."

Mackenzie scowls and taps her wrist. "We're five minutes early, *actually*."

She just turned seventeen years old, and her sassiness has followed exponential growth. I head for the counter and pull out three T-shirts and three aprons for the girls, tell them to change, and start checking the computer and cash register to make sure everything is in order.

We do one last sweep of the store, making sure the doggie play area is set up properly, bowls of water are laid out, and on the other side of the space, that all the outfits and bow ties and accessories are displayed to their advantage.

Penny slides beside me and rests her head against my arm. "It all looks so good. I can't believe it's mine."

I kiss the top of her head. "I can. You're amazing."

Our three workers reappear wearing their new uniforms, and Penny claps her hands. "Great! Let me show you what I want you to do."

Before I know it, my alarm goes off, and it's time to open the doors.

"Ready?" I tell Penny.

She glances up from the box of spare leashes she got from a leather worker she recently hired, turning her gaze to the door. "Oh my goodness," she breathes. "Are all those people waiting to get in here?"

I follow her gaze and see a line forming near the door. My lips curl. "They sure are," I answer.

"I'm going to puke."

"Do it in the bathroom or the back alley if you must," Mackenzie cuts in. She nods to the door. "You want to do the honors, Penny?"

My wife straightens up, hooks an apron over her head and ties it around her waist, and then lets a slow smile spread over her face. "Yeah. I do."

"I'll be the camerawoman," Amy, Mackenzie's best friend, adds as she grabs the phone from the desk. "We're going live in three...two...one..."

Penny throws me one last glance, her smile so beautiful it makes my heart ache, and then she heads to the front of her pop-up store and unlocks the door.

As a dozen people stream in and start exclaiming over her wares, pride and love war within me. I can't believe Penny's my woman, my wife. I can't believe I'm the lucky guy who gets to see her laugh and smile with customers who gush about things she designed. I can't believe I married her and had a kid with her.

I didn't think life could get this good.

Then a bark happens, and one of the displays goes crashing to the ground. Chaos erupts as two dogs start an aggressive dance with each other. Bow ties go flying. Dog owners try to intervene. Penny lunges for Bear, who's advancing like he wants to put himself between the two dogs.

Finally, the owners get control over their dogs, and Mackenzie and the girls get to work fixing one of the displays.

Red-faced, Penny meets my eyes and cringes. "What a disaster."

I nod at the cash register, where half the people in the store are lined up in front of Amy with arms full of dog clothes and accessories. "I wouldn't call it a disaster."

My wife gets that look on her face that I love so much—a mix of awe and joy and hope. It's the way she looked when she saw the pieces of Tim's crib on the floor.

I sling an arm around her shoulders and pull her in for a quick kiss. "I need to go to work," I tell her. "But I'll be back in a couple of hours."

She nods. "Go. I love you."

"Not as much as I love you." I kiss her forehead, then leave out the back door.

THAT EVENING, after the pop-up store is closed and Penny, the girls, and I have prepped the place for the next day, we head home and meet our wonderful nanny, who tells us Tim went down ten minutes ago. As the nanny leaves, Penny and I duck our heads inside the bedroom to watch our son sleeping soundly.

"I can't believe he's eighteen months old already," she says, clinging to the doorframe, eyes luminous.

"About time to give him a brother or sister."

Penny's head whips toward me. "Excuse me?"

I wrap my arm around her waist and drag her out of the bedroom, closing Tim's door as gently as I can. I press her against the wall and rest my forehead against hers. "What do you think?"

"I think you wouldn't be so excited about that thought if you had to carry and deliver a watermelon-sized baby yourself."

I run my lips up her neck and relish the way she shivers. "Okay." I kiss her neck. "Whatever you want, Penny."

Her fingers tunnel into my hair, and she lets out a beautiful gasp as I nip her jaw. We kiss, slow and tender, until her body's writhing against mine. I let my hands slide down her sides and around the small of her back to pull her close.

She moans at the feel of me, hard and ready against her stomach.

"Were you serious?" It comes out between pants.

I pull back slightly, my hips still pinning hers. "About what?"

"About wanting another baby?"

Her face is so earnest, so beautiful, that I have to cup it in my hands. "I'd want half a dozen kids with you, Penny. I've lost my mind, and it's your fault."

She laughs, her hands sliding down my arms to wrap around my wrists. She turns her head and kisses the center of my palm, then turns her gaze back to meet mine. "How about two," she says. "Three kids, max."

My heart beats double-time. "You're serious?"

"I'll stop taking my birth control pill. If it happens, it happens."

Happiness forks through me like lightning. I haul her into

my arms and carry her to our bedroom, then get to work making babies with her.

LESS THAN A YEAR LATER, Penny gives birth to twins. I'm the father of another boy and a girl, both beautiful little redheads with big, blue eyes. They're perfect, just like their brother— and their mom.

ALSO BY LILIAN MONROE

For all books, visit:

www.lilianmonroe.com

Manhattan Billionaires

Big, Bossy Mistake

Big, Bossy Trouble

Big, Bossy Problem

Forty and fabulous

Dirty Little Midlife Crisis

Dirty Little Midlife Mess

Dirty Little Midlife Mistake

Dirty Little Midlife Disaster

Dirty Little Midlife Debacle

Dirty Little Midlife Secret

Dirty Little Midlife Dilemma

Brother's Best Friend Romance

Shouldn't Want You

Can't Have You

Don't Need You

Won't Miss You

Military Romance

His Vow

His Oath

His Word

The Complete Protector Series

Enemies to Lovers Romance

Hate at First Sight

Loathe at First Sight

Despise at First Sight

The Complete Love/Hate Series

Secret Baby/Accidental Pregnancy Romance:

Knocked Up by the CEO

Knocked Up by the Single Dad

Knocked Up...Again!

Knocked Up by the Billionaire's Son

The Complete Unexpected Series

Yours for Christmas

Bad Prince

Heartless Prince

Cruel Prince

Broken Prince

Wicked Prince

Wrong Prince

Lone Prince

Ice Queen

Rogue Prince

Fake Engagement/ Fake Marriage Romance:

Engaged to Mr. Right

Engaged to Mr. Wrong

Engaged to Mr. Perfect

Mr Right: The Complete Fake Engagement Series

Mountain Man Romance:

Lie to Me

Swear to Me

Run to Me

The Complete Clarke Brothers Series

Extra-Steamy Rock Star Romance:

Garrett

Maddox

Carter

The Complete Rock Hard Series

Sexy Doctors:

Doctor O

Doctor D

Doctor L

The Complete Doctor's Orders Series

Time Travel Romance:

The Cause

A little something different:

Second Chance: A Rockstar Romance in North Korea

CPSIA information can be obtained
at www.ICGtesting.com
Printed in the USA
BVHW030956210223
658925BV00002B/61